NEW HOPE FOR THE LITTLE CORNISH FARMHOUSE

ALSO BY NANCY BARONE

No Room at the Little Cornish Inn

NEW HOPE FOR THE LITTLE CORNISH FARMHOUSE

Nancy Barone

Just when she thought she'd written all she knew about love…

An Aria Book

This edition first published in the United Kingdom in 2020 by Aria,
an imprint of Head of Zeus Ltd

A CIP catalogue record for this book is available from the
British Library.

ISBN 9781838938031

Typeset by Siliconchips Services Ltd UK

Cover design © Cherie Chapman

Aria
c/o Head of Zeus
First Floor East
5–8 Hardwick Street
London EC1R 4RG

www.ariafiction.com

To my beloved husband Nick with love. I couldn't have done any of this imaginary-world stuff if you hadn't been there to take care of the real world outside – and to be my creative sounding board as always.

1

It's Complicated

Nina Conte has written three novels and lives in a rambling farmhouse on the outskirts of a Cornish seaside village with her two children and their dog Minnie.

That was my life on paper. More precisely, in my author bio.

Because in reality, my existence couldn't be any more different than the idyllic picture my agent had painted.

Indeed, there were three novels, two children and one dog – no lie there. But the "rambling farmhouse", Cornflower Cottage, had been (and practically still was) a ruin that my erstwhile husband Phil and I had bought three years, ago with the intention of doing it up while we roughed it on site with our children in a caravan for the summer.

That had been the plan three years ago. Chloe, who was ten at the time, and Ben, only five, were absolutely thrilled about our new Cornish adventure. And so was I. But one rainy afternoon, only two weeks into our new life, amidst plumbers and roofers and glazers, Phil walked out on us.

There had been no *Goodbye, I'm sorry, it's not you, it's me, I'll come back for my stuff, We'll take turns with the kids*, et cetera. Nothing but an *I'm not doing this anymore.*

So I'd watched, completely numb with stupor, as he marched through the rotting oak front door that had been hanging on a hinge and a prayer for the last three hundred years, and strode straight off the mess that was the building site – and our lives.

In his haste to go, however, he hadn't forgotten to empty out our joint bank account, leaving me absolutely nothing for the children, not even for a food shop, let alone the hefty renovation bills that were coming in like flyers through a stuffed mailbox.

It was a good thing I had already paid for Ben and Chloe's first year at Northwood Academy, one of the best schools in Cornwall, and the main reason we'd moved here. But as far as everything else was concerned, we had nothing left for the next three months until my royalties came in.

And, as if Phil had cast a *Macumba* on us, the second he disappeared over the horizon on his motorbike, our caravan, containing our every worldly possession, including the kids' brand-new school books, uniforms and PE kits, suddenly caught fire.

I remember half-carrying Ben and Chloe from the caravan to the front yard, which was a mud-rink from weeks of rain. My neighbours and the locals from the village were there in a moment to help put it out, and that was how I met most of them.

But they needn't have bothered, because the minute they arrived, an almighty hell broke loose from the skies, drenching everyone to the bone while I wrapped Chloe and Ben in my

Mac, the only possession we now had left in the world, apart from the roofless ruin we had hoped to call home.

Luckily Jack Marrak, the farmer from Crooked Hill Farm, my nearest neighbour on my left and up the road, put us up in his beautiful farmhouse while he and a few others from the village helped make the building watertight. In the space of a half hour, his entrance hall had been submerged with goods of every kind, from clothes to toys.

And since then, we have been an integral part of the village of Penworth Ford, a community of only seventy-five souls, with my new best friends Emma Perkins living on my right in Hyacinth Cottage and Jack as my pillars. Jack had done as much work as he could with a couple of his friends, such as stripping the floorboards in some of the rooms, repairing the windows and fixing the locks so Phil couldn't get back in should he have chosen to. Not that there was any danger of that.

Jack had continued to work relentlessly for weeks fixing the log burner and the boiler before the winter set in, while Emma had provided the free childcare while I worked in a restaurant. All for the price of a weekly neighbour dinner. And now I reciprocated by providing dinner and babysitting as she worked.

'Mum, I think my clothes are shrinking,' Ben said as we tried to get his trousers over his leg brace this morning. The doctors said he would always have one leg longer than the other, but I refused to believe it. The fact that he couldn't even walk without it (for now) didn't stop us from believing he would run like the wind one day.

And his trousers were actually not shrinking. He was simply growing faster than I could clothe him, and the school had been adamant – no wide-legged trousers (were they afraid my eight-year-old was going to introduce a bazooka into the school, for goodness' sake?), so every morning we had this palaver.

'One more time, darling,' I urged him as my bloody mobile rang. I'd have left it gladly, but it was my accountant, Menacing Mike, formerly dubbed Marvellous Mike when there was money in my account.

I tapped the green circle on my screen. 'Hi, Mike,' I chimed like a dream-catcher warding off evil spirits, hoping that some good karma would work its charm and come back into my life. 'What's up?'

'Up? Nothing's up, Nina. But I can tell you what's down. Your royalties. They're dwindling.'

I felt my stomach start to burn again for the third time that morning. 'What, so soon?'

'It's been three years since your last book, Nina. You need to come up with something new ASAP… or else,' he counselled as I jammed the phone between my shoulder and cheek as Ben and I finally managed to pull his trousers on.

'Do your tie up now, darling,' I whispered.

'It's sort of knotted, Mum,' he apologised and I looked down in dismay. Of all mornings, he'd somehow managed to tangle it so badly that it would not come undone.

Chloe, on the other hand, was already sulking at the top of the stairs preparing a tantrum of biblical proportions because she couldn't find her favourite blue tights, the *sheer* ones. God, how I hated Mondays. It was like being dragged back to hell after a few minutes' paradise called The Weekend during which you were allowed to forget your troubles. But unfortunately, it never lasted.

Sorry, Ms Conte, it's Monday again. You can't stay here in Paradise. No, Ms Conte, please stop bawling and do let go of the Pearly Gates and come down this way, through the burning doors, please.

This happened every seven days. Even God got a break more often than me.

'Look in your mesh bag,' I called up to my pre-teenager.

She yelled back, 'Mum, where do you think I've been looking – the fridge?'

On days like this anything was possible. It wouldn't be the first time anyway. I personally had a potted history of putting my reading glasses in the (hot) oven, my day-planner in the hamper and my keys in the bread bin.

'Then wear socks for today.' I looked down at Ben. 'How on *earth* did we find ourselves in this mess, my boy?' I asked and he looked up at me with those angel eyes and grinned.

'Don't blame me,' Mike shot back, thinking I'd been talking to him. 'I'm not the one with the heart of gold.'

Jesus, I'd almost forgotten he was there. I must stop blanking out like this. And by heart of gold, he meant a brain the size of a piece of lint and *how* could I have not seen that my husband had so cleverly planned his escape?

'How bad is it really, Mike?' I asked, although I was well aware of my options at this point:

1. Lose my dilapidated and heavily mortgaged home if I missed any more payments (very likely) and move under a bridge;
2. Take my kids out of Northwood Academy (not happening);
3. Ask Jack for a loan. I knew he was well off, but I wasn't doing that. He had already done enough for me.

4. Ask my agent for an advance. But an advance on what: my supposed next big fat failure?

While living in London, I had dreamt about leaving my childish, undependable and irresponsible husband for years. Unable to do so because the children were still besotted with him, I instead began to write about my fantasies of a new life. A Cornish life, to be exact. And possibly a new Cornish husband. The result had been three romantic comedy novels.

But then, when Phil had unexpectedly left *me* instead, without a care about the kids whatsoever, writer's block had struck with a vengeance, and the creativity had drained from me. How the heck was I expected to continue dreaming about love and Mr Darcy-ish male leads after Phil, who had once claimed to love me, had pulled such a stunt on me, breaking not only our vows, but also my heart? I simply didn't believe in Happily Ever After anymore, so who did I think I could kid?

My agent Alice Hopkins always said I'd be fine if I wrote another book. It was easy for her to say. But it was no longer my writing that filled my children's bellies. It was my cooking Sicilian *arancini* for restaurants.

Luckily for me, the orders came in steadily (I'll give you the recipe later, promise). I prepared them after dinner, two hundred per batch, and left them in my freezing pantry because there was no space for them in the fridge. These fifty kilograms of food had become, as it were, my lifeline, so I killed myself with work twenty-four-seven to make sure I never ran out. The trouble was the restaurants only gave me thirty per cent of the earnings, when I did all the work and even delivered them to their doorstep.

'Nina, I just told you how bad it is. Get writing again – *or else.*'

'Mum! These socks are black, not blue!' Princess Chloe hollered from the top of the stairs. 'I'm not going anywhere in these!'

Oh God, just swipe me off the face of this earth now. 'Check my drawer!' I shouted back. I was glad school was almost out for the summer. Then we could actually find the time to do things as a family, rather than be this horrid and harried assembly line consisting of morning calls, roll calls for items of clothing that have gone AWOL, breakfast tantrums, missing, or rather "forgotten" homework due on the day, and having to back up a hundred yards because Chloe had forgotten her ballet slippers.

'Is there no one you could ask for a loan?' Mike suggested. 'I think that's the only solution at this point, I'm afraid.'

'Can I get back to you about that? I have to take the kids to school.' For as long as I could afford the fees, that was.

He sighed. 'Right. Keep me posted, then.'

'I will,' I promised obediently as I rang off.

And since I didn't personally know any loan sharks, my next best option was to hightail it to my bank on the high street and beg the manager for an extension on my existing loan.

Maybe I needed a guardian angel. Maybe in this very moment, they were looking down on me tsk-tsking and muttering, *Don't give me that one with the battered, crappy car and the stroppy daughter – she's an overtime job.*

I checked my watch – if it hadn't stopped again I had precisely twenty minutes to unravel Ben's tie from around his neck, solve Chloe's fashion dilemma and drive them off to school *and* deliver my *arancini* across the county before I got to the bank to do some major on-my-knees begging, provided the old banger didn't clonk out in the process (my car, not the manager).

After the said twenty minutes, Chloe finally came down and stuck her head in the fridge.

'I've already packed your lunch, sweetheart,' I called over my shoulder as I freed Ben's neck and tied a proper knot.

As Chloe rummaged through the fridge despite the last piece of information I'd given her about her lunch, it gave a familiar, loud bark.

It did that when it was empty. Not that it *was* empty by all means. But nowadays, we lived a little more frugally, tending towards healthier choices. It worked with Ben, but Chloe was a junk food freak.

Chloe slammed the fridge door as the bark became a Kennel Concerto. 'Oh, God, it's not started that bullshit again, has it?' she whined.

'Chloe, mind your language please.'

She rolled her eyes. 'There's no one else here, Mum.'

'*We*'re here, and I'll not have you talk like a stevedore, thank you.'

Chloe sniffed at the fruit and vegetables and groaned. 'There's never anything to eat in this house,' she declared.

Here we go again. 'You say that every time. There's plenty of food. There are Jack's apples, pears, peaches and three different kinds of berries.'

'Exactly, most of it's from the orchard.'

I lifted an eyebrow. 'Everyone should be so lucky to have an orchard like us. We have almost any kind of fruit you—'

'But I want something store-bought, like biscuits or cake.'

'We have biscuits in the pantry.'

'Ugh, there's only Jaffa cakes. No thanks.'

'And I've just picked some blueberries to make some jam and a pie.'

Silence. Because she actually liked my pies, there was nothing she could really say to that.

'The last one you made was wonky, and the jam wasn't sweet enough,' she countered. Trust her to have the last word.

'Mum's pies are beautiful and her jams are excellent,' defended Ben as he sauntered back in, his limp worse than usual as he reached for an apple from the fruit bowl. 'It's your mouth that's bitter, Chloe. In every way. So let off and leave her alone.'

He winked at me and I melted. I loved both my children, truly I did. Ben was my baby, the one who dealt with a disability, and his was the smile that got me through the bad years with Phil. And Chloe was my first and I'd always cherish the years we had on our own and the bond we'd created. The bond between mother and daughter that no one can break, even if lately she was trying her best to make me pay all over again for letting her dad walk away.

Whatever I did, it was never good enough for her, whereas her dad had only to crook his little finger and she'd go running to him. The divorce, even after three years, was still ongoing, as Phil was finding it difficult in the end to sign on the dotted line.

Chloe looked me up and down. 'And please tell me you're not going to drive us to school dressed like that,' she scoffed.

Yikes. She was right. Cargo pants and crocs were not a good get-up when appearing in the society of the Northwood Academy mothers. Nor for begging for a loan.

So I ran upstairs to my bedroom under the eaves and threw my best suit on (the pseudo Jackie O dress and matching cropped jacket I wore at Aunt Elena's funeral), literally dragged the kids into the car, grabbing the pile that was today's post on the way, twisted my hair into a bun that I secured with a stolen IKEA pencil that disappeared in my messy black rat's nest and threw up a silent prayer that yesterday's engine stalling was not a sign of today's death.

Hopeful that up there someone was listening, I heaved a huge breath and turned the ignition key with one eye scrunched up. Dead flat, of course. *No, no, no! Please God, spare me this one time. I'll take this piece of junk to a mechanic's, I swear to you, but please don't let it die right now. Not yet. I can't afford a taxi.*

'Mum, we're going to be late!' Chloe shrieked right next to me and I swear I felt the physical tear in my eardrum.

I stopped long enough to wipe the hair off my already sticky forehead. 'No, we won't. Old Lottie's just being a little fussy today, that's all.' *Come on, you old, useless bitch, get a move on, or I'll tear every wire out of your twisted, useless metal carcass.*

But when telepathic abuse didn't work, I tried reasoning with her. *Please, please, old Lottie, old girl? Have a heart. I've got fifty kilos of arancini to deliver all over the county before lunchtime! You've been a member of this family longer than my own children. Please help me out here?* But the trollop wasn't interested in the least.

God, what I wouldn't have given for a leisurely cup of coffee and some buttered toast on a nice, unchipped plate and a quiet kitchen all to myself, with the kids upstairs or, better still, in a parallel universe. For at least thirty minutes.

Just enough time for me to take a couple of deep breaths in absolute solitude. That *would* have been heaven.

But enough of dreaming. I had more impelling matters to tend to, like getting the day back onto the right foot. You know: Keep calm and carry on and all that. But I actually felt like bashing the car over the hood like John Cleese and screaming at the top of my lungs so they'd hear me all the way down the village. The image of me actually hitting this clunker with a branch made me giggle.

Ben leaned over the seat. 'What's so funny, Mummy?'

Chloe crossed her arms and gave me a filthy look as I tried the engine again and again and at every useless turn of the key, instead of breaking down into tears as would be expected, I cackled in delight as if I was insane. At this point I had to be. Or maybe it was just some twisted coping mechanism. Which frightened Chloe.

'Can I please go get Jack?' she begged.

Meaning our neighbour on our left, and our knight in shining armour. The one who had practically single-handedly made our farmhouse watertight years ago.

Even if we couldn't see Jack's farm because of a bend in the lane, it was comforting to know that he was always there to lend a hand.

'Just one more try,' I pleaded, more to the car than to Chloe, but she opened the car door and was off like a shot up to Jack's farm before I could stop her.

'Maybe it's the carburettor,' Ben suggested.

'Well, it certainly sounds congested,' I agreed. 'Let's just hope Jack's still in.'

And in he was, because about three minutes later Chloe appeared, her lowered hood bouncing around her shoulders as she rounded the bend, followed by Jack – tall, capable and strong – rolling up his sleeves while pushing back his dark mop of curls. And I already felt better. If anyone could help, it was him.

'Hey,' he said as he rested his hand on the hood. 'What's wrong with her this time?'

'I wish I knew. I'm so sorry, Jack!' I called through the open window as I popped the bonnet. It was a ritual between us by now. We'd be late and he'd come to the rescue. Textbook Monday mornings.

'No worries!' he called, his dark eyes twinkling at me through the windshield just before he disappeared into the bowels of my Ka. Good lad. He knew when it was time to chat and when not to. Not that he was much of a talker, Jack.

'Try now,' Jack said, and I turned on the ignition. The engine gave a phlegm-y cough, a sputter and then roared into life like it was a fricking Ferrari. Go figure.

I stuck my head out the window to gawp at him as he closed the bonnet with a firm, satisfied shove. 'What did you do this time?' I asked in utter awe.

'It was just a loose wire. Off you go.'

Ben stuck his head out the window behind me. 'You're a genius, Jack! Maybe you might want to take a look at our barking fridge while you're at it?' he asked as I blew him a kiss and manoeuvred out onto the road.

Jack's eyebrows lifted. 'Barking fridge?'

I laughed out the window as I turned the steering wheel. 'Yeah, it's our new thing. Don't worry about it. Thanks, Jack. I'm making shepherd's pie tonight, care to join?'

'Sure,' he said with a grin as he wiped his now sooty

hands on a rag hanging from his back pocket. 'Have a great day, guys.'

'Bye, Jack!' Chloe and Ben called in unison as I charged down the hill, less than fashionably late for our day.

At the gates of Northwood Academy, I pulled up alongside all kinds of sport and luxury cars, waved goodbye to my precious cargo, Ben blowing me fish-kisses and Chloe pretending not to know the crazy lady in the Ka flapping her arms like a headless chicken. That was my beloved brood, off to build their futures. And now to make my rounds of the restaurants, and then to the Hallowed Halls of Terror, i.e. the bank.

2

As Good As It Gets

'I'm sorry, Mrs Jenkins. There's absolutely nothing I can do for you,' the bank manager said right off the bat, leaning back as if we were already done. Maybe he was, but I was only starting.

'It's Conte, actually. Not Jenkins.'

'Well, I'm sorry, Ms Conte, but you are not eligible for another loan. With no substantial income and your present outgoings we cannot *possibly* lend you any more money than we already have...'

Was it me or was he actually enjoying this? Human Resources should stop recruiting from the deepest pits of sadistic bastards. So I was not eligible. He was saying *no*. And even if he was only doing his job, I resented him for his attitude. I resented his smile, his expensive suit, his shiny watch and his long white fingers. Fingers that had never done a real day's work in their life.

He leaned forward, probably alarmed by the deadly look on my face.

'Do you have any other income besides your royalties and your cooking?'

'If I did I wouldn't be here, would I?' I snapped, only to apologise. 'Sorry. That was out of order.'

He watched me with surprised eyes that seemed to grow wider. And suddenly, kinder. 'No worries. I'm just trying to think…' He leaned back, steepling his index fingers and jamming them up into his bottom lip. 'Have you any other assets?'

Please see previous retort. I shook my head. 'We had a flat in London but we sold it to pay for… some other things…' Meaning Phil's gambling debts. My eyes, suddenly heavy with moisture, dropped to the dark grey carpet patterned with the bank's logo.

If there is an even number of hexagons on the carpet from here to the door, I'll be okay, I told myself.

When he finally sighed and shook his head, I stood up, forced a smile and shook his outstretched hand firmly to let him know that I was no wimp. I would survive this one as well. Somehow.

On my way home, I remembered we were out of milk, so I stopped off at old Alf's Post Office, or, as the sign had read for the past few years, Post Of ice.

After a morning of running around so other people could eat, I rummaged around in my bag until I found the slice of toast I'd wrapped in a paper towel and tore off a bite as I tried to ring Alice to check up on my royalties that were soon due. But I got my provider instead:

Unfortunately, you don't have enough credit to make your call.

Ooh, *goody*. What next?

As I squeezed the last of my coins out of my bag to pay for the milk, my mobile rang again. I chewed and swallowed.

'H'llo?' God, who was it now, Mephistopheles claiming my soul? Close. 'Good morning, Ms Conte. I'm calling from Northwood Academy...'

I jammed my little stash back into my bag, suddenly not hungry anymore.

'Sorry to disturb you, Ms Conte...' *Not in the least. You just caught me in the middle of writing my suicide note...*

'... But there seems to be a problem with this term's fees...'

I swear I almost fell back against the dairy counter. 'What? I mean, I beg your pardon?'

'Your cheque wasn't, erm, honoured.'

Oh God. It was the beginning of the end. This was the first time ever a cheque had bounced. How on earth had I fallen so low?

'You'll want to pop by and rectify by noon, Ms Conte...'

Was that a threat? Next she was going to tell me how many kids were on the waiting list to get into Northwood.

'Thank you. I will,' I assured her, and hung up, only for my mobile to ring again.

'Hello?'

'Ms Jenkins?'

I rolled my eyes. 'It's Conte,' I said for the second time in a day. 'Nina Conte. Who is calling, please?'

'It's Ray Givens, from C&C Surveyors?'

Who?

'We have been contacted by your husband, Mr Philip Jenkins, to evaluate your home for the sale? When would be a good time to come round?'

Phil? Sale? Oh my God in Heaven.

'Ms Conte?'

'I'm sorry, Mr… er, sir, but our home is not for sale.'

'Do you not live at Cornflower Cottage in Penworth Ford?' he insisted.

'Yes, but, again, our home is not for sale.'

Silence, and then: 'I'm sorry, there must have been a misunderstanding.'

'I'm sure there was. Good day,' I said and hung up.

The *bastard*. What the hell did Phil think he was doing, putting up our home for sale?

Enough of this crap. It was now official. Without a loan, I couldn't go on this way. I needed a second job if I was going to keep the house. Because as far as my writing career was concerned, for the life of me… I simply couldn't write another word about love.

'That son of a bitch!' Emma cried when I told her about Phil's latest act of chivalry.

A single mum herself, she worked as a wedding planner for a firm in Truro and avoided her own ex like the plague. Her goal was to start her own company, raise her daughter Chanel, and meet the man of her dreams. And meet him she would, because she was as determined as hell to bag an eligible bachelor who had it all – the looks, the money, and, above all, someone who loved Chanel as well.

'He can't do that! He can't just put your house up for sale without your signature.'

I squished my heavy eyelids with the tips of my fingers, every drop of energy drained from me. I needed to talk to the arsehole pronto. Use logic and persuasion. And possibly bring my butcher's knife along, just in case.

'And now we know why he's been dragging the divorce all these years,' I sighed. 'He wants as much as he can take from me.'

'Why doesn't he man up and get himself a job rather than trying to sponge off you?' she asked. Emma had been crazy in love with her husband Adam, but had kicked him out when she caught him cheating. Chanel wasn't interested in ever seeing her father again, but I suspect that had a lot to do with Emma's influence. Chanel emulated her mum in almost everything. They shared each other's clothes and secrets and they were more like sisters than mother and daughter. But it worked for them. Me, I didn't have the guts to explain to my children what their own father had done, partly because I didn't want to break their hearts any further.

'Well, if you need any help, I'm here for you,' she said as Callie, our stray pup, crawled across the floorboards towards me, lodging herself between my feet.

'Thanks, Emma, I'll be fine.'

What else could I do? Hire a hitman? I couldn't afford one. Talking to Phil was all I had left, despite the fact that listening had never been his forte. He had the IQ of a doorknob and the attention span of a guppy.

'I'll make sure he doesn't get his hands on my royalties, for one thing. Luckily I've opened a separate account for that, but as we're still married, I don't know what he'll do.'

'Christ almighty, Nina. If you need anything. Anything at all…'

I smiled weakly. 'Thanks, Em. I'm looking for another

job. I don't know that they'd choose me instead of a twenty-year-old, but I have to try everything.'

'Which reminds me,' she said, pulling out a brochure from her bag. 'I thought this might interest you.'

I frowned. 'Poldark Tours? I rather think this is your cup of tea.'

'They're hiring.'

'Oh?' If I could work for them in the mornings after dropping off the kids, maybe I could be home in time for them when they got in, and then continue prepping my *arancini* in the evenings.

'Yeah. They're looking for a tour guide fluent in Italian. Apparently Italians have cottoned on to the show. Something about tall, dark and handsome rings familiar with them, I guess. Anyway, the job sounds like it was made for you.'

'Indeed it does. I'll have a read. Thank you.'

'But you need to have seen the series and know it inside out.'

Which I hadn't, except for a few excerpts Chanel had shown me on her phone. Mother and daughter were both obsessed.

'Who's got time for TV?' I groaned.

She looked at me, her eyes misting over. My Emma. 'I *hate* him for everything he's done to you,' she whispered. 'I wish he fell down the Trevose Head hole, and that the gulls picked every scrap of flesh off his bones.'

And that was two of us.

'Jesus. I think we need some wine,' she said. 'Drown our sorrows and all that.'

'Too early. How about a nice cuppa instead? I've just

bought some really good brownies from Old Nellie's. Here,' I said, opening the lid off the cake tin and switching the kettle on. 'Eat up.'

At those words, Callie and Minnie scrambled from their sleeping position to a begging one, their eyes following every bite Emma took.

Emma ran a hand through her angelic blonde curls and sighed. 'Chanel's driving me nuts with her obsession with fashion.'

'I thought you were happy that she takes after you.'

'I was. But she copies everything I say and do. I want her to have her own personality. She looks like a mini-me.'

I laughed. 'She'll grow out of it. If anything, at least you two get along. Chloe counters every single thing I say. To her, you are the cool mum.'

'How about we swap, then? Just until they're adults?'

'Oh, I'd gladly take Chanel – and Chloe worships the ground you walk on.'

'This game is just too hard, Nina. I'm getting old. Look at me.'

'Nonsense. You're gorgeous,' I said. She was. Fashionable, trendy with a face that wouldn't look out of place in a magazine.

'Once upon a time, maybe, but have you seen the wrinkles under my eyes? I'm absolutely knackered. This life is killing me.'

And she only had one kid and a good, stable job.

'How the hell do you manage?' she asked and I snorted as the kettle boiled and I made our brews.

'As you see, I don't. Here.'

She took a sip of her tea. 'Thanks. Sometimes I wonder what it would be like to get back together with Adam, just so he could deal with some of the parenting. But then I remind myself of what he put me through.'

I nodded. 'I know, Em.'

'And when I look around me,' she said, reaching for a brownie, 'I see that the pickings are slim. Mhhmmm, these are good!'

'I've put some more for you in a Tupperware.'

Emma was on the prowl, but I had neither the time nor the will, because the minute I took my foot off the pedal and got distracted, it was the moment the kids needed me most. I simply couldn't do it. And besides, I had lost my, let's call it, uhm, mojo. And it was fine. But Emma? She had a life, and in a way, I lived vicariously through her, and the restaurants she took her clients to, along with the castles and country houses and amazing venues she worked at on a regular basis. She was always glamorous and her make-up flawless. She was the person I had always wanted to be.

'In any case, you shouldn't have any problems at all,' she said. 'You're so gorgeous you don't even need make-up, with your long black hair, pink pout and perky boobs. Mine need hiking up with a crane in the morning.'

I laughed. 'Nonsense. You are beautiful, Emma.'

'I used to be. When was the last time you saw me without make-up?'

'I can't recall.'

'Exactly. And you won't either, not even at school events. Especially at Northwood school events, where all the single daddies are lurking.'

'Ugh,' I said instinctively. 'Single daddies…'

'It's a shame there aren't any handsome ones around at the moment. Better wait for the next round.'

'The next round?' I echoed.

'Of divorces. Chanel brings home the full account of whose parents are splitting up, whose mum is getting married again to whose dad. By the way, Paul and Belinda Carruthers are having problems.'

'Shame. They seemed happy.'

'Exactly – seemed. Divorce is on the up, so next term… I'm banking on the wealthy Northwood fathers. Someone's got to be viable, sooner or later, and when they are, I'll be there – either as a wedding planner or a candidate. You should, too, Nina.'

I had always wondered how she hadn't yet bagged herself a man, what with all her connections. 'Nah,' I said. 'Divorced dads are too bitter. Almost as bitter as me. But seriously, Em, I thought you were holding out for the perfect man, someone like your Ross Poldark.'

She pointed her brownie at me. 'No one is like Ross Poldark.'

I grinned. 'You and your ideal men.'

She slapped her forehead. 'Shit, I forgot I have some calls to make before my suppliers close for the day. Gotta go. Thanks for these, luv, and everything else. I don't know what the hell I'd do without you,' she said as she shoved the Tupperware container into her bag and kissed me on the cheek, suddenly re-energised in the knowledge that she wasn't the only parent floundering, and that we'd get through everything together.

'And don't forget to ring up for the job,' she said as she bustled out the door.

Ah yes, the job. I only hoped I wouldn't have to wear period costumes and such. With my luck, I'd be the bloody maid. But first, I had to pay a call to a certain thorn in my side.

'Hey, beautiful,' Phil drawled when he answered the door of his flat in his boxers, his hair sticking out in every direction and the acute stench of liquor punching me in the face.

I pushed past him. 'What the hell do you think you're doing, trying to put the house up for sale? Your own children's home? What the hell is wrong with you?'

He looked contrite, pulling at the bottom of his T-shirt like a two-year-old about to burst into tears. 'I'm sorry, babe, but I needed the money…'

I stepped back as if he'd slapped me. 'Phil,' I said as calmly as possible, because murder was looking pretty good from where I was standing. 'You don't contribute one penny in child support and *you* need the money? Why should the children pay for your stupidity, and after all you've done to us?'

He shrugged, scratching the back of his neck like when he was at a loss for words, which didn't happen very often.

'I'm sorry, babe,' he repeated. 'I'm in big trouble. These blokes, they had my back, yeah, and now… they don't have it anymore. I owe a lot of money.'

Dear God, why hadn't I married a real man, one with a brain and a heart and some backbone and not the rejects of *The Wizard of Oz* all rolled into one?

'Well, you'd better start thinking, Phil. Because I'm not selling the very roof over Ben and Chloe's heads just so you can gamble it all away again.'

'What about moving the kids to Childress Academy, then?' he suggested. 'That's free, and we could split the dosh that's left.'

I stopped and stared at him. 'There *is* no "dosh" left! You took it all, don't you remember, you idiot? And there's no way in hell that I'm taking the kids out of Northwood just to pay your debts.'

'But technically, they're our debts, Nina. Hey, what about your royalties? I'm entitled to those. I was living with you when you wrote those books. I suggested the names to you. I have a right to half your earnings. You and I are still married.'

Man, that butcher's knife was looking real good now.

'But we aren't married *here*!' I cried, beating my chest above my heart. 'All you did was sponge off me the minute the royalties started coming in. You've already had your big fat share of my earnings.'

'But my debts...'

'You should've thought about that before you started gambling our lives away. Now back off before I feed you to your creditors myself!' And with that, I shoved past him and out the door, driving all the way to Northwood to pick the kids up under the steam of my fury.

'What happened to you?' Chloe smirked through her braces as she got into the car.

'Hiya, Mum!' Ben said as he got into the back seat. 'Chloe's ticked off because she got made fun of for her socks.'

'Everyone only wears tights in Year Eight,' she seethed, crossing her arms and refusing to look at me. 'I had to go hide in the loo for the entire first period just so I didn't have to hear them laugh.'

God, please grant me the strength to not be cross with my daughter just because she reminds me so much of Phil!

'Well, maybe you want to be more organised with your things in the future,' I suggested calmly. 'From now on, what doesn't go in the laundry bag doesn't get washed.'

At that, she turned to glare at me, then turned to stare sullenly out the window and muttered, 'I hate you. It's all your fault Dad left.'

My heart stopped for a split second. If that was true, they should've been *thanking* me, but I wasn't about to go into rhetoric about their father's shortcomings. It was totally unedifying and I wasn't paying good money so I could turn my kids into trash.

'Chloe, don't be a bitch,' Ben interjected.

'Ben!' I gasped, turning in my seat. 'Where did you learn that language?'

'At school, of course. Listen, Mum, Chloe's just upset because Simon's seeing someone else.'

'Who's Simon?' I asked, although somehow I felt I should've known. These kids today did their very best to keep things to themselves.

'Mind your own damn business,' she snapped.

At that, I checked the rear-view mirror and pulled over again.

'Why are we stopping?' she asked in a panic. 'I have to go home and change before I go out with my friends!'

'First of all, young lady, you're not going anywhere

without my permission. Second of all, we are going to sit here until you apologise to me and Ben for being rude.'

She snorted. 'Yeah, like that's happening.'

Ben caught my eye in the rear-view mirror and shrugged as if to say, *Let it go, Mum*. But I was sick and tired of being walked all over and if I didn't nip her behaviour in the bud now, it would grow into one huge, ugly monster tomorrow.

So I used my inner Voice of Wisdom. 'We all have problems, Chloe. But we don't take them out on you.'

'Whatever…'

'I'm serious, Chloe. We're going to sit here until you apologise.'

'Apologise for what, ruining your life?'

I blinked. 'What are you talking about?'

'You think I don't know that if you didn't have us your life would be easier?' Oh, God, she truly was having one of her beauties today.

I gasped. 'Where on earth did you hear such nonsense?'

'Everyone at school says so. Their parents say that you used to be a famous *Sunday Times* bestseller, and that with the money you earned with your stupid books you would be living it up if you didn't have Ben and me. So why don't you just leave us?'

'Leave her alone, Chloe,' Ben chided so gently I wanted to grip the steering wheel and bawl my eyes out. My little guy, the one who had suffered since he was born, always on my side, whilst Chloe seemed bent on making my life a misery. 'Can't you see how hard she works, Chloe? Give her some slack and apologise.'

But Chloe continued to stare out the window at the passers-by and I could see my own stubbornness in her high, fair forehead, in the delicate pout of her mouth as she tortured the hem of her uniform with her long, slim fingers.

Chloe was still a girl, not even a teenager, technically, and yet her peers were pushing her along faster than she could go. This Simon guy didn't seem like much of a catch if he'd already turned his back on her because of her socks.

'Chloe?' Ben said and she groaned.

'Right.'

'Right, *what*?' he persisted. The kid was a sister-whisperer.

'I'm sorry,' she muttered. 'Can we go home now?'

I sighed and turned on the ignition on my first try. That was as good as it was going to get today.

3

Something's Gotta Give

An hour later or so, Jack came over early to take a look at our barking fridge. I had resolved to leave him with it, but I was so worried that I couldn't help but hover over him as he prodded at the tiny bits in the back.

'So what's wrong with it?' I finally asked when he put the cover back on.

'Nothing, if you don't consider old age. How long have you had it?'

'Since before Chloe was born.'

He dipped his head. 'Then there's your answer.'

'Is it dangerous?'

'No, not the fridge per se, but you might want to look at the wiring back there; it doesn't look too happy.'

'Oh, God, really? Phil rewired the place when we moved in.'

Jack refrained from what was obviously on his mind. 'Just have it looked at as soon as possible, okay?'

'Kay,' I promised, wondering where that money was

coming from. And where it all went, actually. And speaking of, a moment later Chloe came back from Alf's Post Of ice, at least a half hour late when I'd only sent her to get a tin of corn with my last fifty-pound note.

'I was about to call a search party on you,' I said, trying not to sound too anxious. 'Did you get the corn?'

As an answer, she dumped it on the island before me and proceeded across the kitchen to go upstairs.

'May I have the change, please?' I asked.

She halted, her back to me. Uh-oh. Not a good sign. Chloe was famous for never lying, but I knew something was up. She turned around defiantly. 'There is no change. I've spent it all.'

All of it? My very last fifty for the month? Hold on, don't have a coronary yet. And remember we have a guest. You don't want Jack or anyone to think you treat your children unfairly.

'Chloe, what did you spend it on?'

She hesitated.

'Chloe?'

She huffed and upended her rucksack onto the island next to my tray. It was strewn with magazines, cosmetics and junk food. Forty-five pounds' worth of it. Jack glanced at me and discreetly disappeared out the back door to give us some privacy.

I took a deep breath, debating rather than spewing out my frustration with her. I was never one to hurt my children's feelings, but right about now, I longed to give her a solid lecture that would open her eyes about reality and the value of money.

And yet, I dared not scold her too harshly. Why should

she not have what her friends had? It was part of growing up and fitting in. Why should Chloe have to suffer just because I had made a bad choice and got myself pregnant at nineteen?

She stood before me, defiantly, but her fragility made me love her even more. Because the break-up had affected her much more than it had Ben, and she bravely, albeit not peacefully, trudged through it.

'Aren't you going to say anything?' she taunted, just begging for an argument. But I waved Jack back in.

'No,' I said. 'Nothing you don't already know.'

'Good,' she said, pushing all her stuff off the island and onto the floorboards before turning away to flounce up the stairs.

I sighed inwardly as I smiled an apology and Jack took the heavy oven tray from me.

'I'll dish up,' he offered. 'You have a seat. It's been a long day.'

'And it'll be an even longer night,' I said with a sigh.

'Never mind. Eat,' he said, filling Ben's plate and then dishing me up a huge portion before serving himself.

'Mum, don't mind her. It's just growing pains, is all,' Ben said as he came in. 'Can I eat this on a tray in the living room, please, Mum? *Dr Who* is on. I promise I won't spill anything.'

I kissed his cheek. 'Of course. Off you go, love.'

Whenever I thought there was no hope and that I was a crap mother, Ben always said something to melt my heart.

Later, Jack commented, 'I have to say, Nina, you handle things with such...'

'Weakness?' I suggested.

'Silly. I was going to say love. Those kids are so lucky.'

I snorted into my wine glass as I made to take a sip. 'Thanks, Jack, but we can both see that what works with Ben doesn't work with Chloe. She just does everything she can to piss me off.'

'She's still angry about the divorce.'

'A divorce that's been dragging on for three years now, Jack. You'd think she'd be over it by now. At least I had thought so. Blimey, was I wrong.'

'These things take time – you know that.'

'And as if that wasn't enough, she blindly sides with Phil.'

'She just does it to hurt you.'

'I know, but why? Why does she want to hurt me and not Phil? Christ, he's the one who broke us. And I'm killing myself here. I can't see what more I could do for them, but she just keeps rebuking me.'

He took a sip of his wine and pinned me with his dark gaze. 'Because she loves you. And it's always difficult to forgive the ones you love the most.'

He got to his feet. 'What you need is a good night's sleep. Forget the dishes for once. Go to bed.'

'But I can't. I still have to prep for my *arancini*…'

I usually cooked all the ingredients the night before so they would be at room temperature the next morning when I actually formed my rice balls.

'I'll help you,' he offered.

'You? But you've been working all day.'

'I'm fine,' he said, clearing the table and starting on the dishes.

'But—'

'This offer is only valid for the next thirty seconds, so quit your whining and get a move on, Nina.'

What could I say? The bloke was an angel. 'You, Jack, will make some woman very happy one day.'

He made a face. 'Maybe. If the right girl came along.'

'Oh, she will,' I called over my shoulder as I stepped into my larder. 'She'd have to be an idiot to not appreciate you.'

I grabbed my ingredients and with Jack's help, began turning raw meat into money.

All the while we worked, cooking and seasoning and frying, Jack was silent but cheerful, humming softly to himself, and it rubbed off on me. It was comforting, knowing I wasn't the only person up at this ungodly hour when the entire village lay snuggled up in their warm beds.

When he left a couple of hours later, whispering a goodbye and patting me on the shoulder, I realised that he, Emma and I represented three failed marriages, literally, in a row. We should have called our Meadowbank Lane Divorce Row instead. Which sounded a lot like Death Row, I mused, my tired mind wandering as I climbed the stairs, listening to the house, silent but for Minnie and Callie snoring by the Aga. Ben had long gone to bed, and Chloe was probably Snapchatting away with Chanel, or even to her dad about what a monster I was.

So I crept up into the nook in the eaves that I had the gall to call a bedroom when the ceiling was so low not even standing wardrobes would fit. I'd had to buy the kind that you'd find in a baby's nursery. The floorboards were wonky beyond trendy, and in November the window casings let in the Cornish winter with a vengeance. No amount of draught excluders could stop the cold air from creeping in.

Apart from a dresser and a bed under which I stored every book I'd ever read, there was room for little else, but I loved my bed nook because of the window overlooking the back garden. I crawled under the covers and, exhausted, waited for sleep. Sometimes it hit me like an HGV, and sometimes I'd stare up at the ceiling, trying to spot the micro cracks that let the rain in. Jack had done a good job with what he had, but had warned me it would soon need replacing. As if I had anything to spare for that.

I sighed, realising I had already entered my sleep routine, i.e. worrying and wondering whether I had put the clothes in the dryer, prepared the kids' lunches, and how much getting the fridge repaired would cost.

How I longed to fix all of the unfixables of this house that seemed to hold together by virtue of my night-time prayers. How I longed to make my children's house safe and warm and welcoming.

I'd always done as much as I could to put them first, but not without an argument from Phil, like the time he'd wanted to have a cellar dug out for a man cave to kit out with a giant flat-screen TV for himself and his beer-drinking buddies, rather than put double glazing in the kids' bedroom windows. Obviously I had nipped that one in the bud.

And just as I was about to fall asleep, the fridge started barking again, waking the dogs who decided to join it in a howling concerto.

4

Crime And Punishment

In the morning, I called in an electrician who, after a look around, assured me it was safe.

That afternoon, I swung by the Post Of ice. Alf had had a bad spell where he kept getting confused, and his doctor had made him undergo some tests for dementia. Everyone rallied to help him keep his shop open, especially Bev, Carol and Deirdre.

They knew everything about everyone, but they were also the kindest, most generous souls you'd ever meet. When Phil left, they had been among the first to arrive with blankets and home-made meals.

'Morning, Alf! Morning, ladies!' I called at the sight of all four of them confabulating behind the counter as usual.

'Ah, Nina!' they all chimed in unison. 'Care to join the committee for the End of Summer festival?'

I stopped, despite being in a super rush (and super foul mood). Any way that I could pay back the kindness that the community had shown me all these years was always welcome.

'Sure, what do I have to do?'

'Sing with us,' Bev said.

Every year they tried that one on. 'Forget it.' (I can't carry a tune to save myself.) 'But I'll cook.'

'Goody!' Deirdre clapped her hands. 'Your famous Sicilian *arancini*?'

'Sure, with pleasure.'

'Excellent! Carol, add her to the list. This year we're being hosted by the Northwood Academy.'

'What?' Carol said.

'The list! Add her,' Bev said, miming the gesture of writing. 'There's the chairperson now,' Bev said with a snort. 'My, if those heels were any higher she'd be cleaning skyscrapers in New York!'

I turned around, just in time to be ambushed by the Village Snob. One of my most heart-felt activities was avoiding people like her.

'*Darling* Nina!' cooed Vanessa, the head of the Northwood parents committee, spreading her arms and air-kissing me. She only started talking to me when someone mentioned I was a *Sunday Times* bestselling author. You know the type. 'The other Northwood mothers and I were just talking about how *you* could contribute to the End of Summer festival! We were thinking you could do a reading of some poems? After all, you are our only village celebrity left after Barth Humperdinck moved away to one of those dreadful jungles in… where was it, Aimée?' she asked with a turn of her platinum head.

'Vietnam,' her hench-girl answered, not even bothering to nod a hello my way.

'Read in public? Me? No, thank you, Vanessa. But I will be bringing some food.'

'Oh, excellent. What are you bringing? Because I've already got Martha Treghenny on the sushi, and Teresa Marsden is doing the pastries.'

'I'll actually be bringing some *arancini*,' I informed her, already relishing the look on her face.

'Oh dear, are they organic? They sound very fattening. Remember that we parents are responsible for projecting an image of healthy eating. Although I suppose they are part of the Mediterranean so-called diet.'

Unbelievable she was, that one. 'Right. I must be off,' she cut short, looking at Alf and his trio who were watching the exchange innocently, but I knew the minute Vanessa and Aimée left, they'd fall apart in hysterics.

'Bye,' they called, and as the door closed, they all hooted with laughter and I grinned. My silly, beautiful tribe.

After that, I dropped Chloe off at the bakery shop with the very last of my coins to buy some fresh bread.

'I'll walk home, I want to look at some stuff,' she barked as she jumped out. 'Oh, and I'm staying at Chanel's for the night.'

Oh, so now she was telling me rather than asking? Better nip that one in the bud as well.

'Sorry, Chloe. Emma's got a long day tomorrow and doesn't have the energy to deal with you as well as her own daughter. Maybe some other time.'

'Bloody hell, why did I have to get the cheapest – and strictest – mother in the universe!' she seethed, giving me one of her filthy looks before she slammed the car door shut, while Ben slid me a glance and squeezed my arm.

'Don't be late,' I warned her.

When I got home, I fed Minnie and Callie, who enjoyed

watching me with her almond-shaped eyes from the space between the counter and the AGA. Minnie, a German Shepherd and too large to fit in such a small space, dolefully watched from under the table, her clever eyes not missing a move I made, waiting for her turn.

As they devoured every single morsel, I leaned back against the counter, watching them. There was something so very satisfying in feeding a pet, something very rewarding, knowing that they felt safe and happy because of you. And that they loved you unconditionally, as opposed to Chloe. At least I was doing one thing right.

I sighed and turned the oven off. My chicken potato vegetable bake was ready.

'Ben,' I called into the living room where he was doing his homework with his back propped up against the settee. 'Can you please set the table, love? What's keeping Chloe?'

'Don't worry, Mum. She's probably drooling over the new cosmetics rack in Alf's shop,' Ben answered.

'He has a cosmetics rack, now?' Alf was one who didn't like change.

'It would be more appropriate to say that the Ice Cream Trio have. God knows why girls put all that guck on their faces,' Ben said. 'It's not like it makes them any prettier.'

I laughed. 'Ben, my boy, you need to learn a thing or two about girls. And precisely what to keep to yourself.'

As if on cue, the phone rang. It was Beverly, one of the Tregarth sisters who had opened, as a nod to Alf's shop, the Post Of ice Cream Parlour. But as they had promised to sell only ice cream and not any of the same goods Alf stocked, he agreed not to make a fuss as, widowed some twenty years, Alf never went without a hot meal thanks to them, and his clothes were always clean and pressed.

'Hello, pet…'

'Bev, hi,' I said, mentally searching my engagements. 'Was I supposed to call you back about something?'

'No, no, luv. Nothing like that. I… er, have Chloe here…'

My eyebrows shot up. I could feel them. 'Yes?'

'We've a bit of a problem…'

'Oh God, is she okay?'

'Oh, she's fine, but Alf's a bit upset. You see, dear, Chloe thought to, er, help herself to the new cosmetics section…'

'Oh my *God*! I'm so *sorry*! I'll obviously pay him back to the last penny. And I'll punish her like she'll never forget. I'll be there in a minute.'

Ben rolled his eyes and removed Chloe's place from the table.

'No need to come down here, luv. Jack swung by to get some cinnamon for his apples. He's going to attempt a pie. They'll be there shortly.'

Jack. Well, at least I knew he'd keep a secret, if any were to be kept in Penworth Ford.

'Thank you, Bev. I'll talk to you tomorrow.'

'Of course, luv. I'll deal with Alf. Don't you be too hard on her. She's just a child.'

'Yes, well, tomorrow then,' I said and hung up. Child, my arse. At her age I was tending to my sick parents and hadn't had half the fun my friends were having. I had been too indulgent after Phil left, and this was the result. From now on it was going to be tough love. As if there was anything such as easy love.

About a minute later, as Ben finished setting the table,

we heard the familiar crunching of gravel under Jack's SUV as he stopped and took off again and in came Chloe with a bang of the door, her face red as she flounced off to her room without even saying hello.

I dished up Ben's meal and wiped my hands on the tea towel. Time for another sermon.

I trudged upstairs and opened Chloe's door without even knocking. She was on the phone with Chanel, of course.

'Tell her you won't be talking to her for a while and hang up,' I said curtly.

Chloe ignored me and continued to talk.

'Now.'

She stared at me, then rolled her eyes. 'Chanel? Gotta go. Yeah, talk later.'

That was what she thought.

'Chloe, what were you thinking? When did I ever teach you that theft was acceptable? We don't steal in this family.'

She folded her arms and rolled her eyes towards the ceiling. 'Yeah, whatever.'

'Do you realise what you've done? You've hurt yourself, gone somewhere you never should have. Because now you can never undo it. And if Northwood finds out, they'll kick you out! And by association, even Ben!'

'Oh my God, *chill*!' she yelled, bouncing onto her side away from me.

But I wasn't letting her off that easily. 'Do you think I work this hard just so I can have my only daughter shoplifting? You'd better be grateful Alf is like a father to us.'

'Oh my God, Mum! They're not family, these people! They're just a bunch of old weirdos who need Zimmer frames to get around and wouldn't be able to survive in the real world.'

'Chloe! How dare you speak of them like that. They love you to bits and we owe them more than you'll ever know.'

'Yeah, yeah, the fire and the blankets and the gifts, blah, blah, blah.'

'And for your information, Chloe, this *is* the real world. Not the glossy paper dolls you see in your magazines, but an authentic world where people work and suffer and come together to help others. Not that you'd be familiar with the concept. I'm so disappointed in you right now, Chloe.'

'You're disappointed? What about me? What about that so-called family you promised us when you brought us into this shitty world? And this house? I hate this dump!' she yelled, pushing the hair back from her face. 'You go on and on talking about what a wonderful village this is and how you love everybody, but does anyone give us money?'

I bristled. 'We don't need anyone's money, Chloe. A hand babysitting the two of you from time to time, which I regularly repay in kind, yes. But we couldn't accept anything more than friendship. Not from these people who have shown us nothing but kindness.'

She threw her hands into the air. 'Babysitting! You see? I'm thirteen!'

'Yes, but you're acting like you're three.'

'And *you're* acting like an idiot. You say we don't need any more money, but you always say no to everything I want!'

I took a deep breath. When she went off on these tangents, hollering never did the job.

'Chloe, if you're referring to the school trip to France, I said I was working on it.' Literally. 'But now, because of what you did, you have proven to me that I can't trust you to walk around in your own village, let alone another country.'

'Yada, yada, yada,' she muttered to the wall. 'I'm going to stay with Dad! At least, he lives in Truro and gives me everything I want!'

I kept my cool. 'Maybe he does. But he doesn't give you what you need, and there is a very big difference. What you did today was very serious, and I'm going to treat you *consequentially.*' There. If nothing, she'd learn a new word.

'Oh, my God, Mum! It was just a bloody lipstick, not a car! You need to get off my case! All you do is nag, nag, nag, just like Dad says. I wish he'd never married you!'

I opened and closed my mouth. Did my children actually think he was the better parent, and the breadwinner? That he gave me money to support them? They were much too young to know the truth about what he'd done to us. But now, I see it had been counterproductive. But could I lay that on my daughter's – and my son's – shoulders? Tell them how he had robbed us blind, and abandoned us in a caravan?

'We're done here, Chloe. You are grounded for a month. No internet. No magazines. And no phone. If you want to talk to Chanel, you can do that at school. From now on, you march to my tune. End of.'

'You can't do that!' she protested. 'You haven't got the balls!'

I took her phone and her magazines and marched towards the door. 'Watch me,' I said, closing her door behind me, switching off the Wi-Fi on my way out.

My own phone bleeped with an SMS from Jack:

Keep your cool as always. You've got this. Jack xxx

5

It Could Happen To You

The next morning Chloe was ready in ten minutes, a record for any teenager, let alone her. Still, she came down at the last moment, her face red from anger, but I refused to feel sorry for her. It was time she bulked up on reality and manners.

There was a heavy silence in the car except for its usual coughing and spitting, but we made it all the way to the school gates where Ben leaned over to give me a silent kiss and Chloe slammed the door shut, but not too hard so as not to create a scene. After all, she still cared about her reputation here.

Personally, I didn't care what the Northwood parents said, because in my home, a good bollocking every now and then was mandatory.

Back at the house, I sat at my War Desk and whipped out my financial ledger to see how deep in the shit I really was.

Mortgage. Car tax. Car insurance. Council tax. School dinners for both Chloe and Ben. A ghastly total, even before I clothed them and put food on the table. Forget about me. I couldn't remember the last time I'd bought anything for myself.

So, with Minnie lying on my feet, I dusted off my ancient Great Ideas notebook and pulled out my coloured pens in the hope of coming up with a new plot for another book.

I turned to my window facing the garden for some inspiration. From here I could also see the front out to Meadowbank Lane, and from the side window I could see the fields and the bend in the road beyond which Jack's farm lay. I loved the fact that this room was triple aspect. Imagine not being able to continue living here anymore and seeing this overwhelmingly beautiful gift. I swallowed the knot in my throat and began racking my brain for a happy, uplifting plot. If only I could come up with yet another laugh-out-loud, feel-good romantic comedy. But the feeling good and the laughing were long gone.

That evening, with nothing but doodles on my notepad, I was elbow deep in the kitchen sink scouring the crispy lasagne bits off the oven dish when I got a call from Alice. Knowing I owed her (and my bank account) that book, I debated whether to let it go to voicemail and go back to scrubbing, which presented far more enjoyment and satisfaction.

But in the end I picked up, already dreading her pep talk about how a husband like Phil had given me the material to write hilarious stuff, which had been my lottery win.

'Finally!' she cried. 'I have news for you, my girl! News that will blow your bloody mind!'

'Oh, God, just give it to me straight – my sales have completely tanked, haven't they?'

'Nope!'

'You're dropping me?'

'Silly. Try again.'

'Someone – that horrible reviewer who always gives me one-stars – she's written the review that will destroy my career once and for all, hasn't she?'

'You'd better sit down.'

'I am sat down,' I lied.

'Okay! You are not going to believe this! *Written In The Stars*...?'

Meaning my very first book. The heroine is in dire straits (sound familiar?) and writes a book about meeting an American poet, her true love. Who turns out to be a real arsehole. In the end she returns to her cottage in the English countryside with her two children and marries the village butcher. The meat man, not the assassin. Or had I changed him to a vet? Yes, I think I had. I never reread my books once they're published, because by the time I've written and done all the edits, I'm sick to the back teeth of them.

'Yeah...?' I prompted.

'Brace yourself! I got a call from a Hollywood producer. He wants to turn your book into a movie!'

I sat down with a thump, nearly missing the chair. Someone wanted to turn my book into a movie? A Hollywood movie, with real actors and sets and... real royalties? But how could that be? There were millions of books out there – how did mine attract the attention of a Hollywood producer? That kind of stuff only happened, to the point, in the movies, and certainly not to someone like me.

I instantly thought of J.K. Rowling. Sure, my books had nothing to do with the Harry Potter series, but if a movie had changed her entire life, maybe mine would go through some sort of improvement as well? I mean, anything was better than this. But to have your book become a film was every writer's (especially a poor writer's) dream.

'Alice, if this is your idea of a joke or some sick, twisted way to get my creative juices flowing again, I swear I will choke you with your own hair extensions. I will shove them down your throat and watch you turn five thousand shades of purple.' It was time to dump your agent when she started playing with your feelings.

She laughed. 'I'm not joking, promise. Things are about to change for you. Big time.'

I pulled off my sudsy rubber gloves and took her off speakerphone. 'He read the book and he loves it. He wants you to work on the script with— Nina? Are you still there?'

I was still there, in the parallel universe where my life had taken all the right turns and I hadn't met the wrong man and I was no longer a struggling single mum. Images of me striding into the secretary's office at Northwood and dropping a fat cheque onto the desk crammed into my mind, alongside thoughts of taking the kids to get new uniforms, new sports equipment, getting the piping and roof fixed once and for all, seeing a proper, specialist doctor about Ben's leg and maybe one about my allergies. Oh, and paying off the mortgage. Hell, no, move straight into a new build. One with a huge garden, the right postcode and... I had to calm down. There was no point in putting the cart in front of the horses.

'How... how has this even happened, Alice?'

NANCY BARONE

'Does it matter, Nina? He's flying us first class to LAX next week!'

'Next week? I can't believe it…'

'Believe it. And get your hair done.'

'My hair? What for? Besides, which producer are we talking about here?'

'His name is Ben Stein.'

Ben. Like my son. That had to be a good omen.

'What difference does it make anyway?' she wanted to know. 'He's a Hollywood producer!'

'What difference does it make? If he's some flake the whole project could go down the toilet – that's the difference. I need someone with some clout.'

'Listen to you, already making demands and you haven't even left Cornwall yet.'

I still couldn't believe it. 'Please tell me again that this is not a joke?'

Alice giggled. 'I'll send you your tickets.'

'Tickets? Plural?'

'I told them you have two kids. They're flying all of us.'

'But… the kids… school…'

'So take them out for the week! It's almost summer, anyway. Now go get your hair done.'

'Again with my hair. Why do I even have to meet these people? If they like my book can't I just sign by proxy and—'

'Nina, stop! Listen to yourself. Your book is going to be a movie. Your whole life just got made, and you don't even want to meet Daddy Long Legs?'

I was hoping for a female director. Someone fantastic like Nancy Meyers. Someone who knows *What Women Want,*

46

that *It's Complicated* and that, eventually, *Something's Gotta Give*.

'Of course I'll meet him.'

'Good girl. I'll call you tomorrow with an update.' And she rang off, leaving me sitting alone in the darkening kitchen still holding my sudsy rubber gloves and a greasy pan, and with a pounding heart.

If any of this was true and the film actually made it to the cinemas (because we know all too well what happens to some movies that never make it off the producer's desk) our whole lives would indeed be made.

I'd be able to afford the kids a new lifestyle and be a new, angst-free mum who smiled a lot and took them to marvellous places and fed them good-quality food bought from Waitrose and independent shops and not the local joint down the road where you had to bring your own boxes.

When the kids were asleep, I sat back in my writing chair under the dining room window. Maybe this really was my lucky chair after all. It had seen me pound out the three novels that, as it turned out, gave me the much-needed money, my only money.

I had already made a mental list of the improvements I'd make in the children's lives and in our home. Even Minnie and Callie would get the best dog food, rather than the cheap store brand they seemed content with. Yes, life was looking like it had remembered me after all.

But then I fell into my own trap and started wondering all sorts of things, like how much of a say I could have in the script? I wasn't a scriptwriter. And how faithful would the movie be to my book? Who would they cast? *Jesus, Nina,* came Alice's voice in my ear. *Who the hell cares?*

But one thing I did care about. Would the kids recognise the storylines I'd so diligently disguised as some other poor cow's misfortunes and resent me talking like that about their father? Just how similar was my anti-hero Bill to Phil? Because while all my hatred for Phil was safely tucked away in between the discreet pages of a book and out of my children's hands, we were okay. But even they would recognise their dad's character on screen: gorgeous and totally useless. I wondered who could play his role? Jude Law would have been perfect. But he was too talented to want to portray a loser like Phil. I mean *Bill.*

The next morning before the kids were even up, I got another call from Northwood, and my hands began to sweat at the sound of the secretary's voice. All I needed was a little more time. Just a little more. I was trembling so badly I almost dropped my phone.

'Ms Conte?'

'Uh, yes, hello there…' I tried to sound cheerful and confident (you know, project some of that good karma while it was still around).

'Ms Conte, I just wanted to confirm that your payment has been received.'

What? How? 'I beg your pardon?'

'The fees, Ms Conte? We've received them. Thank you.'

'Oh. Okay.'

'Sorry for the misunderstanding.'

'No – uh – problem.' I put the phone down, my heart

beating to a million different rhythms. What the hell was *that* all about? How the hell had the money got there?

I called my bank immediately and spoke to someone named Parminder Rabash, whose name I'll never forget, because he kindly explained to me that I had received an advance of ten thousand pounds from my agent, Alice Hopkins. I thanked him, blessed him, anointed him with all my best wishes and dialled Alice's number.

'Have you gone absolutely mad?' I cried. 'You know I can't pay you back.'

Alice laughed. 'I don't expect you to.'

'Alice, thank you from the bottom of my heart. But what if my deal falls through?'

'It won't. But, honey, let's ride the wave for now, yeah?'

I closed my eyes and grinned, breathing deeply. 'Yes. Thank you so much, Alice.'

'No problem. Now go and buy yourself and the kids some snazzy duds. You can't wear your wellies or your Crocs in LA.'

I grinned. 'Why not? I've seen the way the stars dress there.'

'Well, first of all because there's no mud in LA. None that you'd see, anyway. Oh, speaking of stars, I need you to send me a new pic.'

I snorted. 'How are those two thoughts even remotely connected? Besides, what's wrong with the old photo?' I didn't have a new one, nor did I have a stitch to wear, and my hair, despite Alice's advice, still needed a good cut. Better to keep the money for important things.

'I like my old one, Alice. I look young and happy in it.'

Six years younger, give or take. Forget that I was miserable, but surely youth could sometimes hide the effects of stress? And as long as it didn't catch up on me suddenly the minute I hit fifty, we were cruising.

'Honey, believe you me, from now on, you will be taking only happy pictures. And the resolution on your old one isn't high enough.'

'Resolution? For what?'

'For your promo pages. Wikipedia and stuff.'

I laughed. 'Wikipedia?'

'Will you stop echoing everything I say? I opened a Wikipedia page for you, so that when people look you up now, they'll see your backlist titles.'

'Huh. I hadn't thought of that.'

'That's why you pay me ten per cent. Also, you need to update your website. I had a look at it and it screams the word "Forgotten".'

Yikes. My website. She had a point. The last time I'd even looked at it was when I'd added the banner "*Sunday Times* Bestseller". And that was many, many *Sunday Times* ago. Did I even remember my password? I must have scribbled it on a piece of paper somewhere, possibly on the back of an old recipe.

'Right. I'll see what I can do.'

'It doesn't have to be too staid this time. Actually, make it romcom-y, to reflect the Hollywood vibe. Wear a pink blouse or something.'

'Alice, I love you, but I don't do pink.'

'Oh, honey, you may not understand it now, but your life is about to change. Big time.'

6

Something To Talk About

'And I'm going to ride in a *plane*? Over the Atlantic *Ocean*?' Ben cried, his arms tight around my neck.

'Yes, my darling, you are,' I assured him and hugged him fiercely. I had also booked a session with an American specialist, Dr Ellenberg, to see his leg, but that was a surprise. The cherry on the cake.

'I'm not coming,' Chloe pronounced, crossing her arms like whenever she was on the warpath.

Ben and I stopped. 'What do you mean?' I asked. 'It's the chance of a lifetime.' Now that I had finally embraced my hopes and dreams without any fear, she went and pooh-poohed it all? Really?

'I'm not going to have any part of you demeaning Dad.'

And here they were, my fears finally rearing their ugly head. Bloody brilliant. Not that she had ever read my books, of course, so I began to wonder who her source was. 'Where did you hear such nonsense, Chloe?'

'Everyone is always talking about you at school,' she said

in a tight voice. The voice that came out when she was truly upset and not just throwing one of her strops.

Crap. Sooner than I'd thought. 'And… what are they saying?'

'That you got your own back with your books. That at least Dad found one way to be of use.'

And then the tears streamed down her face. 'Why do you always have to make me the laughing stock of my school? Why can't you just be like the other mothers and have a proper job?'

Ooh, I could see this was going to be a mother of a tantrum. Ben saw it too and released himself from me and slinked off upstairs. Smart kid.

'Chloe, sweetheart, please try to understand that this is the best thing that has ever happened to us.'

'Nothing good has happened to us since you kicked Dad out,' she insisted.

Was that the yarn he spun to our children? That I was the big bad wolf? 'You might not remember, but he left of his own volition, Chloe.'

'I don't believe you.'

I stretched out my arms and took a deep breath. 'Chloe, sweetheart, come here.'

She glared at me in response and I sighed. I knew this conversation was coming, only I didn't know it would be so soon. Chloe had been content, until now, to live this life, just the three of us, perfectly happy and serene, seeing her father twice a month. But as he sank his fingers into her young mind, Chloe had begun to turn against me.

And after he had finally gone through all of our savings and moved to Truro because he didn't have the gall to show his face in Penworth Ford after what he'd done, all the unanswered questions and doubts had come to the fore. He was still in debt, lived in a rented flat he paid for God knew how, seeing as he didn't work anymore. At least not that I knew.

Whether they were really Chloe's doubts or prompted by her school friends, and their curious mothers, was another issue.

When Chloe refused to move towards me, I sat next to her on the settee facing the garden. The daisies were out, gloriously bright like stars in a dark sky.

'Chloe,' I ventured. 'Please understand one thing. My books are not about your father and me.'

She snorted, her eyes still lost on the garden, and once again I saw myself in her. The delicate but angry brow, the full but grim-set lips and the gathered tears that refused to spill.

Was this what I was to expect in the future? A rebel of a daughter? Was she going to become one of those furious girls who ran away from home and never returned? Please God, help me make her understand that I love her and that I only want to keep her safe?

I was doing my damnedest to keep her from the ugliness of the world, but she would one day, all too soon, see it for what it was. A mixture of wondrous, tremendously beautiful but bad things and bad people like Phil. Simon from school would look like the angel Gabriel in comparison.

'Well, then who is it about?'

I shrugged. 'Someone like me. And most women today. But it's made up. It's fiction.'

'But everybody says it's all true…'

'Who?'

'The mothers at Northwood…'

'What do they know, Chloe? Most of them haven't even read my books. Nor do they know what happens in other people's homes. Not even you and Ben know all the details of how your father left, so how can perfect strangers, let alone the Northwood mothers, know?'

But she just stared ahead, refusing to rejoice for us.

The first person I called was Jack. Or rather, the first person I told. He had stopped by with a whole bushel of early summer peaches and I just had to share it with him, and the look of pure wonder – and then delight – on his face was a gift of its own.

'I'm so proud of you, Nina,' he said, giving me a bear hug. 'You truly are Wonder Woman.'

I laughed, finally feeling my ribs expanding for the first time in many many years with something akin to joy.

'Have you told Emma?' he asked.

'The kids went round to bring her over. I want to see her face. And I've just made cannelloni for dinner. Are you interested?'

'Always. And to celebrate,' he said, whipping out a bottle of his prime cider, 'a bit of bubbly!'

I clapped my hands. 'Ooh, yummy! But how did you know?'

'I didn't. I just thought the three of us could have a drink tonight.'

'Yes, let's get sloshed!' Not that I would, with my kids around. But if I did, Jack was the kind of bloke who'd carry you upstairs and pull the covers up to your chin and sit by your bed all night to make sure you didn't choke on your own sick.

'But when you get back from Los Angeles I want to cook for you and the kids myself. And I'll bring it over so as not to disrupt their bed routine. How's that?'

I suppressed a groan. As much as I loved him, Jack could not cook to save himself. His various attempts had resulted in burnt chicken, which was bright pink on the inside, and mashed potatoes, which were still raw. And still to this day, I don't know how he had managed that one. But he was indeed the perfect friend. He knew my kids inside and out. He'd be a great father one day. 'You, my friend, are a man to marry.'

He beamed. 'I am, aren't I?'

'Except that you can't cook to save yourself, so I'll provide the food; you just bring the booze, okay?'

He laughed. 'Works every time!'

The front door opened and banged shut. 'Nina! I'm hungry! What's this secret you've got to tell me? Hey, Marrak,' she greeted, clapping him on the back and seeing the bottle. 'What are we celebrating?'

'Oh, nothing much,' I said with a shrug. 'Just a Hollywood deal for *Written In The Stars*.'

Emma's face – I would never forget it. It went from confused to eyebrows into her scalp, then all teeth and tears as she threw herself at me, jumping up and down, whoop-whooping, and soon we were all a jumble of arms and legs and even Jack got kissed while, in the background, Chloe shrugged at Chanel in disgust.

'Oh my God, Nina!' she finally cried, then clapped Jack on the back again.

'Ow,' he said. 'Easy, Em.'

But she ignored him. 'Do you know what this bloody means? That we know a real celebrity! I want front-row seats at the Oscars when they call out your name! Oh, my God, we're so bloody proud of you, aren't we, Jack?'

'Absolutely proud – but not surprised,' he said softly.

'Thanks, guys. Let's eat! I've got trays for the kids so they can eat in the living room while we—' I held up the bottle of cider and whispered, 'get pissed!'

Not that we ever did. Jack wasn't much of a drinker and I always had my kids in the house and Emma only let herself go once a year on one very specific night.

Jack shook his head and opened the bottle while I dished up the food for the kids and then for ourselves.

All evening we talked and dreamed, all the while eating and laughing. God, it felt good. It didn't hurt to laugh anymore.

At midnight Jack got up. 'Sorry to kill our buzz, ladies, but I've got an early start tomorrow.'

'Going? Aww, you sure?' I asked. I didn't want the euphoria to end.

'Another time. Go and get yourself some rest. You want to be fresh for Hollywood.'

'Yeah, I guess you're right. I'll call you guys from LA?' I giggled. 'Gosh, listen to me, I already sound American!'

'You are a star...' Emma swooned, hugging me.

'Break a leg,' Jack said, kissing me on the cheek. He smelled like chocolate. 'Have a great trip.'

'You too, Jack. You're not going away on one of your own business meetings? You'll be here when I get back?'

He held my elbow with his free hand and peered into my face with an amused twinkle in his eyes. 'I'll be here when you get back.'

'Okay, Jack. Night, Em...'

'Night, Nina.'

I was still chuckling as I closed the door.

House secured and dogs tucked into their baskets, I crept to my room, dizzy more with happiness than cider. Yes! For the first time I was not merely happy, I was elated. Hopeful. Bursting with energy! Sleep? Who was tired? I could actually start a new book tonight! Come to think of it, I could even *finish* a new book tonight!

But I didn't, luckily, because it would have been nothing but drunken drivel.

The next morning as I ran my pre-trip errands about town, there was still a feverishness in me that hadn't disappeared along with the cider fumes.

The news had really gone viral as everyone, including the bank manager, congratulated me.

Alice had done a fabulous job in publicising the news and there was even a headline on some local papers with the new picture I'd sent her. (No makeover, no haircut, just me. Minus the glasses. Sometimes less is more. And the resolution was just fine.)

'*Cornwall writer in talks to secure a Hollywood deal,*' Alf read aloud when I stepped into the Post Of ice. 'It was about time you got your own back, luv,' he said, giving me a pat on the cheek.

'Aww, thanks, Alf.'

Now all I had to do was worry about protecting the kids from the monumental invasion of their privacy that would most certainly ensue, especially if the deal went through.

I only hoped that Phil never read about it and that he stayed away from the internet and any kind of media. I didn't know what he'd be capable of doing.

For days, everyone I knew continued to call and text, congratulating me and asking questions and wishing us well. And I felt... *stronger*. More confident, and it wasn't just the prospect of earnings. I had been given a second chance to make my children's and my life right.

With Alice's advance, I paid the school fees for the rest of the year, bought them new uniforms, and sports kits, and set aside some money for the consultation with Ben's American surgeon.

Then I drove to Falmouth, surprised that Lottie didn't cough once on the way, and paid a mechanic to give her a good look, once and for all, followed by a trip down to B&Q to buy stuff for the house, like a couple of new dog baskets and cushions for Minnie and Callie, a mirror and a pink clock radio for Chloe and an inflatable car-shaped reading chair and a new pile rug for Ben. And for myself, coloured pens, sticky notes and a pile of notebooks with the words Bright Ideas on the cover, because good things always came in threes.

7

Hollywood Dreams

Because I had sole custody of the kids, I didn't need Phil's permission to take them out of the country. So I called the school to inform them we'd be away for a week.

'I hope you've packed your sunscreen, Ms Conte!' the secretary answered. 'And give George Clooney a kiss from me!'

'Uhm, thank you. Will do.'

I put down the phone. George Clooney? As if. I wondered who they'd choose to play my fictitious hero? Probably some young, rising model turned actor. But who could play Stella, my heroine? Come to think of it, who the hell would want to feature in cargo pants, Crocs, glasses and a ponytail for three-quarters of the movie? What actress would want to look like me? I mean Stella.

On the eve of our departure I packed the kids some basics. There was no way they were going to need their macs in California this time of year. Besides, I didn't want them to stand out as Brits abroad usually do. We'd go with whatever we felt comfortable with. Chloe would be all over the department stores pretending she was nineteen instead of thirteen. I had to keep a close eye on that one.

I sighed, but this time it was a happy sigh. Could it be? Could things really be taking a turn for the best for us, after all this time? Dared I hope as much? But I resolved that, whatever happened, even if the whole deal died a quick death, I would still stay upbeat.

And Ben – my throat contracted at the thought of him. Would they be overly kind to a kid in a leg brace? I didn't want him to feel any different, and already I imagined California kids on rollerblades whizzing past him, making him feel teeny tiny. What could I do? I would give the whole of the film proceeds (there I went again, dreaming) to any doctor who could make my son stand on his own two legs and kick a ball without falling over. And so would Chloe – I knew that for sure, because, as shallow as she sometimes seemed, she loved her brother fiercely and would kick anyone's arse if they dared to mistreat him.

Enough, I scolded myself, swiping at my cheeks. This was a *good* thing. The opportunity of a lifetime. I had written the book and I deserved the chance to make my kids happy after all we'd been through. Things were finally going to be good.

The next morning the car arrived bang on time to take us to Heathrow airport where we'd be boarding a direct flight to LAX. Listen to me – until yesterday Lax was my nickname for laxatives and now I was already slipping into the lingo. I could already picture a casual conversation with the folks at The Post Of ice and The Post Of ice Cream:

'*Where are you jetting off to this time, Nina?*'

'*Oh, nowhere special, Deirdre. Just to LAX.*'

'*Oh, how wonderful, Nina! And what will you be doing there?*'

'*Oh, same old, same old. Writing my successful scripts.*'

'*Oh, aren't you the pride of Penworth Ford now?*'

'*That's right, Deirdre. No more Monday morning coronaries trying to get the kids to school, my arancini to the restaurant on time, completely bypassing the pressing phone calls for money, which I now have, thank you very much!*'

It was nice to dream.

Ironically, the day of our departure was a Monday morning, only this one saw us washed, fed and dressed way ahead of schedule. Chloe had her favourite jeans on and all her magazines (I gave in in the end, fresh start and all that) and Ben had his crossword puzzles and his portable dictionary with him. Chloe rolled her eyes but gave him a fake punch in the shoulder.

'Ready, sport?'

'Hollywood, you ain't seen nothin' yet,' he answered. Oh God, listen to these two, I thought. Had they been bingeing on American sitcoms while I wasn't looking?

Alice was already at the airport in an exquisite cream-coloured pants suit. Me, I had done my best in a linen dress, which turned out to be a horrible idea, because as we climbed the steps into the jet I could feel the sweat sticking my wrinkly outfit to the back of my damp thighs. Maybe I should've worn trousers, but Alice had said to dress smart. It only dawned on me then that she meant for the meeting, not the flight. Duh.

'Is there any news?' I asked her as we buckled up, Ben and Chloe on my left, Alice on my right.

'None. Just that we have an appointment with Ben Stein on Wednesday afternoon.'

I nodded, making a mental note on what I was going to say about the book. Of course I'd totally deny it was autobiographical – what the hell did they know about divorced mums in Cornwall anyway?

As the plane's engines roared to life, Chloe paled and she turned to me, her eyes huge in fear. I leant over Ben, taking her hand, which she gripped. 'It's okay, Chloe. You are safer here than in a car.'

'Especially Lottie!' Ben added, craning his head to see out the window next to him.

'These planes are built to take off and land a million times a day, and every time they get checked thoroughly. It's perfectly safe.'

She nodded, the rational side of her clutching at my words, but her hand still gripping mine.

'Sorry,' she said, biting her lip. 'Please don't tell anyone.'

'Of course not, sweetheart.' Didn't she know that I lived for her and Ben, and that I would never do anything to humiliate them? Because if she didn't, it was something I needed to work on even harder.

As the plane soared into the air, Ben's face practically burst with excitement as he craned his neck to take in every inch of the view. Chloe gasped and I made a show of breathing deeply.

'It's all right, we're fine. Look around you, everyone's happy. And if you're still not convinced, look at the flight attendants. They do this so many times it's actually nothing at all to them anymore.'

'Look, Mum! Windsor Castle! And... *Legoland*? Mum!'

Ben was gaga over Lego. 'Hmm,' I said. 'We're going to have to check that out when we get back to England.'

He gasped. 'Really, Mum?'

Really, Mum. If I couldn't do that for him now, where was the joy in making money? Of course, on the outside, I'd still be the staid, strict-ish mother who was their guide and driving force. But inside, I allowed myself to be naff and daft, making lists of all the things we'd actually have the money and time to do. It was fun!

I sat back, still holding Chloe's hand. 'And maybe a trip to the Victoria and Albert Museum?'

Her eyes bulged even more, only this time with incredulity. 'You mean a trip to London?'

It was ridiculous that we were going to America while they'd only been to London once. 'Yes. We'll plan it when we get back. Maybe we could even fly from Newquay – what do you think?'

She thought about it, looking around. 'We would have never been able to do this before your book got noticed by Hollywood, right?'

'Exactly. So maybe writing it wasn't a bad thing after all?'

She bit her lip. 'I don't know yet. I'll think about it.'

It was going to take me more than a tour of some snazzy film studio to win this one over, as she was determined to maintain the upper hand. But I was just as determined to turn her into a happy and polite person. Well-read wouldn't be bad, either. I smiled. 'You do that, sweetie.'

Would you believe me if I told you that as we exited LAX hours later, it was pouring down with rain? I thought it never rained in California. Wasn't that how the song went?

When we were met by a stretch limo, for once Ben was

at a loss for words, lapsing into a repeated 'Wowww! Mum, *look*! Look at the size of the roads! And look at the skyscrapers!' while Chloe sat in absolute silence, her blue eyes enormous with wonder. No, I didn't think we were in Cornwall anymore.

As the rain lashed at the car, we pulled up under a mega-glass awning at a swanky hotel.

The kids weren't the only ones impressed by the sleek luxury of our surroundings. A long white counter that wouldn't have looked out of place on the deck of The Starship Enterprise served as the reception while young gorgeous people of every colour but one size spoke into headsets or to equally swanky people pouring in and out through the sliding glass doors.

'Will you be having dinner in the hall or in your rooms?' a pretty Asian receptionist asked me. She was so beautiful she could've been a star herself, which, a glance around me revealed, was pretty much the norm here.

'Uhm, in the hall, please.' I scouted around for someone as normal-looking as me and found absolutely no one. Who was I kidding? I pulled my jacket closer over my abundant chest and followed Alice and the kids who were following a porter into a lift. I mean, an *elevator*.

'Thirtieth floor,' he informed us as the doors pinged open practically a couple of breaths after climbing in.

This was the closest we'd ever come to my idea of paradise.

Our suite was the size of the ground floor of the farmhouse back home, so white and glossy I was afraid we'd dirty it with our luggage and travel shoes.

I felt like Vivian in *Pretty Woman* in the luxurious hotel room.

'Dibs!' Chloe called as she launched herself onto the white comforter of the queen-sized bed in the far corner of the room, leaving Ben and me to share the other queen. Which was fine by me. Any excuse to cuddle up to at least one of my kids without seeming too s-motherly was a bonus.

Alice and I watched the kids ooh-ing and ah-ing. And then they started to argue over the TV remote.

'Chloe, Ben, settle down. We don't want to make ourselves known here as well, do we?'

Alice laughed. 'But that's exactly what we want! For everyone to know who you are and what you've written. This is your time, Nina!'

I grinned. 'You're right. My destiny will be written in the stars, just like my heroine's.'

'That's the spirit,' Alice agreed, looking around, perhaps no longer unaccustomed to so much space after having to squeeze into her own London flat. 'I'll be next door,' she said, 'washing the aeroplane smells out of my hair.'

The exact opposite of me. I didn't want to erase a single moment of this dream come true.

'Can I have a burger, Mummy?' Ben asked as we later pored over the menus in the hotel restaurant. Outside it was still raining, but inside, we were Walkin' On Sunshine.

Chloe rolled her eyes and said, 'Ben, we've got to act just a little bit more sophisticated now that we're in America...'

'Don't be silly,' I said. 'Just be yourselves. Right, Alice?'

Three sets of eyes swung to her checking her teeth in the cutlery. 'Hm? Yeah, sure. Listen, I've been meaning to tell you—'

'*There* they are,' came a jolly booming voice from behind my back. *Behind my back* being the operative words, as I would soon find out.

Alice cleared her throat and stood up. 'Nina, kids – this is Mr Ben Stein.'

I half-rose like I'd seen in a movie and he gripped my hand so tight I thought he was trying to pull me out of my seat. He was a dead-ringer for Jason Alexander from *Seinfeld* but he was, at the moment, giving me the vibes of his other role, the horrible lawyer in *Pretty Woman*, the one that tries to shaft Richard Gere and, incidentally, Julia Roberts. Now *she* was a street-wise girl if there ever was one. I decided to go with my gut and be wary, because this man had our future in his hands.

Why hadn't Alice mentioned this encounter? Weren't we supposed to be meeting the next day? Or – God help us – had the deal been called off just as we'd been flying in or something? I needed to know now. I was a big girl. I could take it on the chin, whatever the news was.

'Sit, sit, sit. Nice to meet you all, finally! And who do we have here, my namesake Ben! Nice to meet you, buddy!'

Oh God, please don't let him be condescending or Ben's going to hate him straight off the bat, I prayed behind a smile I wasn't feeling. Already alarm bells were ringing and I made a mental note to chew Alice out for this later. I don't know why, but years of watching my back had sharpened my sixth sense, and it was very ill at ease at the moment.

'Are you all ready for this extraordinary adventure?' Ben Stein asked no one in particular but making eye contact with all of us in turn.

Chloe shrugged. 'I want to know who's going to be acting in it. I've got a bet at school.'

Ben Stein laughed. 'Oh, really? Who's your money on for the male lead?'

'My mate's mum says it's going to be Ashton Kutcher and maybe Kate Winslet.'

I snorted my coffee, narrowly missing Ben Stein's sleeve. 'Sorry,' I said, but continued to chuckle to myself at the mere thought. Me, portrayed by Kate Winslet. I only wished.

'Does that tickle your fancy?' Ben Stein asked in an exaggerated British accent. 'Who do you see, Nina? Or should I call you Fab, because you certainly are fab, young lady.'

Fab and young? Give me a break.

'Two fibs in one sentence, well done. You're not a Hollywood producer for nothing,' was the dumbest thing I could say, but I said it. Which, luckily, made him laugh. Unless he was an Academy Award winner for acting as well.

'Nina, I wanted to meet you and your kids before the official meeting tomorrow because—'

Uh-oh, here it came.

'We're having a bit of a problem at the moment.'

I could feel my Bloody Mary turning into a Bloody Ben (the older Ben) in the pit of my stomach. Why didn't he just come out and say it – the movie was a no-go. I chanced a glance at Alice who was too busy with her own Bloody Mary to meet my eyes.

'Oh? What kind of problem?'

'Just... producer stuff. Executive decisions.'

'Meaning?'

'Meaning that we don't want to change anything about your book. We love it just the way it is.'

I don't know why, but I exhaled. But of course I know why. I was terrified they'd Hollywood the book all up. Make the female lead be someone absolutely glamorous like Scarlett Johansson or Charlize Theron. The book had worked because it was about a normal woman.

The guy, admittedly, would have to be half as handsome as Phil had been. And have the same boyish charm. Not to mention the new love in Stella's life. Good luck pulling that one off.

'Who would you see in your role, Nina?'

I coughed. 'Uh... I'm not in the book, Ben. The heroine's name is Stella. It's a work of *fiction*.'

Ben Stein bowed. 'Yes, yes of course. We need someone super-talented to match the male lead. Someone who can step up to the plate – a consummate actress that normal women can relate to at the same time. Have you got any names off hand?'

They were asking me? 'Uh... I dunno. Maybe Reese Witherspoon?'

He nodded. 'Nice, nice. Anyone else?'

I darted a glance at Alice. 'What do you think, Alice?'

She jumped as if I'd startled her in the shower of her own home and then shot a glance at Ben Stein, while my Ben followed the conversation like it was a ping-pong match. Chloe, I noticed, was lost in contemplation of the fashion scene around her. Something was not right. What were these two up to?

'Me?' she asked. 'I don't know, really. It's up to you, Nina.'

'No, it's not,' I answered.

'What if it was?' Ben Stein asked.

I stared at him.

'What if I could get you anyone of your choice?'

Was I dreaming, or would the restaurant suddenly reveal the *Candid Camera* crew? But then again, who was I that they'd be playing a joke on me?

'You're the producer. Anyone you choose will be fine by me. Well, except for maybe Cher or Liz Taylor.'

Ben Stein guffawed. 'That's more like it. I just wanted to know if you had an idea of who you wanted or didn't want.'

I shrugged. 'Who's in the running?'

'I can get you anyone you want.'

'Right. Wow, uhm… thank you.'

Ben Stein stood up. 'So, I'll see you all at the studios tomorrow! Sleep tight, kids.'

Alice nodded and polished off the last of her drink, raising her hand for another one.

'What the hell was that all about?' I hissed when he was out of earshot.

'What do you mean?' she asked innocently.

I rotated my head in an exaggerated gesture. '*No* producer goes to all the trouble to meet some obscure author the day before an official meeting. So what's going on, Alice? Why do I feel I've just been tricked?'

She gulped and put down her empty glass. 'All right. I can't tell you everything yet, but I feel that trust here is an issue.' She took my wrist. 'Nina, trust me when I say you will thank me tomorrow.'

'Thank you for what?'

'I can't tell you. But Ben is in it completely. He's one

hundred per cent behind this project. But so is someone else. Someone I somehow feel you'd prefer, but I'm holding out for the highest bid.'

'There's a bidding on my book?'

'Not really. They're willing to produce it together, but there's a catch.'

'But of course.' How stupid of me. After all, this was Hollywood, land of lies and compromises, right? 'What's the catch?' I persisted and Alice hung her head. Bingo. *Man*, not here three hours and already I was Hollywood-savvy.

'Alice?'

She groaned. 'The other producer is threatening to walk unless he gets his say in a few things.'

'Walk? Oh, I get it. He's got some protégé to pimp. I understand. As long as she's good and doesn't make the movie tank, I'm okay with it. I just want to sign the contract and get on with writing the script.'

Alice hugged me. 'Everything will be okay. Just trust your gut.'

'Are you going to tell me who the other person is?'

She grinned. 'No, not yet. I'm going for the shock effect.'

'Shock effect? Alice, I'm barely hanging on here...'

'It'll be fine, you'll see. Just do what I say and you won't have to worry about a thing for the rest of your life, baby.'

Enough of all the drama. All I wanted to do was sign my name on the dotted line and go back to Penworth Ford before the kids got too homesick. And, obviously, enjoy the royalties. Maybe even start on that new book with my new-found confidence. And the comfort of a new heating system. It was funny how you could suddenly get creative when you weren't worried about survival all the time.

8

Once Upon A Time In Hollywood

The next morning I got up early and showered before changing into my meeting outfit. I took extra care with my hair and make-up and donned my favourite LBD that did wonders for my figure. When the car and nanny arrived, I hugged Chloe and Ben fiercely, reminding Ben to watch his step and Chloe to watch her mouth.

'Can you give me a heads-up?' I asked for the third time that morning as I slid into the limo next to Alice, but she put her finger on her lips and tilted her head towards the driver. I groaned. 'What *can* you tell me?'

'That we're on our way to see the team of producers for a preliminary meeting.'

No surprise there. And yet, I had to ask myself how much I trusted Alice. Which was sad. She'd been my friend years now. Gosh, one night in LA and already I was looking over my shoulder. The place rubbed off on you pretty easily, I had to say.

In ten minutes we arrived at the headquarters of TakeFive

Studios and were beamed up to the penthouse floor. As the elevator swooped up, I wondered what I was getting myself into, if this was too good to be true and whether I would find myself out on my arse within the hour and on a plane back to England where all my problems would be waiting for me. Only there'd also be the humiliation of returning empty-handed. It would take me a little longer to readjust to my old life.

'Act like you don't know him,' Alice whispered into my ear as we were being ushered into a large white office where a bunch of people were sitting and it became immediately clear that I was overdressed in my LBD.

'What?' I whispered back without moving my lips. Act like I didn't know Ben Stein? Why? Oh my God, what the hell had she done?

'Ms Conte, what a pleasure to finally meet you,' he drawled, holding out his hand. I stared at it. 'I'm Ben Stein. This is Anna Weiss, Marty Roth and this here is—'

I looked over to a man holding his hand out to me. And almost had a coronary on the spot.

Luke O'Hara, the most famous and talented actor of the moment, was waiting for me to shake his hand. He was different in person, his familiar blue eyes framed by those lusciously long and dark lashes, the almost red full lips framed by a strong, square jaw – the jaw that made women all over the world swoon.

I hoped he was wanting the role of my hero. He'd be perfect. He could convince anyone he was just a regular guy caught in the bod of a Hollywood superstar. And the only actor that could pull that one off was indeed him, the healthy, all-American lad the whole world was in love with. His performances had ranged from those as a violent drug addict, to an English Lord, to Che Guevara, and was even top of the list for being the next Sherlock Holmes. Luke O'Hara was a mixture of both extremes that had you wanting every side of him. And, in the movies, you'd hardly recognise him because he was a real chameleon.

'Hi, nice to meet you,' was all I managed to say, albeit, I must hand it to myself, looking rather blasé, as if he was just the bloke next door.

But actually, I'd seen an interview on TV a few months back and knew he was, as they say in Hollywood, The Big Time. From his broad smile and easy-going manner, he looked like a fun fellow.

'Hi, Nina. It's good to meet you, too. Have a seat.'

And then as I made to sit down, I slipped and landed in front of the chair, and the next thing I knew he was holding my forearms and guiding me to my seat.

'You all right?' he asked and, stunned, I nodded.

'Sorry. Didn't expect to see you. Well, maybe catch a glimpse of you at Hard Rock Café, or maybe on a bus tour going past your home or something.' So much for my British poise and stiff upper lip.

He laughed in the voice that made women shiver in delight. 'You really are funny. See, Ben? I told you she'd be funny.'

I glanced at Alice who was turning a million different shades and was as emotional as I was. I remembered a crack she'd made once about locking him in her office and having her wicked way with him, and I giggled. All eyes turned to me.

'Sorry. I was just... sorry.'

Luke smiled warmly. God, could a man really be this

beautiful up close? He looked like he didn't even have any pores. Too handsome to be real, and way better, if even possible, than on screen. He looked thinner. Younger. *Sexier.* And, because I was sitting right next to him despite Ben's attempt to offer me a seat next to him, I could literally smell his cologne.

Okay, cut it out, you must be thinking. *No one is that perfect.* And you'd be wrong. Physically, he was perfect. Even Calvin Klein underwear had told the world so a few years ago, and judging by the fitted cotton T-shirt he wore and the low-riding jeans, he still was. But what the hell was he doing here? Wasn't it too early for casting? And then, through the misty fog that was my mind, I got it. He was the other *producer.* Was he the one ready to walk? Why?

I tore my eyes from him long enough to glance at Alice who winked at me.

'Nina, something to drink?' Luke offered, gesturing towards pitchers of various colours in a bid for me to choose. I cleared my throat as delicately as possible. 'Uh, just water, please.'

He poured me a glass as all around there was dead silence. I was being observed. What the hell for? *I only wrote a book; get on with your jobs, for Christ's sake.* The sound of the water slushing into my glass ended and Luke smiled warmly. What the hell was going on here?

I swallowed as silently as possible and Luke, who seemed to be chairman of this meeting, searched my face for a sign that I was ready. I gave a slight nod and he sat back.

'I'll cut to the chase, Nina,' he said. 'The movie is in danger.'

There we go. I knew it. One minute in and it was already

a no-go. It had been too good to be true. There went Ben's operation, the last few years of Northwood School, and of course, the renos to the house. I slumped in my seat. 'H-how…?'

'As one of the producers, one of my conditions is that I co-write the script with you. It makes sense, don't you think?'

Oh God oh God… I'd have to write the script with *him*? 'Absolutely,' I agreed with an emphatic nod.

He grinned. 'Good. I'm glad you agree. Thank you.'

'You're welcome. And the other conditions?'

For some reason, he looked at me with what could only be described as pride and I sat taller in my chair. He looked around at all the other faces.

'The other condition is that we see this story from a second point of view.'

Meaning an omniscient narrator? I didn't know how much good that would do as it had been written in the first person. My heroine Stella White told the story herself, giving sometimes funny, sometimes sad insights. 'Could you be more specific?'

Luke got up and began pacing the room, all eyes on him, and you could tell he was used to the attention.

'Well, you usually see chick flicks from the female point of view, right?'

Duh. 'Ye-es?'

'Which results in women empathising with women.'

That was the whole idea. Women reading women's stories and identifying themselves in them. It was called female solidarity. I was too polite to say, *And your point is?*

He studied my face. 'What if we show how Bill had a

hard time, too? What if we show how the man is not always the bad guy?'

Uh-oh. Red Phil alert. How did I get out of this one? 'But he is.' I didn't want to come across as a misanthropist, but I wasn't doing a very good job at it for the moment. I coughed. 'At least in my case.'

His eyes widened.

'I mean, my heroine's case.'

He dipped his head. 'Yeah, but hear me out a minute.'

I was a guest in a producer's office on the top floor of a skyscraper in LA, being titillated by a golden carrot. The option was going home empty-handed. Did I have a choice?

'There are as many men out there as women who have been devastated by divorce. As you just agreed, men are not always the bad guys.'

I leaned forward in my chair. 'What exactly are you saying? That Stella is to blame for the break-up?'

He dipped his head cautiously. 'Not solely. It's my firm belief that there are always two in a marriage, and two in a divorce.'

'Unless there's a third person,' I interjected.

'But this wasn't Stella's case, was it?'

'No, but…'

'Their problem was Bill's drinking, right?'

And Phil-andering. And gambling. 'Well, yes…'

'So I'd like to analyse their story from both points of view and see what drove him to drink.'

'Uh, his weakness?'

He grinned. 'Of course, but we all know that a good wife makes a good husband and—'

I cleared my throat, shaking my head. 'And you want people to think it was Stella's fault? Absolutely not.'

I could almost hear Alice's sharp intake of breath. I didn't get it. Did she want me to side with him? Then why let me meet up with Ben Stein? To keep them both happy, I guessed. What a true poker player she was. She wasn't asking for ten per cent for nothing. But I wished she'd just sat me down and told me like it was. She wanted me to bag a contract, I understood that much, and she didn't care what compromises I had to make. Just as long as the dosh flowed. But what about my story, the true essence of it?

The cad stopped and ran a hand through his sandy blond hair. 'Sorry, I didn't mean it that way.'

'I take it you're not married, Mr O'Hara?'

He blinked. 'Divorced.'

'Ah. Bad break-up?'

He shrugged and grinned. 'Aren't they all?'

I shrugged back. 'Perhaps. But some are worse than others. And Stella's was one of them.'

'We could all say that, Nina.'

'Oh, yes, definitely. But how many of us wouldn't be biased?'

'This could be the first movie that honestly respects both points of view. It could be ground-breaking in that way.'

Highly unlikely. But in any case, why did it have to be my movie that had to be the forerunner of this new – and risky – trend? Why couldn't I tell my story as it was, for Christ's sake?

'But I didn't write it to express or respect his point of view. I wrote it to express my own.'

He crossed his arms. 'Your point?'

'Simply that this is a story written by a woman for women. If you want to defend your gender from all sorts of accusations, go write your own sob story.'

Again, his eyes widened and I mentally slapped myself. Had I just said that to a Hollywood big gun who was offering me a chance to change my family's life around completely? Good God, was there no end to my stupidity? Or my instinctiveness? I had better learn to turn my brain on before I spoke, or it would be the death of me.

He threw his head back and laughed. 'Ben, I love this lady!'

For the first time, Ben spoke up. 'So do I. But you're going to ruin her story if you even try something so stupid. Take it from me, Luke. What you're trying to do is just not done. You're mixing two totally different genres that don't go together. Like...' Ben turned to me. 'What is it they say in England?'

'Chalk and cheese.' Two incompatible things. A bit like my Sicilian rice-balls in Cornish restaurants. Phil had pooh-poohed it from the start. Only he'd been wrong.

'Ben – you need to take a risk every now and then,' Luke said.

Ben Stein reddened. 'With all due respect, Luke, you can take a risk with John Grisham or Tom Clancy, but we're talking here about a mid-lister no one's ever heard of before...'

Mid-lister? I sat up. 'Actually, all three books were *Sunday Times* bestsellers.' I glanced at Alice who widened her eyes and slightly shook her head. I got the message.

'Ah, mid-lister she may be, but she's a total laugh-lab!' Luke said.

Was he not listening to me? Laugh-lab? I whipped my head around, caught in the crossfire. Both were slagging me off for different reasons and Alice was doing absolutely nothing to cover my back. All she wanted was to see whose court the ball landed in.

Luke gestured towards me. 'Believe me, she can pull off comedy like no one. Just look at her. Look at that *face*.'

Unbelievable. He had me flown all this way just to have a laugh? How could someone who looked so fantastic be a complete monster? He was supposed to be every woman's dream. Every woman's minus *this* one.

I knew it had been too good to be true. How dare they drag me all the way across the Atlantic just to humiliate me? I'd put my heart into that novel – three years of my own personal hell of *Should I stay or should I go*, during which even throwing myself off Gwennap Head seemed like a better alternative than living like that, and I wasn't about to let them laugh at me. This was *my* life I'd poured out, my feelings, my kids' feelings and their expectations too.

I'd had enough of my ex-husband taking advantage of me all these years, trying to demean me and attacking my dignity. I rose to my feet. 'Excuse me,' I muttered and headed for the door.

'Nina?' Luke said.

I shot him a glance and shook my head, my eyes burning with unshed tears, and closed the door behind me.

9

The Devil's Advocate

I regretted my reaction the moment the door clunked shut behind me, like a vault full of gold bullion, lost to me forever. What the hell was wrong with me? What the hell was I doing, abandoning a conference room full of Hollywood producers who wanted me to co-write a script based on my book? Would I rather go home and watch the rain trickling through my roof? If a little rudeness towards my persona was the price I had to pay for my children, shouldn't I pay it? After all these years and all these promises to myself that I would make it good for them, and I snubbed it all for the sake of a moment of humiliation?

I swiped at my cheeks with one hand and banged on the lift button with the other, willing it to open and take me straight back home like in a time machine, when things weren't going great but at least I didn't have people actually deriding me so openly and unashamedly.

How the hell was I going to break it to the kids? And

what the hell was Alice thinking? Had she sold her soul to Hollywood already? She knew that we as a family needed this deal like we needed our next breath. For Ben, for Chloe, I had needed to see this through. And I realised that, if I went back in there and apologised, this would only be the beginning of a series of compromises. But I hadn't flown all the way over here just to go back to Cornwall empty-handed. What had I been thinking? Was my dignity really more important than my children's lives? No contest. But now, was it too late to go back in there and eat humble pie? Could I just knock on the door? Would they snort? Guffaw? Tell me I'd missed my chance?

'Nina—' came a voice behind me. Alice.

'You knew all about this and didn't tell me?' I hissed. 'You're supposed to be my friend. I *trusted* you.'

'Before you say anything more,' Alice said, taking my hands in hers, 'listen to me. Ben Stein doesn't want you writing the script, but Luke does. Think of the difference it will make if you are hands-on. You will be a scriptwriter, and you will be making connections in Hollywood – isn't that every writer's dream?'

I bit my tongue. 'Yes.'

'And would you not – in one single second – secure the future of your children in every way?'

'You know I would.'

'Then why do I have to stand here and have this conversation with you when we both agree it's the best thing that's ever happened to you?'

'Alice, I *do* know.'

'Well then why are you playing bloody hard to get?

You deserve this. It's your one chance to right all of Phil's wrongs and show him how strong you have always been. I don't understand you.'

I didn't understand me either. Perhaps I simply wasn't prepared for such a sudden reversal of fortune. I wasn't used to having a chance at anything anymore. One minute I had been plastered to my basement floor sobbing my eyes out into the fleece rug so the kids wouldn't hear me and the next... I was sitting at a conference table with Luke O'Hara in Hollywood. How did that even begin to make sense? I was still trying to cope with that much, let alone a life-changing event like this.

But Alice was right. Nothing as monumental as this would ever happen to me again.

'Just listen to me and listen good, Nina. I am your friend and I am begging you to not be an idiot and blow it all away.' She squeezed my shoulder. 'Are you with me?'

I sighed. More out of terror than doubt. You might think I didn't deserve something so great happening to me. And I'd say you were probably right. Maybe that was half the problem. I didn't believe in myself enough. Luckily, Alice did.

I dried my eyes and huffed. 'Okay. I'm sorry. I'm with you.'

'And you'll agree to Luke's terms?'

'Have I got a choice?'

'Sure. You can go home and watch Ben Stein do whatever he wants with your story. And the opening credits will read "An adaptation from the novel by...", when it could instead read "Screenplay by Nina Conte and Luke O'Hara". You choose. And besides, Luke wasn't laughing at you! He was laughing *about* you. It's different; can't you see that? He loves your sense of humour!'

'It's true, Nina…' said Luke, closing the conference room door behind him and coming to stand before me, his face contrite.

But then, that was what actors did very well. Look something they weren't.

'I'm sorry if I wasn't clear. What I meant was that you are funny. Refreshingly so…'

His face was solemn, like a little boy's, his voice low, just like in the scenes where he apologised to his female lead for being a jerk and gave his heart-felt rendition of sorrow. It was his trademark: his voice failing at the end of each sentence, like it was too hard for him to speak after all the pain he'd caused. It worked like a charm on screen. In real life, not so much.

I could've said something like: *Save your talent for your movies,* but it would've been too cheesy. Besides, he was right. Look at me. I *was* a barrel of laughs. For someone else, at least.

Alice stepped forward. 'Nina, come on. The man's got everyone against him because of you. He's ready to risk a lot of money.'

Oh, so that was his beef.

'Tell you what,' he said. 'Let's not go back in there. Let's go to your hotel and hash it out over lunch, just you and me. Let me talk you through it all.'

'You mean *persuade* me,' I corrected him and Alice and Luke grinned at each other as he put his hand on my shoulder in a gesture of close friendship. God, he was so *American.*

'Great. Now I'm going back in there to tell Ben he's out on his arse because I don't need his money. I'm going solo.'

'What?' Alice almost shrieked. 'Do you have any idea of how much money this is going to cost you? You can't do that! You need him on board. What if it tanks?'

Ah, so not even she was all that optimistic after all. Good to know.

'It won't. Nina's book is brilliant.'

'I know it is and you know it is. But you shouldn't take such risks without the Stein Safety Net. You need Ben. Try to convince him at least!'

Without turning to look at her, he said, 'Risks are there to be taken.'

She shook her head miserably as she understood he was determined. Me, I had no idea what was going to happen, but I as sure as hell was not going home without my contract after all that.

'I hope you know what you're doing,' she warned him.

'I know exactly what I'm doing, Alice,' he promised, still smiling at me. 'And you, Nina – if I can convince you to have joint custody of the point of view, you'll get much more than you bargained for.'

I very much doubted that, but kept my gob shut for once.

10

Alice In Wonderland

You can imagine the state I was in by the time I sat down with him at a restaurant table. On my own, without Alice as my backup – and our foil – I felt totally, completely vulnerable. You think I'd be over the moon lunching with a Hollywood actor. Trouble was, I felt so spaced out by it all. This was truly surreal, discussing my book that was to be turned into a script, writing shoulder to shoulder with a celebrity, for who knew how many months? Not to mention the financial benefits.

Because, if truth be told, the money was already mentally spent, no joke. I'd already mended the roof, paid the tuition fees for both Ben and Chloe up until their final years and even paid off the mortgage. If you're going to dream, dream big, correct?

Besides, whatever sum I'd get out of it once Alice had her cut – and her advance back – was always way better than what I had now. Nada. Zilcho. So seriously, whatever the studio's advance on the script would be, it would finally go on the kids. Chloe would soon need braces, and she had been pestering me to send her on that school trip to France, while I knew Ben could do with a new bed.

He was growing at the speed of light, which made me fear all the more for his leg. Would he continue to grow while his leg didn't? I'd heard so many different opinions from a gazillion different doctors, and no one seemed to agree. Some said he'd grow out of it, others said if he grew any taller he'd end up with a crooked spine on top of everything else and others predicted all sorts of horrifying ends.

I couldn't let anything bad happen to my baby. He was so cheery and fun-loving, and it made me want to bawl even harder. *Please,* I prayed, *if only to cure him, let this whole deal go well.*

'This is not going to be easy, is it?' Luke said.

I looked up, half-terrified I'd missed something vital. 'I'm sorry?'

'Your face…' He laughed his famous laugh as we were waiting for our steaks.

'Yes, I know, you find me funny.'

He leaned in, fixing his cool blue eyes on me. 'And beautiful.'

Well, he sure knew how to work it. They didn't pay him actors' wages for nothing. I leaned away from the table, reaching for my San Pellegrino water.

'Are you going to try to charm me into seeing things your way?' I asked. 'Because I'm not susceptible to male charm.'

He shrugged. 'Lots of lesbians love me, too.'

'I beg your pardon? Do you think—?'

'I don't think anything. Besides the fact that you are a tough nut to crack.'

'And why's that?'

He took a sip of his beer and swallowed. 'Because you're not the type to be dazzled by city lights. You believe what you believe in.'

I was surprised he'd got that about me already. Or was it a ruse?

He put down his glass, his eyes never leaving my face. He was studying me. Choosing his next words. So would I, I guess, if I had thousands of dollars riding on the cooperation of a writer/housewife.

'Can I ask you a question?' I blurted as I set my glass down, happy to see I'd kept it steady and not spilled it over my LBD. I still couldn't believe I'd got so dressed up in the morning, even if it was the most important meeting in my life.

Luke tilted his head, glancing up as he had many a time from the silver screen, only it had always been for the benefit of his heroine, the woman who would be charmed within an average timeframe of ninety-six minutes. He slapped his cheek lightly and sighed. 'Oh, man, this is gonna hurt big time, I can feel it already!'

I shrugged noncommittally. If anyone here was *gonna hurt*, it was me, and the kids.

'Why – not that I'm complaining because believe you me, this offer has arrived in the nick of time – but why on earth would you want to produce a female-led romcom? I mean, wouldn't someone like, I don't know, Nancy Meyers better fit the bill?'

He shrugged. 'I got to it first.'

'Yes, but why? You admitted yourself it's not your cup of tea.'

'No, I only said it should be told from both points of view.'

'Then why don't you talk about your own experience? You have the money, you have the connections, obviously.'

He grinned. 'That may be true. But I don't have your talent.'

My mouth opened. 'You mean you don't write?'

He shook his head, looking very much like the Cheshire cat. 'Nope.'

'Not at all?'

'Not even shopping lists.'

'So let me get this straight. You want me to write your point of view? Even if mine is diametrically opposite to yours?'

He nodded. 'I've read all your books.'

'I've only published three.'

'I know. They were great. They are great. You write like a dream.'

'Thank you. But you must understand that I can't write what I don't believe in.'

'So you're not gonna give this poor ex-husband, along with all the ex-husbands in the world, a chance to have his say?'

'Why don't you get someone else's—' I shut up immediately, not wanting to sound like I didn't want the contract. I wanted it, and how. But I had no idea how we were going to rub along, if at all.

And then he put his hand over mine. It was warm. 'Was it that bad, Nina? The break-up?'

I stared at his long fingers as they gently gripped mine. On what planet had I ever imagined having lunch in Hollywood with Luke O'Hara in the flesh, holding my flesh—I mean, my hand? Certainly this was all one misogynistic bastard of a dream that would leave me shattered the moment I woke up? I didn't have time for ogling famous men on the internet, but now I'd have to find it because I needed to know *exactly* who I was dealing with. The man behind the face.

I shrugged. 'Yes. It was bad. But I'm over it.'

'Then what is it? Do you not trust me? I promise not to be a total control creep.'

I smiled. 'No, it's not that. I was just thinking of the benefits for my children. I'm pretty much broke and this would mean changing their life around completely.'

He nodded, squeezing my shoulder. 'I understand.'

Yeah, sure, I thought.

His eyebrows rose. 'Don't give me that look, Nina. I really do understand. My family was so poor we couldn't afford anything. And they worked so hard, you know? But there was just no way they could dig us out of it.'

'Really? I didn't know that. Not that I know much about you. I confess to not being a—'

'A fan?' He grinned. 'I had an inkling of that!'

I snickered and took another sip of my San Pellegrino. Gosh, even the water tasted better here.

He took a draught from his beer, still grinning at me. He had an addictive laugh and I found myself saying funny things just to hear it.

'So do you agree, then?' he said and I sobered up instantly, remembering why we were actually there.

'Yes.'

'Fantastic! I'll have the papers drawn up. You'll be happy

you stuck with me and not Ben. He's much too traditional and conventional. Congratulations to us!' He clinked his glass to mine, that charming look on his face just as the waitress arrived. 'Ah, our food, just in time! Thank you... Danielle,' he greeted her, reading her name tag with a dazzling smile and she smiled back, apparently used to seeing Hollywood stars, but still star-struck by him. And it hit me again, where I was, and why.

'So, if it's all the same to you, I'll come to England,' he said, out of the blue.

'Oh? Excellent.' That way I wouldn't disrupt the kids' lives.

'I'd bring Jessica, of course,' he said as he took another swig of his beer. 'My girl and I are inseparable.'

I couldn't resist asking. 'Jessica?'

He swallowed and nodded, cracking his fingers. 'My daughter. She's thirteen and the best thing that's ever happened to me.'

'I didn't know you had a daughter.' As a matter of fact, I didn't know a rat's arse about him.

'She was born blind. Lauren and I were two kids out of drama school. When we found out that Jessica was blind, it was too much for her. So she left. I haven't seen her since.'

I stopped eating. 'What, not even phone calls or emails?'

He shook his head. 'Nothing. Better that way. At least Jessica wasn't... you know...'

Hopeful was the word I'd had in mind, but kept quiet.

He searched for the right expression, and then, having found it, rubbed the back of his neck. 'Led on. Jessica knew from the start it was just me and her.' He looked up with a grin. 'But actually, it wasn't that bad at all. Jessica's a great kid, the way she lives with her disability.'

'She sounds like a strong girl.'

'She is. And you? What are your children like?' he asked, and I smiled.

'Chloe is thirteen, too. She's much smarter than she thinks, and is a real rebel. Determined. Clever. Free-spirited. Ben is eight, and he loves words and cars. Anything motor-driven, really. And he has a disability as well.'

'I'm sorry to hear that.'

I shrugged. 'He wears a leg brace because one leg is shorter than the other. Some doctors say it's a bone issue, others say it's just a ligament or a muscle. Some say to wait, while others—' I stopped. 'I'm sorry, this is not—'

'No, it's fine. I wish I had had someone to talk to who wasn't a shrink,' he said, then made a face at his own admission. 'That sounds real sad-ass, doesn't it?'

'All parents are sad-ass,' I agreed.

'Was it hard, with Ben?'

I looked up, surprised. 'Ben? No, not at all. He's a dream. Chloe's my bigger worry, to be honest.'

'Chloe? But she sounds so lovely!'

'Trust me, she was a real nightmare to raise. Especially after the break-up. Everything was my fault. Ben has always been mine, while she was Daddy's girl, you see.'

He harrumphed. 'So is Jessica, but not by choice. I was all she had.'

'How did you manage… everything?'

He smiled. 'One day at a time.'

'But Jessica, may I ask, is there no…?'

'Operation? No. We've been to the best doctors, all over the world. Jessica is missing a nerve that cannot be re-created in a lab. At least not yet.' The muscles in his jaw tensed and I recognised my own pain for Ben. 'But when that day comes, she'll be first in line…'

For a while we exchanged parenting nightmares, which made me relax a little more, and I realised I had a very decent human being before me.

'I'd like to meet them,' he said.

I rolled my eyes. 'Careful what you wish for.'

He chuckled and looked up. 'You know what? I think I'm going to love Cornwall. You make it sound so… epic in your novels.'

'I must confess, I never thought you'd come to Cornwall.'

'Did you think we were going to email each other the dialogue beats then?'

I laughed. 'No, of course not. I thought—I really didn't think of the practicalities. I never thought we'd agree on anything at all, really. But you in Cornwall?'

'What's wrong with that?'

Come to think of it now, the very thought of Luke O'Hara in Cornwall made me want to giggle. And hurl at the same time. Would he be hunted by the villagers? Stalked by Vanessa? Loved to death by Deirdre? Shocked by Old Nellie's potty mouth?

I shrugged. 'I don't know. You live in LA where the cars are fast and people are obsessed with the way they look and what they eat. I can't see you sitting in the village pub and bingeing on pasties. You'll die of boredom.'

He threw back his head and laughed. 'Ah-ha, that's where

you're wrong. I'm an Iowa boy and I'd like nothing more than to feel the Atlantic winds in my hair.'

Iowa? Google would have known that, but somehow I felt that checking it out would be betraying his confidence. Silly, I know because all over the globe were Luke O'Hara experts who knew his shoe size and had never even met him, while I'd be working with the guy and felt guilty about the slightest curiosity. That's the way it was with meeting famous people, I guess. You didn't want to seem to be invading their privacy.

He grinned. 'Your face…'

I sat up. 'What?' Did I have salad dressing on my chin or something?

'You really don't know jack about me, do you?'

I shrugged. 'I haven't got much time for Hollywood gossip.'

'Me neither. I hate it when people think they can impose on your privacy just because you're an entertainer.'

I studied him, trying not to at the same time.

'You're doing it again.' He laughed.

'Doing what?'

'Asking yourself questions about me when all you have to do is ask me.'

'Sorry I gave you that impression. I'm not the curious type,' I lied.

'Well, that's a relief.'

'Are you always so biased towards us commoners?'

'You are anything but common. What do you mean?'

'I mean that when you meet someone, are you always thinking that they can't see you as a normal bloke?'

He considered it. 'You're right. I've become jaded. Hey, would you and your kids like to come and meet Jessica, maybe break the ice before we come to England?'

Would you have needed to think about it? 'We'd love to, thank you.'

'Then why don't I swing by and pick you all up tomorrow?' he said as he helped me out of my chair and walked me to the lift. 'I can whip up something for lunch. Have the kids bring their swimsuits. We'll all go for a swim and maybe roast some marshmallows around the fire in the evening, after dinner. Would you like that?'

A whole day at the O'Hara mansion? What did one say to something like that?

'Cool.'

At the lift, he turned. 'Nina, thank you. I know this is gonna be a great movie! You are the best!'

I blushed despite myself. 'I bet you say that to every writer.'

He chuckled. 'I wish. No, just you.'

I raised a hand to say goodbye as the doors closed, but he lurched forward and blocked them. 'I almost forgot – what's it called?'

'What's what called?' I asked.

'The pub where I'll be eating pasties. Just so I can picture it.'

'There are several in Penworth Ford. Our local is The Bobbin' Buoy.'

'Then I'm looking forward to it becoming my local, too.'

11

California Dreaming

'A swimsuit? For the ocean or for a pool? Lucky I packed both, although I'll bet they have a pool! Everybody in LA has a pool,' Chloe cried. 'I can't wait to tell Chanel and send her some pictures!'

'Ah, that's the thing, darling. No pictures. Luke values his privacy, and I only think it's fair to respect that.'

'But, Mum!' she protested. 'Everyone posts pics!'

'Not Jessica, I don't think.'

'How do you know?'

'Well, darling, because Jessica is blind.'

Chloe sat back, eyes wide. 'Blind?'

'Yes.'

'But how does she, I don't know, put her make-up on?'

'I don't know that she wears any. After all, she's only thirteen, Chloe.' Meaning, *You, my dear, are way too much in a hurry to grow up.*

She rolled her eyes. 'God, and I'm going to have to lug her around Cornwall?'

'She's not a trolley, Chloe. She's a lovely girl who has had a difficult life and who has suffered greatly and with tremendous dignity.'

Chloe snorted. 'Yeah, I'd like to suffer like that in a California mansion.'

God, the headaches she always gave me. It was no wonder I was getting wrinkles.

'I hardly think she'd put make-up on secretly and try to scrub it off before she gets home like you do.'

'Mum!'

'Exactly. Mum. Not Stupid. Now go brush your teeth and get into bed. You, too, Ben.'

I could see it on his face. *Monster Trucks* was on and he wanted to watch it to the end. He never asked for anything, and even now he was reaching for the remote to obey me.

'Oh, go on, then. Maybe just a little longer,' I offered, tucking him in.

He beamed at me and lifted his arms to circle my neck and I smelled Bold laundry detergent and toothpaste. And home. I held him fast to me and gave him a raspberry, which made him giggle. He may have been academically bright and mature for his years, but he was still my eight-year-old who needed to be reminded of one thing.

'I love you a million gazillion,' I said, then turned to bend over Chloe. 'And I love you a *gazillion* million.' But she put her hand up to stop me and yawned.

Crikey, not even LA had mellowed her.

'Mum!' she ground out. 'Alice is knocking on the door!'

'Oh. Goodnight, then, don't stay up too late. You want to be fresh tomorrow.'

'Yeah, yeah,' she mumbled and turned to face the wall.

I moved into the living area and pulled open the door to see Alice in her nightgown and robe.

'I can't believe you're really going to his house!' Alice cackled in delight when I told her our plans for tomorrow in front of a bowl of crisps and a beer on the settee. Sorry, *couch*. 'I'm so frickin' jealous!'

'I guess he wants the kids to bond before they get lumbered together. I'm worried about Chloe's attitude towards his daughter Jessica, who is blind, so...'

'Listen to you, talking about Hollywood's heart throb as if he was your bosom buddy!'

'Ha ha, very funny. I just can't believe we will be working shoulder to shoulder.'

She beamed at me. 'You sooo deserve this, Nina!'

'I know, I do, right? Sorry for doubting you,' was all I could say. It was difficult for me to accept that I was finally getting what I had worked so hard for – and more. I just hoped I didn't soar too high. Because the higher I climbed, the harder I'd fall back down splat on the pavement.

After we'd had a quick drink and Alice went back to her own room, I tried to follow my own advice and get a good night's sleep, but it was proving rather difficult, so I pulled out my laptop and went onto YouTube to watch some of his interviews.

It was like being a Peeping Tom, getting to know him without him knowing me. From the comfort of my chair, I could peruse and spy on every (well, almost) inch of him without getting caught. I could see the hues of his skin change with fury when he punched his enemy's lights out, or see his eyes turn from blue to green in the sunshine, or hooded with passion when Julie Shipp slowly unbuttoned his shirt in that famous sex scene in that time-traveller, *Yesterday Waits For No One*.

Didn't he feel awkward, knowing that his face and body had no secrets to people all over the world? That every woman knew he had a scar on his back and other outrageously intimate things like, say, the shade of his nipples? And didn't it bother him that he had no private life? That everyone – bar me – knew all about his girlfriends, past, present and imaginary?

I would feel vulnerable, knowing people on the net were tracking down my every movement, holding polls for which of my dates had the best chance of becoming that special person in my life. These things were personal, no matter what you did for a living.

So I moved on to more harmless things, like his filmography. There were his spy movies, such as *Strangers*, and his psychological thriller, *The Man From Nowhere*.

His romcoms included *Finally You*, *Meet Me In Boise* and *A Year Without You*.

And his portrayal of Heathcliff? I'd never seen anything so gut-wrenching. The bugger was indeed talented.

The information about him went on and on, and in the space of a few hours, I knew as much as anybody else about Luke O'Hara.

He was the youngest of four and his aunt had been the one to sign him up to drama school as a birthday gift.

He'd dated just about all of his co-stars, the most famous models of the moment and even royalty, both genuine and self-assumed. But the more famous he became, the more he seemed disillusioned. Who was he, really? I checked everything – Wikipedia, IMDb, YouTube – anything I could find, to better understand whom I was dealing with.

Little did I know back then that it would take more than the internet.

12

Glass Houses

You know when you're living a moment you wish could last forever, and you stop for just a sec to wonder if it's even real and then tell yourself not to worry about that right now, and to just enjoy it? Well, nothing like that had ever happened to me ever before, so it caught me by surprise.

Because when in my entire life had I ever thought I would be cruising along the California highways in a black convertible, the wind in my hair, sitting beside a guy who had (really) leapt off the pages of *GQ*? I mean, really, could the scene *be* more clichéd?

And yet, there I was, Luke at the wheel, my kids in the back, driving to his mansion to meet his daughter. Ben was even more ecstatic than myself, albeit for different reasons, his hands clutching the back of my seat, marvelling at the dashboard.

'Wowee! This is the BMW 4-Series M4 Trim! It's the most powerful and most expensive in the line-up!'

'That's right, Ben!' Luke grinned as he shifted into a

lower gear in preparation for the steep hills awaiting us. My stomach lurched as I looked beyond Luke to the edge of the road. Apart from the fact that we were on the wrong side of the road, we were about two feet away from the gaping abyss.

'Don't look down, Nina,' he said, but I could barely hear him with the wind whipping about our heads.

Not that I had intended to, but the sea was such a beautiful cobalt blue, and the coast so large I couldn't help it. In a way, the expanse reminded me of home. Mullion Cove, Soapy Cove, Predannack Wollas. Soon I'd be back home to see it all again. If we didn't pitch straight into the ocean.

'I bet Cornwall's even better!' Luke called over the breeze.

Ah, no contest there indeed. But how to be polite? 'It's different!' I called back, tossing a look at Chloe who was busy taking selfies. She really worried me. When I was her age, I still played with dolls. Granted, they spent their time kissing and gossiping about Ken and Big Jim, but still. I had a story to tell, while my daughter was always completely engrossed in herself.

Was it my parenting that needed addressing, or were all kids like that? Certainly all of Chloe's friends in school were, but then again, all you had to do was look at their Northwood mums like Vanessa and Aimée, with their pearls and yoga classes and macrobiotic/bio/non-fat foods. It made me sick just listening to how Hugo, Heath and Horatio had made the top of the team, and how Persephone, Perpetua and Portia were at the head of their Literature classes, whilst they could barely spell their names.

'Here we are! Jessica can't wait to meet you guys!' he

called as we got to the top of a steep drive where a two-storeyed glass and white-rendered monolith came into view, dominating the landscape and sparkling as it caught the rays of the morning sun. It had stopped raining only last night, and the air smelled cleaner and fresher, just like hope and new beginnings.

I tried not to look too impressed as Luke led us in via the foyer from where through enormous glass walls, I feasted my eyes on the ocean meeting the strip of multi-million-dollar mansions in Santa Monica and caught a glimpse of a huge infinity pool that looked like it spilled down into the ocean.

Evidently Luke's talent as an actor had paid off. From whichever way I looked at it – from his talent to his fame to his house – his whole life was perfect. Or almost, because it was a shame that his daughter couldn't see it.

'Oh my God, will you look at the pool?' Chloe squealed, then checked herself, remembering she considered herself the posh one. Whatever had given her that idea, I would never know.

'It's so cool, Luke!' Ben agreed, making an impressed face, like an adult tasting a good wine he approved of.

I guessed it was my turn. 'It's absolutely breathtaking,' I added in earnest. What else can you say about paradise?

He stuffed his hands in his pockets. 'Thanks, but I'm selling it. This place is not fit for Jessica. I want something more cosy that she can feel her way around. Plus we're almost never home. Seems a shame for her not to be able to enjoy the view.'

'Luke – there you are. Jessica's been waiting for you,' said a voice that seemed to drift down from the sky.

I looked up to see an elderly woman descending the glass stairs, and a pretty dark-haired teenager behind her.

Luke's face lit up. 'Where's my girl?' he said, moving up the stairs and scooping her into his embrace. 'Jessica, I want you to meet Nina Conte and her children, Chloe and Ben.'

'Hello, Jessica,' I said, and she extended her hand for me to take. She had a beautiful smile, quite like her father's, only her colouring was different. She must have taken after her mother.

'Hey,' Chloe said casually, eyeing her surreptitiously. 'I'm Chloe. This is Ben.'

'Hi, guys!' she said. 'Wanna see my room? You can see all the way out to Catalina from there on a great day like today! Come on!'

As Jessica navigated her way up the banister, they eagerly followed. She was right. Today was a good day.

'Nina, this is Martha,' Luke said. Everything about her was white, just like the house, from her hair to her linen trousers. 'She's Jessica's tutor, nanny, cook. You name it, she's an ace.'

The woman grinned and rolled her eyes. 'The man is pure adulation. Nice to meet you, Nina. Are you Italian?'

'Yes,' I answered. 'Sicilian English.'

'Then maybe you'd like to give me a few tips on some of your specialties?'

'I'd love to,' I agreed. Anyone who loved to cook was a friend of mine.

After a tour of the house and gardens, which left me completely gobsmacked, we sat down to lunch, by which time I was ravenous. Martha had made an exquisite Caesar salad, a carbonara pasta dish and a large apple pie from scratch, and I wondered how long before Jack's apples would be ready to harvest.

It was all delicious, of course. Martha was very graceful and Luke was entertaining and the kids were on their best behaviour, including Chloe. Until… she wasn't.

'What's it like to be blind?' she asked Jessica out of the blue while she chomped on her dessert.

I swallowed. 'Chloe…'

Jessica turned my way and smiled. 'It's all right, Mrs Conte. I don't actually get much of a chance to talk about it. Everyone seems to think I can't accept it. But I do. I was born this way, and don't know any better. That view, for instance. Imagine not seeing it. Can you?'

'No…'

'Sure you can. Close your eyes – you, too, Ben – and tell me what you can detect through the open doors.'

Luke's eyes swung to mine, and he smiled, a proud fatherly smile, and my heart went out to him. He was so lucky to have such a lovely daughter.

'The waves,' Chloe said.

'The ebb and flow,' Ben said.

'Ben, stop showing off,' Chloe said. 'The wind… not strong, but steady. A little like the Cornish winds.'

I didn't know my daughter had even acknowledged the Cornish winds. Huh.

'And… seagulls?' she added.

'Yes, that's right, Chloe. Now open your eyes.'

They did.

'Can you see the wind and the seagulls from where you're sitting?'

'No,' Ben answered. 'But I noticed them as soon as I closed my eyes!'

'That's right, Ben. I use my other senses. I can tell when my dad is sad or tired or upset, by just listening to his breathing, and the tone of his voice.'

'You never told me that,' he said, slightly unnerved. 'I thought I fooled you. I'm an actor, after all.'

Jessica giggled. 'Not a very good one, Dad!'

Oh, how I wished my children could have a similar relationship with their own father. But then again, Jessica must be longing to have a mother.

As Luke promised, after lunch, we went for a frolic on the beach, which was so different from our Cornish beaches. With Ben and Chloe's help, Jessica built a sandcastle three foot high, complete with a moat and seaweed for the drawbridge chains.

'It looks sturdy enough,' I admired, and Jessica's head swung in my direction. 'Yes, and not a sliding glass door in sight. All cosy and safe.'

I looked at Luke, and his lips pursed in thought.

'That's why I'm selling it, you see,' he explained as the two of us took a short stroll down the beach, the kids further ahead. 'What's the point of having a huge house full of vistas, staircases and glass that could harm her if she took a wrong turn, and most of all a house that she can't enjoy? I want something more tactile for her, something smaller, cosier, warmer.'

I was silent, but nodded.

He stopped. 'You don't like it either, do you?'

I looked up and halted just before him. It was already surreal, being here on the private beach of one of the most famous actors on the planet. But having him ask me for my opinion was way off the charts. And I was supposed to tell him the truth?

'It is magnificent, with all the views and everything. Gorgeous, in fact. But I have to agree with Jessica who appreciates something much more, as you said, tactile. Walls she can run her hands along without worrying about smudging massive glass expansions. Flagstone floors that accompany you throughout your house and dip in the most worn spots. Ancient hearths that tell you the secrets of many a dweller before you while you surrender to their warmth, surrounded by friends and family…'

Luke smiled. 'We definitely know who the writer here is,' he said. 'You sounded like you were talking about a place that really exists…'

'It does. It's my home.'

13

About A Boy

The next day was the day of Ben's appointment with a specialist. The true highlight of our trip. We were escorted into a dimly but elegantly lit office that looked more like a lounge, and were served hot and cold drinks while Dr Ellenberg clearly stated Ben's situation after examining him thoroughly.

'I'm sorry, Doctor, if I ask again, but I need to be sure. Are you saying that with this operation, which is not as invasive as we thought, my son will be able to walk without a brace?'

'Ms Conte,' he said, removing his glasses, and for a moment I dreaded I'd misunderstood the contents of the entire twenty-minute consultation. 'Your son's ligaments are shorter than they should be, and that's what's causing him to limp. His bones are perfectly well proportioned. With an operation, he'll be running around like any other boy in six months' time. Of that I can assure you.'

I don't know what happened to me, but all of a sudden it

was as if the puppet master keeping me constantly upright just pulled the wrong string and I collapsed. My shoulders shuddered as I silently wept, tears running down my cheeks and into my mouth, salty and hot, all the while cursing myself for being unable to keep it together.

He leaned forward and patted my hand. 'Ms Conte, you have every reason to cry these tears of joy. Your son will be just like everyone else.'

Oh, if he only knew. Ben was never going to be like anyone else to me. He was far stronger, far more mature, far more loving than anyone I'd ever known and I was so proud of how he'd put up with all the pain all these years, my brave, brave little boy!

'Just come back when you're ready and we'll start the paperwork and have him done within the week,' he concluded, shuffling his papers into a neat pile.

Meaning, *Come back when you have the money.*

And soon I would, just as soon as the studio paid my advance on the script. Because Alice's ten grand had been spent on the kids' education. As cautious as I was by nature, I couldn't help but taste the flavour of accomplishment.

It had been years since my last lucrative achievement that was beneficial to my children, and finally I had succeeded. The tiny margin of things going wrong existed, I knew, but for once I wanted to be completely optimistic and oblivious to any chance of it not going well.

My time had come. My book was going to become a movie, and with that giving me confidence, I knew I would manage to find a fourth book in me. All I'd needed was someone to believe in me again, and I now had Luke O'Hara to thank.

★

Before our departure back to England, Luke and Jessica offered to take us to Rodeo Drive.

'Er, we'd better give that one a miss,' I said. With T-shirts at four hundred dollars a pop, Chloe was better off eating ice cream on the pier like the rest of us mortals.

Only they pranced around in tiny outfits, all smiley, like guests at a plastic Barbie and Ken party. I'd much rather have been back at home talking to Alf or to Bev, Carol and Deirdre – the Ice Cream Ladies – or Jack and Em, real people. My people.

As we were strolling down the Santa Monica Pier, my mobile rang. It was, what a coincidence, Jack.

'Hey, how's it going?' came his breezy voice. He sounded happy.

'Jack! Absolutely fantastic! We'll be home the day after tomorrow.'

'That's great, Nina! Did you play hardball?'

I laughed. 'Yeah, pretty much, although Alice did most of the playing. Luke O'Hara wants me to co-write the script.'

'Luke O'Hara, the actor?'

'Yup!'

'That's excellent news, Nina. You so deserve this.'

'I know, but I'm not sure I can—'

'Nina,' came his deep voice from across the ocean, making me even more homesick. And it had only been a few days. 'You've got this.'

I smiled. Good old supportive Jack. 'Thank you. So I'll fill you in when we get back. How are Minnie and Callie? Thanks for taking care of them, by the way.'

'They miss you terribly.'

Awh. So did we. I hadn't realised how much I would miss them, like my own children. I couldn't wait to wrap my arms around their warm furry bodies and see them yapping for joy.

'How's everyone? How's Emma?'

'We had dinner last night at my place.'

'Did you miss us at all?'

Silence. 'Of course we missed you, Nina. We miss all of you. But we'll have a nice dinner when you get back, okay? Emma and Chanel will be there and it'll be like you never left.'

'I'll bring something over, too.'

'Can't wait,' he mumbled, or I thought that was what he said.

'Jack? You still there?'

'I'm here,' he reassured me.

''Kay then.'

'Give the kids my love. And why the hell not, Alice too. She deserves it.'

I grinned. 'She'll be gushing, then. Bye.'

'See you soon.'

He and Emma had had dinner without me – that was a first. I hung up with the strange sensation that I had missed out on something by being here.

After another day of sightseeing and buying souvenirs for practically everyone in the village, there was nothing left to do but pack up and go home. And wait for the lawyers to draw up a contract.

The morning we were to fly out, Luke and Jessica came to the hotel lobby to say goodbye with snack bags. Proper sweet, old-school kindness. Mine contained Hershey kisses, walnut cookies, Wrigley's chewing gum and also a small bottle of San Pellegrino water.

'I noticed how you were savouring it the other day,' he said with a shrug. Maybe there was hope for this American yet.

'Thank you.'

'So… see you when we get to Cornwall,' he said, shaking my hand. 'In a few weeks we'll be in England and getting to work.'

'See you back in ol' Kernow,' I chimed back, mentally raising my eyebrows. That was *it*? A handshake, after we'd had lunch twice, once in his own home, and our daughters had practically become blood sisters? Must be my Italian temperament. Once we broke bread with someone, we were buddies for life. I guess Hollywood did the opposite to people.

As we were going back up to our room, he called me. 'Hey, Nina!'

I looked back. He grinned and waved. 'It's gonna be great, you'll see…'

'I just can't wait to get started,' I called back. The start of a completely different life for us.

14

The Bucket List

On the flight home Ben was sick three times, poor soul, and I was about to collapse from exhaustion as I kept waking up from my uncomfortable, constrained position to check on Ben. Chloe had several naps this time, sleeping like an angel, and Alice snored practically all the way home, the lucky cow. I guessed the security of that kind of money coming her way induced her into a deep, serene sleep.

As I was finishing off a delicious cup of coffee, Chloe opened her eyes and looked up at me. I swear she looked like when she was three. 'Are you okay, darling?' I asked.

She stretched and nodded.

'You had a good time with Jess, didn't you?'

'Yeah. She's really cool. I didn't know a blind person could be that cool.'

I bit my lip to keep from retorting with a moral lesson. It was a miracle she had even told me that much. If not towards me, I noticed that LA had mellowed Chloe slightly. She didn't snort as much. I only hoped it would last.

'Do you think she's a happy girl?' I asked and she looked at me cagily.

'She'd be happier if she could see,' she retorted.

'I didn't mean that, Chloe.'

'Yeah, well, I'm not going to share her secrets with you.'

Here we go again. 'Ah, so you really are that close. I'm glad.'

'Whatever,' she said and turned away to go to sleep again. And that was the end of that. If Luke had had a tough time raising Jess on his own, I realised that my battle was still an ongoing one, and would be for a very long time.

By the time we landed in Heathrow I could barely keep my eyes open, and when Alice, who was as fresh as a daisy, offered to help us get our bags to the train, I almost wept with relief.

It was still, what with transfers and all, another eight hours to our front door, and I was dreading it, because, let's face it, I wouldn't be able to sleep this leg of the journey either while having to keep an eye on the children. In a city like London, a mother's work was never done.

If I was an absolute wreck now, I could imagine what I would be like by the time I got these two home. All I wanted to do was pass out, but it was up to me to get them home safe.

As we were spilling out of Arrivals, me holding Ben upright, along with three holdalls around my neck and my clothes pulled every which way but the right way along with my hair, Alice stopped in her tracks.

'Oh my bloody God!' she swore.

'What? What did you forget?'

But she just looked ahead and I followed the direction of her gaze. It took me a while to recognise him, with his dark mop of curls shortened and clean-shaven face. I was so shocked I didn't even have the strength to speak at a normal volume, and it came out as a croaked whisper. 'Jack…? What are you *doing* here?'

The kids suddenly recovered and clung to him as he in turn enveloped them in his arms. 'Hey, you guys! Did you have a good time?'

'Awesome!' Ben cried and Chloe laughed. 'That's what they say in LA, and they say it, like, all the time!'

His eyes met mine, almost apologetically, his long dark lashes fanning his tanned cheeks. 'I figured you'd be exhausted so I thought I'd meet you. Huge congratulations again, by the way.'

I moved to hug him, but I was weighed down by all the bags hanging from me. 'You're my hero,' I gushed. 'I can't believe you did this!'

'*I* can,' Alice said, jangling her keys, in a hurry to get home herself now, seeing as the ballast had been passed to him. 'So as you're in excellent hands, I'll just let you get on with it. Congratulations again, doll, and I'll call you tomorrow. Kids, it's been… interesting. I didn't think I'd like you so much.'

Chloe and Ben laughed and waved as she tottered off, then turned again. 'Don't forget you need to update your website now!'

Website? It was the last thing on my mind.

'Right,' Jack said, lifting all of my bags from around my neck. 'Let's get you three home. You must be knackered to the bone!'

'Not too bad,' I said and then yawned. 'I still can't believe you're here! I thought I was hallucinating!'

He slid me a happy grin. 'The exit's this way.'

This was so Jack, going all the way for other people. Everyone in town loved him to bits, and it wasn't hard to see why. He was completely selfless. I simply didn't understand that silly cow who had dumped him.

Once we were in his SUV, it started to rain. 'Welcome back to Kernow summers,' he quipped, then turned to Chloe in the back seat. 'Honey, there's a basket in the back with drinks and snacks. Would you mind?'

'Ooh, thanks, Jack!' she cried, twisting to retrieve the bounty.

'And there's hot coffee for you and some baps and muffins and stuff,' he said to me.

'Coffee's fine, thanks, Jack. You've thought of everything. If you knew how to cook you'd be perfect marriage material.'

Again, he slanted me a funny look. He looked so different, without his beard, and there were dimples I never even knew existed.

'You look… amazing,' I said in earnest and his eyes swung to mine in a shy grin before they went back to the road.

'So do you. But then, you always do.'

'Liar,' I chuckled as I took two travel mugs from Chloe and rested them in the receptacles and stretched out luxuriously. This might not be a BMW convertible, but it was roomy and solid and just as comfortable, if not more. It was already home.

'Chloe, Ben, mind you don't spill anything,' I cautioned. I wasn't that deliriously exhausted that I'd forgotten my manners.

But I did fall asleep, and when I came to, I knew I'd slept because I had that funny taste in my mouth. Inside the vehicle, it had become quiet as Chloe and Ben had finally fallen asleep too.

'Sorry, I passed out,' I said, rubbing my eyes. 'I'm not much in the way of company, am I?'

'You're fine,' Jack whispered.

I stifled a yawn. 'You don't need to whisper, they're out for the count.'

'Seems so,' he agreed.

The rain was coming down in sheets now, but his driving was steady, without the bursts of energy of Luke's sports car, so I lay happy in the knowledge we would get home safe and dry with Jack.

It was like being inside an unbreakable cocoon – warm, safe and quiet. I pictured having to face the same journey with Lottie The Shitty Car and suddenly shivered in horror. She'd have abandoned us on the A30 without a second thought.

'Cold?' he said softly, reaching for the heating. 'There are a couple of throws in the back.'

I shook my head dreamily. 'I'm fine, thank you, Jack. It was so kind of you to drive to the airport just so we wouldn't have to take a train.'

'I'm glad to do it. Emma wanted to come, too, but she had to work.'

'Did you and Emma have a good time the other night?' I asked. 'I so wanted to be there with you guys.'

He cleared his throat. 'Nina, there's something you should know—'

The Cornwall county border sign flashed by and our beautiful green hills and hedgerows came into view.

'Oh, how I've *missed* Cornwall!' I cried under my breath.

'Well, it wasn't the same without you. Even Alf has had a few bad moments.'

'No! What happened?'

'He went out and got lost. Hugh the postman found him on the coastal path at Soapy Cove.'

'Oh my God, he could have—' I didn't even want to finish the thought.

'So the Ice Cream Ladies have stepped up to the plate as usual, keeping his business open while he recovers.'

'Will… he?' I asked.

Jack shrugged his shoulders. 'He seems fine again now. It just comes and goes, you know?'

'I'll go see him tomorrow morning. I'm so sorry!'

'See what happens the minute you leave us, Nina? Everything just falls apart.'

'Well, luckily, I won't be going anywhere.'

He turned to me. 'You're not going back to Los Angeles? To write the script?'

'Me? No, Luke O'Hara will be coming here.'

'Really? A Hollywood star in our midst? That should be interesting.'

'And at my dining room table, to boot.'

'You'll do a proper job.'

'You think?'

'I know.'

'What did you want to tell me just now?'

His eyes lost their twinkle and his mouth clamped shut. 'It'll keep.'

When we got in, loaded with our bags, Emma and Chanel were there with a *Welcome Back, Hollywood!* banner.

'It's so good to see you,' Emma cried. 'My best friend, the scriptwriter!'

I hugged her back, catching a glimpse of Jack beaming at her, while Chloe dragged Chanel upstairs to tell her all about her adventure and Minnie and Callie were yapping for all they were worth as they jumped and licked our faces.

'Hello, my beauties!' I cooed as Ben sank to his knees and let them lick him.

Compared to Luke's place, the house seemed dreary, and the furniture dark, but it was my home, my safe place.

'Sit yourselves down, I'll be ten minutes with dinner. Jack, would you crack the wine open please?' I said as I pulled out the freezer bag that I had prepared for this very evening: cannoli, parmesan eggplant, rosemary-baked potatoes with caramelised onion and carrots and a tiramisu to top it all off.

'Ah, I'd love to, Nina, but can it wait until tomorrow evening?' Jack said regretfully. 'I have an early meeting with some organic distributors in Bude in the morning.'

I stopped, eyeing Emma who was looking over Chloe's gifts to Chanel, and pulled him closer to me, using the fridge freezer door to screen us. 'You have to. Why do you think I made sure I was back today of all days?'

He blinked. 'Why, what's today?'

'The thirteenth of July?'

And then it dawned on him. 'Shit. Sorry, I completely forgot.'

'No worries. We just need to keep her from getting too drunk again. That's when she reaches the stage of self-pity.'

'Right – let me make a call, then.'

'Thanks, Jack. You are the best friend a woman could ever have.'

He raised his eyebrows critically. 'Not sure if that would be read as a compliment by most men.'

'Of course it's a compliment. Now go make your call and get that bottle open. Chloe? Come and set the table please!'

As promised, exactly ten minutes later we were all seated around a table full of food and laughter, and Emma, despite her mind alighting on that bad memory every once in a while, was determined to celebrate my good news like the great friend that she was, pushing her own woes aside.

'Is it okay if Chanel stays the night?' Emma asked. 'She's missed Chloe.'

'Of course!'

'Thanks,' she said, then hissed, 'I need a break!'

After dinner, the girls absconded to Chloe's room while Ben – wide awake and wired yet delirious with jet lag – migrated to the dining room to watch his science documentaries on TV.

It was late, and we were all tired for our own reasons, but the pleasure of being with one another after an entire week, and sharing the good and the bad moments beat everything else.

'This is nice,' Emma slurred, and after a while of companionable silence, fell asleep against Jack's shoulder.

He shot me a glance. 'I daren't move.'

'Poor Em, it gets her every year. She's been through a lot.'

'So have you,' Jack whispered.

'We all have. Even you, with your own divorce.'

He made to shrug, but sat still under Emma's body.

'Do… you still think of Clarissa?' I ventured.

Jack looked at his feet that were propped up on the coffee table before him.

'Only when I hear someone say her name. Otherwise, I have completely erased her from my memory.'

'And are you happy, Jack?'

He slanted me a lazy, tired look, but there was a smile on his lips. 'Happier than I've been in a long time, Nina. You?'

'I'm definitely working on it.'

'I don't know why she left you, but I do know that it was her loss, in any case, Jack,' I said and truly meant it.

What kind of idiot would dump Jack? He was kind, intelligent, and quite frankly, very easy on the eye, with his dark hair and dark eyes. He was a jeans and T-shirt kind of bloke who worked hard for a living, using both his muscles and his brain, and his appeal to all the women in the village was his sexy smile and his easy-going attitude and manliness. And the funny part was that he wasn't even aware of the effect he had on them. His was a power that he kept banked under years of self-control. He was never loud, never angry, never overly silly.

He gave a light toss of his head because he couldn't shrug. 'She hated the countryside – all the mud in the winter, the harvest with all these damn apples and pumpkins that needed harvesting.'

'Uh, duh?' I said and he rolled his eyes.

'In any case, when something's not meant to be, it's wiser to just let it go,' he said.

Emma stirred in her sleep, muttered something, and we both waited for her to settle again.

'Apart from her wedding anniversary today, is Em okay?' I asked.

His eyes swung to mine from above the rim of his glass.

'What do you mean?'

'She seems… odd. Like she has a secret. Has she got a new man or something?'

He swallowed and put his glass down, making sure not to jostle her. 'Seems all right to me. Maybe she's just working too hard.'

I took a sip of my wine. 'Well, hopefully we're looking at sunny days ahead.'

'To sunny days, then, Nina,' he whispered.

'To sunny days, Jack,' I whispered back.

Emma stretched, yawned and opened her eyes. 'Oh, God… how long have I been out?' she asked.

'Not long enough to sleep it off,' Jack answered with his usual sarcasm.

'Yeah, yeah,' she said. 'Play the indifference card, you two. Don't think I don't know why you had me over tonight even if you only just got back home. And you with your business meeting tomorrow. You guys are the best.'

I patted her knee, and Jack, who was against anything that could be described as gushy or cheesy, gave her head a light shove sideways as he always did in similar moments. Jack eyed me, knowing what was next.

'O' course I have Adam to thank. If he hadn'ta left me, I'da never moved to Penworth Ford and met you lot,' she slurred. 'And if I'da never met him, I'd a never fallen in love with him and had his baby,' she said, her voice cracking now.

I hugged her. 'It's all right, Em, it's all right.'

'And if I'da never had his baby, I'da never put on the baby weight, and he'd never lost interest in me,' she sniffled as the tears came.

'Em,' Jack said. 'It's not your fault. He lost interest in you because he's a wanker – you know that. And you're better off without him.'

She was now sobbing, and I hated her husband for what he'd done to her. I wondered how long it would take her to recover.

'Would you have left me, Jack?' she sniffled. 'Just because I'd gained a few baby pounds?'

'I told you – he's just a wanker.'

She snuggled up to him, and I could see the fragile curve of her back. 'You would never leave me, would you, Jack?' she wheedled, moving in to kiss his cheek.

He rolled his eyes. 'Of course not.'

'No, you wouldn't Jack, and you know why? Because you,' she said poking him in the chest, 'are one of the good ones. You're good-lookin', rich, and sexy as hell. By the way, Nina, did I ever tell you that Jack has a huge—'

He stood up, catching her as she slid off his lap.

'All right, all right, Missy, you've had too much tonight. Let's get you next door,' he said, propping her up in his arms like she weighed absolutely nothing.

'Give her a couple of aspirin,' I said. 'That usually makes her feel better.'

'I know,' he said.

Emma looked at me through her dazed drunkenness as if she was seeing me for the first time. 'You're so prettyyyy,' she said. 'Isn't she pretty, Jack?'

'Absolutely,' he said, rolling his eyes.

'And she's so kind.' She turned around to look at me over Jack's shoulder. 'You deserve good things to happen to you, Nina. And I'm a horrible person...'

'That's enough now,' he said, whisking her through the front door as I held it open for them.

'Night, Hollywood,' she called, suddenly happy again, waving, then turned to look at Jack. 'Oh, look, my ride's here! Hi, lover boy!'

'Okay then, see you tomorrow, Jack. Thanks so much and good luck with your distributors tomorrow,' I said as I waved them off.

'Thanks, Nina. Welcome back. Don't worry about her. I'm proper proud of you.' And with that, he disappeared into the night.

Poor Emma. She, too, had been through a lot. But at least she had us now. With a sigh, I loaded the washing machine with our darks and sat at the dining room table where my encrypted-against-beady-little-eyes Bucket List was still pinned to my cork board the way I'd left it a week ago:

Guru was Ben's operation

Miracle meant Write next book

Filter meant Filter Phil out of my blood system

Soldi was Italian for money

De-royalise had nothing to do with my royalties, but rather getting Chloe off her throne where I was concerned.

And now, sitting where I always sat, Los Angeles once again seemed as far as it always had been and that a whole lifetime had already gone by, and that I had never left at all. My daisies were still flowering nicely, and Minnie and Callie settled again into our evening routine. Only one big thing had changed, and in a moment of indulgence towards myself, and just for the fun of it, I added to my list, *Get a big fat Hollywood movie deal*. And with immense satisfaction, crossed it off my list.

15

My Neighbour's Secret

Being back home in Penworth Ford was like running a victory lap in the market square. Everywhere I went, people kept congratulating me about the movie, from the village butcher to the vicar.

'Is it true you and Luke O'Hara are going to write a script together?'

'How long are you and Luke going to be together?'

And, the most hilarious of all, from the local movie buffs, 'Are you going to star in the movie like Nia Vardalos? You'd make a great Stella!'

If they only knew. Stella *was* me, made from my boiling blood, broken heart and shattered bones. She was the war-torn heroine I never let out except for at night, under the eaves of my tiny bedroom where I kept all the books I'd ever owned, from *Charlotte's Web* to Kafka (never got past page thirty) and Katie Fforde (read 'em all). That was my lair, where I hid away from the world.

My first stop was to go and see how Alf was. I was surprised to find him reading his usual paper at his counter.

'Ah, look what the wind's brought in!' he called.

I put my gifts down and rounded the counter to hug him. 'Alf, are you okay?'

'Why wouldn't I be?' he snapped as he folded his broadsheet into a tiny lump. 'Never been better, despite these three crones molly-coddling me all the time.'

Beverly clapped him on the back lightly. 'You love it!'

He shrugged.

'I've missed you lot,' I cried, hugging them all. 'Here, I've brought something for you. Anchor Beer for you, Alf. See's chocolate for you, Carol; saltwater taffy for Deirdre; and some Napa Valley wine for Bev.'

'Spot on!' cackled Alf with satisfaction. 'Thank you, luv.'

He seemed okay to me, but I did detect a sliver of worry on the trio's jolly faces.

'Oh my word, I've never seen so much luxury,' Deirdre said as they went through all the bounty. 'And you thought of us!'

'Of course!' I exclaimed. 'You are my family.'

'What did you get Emma and Jack?' Bev asked, and Deirdre elbowed her. 'That's not polite to ask. Thank you, pet, for all this. We'll make sure Alf doesn't go through it in one night!'

I leaned forward and looked my ladies in the eye. 'You call me if there's anything… I mean anything, okay?'

They slid a glance towards Alf, who was checking the label of his beer, and nodded. 'Don't you worry, pet, he's in and out of it as the days go by. We've got the number for

Brian's surgery just in case, but we will keep you posted should, uhm... you know.'

'Okay. Thank you. I mean anything, remember. I'm here for you.'

Deirdre swiped at a tear as usual, and gently nudged me towards the shelves. 'Go do your shop, pet. You've got a busy day, I assume.'

'That I have,' I agreed. 'Apparently I have to resuscitate my old website. That'll be interesting, seeing as I have no techie skills whatsoever. But how about we meet for cakes and tea at Old Nellie's sometime this week?'

'Ooh.' Carol clapped her hands. 'A chance to get away from the ogre, yes, please!'

But Alf didn't hear her, or was simply ignoring her, so I took a basket and grabbed my milk, eggs, bread, fruit and veg.

The rest of the day was spent in total, lazy bliss just basking in the warmth of a bright, shiny future.

At five o'clock I started dinner, looking out the window for any sign of Jack. He was the only one to use the door into the kitchen, which was usually where he would find whatever it was that needed fixing.

After dinner, while we polished off our desserts and sipped our coffees, Jack snapped his fingers. 'Oh, Nina, before I forget—' he said, pulling his mobile phone out. Was he going to show me a picture of his hot date? I wondered if he'd run her past Emma, at least. He did nothing without our approval, this one.

'About your website...'

'What about it?' I said as I topped up our coffees.

'The Ice Cream Ladies mentioned you might need a

hand, so I looked it up. NinaConte.com is a shambles. So I've done a dummy page for you, just to see if you like it.'

I put our mugs back onto the table, my eyes scanning the screen. It was gorgeous and delicious, like cupcakes of the brightest colours. He'd used the perfect font, the right tone; it was rich and yet linear.

I scrolled down and checked my menu as I sat back in satisfaction. 'This is amazing!'

'Thank you. So is the writer.'

'How am I ever going to get even with your kindnesses if you keep topping them up?'

He grinned, showing a slightly crooked incisor, which only added to his charm. 'Silly sausage.'

'I'm serious, Jack. You are always there for me, and what do I do for you? What can I do for you apart from a stupid dinner?'

'There is one thing you could do for me, Nina,' he said. 'You could smile more. Enjoy your life.'

I didn't even need to think about that one now. 'I will,' I promised him. 'You're the best, Jack.'

'I know.'

16

A New Life

After two weeks, I still hadn't yet received my contract in the mail. 'Chloe, are you and Jessica still voice-messaging each other?'

'Yeah, why?'

Is her dad still alive? And does the postal service still work in that country? I wanted to ask.

'Nothing, just wondering.'

Ben came to put his arms around me. 'It'll come soon, Mum, don't worry.'

'Thank you, my darling.'

'By the way, Mum, I promised Jack I'd help him with a project of his. Can I go over there after tea from now on?' he asked.

'Every day? What about your homework, darling?' As if I needed to ask.

'I always finish my homework at school. Is it all right if I go?'

His need to be with a male role model, one that I couldn't

ultimately provide, stabbed me in the heart. But I was also grateful to Jack. I smiled. 'Of course you can go, love.'

'Thanks, Mum! Jack's right. You are a star!'

I laughed. 'Have you two nothing better to talk about than your mother?'

'Sure we have. We talk about motors, and we build things together.'

'Build things? Like what?'

'Last month he showed me how to build a water clock! There are sixty cups that take sixty seconds to fill, and when the first one empties into the second, the next minute strikes. It's amazing!'

'Oh, that sounds unbelievable, Ben! Can I come round and have a look?'

'Not until we're done!' he warned me.

I laughed and folded him in my arms and he pressed his face into my neck.

'I love you, Mum!' he chimed as Chloe rolled her eyes and went back to her mobile phone. Ben was like that, honest in his affections, and unheeding of what people thought.

'Oh, my darling boy, I love you more!'

'Get over yourselves, you two,' Chloe muttered.

'Sweetheart, I've been meaning to ask you,' I said, turning to Chloe. 'You haven't sent Chanel any pictures of Luke's daughter and home, have you?'

She shrugged. 'I haven't talked to Chanel in weeks.'

'Weeks? Why? She's our next door neighbour and your best friend. How could you even manage that?'

'Chloe's always voice-messaging with Jessica these days,' Ben informed me.

'But what about Chanel?' I insisted.

Chloe shrugged again. 'Chanel is jealous that I have a celebrity friend and she doesn't.'

My mouth fell open. 'Chloe, I'm happy that you and Jessica have bonded – that's brilliant. But please don't forget who your people are.'

'Yada, yada, yada,' she muttered as she disappeared up the stairs and into her room. Teenagers. You just couldn't win.

That night Emma came over, looking haggard.

'Are you all right?' I asked as I poured her a glass of Merlot.

'No, I have to tell you something, but I'm afraid it will ruin our friendship.'

I stopped in mid-pour. 'Oh, God, is it Chloe? Has she been rude to Chanel? I'm so sorry, she's been a brat for weeks now and does nothing but voice-text Jessica, but Chanel does not deserve to be treated like that. I've had a word with Chloe who is going to apologise and...'

'Don't worry about it,' she said.

That was Emma. Always downplaying things, when I knew she was as upset as I was by Chloe's behaviour.

'Em?'

Emma had buried her head in her forearms on the table.

'There's something else, isn't there? What's wrong?'

She looked up at me. 'You know I love you, right?'

'Of course. And I love you and Jack, too. I love our little Three's Company thing. And I apologise if in the next few weeks I'll be busy, because Luke O'Hara will be arriving soon – I hope – to work on the script. But once Luke and Jessica have gone I can go back to my normal life and we can resume our dinners together with Jack.'

'You're avoiding him, too?'

I sighed. 'I'm not avoiding anyone, Emma. There is so much work behind this script that I didn't expect. I am overwhelmed, is all, but I promise you things will get back to normal.'

'It's not just that, Nina…' she said.

I sat down. 'What is it then, Em?'

She hesitated, biting her lip, and then smiled. 'Don't listen to me, Nina, I'm just cranky and exhausted,' she whispered. 'And I've only got one kid and one bloody job. How do you do it? Because I can't take it anymore…'

It was like looking in the mirror during one of my cold nights up in the eaves by myself, listening to the rain pinging into the bucket and wondering how much longer I could get away with it before the roof buckled under the pressure of the next storm. It was a waiting game, and the object was to see it out.

'Of course you can, Em,' I soothed. 'You're just having a mother's moment, is all. We all do. Even married people are exhausted. I know I was.'

'But at least back then you had someone to share your problems with,' she insisted, taking a deep breath. 'Don't you ever wake up in the middle of the night, hankering for a warm, strong body to anchor yourself to, if not for some good, hard sex?'

Good question. It was the answer that was bad. Because no, I didn't. I was completely dead in that department. But as far as loneliness was concerned?

'Of course, we all do, Em. But just have faith. You will meet someone fantastic, because *you* are fantastic. You just need to put yourself out there a bit more. Let's go to the

Northwood parents' parties. There's some new dads this term,' I said, ruffling her hair.

She lifted her head. 'I'm not going with you.' She pouted. 'They'll all be gaga over you. If I didn't love you, Nina, I swear I'd hate your guts.'

'What a daft idea, Em! Besides, you know I don't feel comfortable with all those pretentious people who only speak to me when they needed something.' (Shit, I'd almost forgotten to make them those *arancini* I promised for the festival.)

'They're actually not that bad once you look past all that,' she defended.

'Then why don't you let someone there set you up?'

'Me? No. What about you? Are you interested in anyone at the moment?'

I laughed. 'Me? I wouldn't recognise romance if it clobbered me over the head with a cricket bat.' And that was the truth.

Days turned into weeks, and still no word from Luke. By day twenty-three, I was just about ready to scream, but Chloe beat me to it.

She came screeching through the front door, not bothering to remove her wellies as a brown trail followed her into the living room where I was sitting at my idle computer waiting for a miracle to happen.

'Mum! MUM!' she screamed. If it hadn't been for the ecstatic look on her face and the complete change of attitude towards me, I'd have cringed at the streaks on the carpet. But what was that she was waving under my nose? A large envelope. My hand shot to my heart. It was either that, or bad news from somewhere. But it had to be my contract. Bad news usually came in small envelopes.

'It's arrived! Your contract!'

'What? Let me see!'

I tore at the envelope and besides a thirty-seven-page contract, there was a hand-written note that I read in one breath:

Dear Nina,

Sorry it took so long, but here it is. With this contract you agree to put up with me. I hope you won't regret it!

I will be arriving in Penworth Ford at the end of the month and will be emailing you details of my hotel.

Can't wait to see you!

Luke x

I looked up at Chloe whose face was bright red with excitement. Meeting Luke and Jessica had changed her attitude big time, and I was grateful for it. Hopefully the encounter would change a lot of other things, too.

17

The Predator

The next day after I returned from dropping the kids off at school for their final week before their summer break, Phil appeared on my doorstep, bright-eyed and bushy-tailed. His hair had been combed back (that was a first in years) and he was wearing jeans instead of his usual track bottoms. His Sex Pistols shirt, however, was stained and crumpled, like someone who had slept in his clothes. I could tell by the look in his eyes that he was on a mission.

'Nina! Welcome back, babe!'

Ah. Of course.

'Thank you,' I said politely. After all, I did once love him, plus, I was feeling much stronger, less vulnerable and more cheerful since the trip to Hollywood. I found that, as I grew happier, the need to hate him diminished.

'Aren't you gonna let me in?' he asked.

I debated, then figured that now I could take him any day.

He followed me inside where he sat himself down at the kitchen table.

'You makin' a cuppa? I'll have a coffee,' he said, and with a sigh, I flicked the kettle on. Not because I wanted him to stay, but because I knew he wasn't leaving until he came out and asked.

He was silent for a moment, listening to the kettle getting into gear, as if mustering the courage to put his plan into action. 'You got any Jaffa Cakes?' he asked, licking his lips and craning his neck as I opened the snacks cupboard.

I sighed inwardly as I filled his cup, listening to him prattling on about his new friends and new ventures. And then he grinned so widely I could see all the way to the back of his teeth.

'So, congratulations on your Hollywood deal, babe!'

I plonked his cup down along with the entire box of Jaffa cakes.

'Don't call me babe.'

'You used to like it.'

'"Used to" being the operative words, Phil. And that was a long time ago.'

He shrugged, ripping off the top of the box with the same gusto he used to pull at my nighties. The thought now repulsed me.

'Not that long ago.'

'Why are you here, Phil? The kids are out.'

'It's you I wanted to see.'

Here we go. 'For?'

He took a sip of his coffee, making an impressed face. 'Mmmhhh, is that a new brand?'

'No, it's still Tesco's.'

''Course now that you've struck gold, you can afford all the luxuries. So, what are you gonna do with all that dosh?'

'Oh, I dunno, Phil. Maybe pay for Ben's operation. Fix the roof you promised to do a thousand years ago.'

'Oh, I can do that for you, babe—Nina.'

As if I'd give him access to anything of importance to me, the kids being a forced exception.

'And I'm cheap, too. I'll give you a good rate.'

I swallowed my coffee, nearly burning the roof of my mouth. Jack had done everything for free, without even knowing us, and this stupid bozo here wanted to be *paid* for doing the labour necessary to shelter his own kids?

'You want money to fix the very roof you abandoned three years ago?'

He shrugged. 'You owe me, Nina.'

I laughed. 'I owe *you?*'

'It's thanks to me you wrote those stories.'

Shit. Had he read them? Did he see himself in them? I turned around, my back to him. Maybe I could upend the kettle over his head. That would certainly distract him.

'I suggested the names to you, didn't I?' he said.

'What names? What are you talking about?' Was he off his rocker completely?

He blushed. 'The names of your characters. I don't remember what we called them.'

'We? Have you even read my books, Phil?'

His face got even redder. 'No, I don't have time to read...'

Thank you, God.

'...but you wrote those books while you were married to me, so...'

'I owe you nothing, Phil. Those stories have nothing to do with you.'

'Still, I'm your husband.'

'Only because you are dragging the divorce on endlessly. Why don't you just sign off on it and leave me be, Phil?'

'Because you're still my wife here,' he said, patting his chest. He should have been patting his back pocket where his wallet usually was. Only I don't think track bottoms have back pockets, do they?

'Come on, Nina! I need the money!'

'Then go and find yourself a job like I did. I'm not giving you a single penny.'

'You sound like Scrooge,' he whined. 'What's a few K when you've got all that dosh rolling in?'

I put down my mug. 'A few *K*?'

'Yeah. All I need is a few thousand to set me up in my new business, Nina.'

Oh, God. I eyed him warily. 'What new business?'

'Polly – a friend of mine – she's an IT genius, yeah? So I asked her to create a thingy—'

'You mean a programme.'

'Yeah. That comes up with all these winning lottery combinations.'

'You mean she has designed a programme that generates number combinations. Based on what criteria?'

'Huh?'

I sighed. 'Based on what criteria does the programme generate numbers? Or are they random?'

He scratched his head. 'I dunno. All I know is that people are gonna rush to buy them and we're going to make loads! And then I'll pay you back.'

Yeah. I'd heard that one before. I was still waiting for

him to return the seventy-five thousand pounds he'd kindly relieved our joint account of. But because he had no earnings and no capital anywhere, the courts were helpless.

And on top of that, he wanted my hard-earned money, without even paying me back what he'd already stolen? Murder was too kind.

'I'm sorry, Phil. I don't have any money to spare for you.'

And between you and me, even if I did, there was no way in hell's chance that I was going to feed his megalomaniac and fruitless ideas on how to make a living when all he had to do was get off his arse and get himself a proper job like the rest of us.

He shoved another biscuit into his mouth. 'I don't believe you, Nina. They paid you an advance, didn't they?'

I bristled. 'Not yet.'

'Good. Maybe I should have a look at the contract when it arrives, seeing as I have good business sense.'

Oh my Lord, please kill me now.

I put the packet of biscuits in a small paper bag and pushed it into his hands. 'I don't need your expertise, Phil. Now go. I've got work to do.'

He stood up, scratching his head. 'But what about my money?'

'It's not your money, Phil. Now piss off.'

'But I still love you, Nina!'

'Tell that to your new flame.'

'But she's nothing like you, babe!'

'Oh my bloody God, Phil. Will you please get out of here?'

'You need me, Nina.'

At the thought of that, I grinned. 'Sure I do. Just like a hole in the head.'

He rolled his eyes, just like Chloe did, and then rubbed his knuckles against a stain down his front. 'Fetch the kids, I'm taking them out,' he said suddenly.

I took a deep breath. 'First of all, you get them every other weekend – when you don't forget or have other plans. And second of all, you don't give me orders anymore,' I said, and, just like that, we were back in the past, when I'd realised what he was and that I'd had enough. That the children and I could no longer live under him like that. We were no longer captives of his dissolute ways, and the children would never again have to be subjected to his mood swings and the erratic behaviour typical of a gambler. Thank God the courts had been on my side, although bi-monthly visitation rights had been even too generous in my opinion.

'And while we're on the subject, how dare you talk to my daughter about our relationship?'

'*Our* daughter. And it's true. You,' he continued, jabbing his index finger into my chest. 'You with all your frownin' and worryin'! You're nothing but a killjoy. And then you took away the sex to top it off! You've put me off sex completely! You've made me a monk, you have!'

Which I found hard to believe. It was a wonder we didn't have an army of little Jenkinses running around the place.

In any case, how the hell did he expect me to think about sex and frolicking around in bed with all the worrying I did concerning our very survival? How could I have been the only one seeing the cliff we had been barrelling towards?

Of course I worried on a daily – no, *hourly* basis – about my children's wellbeing and happiness. No one else would bother to. If I'd had someone to share the burden of my daily grind and worries with, someone to talk to in those brief moments before dropping off to sleep in sheer exhaustion, while he was gambling away all our money, I might have been able to take my foot off the pedal and have a go at living a decent, even happy, life. But now, things were finally going to change.

'And thanks to you, I'm not interested in a serious relationship anymore!' he continued to yell.

'You never were, Phil. And if that's still true, I'm glad to have been of service to some poor woman who's just dodged the ill fortune of meeting you.' And with that, I pulled him up and marched through the front door.

'Nina!' he called as I closed the door in his face.

With Phil removed as a major influence, I did my best to educate my children and teach them respect for others and themselves. They went to the best school in the county. They were surrounded by top-quality people with integrity and hearts of gold. I could only do so much on my own, provided he didn't influence them negatively any further.

There was another knock at the door, and thinking Phil would have the gall to return, I swung it open, ready to resume the battle.

It was Jack, watching Phil getting onto his bike. The last time they had met was when Jack had told him to stay away from us outside visiting days and Phil had told him to, let's say, Eff Off.

But this time Phil simply glared at him and drove off, leaving a pound of rubber on the tarmacadam.

'Hey, you okay?' Jack asked as I moved aside to let him in.

'God, what I wouldn't do to erase him from my past. Jack, be very careful who you marry, because once the kids come, that's it. You can never get rid of your ex.'

'Can't you get a court order?'

'I would, but the kids would never forgive me. They don't know what he did, and I don't want to break their hearts.'

'That's a mother's love for you, keeping her children safe at all costs. You are a star, Nina.'

'To be honest, I don't feel like one,' I huffed, suddenly tired of everything. 'You know what? Maybe I should just dump Chloe on his hands twenty-four-seven. See what a great job he does.'

'As if you'd ever do that,' he said loyally, nudging me.

'Ooh, sometimes I just want to clobber him over the head, so neither of us would have to remember we were actually married to each other once.'

'Marriage is not always bad,' he said. 'If you meet the right person, that is.'

I stared at him. 'Jack! Are you… in love?'

'Nina—'

'Oh, my God, who is it? Tell me, tell me!'

'There's nothing to tell.'

'Ooh, you dark horse! Does Em know? I'll feel left out if you've told her and not me!'

Jack moved away and huffed. 'Will you just let it go, Nina?'

Today was Wednesday, the day that Olly and Joe, Ben's best friends, always came over to work on a long-standing school project, which was due at the end of the year. They had met at Little Acorns nursery school and had stuck to each other thanks to a common love of cars and crossword puzzles. Yes, ladies and gents, my son is a self-confessed, popular nerd and I am over the moon about it. During some tests at school he scored at university student level, Olly and Joe not far behind. They were not the typical, quiet, isolated nerds, but rather enjoyed everyone's company and everyone enjoyed theirs. Smart enough to be set as a standard, but not too much so as the other kids would resent them.

Ben was an original child, unique in many ways, and he made me proud every day.

He's going to turn out a prissy one day, he is, Phil had scolded me when Ben had mastered making muffins. *It's a good job he likes cars or I'd be very worried.*

Ben must be free to do whatever he wants in life, I defended. But deep down in my heart, I knew that until his leg was operated on, he would never be able to do that. He enjoyed watching sports and cheering everyone on, often jumping up and down with sheer glee when someone scored, but then in the next few days he'd become all pensive.

Now, intellectually and socially, I knew that Ben would do well in life. What I wanted was for him to feel the joy of his feet pounding on the ground as he ran laps around the school playground or played tag and later in life, ran to catch the train for his first job interview, or to see off a friend or even propose to his girlfriend the old-fashioned, romantic way. Ben *had* to be okay. There was no way I could ever be happy knowing that my little man wasn't enjoying his young life to the full. And I would see to it that he did, even if it meant selling the shirt off my back.

18

The Odd Couple

Luke and Jessica were scheduled to arrive on 1st August, and in the week before that, I was in a funny new kind of hell that most women would liken to menopause, i.e. hot flashes, memory loss (had I ever got round to cleaning out the box room?) and mood swings (what kind of crappy movie is going to come out of this?).

And of course, self-doubt: How the hell do you prepare yourself to write a script, when you've never written one before in your life, with a man you've just met who, incidentally, wants to change at least half of it?

And how on earth do you prepare your home for a Hollywood star? Where would we write – on the kitchen table? I looked around and suddenly the things that hadn't mattered before were humongous issues now, like the noisy pipes, the five-minute delay before you actually got any hot water and the green bathroom suite. My tablecloths were all faded with washing, most of my mugs were chipped and the back door screeched like a banshee when you opened it.

And the fridge barked as usual, but for once, it was the very least of my worries.

The morning Luke was due, I was one huge mass of nervous jelly. I had pulled the dining room table closer to the window, exchanging it with my War Desk which was too tiny, retrieved the two good chairs, while pulling out notebooks, writing pads, coloured pens, highlighters and even Post-it Notes in case Luke was old-school. I had no idea how he worked.

And as I fidgeted like a schoolgirl before an exam, it dawned on me that this could really tank if we didn't work well together. My family's every hope lay in the success of this project. So I had to be as professional as possible. And speaking of which, I realised, glancing at my watch, that Luke was late. It figured. Stars always made an entrance, I knew that, but wasn't that supposed to be limited to the red carpet?

I drove over to the village of Little Kettering where he would be staying, bringing along a bottle of Jack's cider and a box of scones for Jessica. I knew that was her one weakness, only she continued with the travesty of putting cream on first. I would make a Cornish girl out of her yet. I waited, chatting away with the receptionist at The Old Bell Inn, my stomach a king-size butterfly cage.

A half hour later, when Luke's taxi finally arrived, he got out, all harried, something akin to a scowl on his face.

Oh, no, no, no, I begged as I watched him pay the taxi driver through the hotel doors. *Please don't be angry.* This is supposed to be the third most beautiful day of my life!

'Hello and welcome to Cornwall!' I sang, hugging Jessica

and wrapping her hands around the box. 'These scones are for you.'

'Thanks, Nina!' she said, feeling her way up my arm to kiss my cheek.

'Hi...' Luke breathed, exhaustion on his face. So much for jet-setters. 'Jet lag is horrible flying east!'

'Oh. Yes, it is.' There went the ultra-original opening gambit I'd prepared, i.e. How was your flight?

As the driver pulled their cases out of the boot, Luke looked around and suddenly jolted forward to kiss me as if he had almost forgotten we were absolute bosom buddies. 'Good to see you, Nina.'

'And you. The kids are at home, preparing you a welcome party.'

Luke forced himself to not cringe.

'Oh, it's just us!' I assured him. 'I mean, of course, what with the papers, everyone knows you're coming, but I'll try to get them to leave you alone while you're in Cornwall.'

'Thanks,' he said, taking Jessica's arm and I followed them into the lobby. 'We'll need to catch up on our sleep first.'

'Of course. So, uhm, I'll let you get on with it. You have my number. Just give me a ring when you're ready for me to come pick you up.'

'I've hired a car locally.'

'Okay, then. Just, uhm, let me know when you want to meet up. Have a lovely afternoon. Bye, Jessica...'

'Bye Nina, thanks for these. So, it is jam first, right?'

'Right. We have a certain way of doing things properly here in Cornwall.' And to Luke I simply said, 'Goodbye' and left.

Talk about ice. Had I crowded him? All I did was show up to greet them, and yet, Luke apparently hadn't appreciated it. Fine. At least now I knew my boundaries.

'Where are they?' Ben asked when I got in, somewhat deflated.

'Oh, they're absolutely exhausted, love, but they're meeting us once they have rested.'

'When's that?' Chloe wanted to know. 'I blew Chanel over today for Jessica. The least she could have done was messaged me.'

'Oh, come now, don't be so demanding. Don't you remember how knackered you were when we came back?'

'Yes, and we had Jack to pick us up. We could have asked Jack to pick them up too, couldn't we, Mum?' Ben asked.

I laughed. 'No, my darling. Luke and Jack aren't even friends.'

And little did I know, those would be my famous last words.

Everything was in place. If they came in the morning, breakfast was to be eaten in the kitchen, facing the garden. Granted, it wasn't the Pacific Ocean, but the English Channel would have to do.

The whole of the next day went by, as I had anticipated, and then I received a text from Luke saying they were on their way. Well, at least he had recovered some of his manners.

I was at the door by the time he rang and flung it open with the biggest of smiles for everyone's benefit. 'Well, hello there!' I said and Jessica lifted her head and gave me a tired but sincere grin.

'Hey,' Luke huffed. 'Sorry I'm late. Jessica had a horrible

night. You must be thinking I'm a real pro. I figured I could get here in time.' And then he looked up at me and grinned his Hollywood smile that melted every woman's knickers. 'I figured wrong…'

'No worries. What's all this stuff you brought?' I asked, eying the bags in his arms.

'My laptop, Jessica's vitamins and stuff… plus some American goodies for everyone.' He was trying to buy his popularity back, but I was a tough nut to crack.

'Thank you. But we have snacks here in England too, you know?'

'Ah, but you haven't tasted junk food until you've tasted American junk food.'

I sighed inwardly. Years and years of hammering healthy habits into my kids, and now?

'Want to see my room?' Chloe asked and then realised what she'd said.

'Sure!' Jessica said, taking her arm and they disappeared up the stairs as Ben shook his head.

'Girls!'

Luke laughed. 'I know, buddy boy! But this summer you and I are going to hang out, right?'

Ben looked at him. 'Of course. Jack can teach you how to drive a tractor and how he harvests his apples. It'll be fun, right, Mum?'

Oh, yeah. Sparksville. I couldn't imagine any men being any more different than Jack and Luke. Like chalk and cheese. 'Absolutely, darling.'

'Who's Jack?' he asked.

'He's our friend. And only the smartest bloke in the village!' Ben boasted, bless his soul.

But it was true. There was nothing Jack couldn't fix.

'Yeah?' Luke said, ruffling his hair, then turned to me. 'And here's some chocolate for everyone and some groceries for the amazing dinner I'm going to cook you,' Luke said.

'But I've already cooked dinner…'

'Lunch tomorrow, then. God, what's the time anyway?'

I grinned. 'Cornwall time. We take things easy here, Luke.'

'This is heaven, you know that, Nina?' Luke said as I poured him another glass of wine with his dinner, the kids having holed themselves up upstairs. After that, I'd open Jack's cider and with a little luck, through the haze he wouldn't see that my walls needed painting, or the green sink and bathtub.

'What is?'

He took a sip and put the glass down, smacking his lips. 'The warmth from the fire, the silence. Your home is lovely. It sends out a great sense of security. And love…'

I giggled. 'Love, yes, loads of it, but security? Uh-uh. Every day is a struggle. If it hadn't been for my books we'd have literally starved…'

His eyes widened. 'Does your ex-husband not…?'

'Who, Phil? God forbid. He bums it off me, if anything. Or, he used to. Not anymore. I'm done being his bank.' And his doormat, for the record, but I wasn't about to tell Luke that. Granted, Luke had figured out that *Written In The Stars* was sort of autobiographical, but it wasn't something an author would easily admit to, was it?

All the same, Luke's face went serious. 'And your kids?'

'At the moment, I'm working on damage control. I try to brainwash them after every visit with the new and latest girlfriend. They come and go like commuters at Victoria Station. Ugh sorry, I didn't mean to max you out on ex-talk.'

'No, it's fine. Can't you do anything? Talk to a lawyer?'

I shrugged. 'Unless he hits the kids over the head with a baseball bat or something, he has access to them twice a month.'

'Can't you get another lawyer? One who will sort him out once and for all?'

'I don't want to put the kids through that, Luke.'

I could see it on his face, the question I'd asked myself so many times: *How could I have allowed things to get so bad?*

The next day, Luke and Jessica were over bright and early, which boded well with me as I was a lark. Also, I hadn't been able to sleep a wink, knowing that today was the first day of my professional life.

The kids took Jessica out into the garden onto the swings, and Luke cast a quick glance out the back window.

'She'll be all right, Luke. They have been instructed to be considerate.'

He smiled at me. 'I have no doubt, Nina. Your kids are cool. So, let's get started!'

'Let's,' I said. 'Care for a brew?'

At his blank face, I rolled my eyes. 'Tea?'

'Coffee in the mornings for me, thanks.'

'And how many sugars?'

'None, thanks. Just a little milk please. And then we can start,' he said, becoming all business-like. Which actually made me feel more comfortable than talking about myself, although you wouldn't know it, the way I yapped on. I guess I was just grateful for some adult company. I hadn't spoken to Emma properly for a while, and Jack was busy working like a dog.

'Sure. I've put a table next to the dining room window if that's okay? Although it's rather small, I'm afraid.'

He pulled out a tablet from his travel bag and tapped it as he sat down by the window. 'I don't need much space. Everything I need is in here.'

'Okay,' I said, feeling a bit nervous. 'I'm new to this as you know, so where do we start?'

'Well, I've reread your book and underlined and made notes.'

'Yes?' Gosh, that was the first time I'd heard anyone do that, apart from a reviewer, my nemesis, who killed my books every time with her scathing comments on my writing. And... she was usually one of the first ones out.

'I gotta say, Nina, your novel reveals more and more each time I read it.'

I laughed. 'That sounds like a great endorsement, Luke.'

'It is. If I am willing to spend millions on it, it means I love it. You are an extraordinary writer. And it feels as though you wrote this part for me. It seems like you have known me inside and out for ages.'

Was that what he thought? I think I blushed, because my face suddenly felt hot. And I was too young for hot flashes.

'I've a confession to make, Luke.'

He grinned as if nothing could upset him. 'What's that, Nina?'

'The day we met, I went back to my hotel room and googled you.'

'Are you serious? You didn't know who I was?'

Jesus, was he full of himself or what?

'That was a joke, Nina. Come on! No need to make a face.'

'Oh. Sorry. In any case, it's not that I didn't know who you were, because I recognised you instantly. But since the kids were born… I really don't remember seeing anything that wasn't from Disney or Pixar. And I don't really buy magazines or even the papers. But I did see you at the Oscars.'

He laughed. 'You mean when I didn't win?'

'Yep.'

He put his hand on mine. 'Thank you, Nina.'

'For what?'

'For writing such a great book, for welcoming us into your home. And above all, for not giving a crap about who I am.'

I rolled my eyes.

'I'm serious. You're the first person I meet who actually isn't…'

'Star-struck?'

'Yeah. I mean, I'm a guy like everyone else, only with more…'

'Money?'

He grinned. 'I was going to say visibility.'

I nodded, and we got back to work.

As it turned out, our first morning of work hadn't been as bad as I'd thought. Granted, we'd hit some potholes (and thankfully not plotholes) along the way, but I had to accept that now my story was evolving for the screen. How much "evolving" it was about to do remained to be seen.

19

Gossip

As would have been expected, the news of the arrival of a Hollywood star in Penworth Ford could not have stayed smothered for long, and soon everyone between eight and eighty (well, ninety-three, actually, counting Old Nellie from the tea room on Fore Street) was gagging for some gossip.

'Is he staying in your house?' Nellie asked me as her granddaughter Annie poured us a cuppa and brought us carrot cake on the house (after all, I was a half-celebrity now, wasn't I? Well, at least in the village).

'No, Nellie. He's booked a suite at an inn.'

'Is he as handsome as he looks on the telly?' Her eyes shone with excitement.

I thought about it. 'Even more.'

'And are you going to sleep with him?'

'Nan!' Annie cried.

I laughed. 'No, Nellie, I'm not going to sleep with him. It's just a business relationship.'

'I think you should definitely sleep with him,' she said with a nod, her silver eyes sparkling behind her thick, foggy lenses.

Annie turned crimson. 'I'm so sorry, Nina! Nan sees intrigue and sex everywhere.'

'She should write a book then!' I quipped, forking some cake into my mouth. 'Oh, my God, Annie, this is delicious!'

'Nan's recipe,' she said, kissing her on the cheek. 'Isn't it, Nan?'

Old Nellie nodded, caressing her granddaughter's face. 'They're cute when they're young, aren't they?' she said, turning to me. 'I was cute when I was young, too! And Charles was the handsomest devil you'd ever seen.'

'Who's Charles?'

'My first love. I was,' she whispered, leaning in, 'the "older" woman!'

I put my cup down. 'Really? What was he like?'

She clasped her hands together. 'A real blinder. Couldn't eat for days, the first time I met him. But… he was married.'

I looked at her, her white, paper-thin skin, spotted hands and wrinkly but dreamy eyes. And it surprised me that I had never thought of her that way. We seem to forget that the elderly once had love lives.

'Nellie! It looks like you were not only the older woman but also the *other* woman, you naughty girl, you!'

How the years take everything away except for the memories. It must have been terrible for her, loving someone for so long, wanting to be with him but also feeling guilty for the pain she would cause another woman if she got her wish. But at least she had loved, and cherished those memories. I had nothing in my heart but disappointment and bitterness. But at least I was now out of the hurting game.

About a week later, as I was getting into the hang of scriptwriting (well, sort of), Luke suddenly got to his feet.

'What's wrong?' I asked. Had I said or done something untoward? Did he not like my rendition of Stella?

'I've been here for days and you haven't once taken me into town. Even Jessica's been a gazillion times.'

'I thought... you would want to avoid the crowds,' I explained, feeling guilty for keeping him cooped up.

'Crowds? The whole population of Penworth Ford is what I have in one evening at a house party. So, are you coming?' he asked.

Well, if he put it that way. 'Okay, then. I'll get my bag. Guys? Would you like to come into town with us?'

'Can we get cake?' Chloe negotiated.

'Of course,' I said, and we all piled into his rental, also because he wouldn't fit in my Ka.

We parked by the village gardens by the sea, which was a stone's throw away from the centre along Fore Street. The village was in a stir. First the book, then the movie and now the star, in the flesh? It was more than anyone could take, especially a backwater hamlet like ours. 'Everyone knows who you are,' I warned him as we walked down the High Street, and oh God, who was the first person we ran into? Vanessa, the Northwood chairwoman.

'Niiiinaaa, helloooo!' she called, waving her bejewelled hands at me, kissing me on both cheeks like they did on the continent. 'And who do we have here, Luke O'Hara? Such a pleasure to meet you!'

'Hi,' he said, shaking her hand.

I cleared my throat. 'Vanessa is—'

'Our children are best friends at school,' she cut in, and I almost snorted.

If Chloe and her Imogen were even remotely friends, then I was Queen Elizabeth the First. I couldn't remember how many times I'd asked Vanessa to tell her daughter to stop bullying mine.

'I'm the chairwoman of the PTA at Northwood Academy,' she said, as if Luke was supposed to know all about the school.

He turned to me for help.

'It's just the school our kids go to,' I floundered.

'Not just a school,' Vanessa corrected me. 'It's one of the best, if not the best, school in Cornwall, if not the entire West Country.'

'West Country?' Luke asked.

'It's just the western part of England,' I explained.

'By the way, Nina,' Vanessa continued. 'I know you're busy with Luke doing your scriptwriting, so I'll come to your place and pick up your *arancini* for the festival.'

Ah. That was a first. 'That's all right, Vanessa. I can bring them to the school just like I do every year.'

'Ah, I insist! We can't keep our celebrities from their work! I'll call you next week then. Goodbye, Luke, it was delightful meeting you!'

And just like that, she was on a first-name basis with him. It had taken me years of slogging away at my laptop to even get close to a celebrity, and she had done it in a nanosecond.

'Likewise,' he answered politely as she lifted herself onto her tiptoes to kiss him on both cheeks, taking him by surprise, but he was very smooth. He wasn't Hollywood for nothing.

As we ambled along, the kids ahead of us, a couple of my fellow villagers stopped to say hi and to welcome Luke to Penworth Ford, assuring him he was in good hands with me.

'Sorry about that,' I apologised as we resumed our way towards the Post Of ice.

'Don't be. I managed to get somewhere with only three people recognising me. And they were so polite! No cameras in my face, no pens shoved up my nose. Just pleasant exchanges between normal people. This is such a beautiful little village, like the kind you see in fairy tales.'

'It is,' I agreed happily. 'Only salt-of-the-earth people here. Well, except for maybe a couple.'

Luke laughed. 'Meaning that woman with the red claws?'

'Vanessa?' I said. 'She's harmless.'

'She's jealous of you,' he said.

'Jealous? Absolutely not. If anything, she feels above us all because she comes from money.'

'So will you, very soon, dear Nina. You'll be so rich you won't know what to do with your money. And you might even buy yourself a mansion facing the Pacific. We could even be neighbours one day.'

'Who? Me?' I said with a laugh. 'Ah, Luke, you are truly entertaining.'

He shrugged. 'If you keep writing movies I want to produce, you will shoot to the top, Nina.'

I stopped. 'You want to produce more movies from my—?'

'Your books? Yeah. I told you, I love them.'

My heart began to pound. 'But you never mentioned…'

He took my arm. 'Let's get through this script first, okay? I just wanted to throw that at you in case you ever doubted my respect for you during one of our heated arguments.'

'We're going to have heated arguments?'

'Lots of 'em, Nina. But that's the way it works in Hollywood.'

'Oh. Okay, then.' I paused just outside the Post Of ice. 'And here is one of my oldest haunts. As you can see, one of the Fs is missing, but Alf is such an original, he decided to leave it that way, and the ladies from the ice cream parlour opposite decided to call their place The Post Of ice Cream, just for laughs. They're a great bunch. Come on in, I'd like to introduce you. Bev and Carol and Deirdre take care of Alf since he was widowed, just out of the goodness of their hearts, and when he was ill they took turns in running the shop for him. They have been with me from the very start here in Cornwall.'

'They sound like a great bunch,' Luke said.

'Oh, they are,' I said as I pushed the door open, and a jingle filled the shop.

'Morning, Alf,' I called, but he just sat behind his paper, as deaf as a post.

'Hi, Alf!' I repeated, and the paper came crashing down to reveal a sullen face.

'Hello, Nina,' he said, and my blood froze at the frostiness in his voice. Had I offended him in some way? Had his Anchor Beer turned out bad?

'Hello, pet,' Deirdre said, sliding in behind the counter, patting my hand.

'Folks, this is Luke O'Hara. We're working together on my script.'

'Of course,' Deirdre cooed. 'Lovely to meet you, Mr O'Hara.'

'Mr O'Hara's my dad, ma'am,' Luke said, turning on the charm. 'Please call me Luke.'

'Oh, my, to be on first-name terms with a Hollywood superstar!' she returned with an equal amount of panache.

'Alf,' I said. 'I was just telling Luke the story about you. Are you ever going to get the F up?'

He glared at me from under those bushy eyebrows that looked like rats' nests. 'When did you start swearin', Nina?'

I laughed. A forced, croaked laugh. 'No, I mean the F on your *sign*. It's been like that for years now.'

'Well, Nina, maybe I don't like change. And maybe neither should you.'

My mouth fell open as my eyes swung to Luke's who didn't miss a beat. 'I'll be at the dairy section,' he whispered and slipped away.

'Oh, Alf,' Bev said, elbowing him in the ribs as she joined us. 'Go on, pet, don't mind this ogre. He's just having one of those days.'

'I am not,' Alf interjected, putting his paper down. 'Nina, we've known you for years now, ever since you became one of us. And you know we don't take kindly to strangers so easily, so you can understand how much we love you.'

I nodded, and suddenly some stupid tears were sliding down my face again. 'I love you too, Alf. I love you all…'

'And we love *you*, pet,' Deirdre – who only needed to see the shadow of a tear to get emotional – blubbered, coming around the counter again to embrace me. 'You are the daughter I never had…!'

'Oh, dearie me,' sighed Carol, who, being hard of hearing, had missed most of the words spoken, but there was no mistaking the tears and Alf's icy manner towards Luke.

'Alf!' Bev hissed. 'When are you going to learn your manners once and for all?'

He shrugged. 'What? I only said the truth! What did I tell you the moment I saw his face in the papers? I didn't like him, I said. And I still don't!'

'You're talking nonsense as usual. And lower your voice,' Bev scolded as Deirdre dried her eyes. 'And where is your Cornish sense of hospitality?'

'Ain't got none for the likes of 'im!' Alf declared, nodding down the aisle to where Luke, reading milk labels, pretended not to hear. If anything, he was a gentleman.

'Shut your mouth,' Bev said. 'Shame on you, at your age. You are going to be nice to him from now on, do you understand?'

'Why should I be nice to that fancy gent?'

'Because he's a friend of Nina's. And because if you don't, you'll be cooking your own meals and doing your own laundry. Right, girls?'

Bev squeezed my hand and nodded firmly. 'Absolutely.'

'Tough crowd.' Luke whistled as we got back into his car.

I turned in my seat. 'Luke, I'm absolutely *mor*tified. I just don't know what's got into him. He's normally a sweetheart, you know? It must be the Alzheimer's. I'm so sorry.'

Luke patted my hand. 'It's okay. He's just protecting his baby.'

I grinned. 'I am, in a way.' It felt so great to be loved.

The next morning, Luke, who had unwittingly stumbled upon Nellie's tea room, arrived with a selection of her best croissants as I was pouring the coffee. Chloe and Ben had come down to retrieve Jessica and take her upstairs.

As Luke leaned against the counter sipping his coffee, the fridge barked and he leapt to attention, swinging his round eyes from the fridge to me. 'What the—I say what the Jesse James was that?' he said in a John Wayne accent.

I laughed and shrugged. 'It does that all the time. Jack says it's just because it's old.' The subtext being that there was no money for a new refrigerator, but it was too late to take it back. However, my finances weren't as interesting to him as my social life.

'Who's Jack?'

'Ben told you. Our neighbour.'

He looked doubtful. 'You mean the farmer down the road? Is he qualified?'

'Well, he was actually an engineer in London. But when he inherited Crooked Hill Farm from his gran, he decided to call it quits and enjoy the good life. He's very happy here.'

'He's not the vet in your book, is he?'

'No, of course not,' I answered. 'It's a work of fiction. Besides, I wrote those before I moved here.'

Not that he believed me. 'Hmm. Is this Jack guy as good-looking as the one in the book?'

I shrugged. 'Handsome? Women seem to think so.'

'And you?'

'Me? I suppose he's rather easy on the eye.'

'Hm, now I'm jealous. Is he as handsome as me?'

There we go. It was only a matter of time until Luke

hammed out on me. Blimey, these Hollywood stars had egos the size of cathedrals.

'He's… a different type,' I considered. 'You're more of a yacht-y, French Riviera type, while he's more of a…' How to define Jack? 'Woodsy type.'

'I was actually joking when I asked, Nina. God, you're so gullible.'

'Oh. Sorry.' I never knew when he was serious. Which was good for his reputation as an actor, but made communication a little iffy at times. I had yet to become accustomed to his sense of humour.

'Don't be. It's what makes you so adorable.'

At that, my face went hot.

'How long have you known him?' he asked.

I took a sip of my coffee. 'Ever since we moved in three years ago.'

'You've been here for three years?' he asked, looking around himself, and I bristled.

I knew he didn't intend anything by it, but the fact was that in all this time we hadn't managed to complete the renovations. But I had painted the kids' rooms and re-carpeted before Phil took what we'd had left.

The rest was… drab. No matter how many beautiful beach-themed cushions and rugs I scattered around the house, it still looked helpless. The original floorboards were one of the house's strong points, but it was still a dump, especially compared to the Nirvana that was Luke's house.

'Hm,' he said, pulling a croissant apart. 'Speaking of characters, I was thinking about your female lead.'

'Stella?'

'Yeah. I think the best scenes are when we see her

vulnerability. We should show more of her in her weaker moments.'

'You mean when she breaks down and cries while vacuuming under the bed?'

'Yeah. And also, I'd show how she could've been more understanding towards Bill.'

I felt my teeth grinding. Here we go again. 'Oh?'

'Yeah. I also want some scenes to depict his struggle. Make him seem much less of a jerk. You know, show the temptation to not drink, the pain he goes through...'

This was not good. If I showed Bill as a nice guy, the viewer would want Stella to give him another chance. I didn't want to give him another chance. He'd had more than enough, and had wasted every single one of them.

'Not a good idea, Luke...'

'Oh come on. Have a heart, Stella.'

'I do have a heart. I don't want— What did you just call me?'

Luke grinned. An open-mouthed, I've got perfect teeth grin. 'Stella. You and Stella are one. But it's great. I'll be Bill, and we can recite the arguments and—'

I huffed. 'This isn't going to work, Luke.'

'Of course it is. All you have to do is try a bit harder.'

'You sound like my husband.'

'Exactly, you see?'

'No, I mean, this male point of view. I know I agreed to it, but it's just not going to work. Hollywood will hate it.'

'Bull. Hollywood loves stories about break-ups. Think *Kramer vs. Kramer*, and *The War of the Roses*.'

He didn't mean the one between the Lancasters and the Yorks, but a much bloodier one, that is, the movie where

Michael Douglas and Kathleen Turner meet, fall in love and, many tears later, end up dead. Sad, but a great movie.

'Don't you see?' he persisted. 'This is a good thing. Male versus female. Husband versus wife. In most divorces, is there anyone who is actually always right about everything?'

'I'm not even going to answer that,' I muttered. 'It just doesn't feel right, in this case.'

'But you're missing the point. It will be good to hear *his* side of the story.'

'How is that a good thing?' I asked. Phil had been the source of our problems, not me. I hadn't been the one to make this big mess that was our lives now. If anything, I was still mopping up after him after him. And thanks to this once-in-a-lifetime chance I finally could hope in succeeding. 'Luke, Bill is the villain in this story, and justifying his actions will only make him more human and... no. I can't.'

I was seriously doubting the outcome of this project, but I had to tread carefully, because if we reached a stalemate, we were in big trouble. And so were my finances and the very fate of my family. How to explain it to him that there was no room for a stinking mess of a man's point of view in my story, without losing this contract, our meal ticket, for the rest of our lives? All I had was reasoning. If only I could make him understand how strongly I felt.

'We are on polar opposite sides, Luke,' I said in all honesty. 'It's not your fault, but maybe I didn't make myself clear. It's my fault...'

He looked up at me, beaming. 'There's my girl. That's the attitude Stella should have.'

I swear I almost fainted. '*What?*'

'Admitting she isn't always right is the first step towards

a sort of understanding. Only then will they be able to communicate.'

No, no, no! This was all wrong. He'd misunderstood. Completely. How to get out of this?

Luckily, there was a knock at the front door, which opened a crack. 'Nina? You guys in?'

Luke turned to look at me as the door widened. It was Jack. Jack, I suddenly remembered, come to take us to Predannack Wollas for a picnic, scheduled weeks ago. How many things had changed in such a short time!

'Shit!' I swore as I jumped up from the table.

He stepped into the room and made a weird face. 'Well, nice to see you too.'

'I'm so sorry, Jack, I completely forgot to tell them, what with Luke arriving and all.'

Silence. Dead silence for a minute. Then Jack spoke.

'Jack Marrak. I've seen all of your movies.'

After a moment, Luke rose to his feet and shook his hand. 'Gee, thanks, man.'

Why did I expect Jack to reply with something like: *I didn't say I liked them?* Because the air was definitely strange.

I cleared my throat. 'The kids are upstairs. I'll go get them. Jack, pour yourself some coffee, and there's croissants. Chloe!' I called as I raced up the stairs. 'Ben!'

Shit. How could I have forgotten something so important? And what about Jessica? Surely Luke wouldn't let a complete stranger take his one and only daughter onto the edge of a cliff?

I found the three of them listening to music in Chloe's room, Ben happily swiping away at titles on Spotify.

'Guys, so sorry, I forgot to mention Jack was coming by to go on a picnic at Predannack Wollas.'

'Cool!' Ben and Chloe chimed. Now, while Ben loved the outdoors, give Chloe her mobile and that was all she needed. While she'd usually much rather stay home and chat with her friends all day, when Jack was involved, she always agreed readily.

'Who's Jack?' Jessica asked.

'Only the coolest bloke you'll ever meet!' Ben said, scrambling to his feet.

'Mum, can Jess come?' Chloe asked.

'We'll have to ask her father, but—'

'You guys coming down or what?' Jack called from the bottom of the stairs.

'Grab your rucksacks,' I said and turned back downstairs to find Jack and Luke in complete silence. You could hear a pin drop. It wasn't going very well, and yet, they had a lot in common. Both successful in their own way, both young and handsome. They should get along like a house on fire, right?

Luke was packing up his laptop. 'Where are you going?' I asked, although it was obvious. These two did not like each other.

'You go, Nina. The kids have been looking forward to this all week,' Luke said.

'Indeed they have,' came Jack's voice. What had I missed, exactly?

'We're going back to the inn for today,' Luke informed me. 'But we'll see you tomorrow.'

'But Mum, Jess wants to come,' Chloe reminded me.

Luke turned to his daughter, caressing her cheek. 'Another time, sweetheart.'

My eyes pleadingly swung to Jack's.

He cleared his throat. 'You should all come,' he said. 'Really, Luke, I've got food for an army, and an eight-seater. Some fresh air would do us all some good.'

Bless his soul.

'Oh, Dad, can we, please?' Jess said.

Luke's face softened, but not completely. 'Thanks, Jack. We accept. But I'll follow you in my rental.'

What was it with male pride and all?

Jack shrugged his shoulders and as the kids cheered, I went to get some extra drinks and snacks for all. Or maybe I should have got some tranquilising darts?

There was a definite sense of... differences between Jack and Luke. Luke, dressed in linen Bermuda shorts and a light blue cotton shirt and looking like he had come straight from his California beach house, watched his footing, as he was wearing expensive leather loafers, not quite ideal for negotiating these rugged coastal paths. Luke was born for luxury, I realised, while Jack was just as at ease with his head and arms reaching inside a broken tractor, studying how to repair it.

Luke kept Jess firmly by the hand, wary of the terrain. I reached out and took Jess's other hand and we ambled along the clifftops.

Jack, on the other hand, had an innate confidence and was comfortable in his walking boots and jeans, easily piggybacking Ben who shrieked in pure delight over his shoulder, his strong hands around my son's chubby ankles.

It was such a beautiful picture against the Cornish sunset: a little boy laughing without a care in the world, knowing he was safe and loved in those strong hands.

To me, laughing and being silly were better than a romance. I didn't even remember what it was like to be this carefree. Finally everything was going our way.

When we found our favourite spot, just by the stone National Trust location marker, we sat down to a meal of British staple foods such as pasties, Scotch eggs, sausage rolls, meat pies and Marmite sandwiches that Luke marvelled about graciously. It had been a long walk and we were content to sit back and watch the children play.

Luke's eyes always darted to Jess, and I could tell he was making huge sacrifices to not jump up every time Jess moved. It was a relief to see how thoughtful Chloe was around Jessica, and how she was always on guard lest she tripped over something. This new friendship could do Chloe wonders, because Jessica was a gem of a girl – sweet, polite, and undemanding. She never spoke inconsiderately and always ate everything she was offered with gusto and grace. She was a true testament to Luke's parenting skills.

Jack, who seemed to have read my mind, turned to him, somewhat less glacial than earlier. 'Your daughter is a lovely girl. You've done a great job with her.'

Luke's face lit up. 'Thanks, man. Have you got any kids yourself?'

Jack's face sobered ever so slightly. 'No.'

'Are you planning on having any?'

Jack took a long swig of his coffee as Luke's eyes swung to mine in question. I raised my eyebrows up at him and shrugged imperceptibly. How was I supposed to know the answer to that question? He was as closed up as a lobster on that front.

'If the right girl comes by,' Jack answered, staring down into his mug. And that was the end of that conversation.

On the way back, we stopped off at Luke's inn and he came up to Jack's window.

'Jess and I had a great day, Jack. Thanks. Thanks to all of you.'

Jack shrugged. 'No biggie. I'm picking apples later this week if anyone's interested.'

Luke's arm came around his daughter's shoulders. 'Would you like that, sweetheart?'

'Oh, yes, Daddy, please!'

Jack grinned. 'Okay then. See you guys?'

'Yay!' the kids all cried to one another as we drove away.

But then in his 4x4, Jack's mood changed. Not that you would know by his cool exterior.

'You all right?' I asked.

'Yep. Did *you* have a good time?'

'I had a great time, Jack, and it's all thanks to you. You sure know how to entertain the kids.'

Something had definitely changed, and by the time we got back to the house, I still had no idea what it was. Was he bothered that the kids were spending so much time with another male role model? But he needn't have worried. They loved him dearly. We all did. So that needed to be sorted out pronto.

'Don't forget breakfast tomorrow, Jack,' I reminded him as we pulled up in front of the house. 'I'm making blueberry pancakes, your favourite.'

He ruffled the kids' hair with a smile as they got out, then he turned to me as I swung out, closing the door.

'Thanks, but no thanks. You and Luke have a lot of work to do and so do I. My orchards and pumpkin crops wait for no one. Plus later I'm meeting someone.'

'Are you sure? What about after that? We could all have Saturday brunch together.'

'Another time, Nina, but thanks. I'll see you.'

I stepped away from the Jeep. 'Okay, then. Thanks again, Jack. Take care.'

He smiled, and I inwardly breathed a sigh of relief. He wasn't angry with me. But for some reason, I figured I'd done something wrong.

20

The English Patient

A few days later, after a hearty breakfast, Chloe and Ben took Jessica round to Jack's as agreed. I refilled our coffee mugs and took them to the dining table so Luke and I could get to work. I needed to get him out of his Your Character Bill Is A Saint mode.

'Thanks, Nina. So tell me,' Luke said as we sank into our working seats. 'Does Stella marry Aidan the vet straightaway, or should we give her some fun with Dylan the playboy first?'

I frowned. 'Another man? No. Stella's not like that.' Just like I wasn't.

'Why not?' he wanted to know.

I shrugged. 'Because I don't want to complicate things.'

He grinned. 'You don't think Stella should have a bit of naughty fun?'

I sat back. 'You mean…? No. This is not about… sex. This is about her journey.'

'Exactly. There should be a bit of spice – a change in her life.'

'There is. It ends well, which is more than I can say for the real world.'

'What a bitter concept you have of life, Nina. Life can be fantastic if you let it.'

'Yeah, well maybe I'd have a sweeter concept if I lived in a glass mansion with a view of the Pacific Ocean.' I bit my lip. 'I'm sorry. That was uncalled for. I know you've had your share of pain with the divorce and worries with Jess and th—'

'Nina, it's fine. I understand you, and you understand me. We're good.'

I studied him. 'Okay,' I said, relieved. The last thing I wanted to do was offend anyone, or, as it were, bite the hand that fed.

'But I still think that Stella deserves to have some fun before settling down,' he insisted.

Fun. Ha. I tried to forge my face into a neutral expression, but I could feel the muscles around my eyes and cheeks tense. I wondered if Stella had enough stamina or sense of adventure to play the field. I certainly had not. When we'd drained our mugs once more, I got up to take them to the sink.

'Let me do this,' he said, rising. 'You sit down and relax.'

'Oh. Okay, thank you.' I watched while Luke washed and dried and even put away the last of the breakfast dishes. Apart from Jack, I had never seen any man scrub the dishes in this kitchen sink, least of all Phil.

But that was about all that Luke and Jack had in common. Where Luke was always clad in baby blues and whites, and poised like the model that he had been, Jack was scruffy and scarred in his collection of jeans and T-shirts from all the rock concerts he'd been to, his beauty hidden by an eternal five o'clock shadow on a good day. Where Luke was classy, with leather-strapped watches and belts, Jack never even wore a watch as he'd once caught it in the tractor door and had been dragged a few yards across the field before he'd managed to free himself. Also, Luke was eloquent – a born entertainer – while Jack was content listening. Plus, Luke looked at ease in the kitchen, while Jack couldn't boil an egg.

'You're mighty handy around the kitchen,' I mused.

He grinned. 'I needed to be, after Lauren left. Not that she was much of a homemaker, really.' He held out a plate of biscuits and I shook my head. He picked one for himself and bit into it thoughtfully. 'But what about you and Lumber Jack over there,' Luke asked. 'What's the deal?'

'Jack? I told you. He's my friend, and an excellent pumpkin and apple grower. His cider is unrivalled in the county. He and Phil had barely spoken two words when we moved in, and were not very fond of each other, but then again, none of the villagers ever liked Phil.'

'Well, if he's anything like Bill in the script, I don't doubt it at all.'

Was Bill like Phil? And was I like Stella? Phil and I *were* Bill and Stella, no doubt about it. But legally, if Phil ever found out? I'd be in Shitsville.

'Luckily Stella is like you,' he said.

'Yeah?' I said. I was beginning to wonder whether Luke would finally see my side of the story, and how wronged Stella had been by her husband, rather than the other way around. Maybe that was it. If Luke met Phil, he'd understand where I was coming from and stop badgering me about poor, wronged, bloody Bill.

'Yeah,' he said, lowering his voice and leaning in with that cocky smile. 'A cool exterior, hiding a pressure cooker of pent-up passion just dying to get out.'

His eyes bored into mine, and I could see they were a darker blue than usual. I swallowed. If I didn't know any better I'd think he was seriously flirting with me.

'I've seen the way he looks at you,' he said and I stopped.

'Who?'

'Jack.'

'No, I told you. Jack and I are just friends. The best of friends, even, but nothing more. Besides, he's seeing someone else, I think.'

'Okay, if you say so.'

'I say so. Now let's get back to Stella.'

'Yes, let's get back to Stella and her thwarted libido.'

'Stop it, Luke, and get serious. We have work to do.'

He gave me a mock military salute as he reached over the counter behind him and grabbed a peach, of which he took a big bite. 'Want some?' he asked, pushing it towards me.

My throat suddenly went very dry.

'No thanks. Concentrate now, please.'

When the kids returned, I noticed that Jessica was looking a bit off.

'Are you feeling hot, Jessica?' I asked, checking her pulse and feeling her forehead. She had a fever, but I also recognised other unmistakeable symptoms.

'Yuh…' she murmured.

'All right, follow me,' I ordered and headed upstairs. 'Put her in Chloe's bed, will you?' I said to Luke and he bent over and tucked her in, bringing the covers to her chin.

'She doesn't look right – I'm worried, Nina,' he whispered to me.

'Don't be,' I assured him. 'All she needs is some rest. That's chickenpox.'

Luke's eyebrows shot into his hairline. 'Chickenpox?'

'Yep,' I said as Chloe jumped back into bed, making a fuss of her, something I hadn't seen since Ben had fallen off the swings at the village gardens and broken his collarbone. 'Let her sleep for now. I'll call the doctor in the meantime.'

He glanced at me, then leaned over Jessica again to kiss her on the forehead. 'Sleep, pumpkin. I'll be right downstairs if you need me, okay?'

Jessica nodded and rolled over and closed her eyes.

'She'll be okay,' Chloe told him. 'I had it and it was actually lots of fun!'

'That's because you didn't go to school and we spoiled you rotten for three weeks,' I said with a laugh. 'Come on, Luke, let her sleep for now.'

I closed the door on our girls and he followed me downstairs, hands in his pockets.

'Are you sure it's chickenpox?'

'Have you never had it?' I asked and he shook his head.

'Oh, Jesus. Let's hope you don't get it too, then…'

He laughed and rolled his eyes. 'I won't.'

'I'm calling Brian.'

'A doctor, I hope, and not the family vet?'

I grinned. 'Yes, our family doctor. He's been coming here forever and he's worth his weight in gold.'

'So he knows you well.'

'Oh yeah,' I agreed as I sauntered into the kitchen to start on a chicken broth. If Jess was anything like my two, she wouldn't want to eat anything solid. I fetched my mobile and left a message for him to come round. 'Knows every single little Jenkins drama.'

'The break-up, too?' he asked.

I shrugged. 'When you live in a tiny village, some things can't be hidden, as hard as you try.'

'You're telling me,' he snorted. 'I live in LA and I can't take a leak without the whole world knowing.'

I eyed him from the cooker. 'Doesn't it bother you?'

'Does it bother me?' He rubbed the back of his neck in thought. 'It never used to, but with Jessica growing up I'm finding it harder to protect her, you know?'

'Do I ever,' I agreed.

As it turned out, my diagnosis of Jessica was right. Brian came quickly, visited her and snapped his bag shut. 'Chickenpox it is.'

'Damn,' Luke said.

'No worries. Just don't let her scratch.'

'Thanks, Doctor,' Luke said and Brian turned and stared at him with sudden interest.

'Are you…?'

Luke smiled. 'Yes, it's me.'

Brian put a hand on his shoulder and gently pulled him forward as if to kiss him. But Brian had no interest in movies.

'As I suspected. You have it, too, I can already see a few spots. Bed rest and plenty of Nina's chicken soup.'

'What?' Luke said. 'I'm perfectly fine.'

Brian turned to me. 'Nina?'

I could see a couple of spots I hadn't noticed earlier. 'I'm on it,' I promised.

After Brian left, I marched Luke upstairs and put him in Ben's room and Ben up with me, grateful for an excuse to cuddle my baby.

'Get into bed. And don't scratch if you don't want to ruin that Hollywood face.' I giggled.

'This is ridiculous. I'm perfectly fine.'

But when I brought him his chicken soup twenty minutes later, he was sprawled on the mattress as if he'd been steamrolled.

'You okay?' I said as I set down the tray on Ben's night table.

'I suddenly feel like a sack of shit,' he groaned in a feeble voice.

'You'll be fine. Eat this.'

'Not hungry…'

'Eat. I'm going to give Jessica hers now.'

He groaned again. 'Don't tell her I've got it. She'll worry.'

'You'll both be fine.'

'And you?' he croaked.

'We've all had it, don't worry. Now eat.'

Conte Hospital was now officially open.

As it turned out, Luke O'Hara was the patient from hell. He was uncomfortable, hot, cranky, thirsty, impatient. But worst of all, he insisted on working in his waking hours, which were not that many, luckily for me. So instead of banging away on my laptop prepping the outline for the next scenes by myself, something even a four-year-old could do, I had to sit in Ben's armchair with a pad and paper while Luke dictated his tips to me.

Some were very clever, others a little clichéd. Rather cheesy, really.

'What do you think?' he asked, taking a sip of water and closing his eyes, finally exhausted into semi-silence.

How to be honest without seeming to be rude or ungrateful? 'It's a little… formulaic.'

He opened an eye. 'Exactly what I was aiming for.'

'But do we want our audience to guess the ending, Luke? Don't we want to be a bit more, I don't know, imaginative?'

'Nina, formulas work. That's what Hollywood is built on.'

'But what about the unexpected? The beloved twist?'

'You mean Stella ending up with Aidan? I think she should go with Dylan the playboy. There's much more scope for imagination there.'

Hang on a minute. Was he trying to change the ending? 'But… but what about Stella being true to herself?'

Luke closed his eyes and groaned. 'I'm boiling, Nina. Would you mind checking my temperature?'

I closed my mouth and got out Ben's electric thermometer. He was boiling, all right, so I went into the bathroom and soaked a washcloth with freezing water and gently replaced it on his forehead. He opened an eye briefly.

'You see? We're getting on like a house on fire, Nina…'

That was exactly what I was worried about – me setting him on fire if he insisted on changing everything, even the ending.

★

After three weeks of nursing a cranky Hollywood star and a lovely teenage girl who was polite and appreciative of everything we did, they were as good as new. But as they were packing to return to their inn, I realised that it wasn't practical for them to drive all the way back and forth every day. Besides, we had already broken the ice. So I took a long shot and bit the bullet.

'I think you and Jessica should stay with us.'

Luke looked at me, eyebrows raised. 'Are you serious?' was all he said.

Oh God, I knew it. It was a horrible idea. There was no way I could offer him the comforts he was used to in his LA mansion. What was I going to cook for him? Soup for the sick was one thing, but three square meals every day? I didn't know what he liked and didn't like. Was he a meat and potatoes man, or a pasta freak? Who knew? And would he still want to sleep in a little boy's bed when he could have luxury service at his inn?

Chloe took Jessica's hand. 'Oh, Dad, can we?' Jessica begged. 'Please?'

Luke smiled at Chloe's sincere display of affection for his daughter, scratched the stubble on his cheek and then turned to me with a huge grin. 'We'd absolutely love to, Nina. Thank you so much.'

I exhaled. 'Jessica can continue staying with Chloe, and you can stay in Ben's bed. Is that all right, Ben?'

My son gave a sharp, satisfied nod. 'Super cool. Mum's got a load of interesting books under her bed.'

Luke's eyes widened with interest bordering on the naughty as I felt my face going hot.

'It's just some classics…' I murmured.

'Oh, for a minute there I thought you had a stash of—'

I clapped my hands. 'Right! Everybody back to their rooms to unpack, then. Jack's invited the kids to Crooked Hill again today. Jessica will be safe in his hands.'

'Are you sure she's okay, going out so soon?' Luke asked.

'It's been three weeks. She needs the fresh air.'

'But how do we know she didn't get the chickenpox from Jack's farm? And what about foot and mouth disease, or mad cow disease?'

I tried my best not to laugh, but it didn't work. 'That was an isolated episode years ago, and besides, Jack grows fruit.'

'No animals?'

'Well, the odd stray, but no. No animals. He owns a cider farm.' As I'd told him before, but somehow he seemed to have forgotten.

'Cider? Cool. Maybe I could buy some off him.'

'And maybe you could open a Californian market for him. Our apples in the West Country are world renowned.'

'Is that so?'

'Absolutely.'

He took my hand. 'This is a gorgeous corner of the world. Thank you for agreeing to have me in your home. You and me together! A sizzling combination, sweets. To flying sparks…'

'To flying sparks,' I agreed, wondering if at that rate how long it would take us to progress from flying sparks to flying crockery.

21

Friends With Benefits

'How's Writer's Paradise?' Alice asked over the phone the next morning.

'He's driving me nuts, Alice,' I hissed into my mobile. 'Sometimes I wonder if he even likes Stella. He wants her more polite, less polite, louder, softer, a procrastinator, a go-getter and I...'

'But this is good,' Alice countered. 'He's putting your heroine through her paces.'

'I thought my editor had already done that,' I muttered as I laid the Pyrex dish on a trivet in the middle of the table.

'But an onscreen Stella is much more alive!' Alice continued. 'She'll have a face, even though we don't know whose yet.'

I wanted to argue that she already had a face even before the movie, but decided against it. Alice and Luke saw things the same way. I guess I was the odd one out, the one who knew absolutely nothing about the big screen. Plus, I wasn't about to quibble with whomever got cast or anything, just as long as she could act and do Stella justice.

I was beginning to wonder whether I'd made a colossal mistake inviting Luke to stay. Jessica was a dream guest, and I was growing fonder and fonder of her every day. But Luke? He was a handful. Of all the producers in Hollywood who could have come across my book, why did it have to be demanding, gorgeous, flirty him?

'Breakfast is ready, Alice. Gotta go. Call me when you're down next month and I'll have something nice for you to eat.'

'I'll bring the wine,' she chimed.

'Sounds like a plan,' I said and rang off. Good old Alice. I owed her everything. It seemed like I owed a lot of people everything: Alf, my Ice Cream Ladies, Emma, Jack. And the only way I could pay them back was to be there for them as much as I could.

When I went downstairs, Luke was already up and stirring coffee. It was still something I'd never get over, something utterly surreal. Imagine coming down the stairs one morning, and out of the blue, some Hollywood star is standing in your kitchen in his boxers (not that Luke was) having his morning coffee.

'Mornin',' Luke said as I padded into the kitchen. 'I hope you don't mind, but I had to check on Jessica. Chloe opened her eyes for a moment and harrumphed – it was so funny. If I'd had a stranger in my room I'd have jumped six feet!'

'No worries,' I said, and we stood shoulder to shoulder, looking out to the garden. The irises were late this year. And I had a whole lot of gardening to do. I felt him turn to me.

'I'm glad I had you to help me look after her, Nina.'

I shrugged. 'You're doing fine. Better than any father I've ever seen.'

'Better than Phil…?' he asked softly and I looked up from my coffee.

'Oh.' I giggled. 'Anyone else would be more broody than him.'

'It's so strange, Nina…'

'What is?'

'That thanks to your book, I feel like I've known you forever.'

I rolled my eyes. 'And I feel like I've known you forever, thanks to Google.'

'Thank God for that,' he chuckled. 'Do you miss not having him around?'

'Who, Phil? You must be joking. The kids do, though. I'm just glad our family life is back on track now.'

'Their life was never off track, Nina. Not with someone like you at the helm.'

'Yeah, well, there were some tough times. Up until a few weeks ago, actually. If you hadn't come along I don't know what I'd have done.'

The scale of what I'd said hit me when I saw the expression on his face. But it was true. I shrugged, hiding my face in my mug. 'My financial situation was so dire I was about to lose the house, the kids' places at school… everything.'

He took a sip, never taking his eyes off me. He had that way of looking at you that made you feel all his attention was concentrated solely on you. He made women feel special, and I had to confess that his charm was beginning to rub off on me. Particularly as he was such a loving father.

'Was… all of it autobiographical?' he wanted to know,

but kept his voice low in case I decided I wanted to pretend I hadn't heard his question. Classy guy, no doubt. A bit nosy, but then again, I knew it was for the sake of the movie. Why the hell would he care about my life otherwise?

'Oh, some things. There was, of course, lots of poetic licence. I am a writer, after all.'

'Hm. What about the cliff scene? Did you really think that he wanted to push you off it? And did you really write that message in your diary to the effect that if you were found dead it would most likely have been him?'

'Of course not,' I said hotly. Phil had never been a violent man, but there had been more than one instance in which I felt he wasn't capable of parenting. I just couldn't risk it. I could feel my blood draining from my face. I should never have left that in there, I now realised.

'Okay,' he said softly. 'We all have our secrets.'

'No, that one isn't true. But it makes for good effect, doesn't it?' I said.

He took a sip of his coffee and swallowed it, and his eyes swung to mine again, studying me. Then his lips widened into a grin.

'Yeah,' he said. 'It does, actually. Listen, tomorrow I'm seeing a friend in London who wants to meet Jessica. We'll be gone a couple of days.'

'Okay,' I said. 'Shall I continue with the script in the meantime?'

'Let's take a break. You've worked hard, between that and nursing me. We'll continue when I get back, okay?'

'No problem,' I said, and decided to invite Jack and Emma over in the meantime. I hadn't seen Emma since Luke had arrived. I wondered who the friend in London was.

★

The next day I saw Luke and Jessica off with a hamper of food for their trip, my hand already on my mobile.

'Hello?' Emma said.

'Em? It's me.'

'Well, hello, Me,' she said. 'What's up?'

'How about dinner tonight at mine? I'll call Jack.'

'What about your superstar?'

'He's gone away until tomorrow night.'

'Cool. Have you noticed that you actually haven't introduced us?'

I slapped my hand against my forehead. 'I haven't? Jesus, Em, I'm so sorry – you're right! I'll do it when they get back. Chanel will love Jessica, I can assure you.'

'Well, actually, Chanel is a bit jealous at the moment. Chloe hasn't called her for ages. And we only live next door.'

'I know, I know… we're horrible friends, Em, I'm mortified.'

'Well, then you'll have to make up for it by having a dinner in honour of your *old* friends.'

'I will. See you later, then?'

'Laters,' she promised. 'But I don't know about Chanel. She's pretty pissed off at the moment.'

'I'll send Chloe over immediately to apologise,' I promised.

'Did you hear?' Em said as she eased herself into her favourite chair that evening. 'Old Audrey is getting married.'

I stopped in mid-stir. '*Audrey* Audrey? The *spinster*?'

'The very one. Jesus, you have to wonder what's happening to the world if eighty-year-old women are getting married and we're not.'

'Oh, I already gave in that department.' I laughed, handing her a mug of coffee. It seemed that Luke had got me hooked on it.

'Ooh, that's hot. But Nina, wouldn't you want someone to keep you warm at night? The trouble is finding someone worth it. If you found someone, wouldn't you risk it all over again?'

I smiled as I buried my nose into my own mug. I knew my friend. This was not about me, but about her own love life. She was on the mooch, if not already just about to close in on someone. Her expression, not mine, because Em always saw love as a game, a conquest, a prize to be awarded to the most valiant.

'Em, it's just not for me. I'm just too busy for a bloke.' Besides, I was closed for business. My parts were weary, not to say dead. No more production chain for me.

'Nina, I can't keep it to myself any longer. I've got news myself!'

'Please don't tell me you and Jack have both found someone. Then I'll be the odd one out.'

She stopped smiling. 'Why would you say that?'

I shrugged. 'I have heard rumours that he's seeing someone.'

She put her mug down slowly. 'Did they… say who?'

I shrugged. 'No, but did you think that we'd be Three's Company forever?'

'No, but—'

'Come on, let's have it, then. What's your news?'

'I'm moving to Truro, lock, stock and wedding samples!'

I gasped. 'Noooo, why?'

'Because it'll be easier getting my own clients. I don't want to work for someone else forever. I want to be my own boss, like you.'

'I'm so proud of you, you've finally done it. Your own business!'

'Thanks, luv. Jack's promised to help me move.'

'I'll help, too.'

'No, you won't. You're busy enough as it is. I can hardly still believe it! My own schedule, my own terms, my own clients! And I'm crapping myself!'

'Nonsense, Em! You'll be absolutely brilliant. You already are! I'd let you organise my wedding in less than a heartbeat!'

'Well, maybe I might, one day.'

'Fat chance. I'm so happy for you and Chanel, but miserable for me and Chloe. Who am I going to talk to in the evenings?'

'I'll only be half an hour away, you silly sausage. In any case, Jack's still around. He'll die before he leaves Crooked Hill.'

'But you'll come over during the weekends and stuff?'

She pursed her lips. 'That's the thing, Nina. A lot of my clients only have time to meet up on weekends.'

'Jesus, Em. Then it really is the end of an era. But a start to a better one for you and Chanel. So we need to celebrate your career move! I've got a cheapola bottle of champers around here somewhere – is that all right?'

'Did you invite Jack?' she asked. 'Is he coming?'

'When does he not come over?' I said.

Come to think of it, it was true. Our girl talk was always limited, always secondary to the practical conversations we had with Jack, such as: *My tap is leaking; what can I use to fix it?* or *Can you bring over a bottle of your best cider?*

Poor bloke, we were his closest friends. And now he was losing one of us. I'd have to make sure he didn't feel too lonely, now that his oldest friend was going.

There was a knock on the door – Jack's knock. 'You can stop slagging me off, you two. I can hear you all the way down the lane!' he warned us as he came in.

'Jack!' I called, throwing my arms around his neck. 'I've missed you! And so has Em here, haven't you?'

They exchanged glances and she coughed. 'Nah, not really. How are you, mate?' she asked, clapping him on the back.

'Ow. I hate it when you do that, Em!'

I looked between the two of them. 'Is there something wrong? What have I missed?'

Emma's eyes widened. 'Missed? Nothing, why would you say that?'

I shrugged. 'You just look like you've quarrelled, is all.'

'Nonsense,' Jack said. 'And throw that shit away,' he said, pulling out a bottle of cider from his jacket. 'This is what we need to celebrate Emma's move.'

'You already knew?' I asked.

'I told you – Jack's helping me move,' Emma said.

'Why do I feel left out? Have I really neglected my best friends so much that I didn't even know one of them was moving away?'

'Easy, old girl,' Jack said. 'Don't get upset. We've all been busy – that's life.'

'*You* knew,' I shot back. 'I'm a terrible friend, caught up in my own life. I'm sorry. It won't happen again.'

'Nina, you're making a big deal out of nothing,' Em said, squeezing my shoulder.

I wiped my eyes. 'I just don't want to lose you guys. You're moving away, Jack'll end up marrying someone who doesn't like us and that'll be the end of that. You guys are my *family*.'

'Well, maybe we should accept that things do change, Nina,' Jack said.

'Jack, will you shut up already?' Emma said. 'Come on, dish up, Nina – I'm starving.'

I stirred my shrimp and courgettes risotto, and tore a few shoots of parsley from one of the pots on my windowsill, ran it under the tap and snipped it, watching it colour the top of the rice. And all the while I was wondering how many more of these meals we'd have as Three's Company, and why things had changed so suddenly.

22

Irreconcilable Differences

Alone for once in the house, I wandered around aimlessly, realising how much I depended on my loved ones to cheer me up on a daily basis because the house felt empty without my children. Chloe was out with Ben in the village, helping prepare for the End of Summer festival. She was definitely growing up fast. Her clothes hung from her chair, her cosmetics, strewn across the dresser, spoke of a girl who was dying to be a woman, the very opposite of me.

All her belongings spoke of her, like her lip-gloss that had sparkles in it. I opened it and dabbed the tip of my finger with it. It smelled like raspberries and the sparkles caught the light, like the sea at dawn, and I promised myself that I would never let anything happen to her, nor would I ever let her fall into bad company, and possibly meet someone like Phil who would enchant her at first, and then steal her youth later. For as long as I lived, Chloe would believe in the beauty of happiness, respect, and love. I rubbed my hands together and went back downstairs to my world of hard graft.

★

When Luke and Jessica returned the next evening, he dropped a bomb on me.

'You want to set my Cornish romcom in *California*?' I wailed.

He waggled his eyebrows. 'Yes.'

'No! The story is set in Cornwall. End of!'

'Chill, Nina. It's an adaptation. Even Romeo and Juliet moved to New York in *West Side Story*.'

'That was different. That was a *musical*.'

'It still counts,' he insisted.

'Great, let's adapt everything. Let's turn Cornwall into California. Let's even move *Poldark* and *Doc Martin* to the bloody San Fernando Valley. And oh, *Rebecca*? Let's set that up in Beverly Hills! Why did you even bother to come all the way out here if you were going to pull this stunt on me?'

'I told you, I needed to see how your life works. And how things developed between you and your own husband, and what drove him away from the love.'

What drove him away? Meaning it was my fault? Ooh, I'd drive some nine-inch nails into this bloke's skull right about now. How dare he imply that I was the reason he left! And I had just invited this jackass to stay in my home?

'Fine,' I snapped. 'You'll see it wasn't my fault. But for the record, I'm not setting this anywhere but Cornwall.' I was about to add, *Take it or leave it*, but then I remembered who called the shots.

He leaned forward to peer into my eyes. Really close. I stared back, like a rabbit caught in headlights. What... was he doing now?

'Are you wearing… glitter?' he asked.

I swiped at my face hotly. 'Of course not.'

He moved closer, inspecting my face. 'Looks like glitter to me…'

'It must have rubbed off from my daughter,' I defended. 'I had nothing to do with it.'

He shrugged. 'Shame. It suits you.'

I sat up despite myself. 'Meaning I'm like a teenager?'

He flashed his famous all-American Hollywood grin, those blue eyes twinkling. 'Meaning you have a sparkly personality.'

I snorted and flipped through the pages of my notebook. Weeks of adapting my book for the screen, imagining my breathtaking landscapes in Technicolor or whatever it was they used nowadays, for everyone to enjoy, and now some American Hollywood playboy who hadn't even heard of Cornwall before wanted to turn my movie into a Hollywood bonkbuster?

'Really, you are very bubbly,' he insisted and I put my book down and gave him one of my Get Real looks and he threw his head back and laughed like only he could. 'Awh, man, Nina, it's only been twenty-four hours and I've *missed* you!'

He meant he missed bossing me around, telling me what to do? I had been very accommodating up to now, but this was the cherry on top.

'Earth calling Nina…' he called.

'This is not even remotely funny.'

'Maybe not. But you are bubbly. Which is why I love this story. It's your characters that make the story, Nina. Where they are doesn't really matter.'

'Oh, good, then you won't mind leaving them in Polperro.'

'But *perro* means dog in Spanish.'

'And?'

He shrugged. There are many Latin Americans in the United States who would have something to say about a village named after a dog.'

'Have you noticed, Luke, that there is life outside the United States?'

'Oh, I like you when you get mad.'

'And do you realise that this is a story about a divorced woman who lives in Cornwall? And that the tempestuous location is the symbolism of the tumult in her heart? And do you realise that many women will relate to that?'

'Ooh, symbolism. I like the sound of that. And yes, I do know that she is a divorced woman. But… who did she divorce from? Exactly – a man. Nina, this is not all about your heroine.'

I crossed my arms. 'And who the heck should it be about, her next door neighbour?'

'Not a bad idea. He's a single bloke, isn't he, that Jack? Maybe we should get him over here and help me inject some masculinity into this story. I could use a hand against you, you know.'

'Ah-ha! So you admit that you are working against me?'

He rolled his eyes. 'Nina, it was just a figure of speech. Like symbolism. You can't be right about everything.'

I knew I should have begged for Nancy Meyers to produce the movie. She'd have made a bloody masterpiece out of my story. But I'd had no other choice. I knew I was lucky that Hollywood's most wanted heartthrob had even heard of me, let alone that we were writing a script together.

'Listen, Luke. If you want a movie about a poor, wronged

divorced bloke, then go and write your own sob story. This one is being told like it is.' There.

He stood up to put on his jacket. Oh, God, where was he going? Had I changed his mind once and for all about investing in me, with all my arguing?

'Luke, where—uhm…?'

'Enough writing,' he suddenly said, pulling me up to my feet.

'What? But we've only just started.'

'If we're going to do it your way in Cornwall, I need to see more, see the places where we are going to set the scenes. Give the location managers a few tips and all. Even if we would be hiring a local company, of course.'

'And while we're at it,' I braved, 'I'd like to ask you a favour.' If he hadn't shut down on me yet, he probably never would now.

'I'm listening.'

'I'd like to approach the council of Penworth Ford for permission to double as Polperro. It would save us a lot of money, and boost my village's economy.'

He shrugged. 'If Penworth Ford looks anything like Polperro—'

'Oh, it does,' I said in earnest. 'At least the west side does. The east has the cliffs instead.'

'Okay, if that's what you want.'

Which filled my heart with joy. Because of my book, there would be money coming into the village. 'Thank you, Luke. Come on, then,' I urged. 'There's a whole lot of Cornwall to show you.'

'Bring it on.'

So I drove him straight to Holywell Bay and dragged him

up the sand dunes covered with marram grass to look out over to Gulls Rocks, that looked like they had fallen from a giant's pockets on his way back from a swim in the sea. I stopped, grinning to myself in satisfaction at the look on his face. If this didn't win him over, nothing ever would.

'We have nothing like this in California. It's so...'

'Iconic?' I suggested.

He nodded. 'We can shoot the love scene here...'

Excellent. The Post Of ice Cream Ladies and Old Nellie's Tea Room could do the catering, and Alf's would provide general necessities. The Old Bell Inn and a few other chosen places could put the crew and actors up. It would be perfect, and Annie and Nell would be getting some good business. Maybe even Em could hand out business cards for her wedding dos, who knew? Lots of people wanted their weddings officiated in Cornwall.

'I have to say, Nina, I never realised Cornwall was such a magnificent place. It's literally a world of its own.'

'Yeah,' I said smugly. 'There's no place like home.'

He smiled at my *Wizard of Oz* quote. 'You, my dear, were born to work in Hollywood. It's lucky I found you.'

'Come on, there's so much more to see.'

A bit later, we arrived in the fishing village of Mousehole and again, he was gobsmacked, and I knew Cornwall was definitely in the bag. All I needed was to feed him some of our Cornish delights, and with a little luck, he'd be completely converted from California Dreamin' to Cornwall Drooling.

'Why the hell would you call a place Mouse Hole though?' he said as he bit into his pasty.

I laughed. 'Careful, that's hot. And it's Mouze-ole, not mouse hole.'

'Ah… what the –uck…? It'th hot!'

'I just told you that. You okay?'

He swallowed, gasping for air. 'I can't feel the roof of my mouth. And why is the crust so bloody thick? In the States we at least fill our crusts with cheese or ham.'

'That is so you don't get arsenic on your food,' I explained.

He stopped chewing, his eyes swinging to mine in alarm. 'Arsenic?'

'This is an old miners' meal. They didn't have time to come up to grass, wash their hands and sit down to a full meal. So their wives made them pasties with thick crusts they could hold in their bare, dirty hands and then discard and go back to work.'

'So the mines were full of pasty crusts?'

'Only until the rats arrived to carry them away.'

'Ugh.'

'Cornish life was never easy, you know. It still isn't.' I would know.

'Toto, I don't think we're in California anymore,' he said with a chuckle.

'Thank God for that,' I said without thinking, as I usually do. 'Sorry. I mean, it's beautiful, of course, but I couldn't live there – it's so crazy.'

He shrugged. 'It depends on what you want in life. I'm at the top of my game now but don't expect it to last forever. When it ends, I'll probably move to England and buy a place like this.'

'Really? England?'

'Sure, why not?' He looked me in the eye. 'There's a lot to be loved here. I can see that now.'

Huh? Was he flirting with me? 'Well, apart from Ben's operation, I swear I never want to go back there again.'

He grinned. 'Except for accepting an Oscar for best screenplay!'

I laughed. 'Yeah, except for that.'

The next day we took the kids for a picnic lunch on Gwennap Head, promising ourselves we'd get to work in the afternoon. I knew the rambling mornings across Cornwall were all part of the research work, but I couldn't help feeling we needed to continue with the script. I needed the money, and the sooner it was finished, the sooner I could book Ben's appointment.

The five of us ambled along, taking in the sights as Jessica breathed in deeply, ecstatic with the wind in her hair and the Cornish summer sun on her face.

'What's that red thing? It looks like a dunce's cap,' Luke asked, pointing into the distance.

Ben smiled, too polite to laugh. 'It's a daymark – like a diurnal lighthouse for the ships. It warns them of the Runnel Stone reef a mile off shore. You see the black and white one, further behind?'

'Diurnal, wow. This kid can talk. Yeah, I see it.'

'As long as the ships can see both of them during the day, they're okay, but if the black and white one disappears behind the red one, that means they're in rocky waters.'

'I didn't know that!' Chloe marvelled.

'That's because you've always got your nose in your mobile phone,' I observed. 'Look up every once in a while, and smell the sea air. Or read a book.' As I said it, her mobile rang and she clicked the off button. I wondered if it was Chanel. Chloe hadn't mentioned her since Luke and Jessica had arrived.

'This is so beautiful,' Jessica said. 'I can smell the salt air, feel the freshness on my face, hear the seagulls. There are at least three circling our heads now, am I right?'

We all looked up and, sure as rain in a Cornish summer, there they were – three seagulls eyeing us, or more precisely Ben's sandwich.

When we got in, Chloe dumped her phone onto the side table in the living room. Now, as much as I was thrilled about that fact per se, I had to find out.

'Chloe?' I said. 'I meant to ask you. Have you been connecting with Chanel lately?'

At that, she rolled her eyes.

Normally, I try not to be too much of a pain in the arse, because I know I really can be with all my rules about respect and manners and responsibilities.

And if on one hand I was thrilled that Jessica and Chloe had bonded, and that Jessica was drumming into my daughter the same manners I hadn't managed to, on the other hand I was upset about Chloe's dwindling friendship with Chanel. I was all for making new friends, but one must never forget the old ones, particularly the good ones, and Chanel indeed was the best friend a mother could hope for, for her daughter. Chanel was definitely part of our family, no bones about it. When Chanel first had her heart broken, it was my shoulder she cried on, me who drove her to get some ice cream, and me who gave her advice on how to (at least seem to) get over him.

But with Jessica's arrival, their conversations had dwindled, and now it was me who normally reminded

Chloe to answer Chanel's texts. So the next day I had a private word with her in her bedroom. 'How would you feel if Chanel met, I don't know, some singer or someone, and completely forgot about you?'

'Like who?' she wanted to know.

'I'm just pretending, Chloe. How would you feel?'

She thought about it. 'She would never do that to me.'

'Exactly. Remember who your people are, Chloe. Call Chanel back immediately and apologise for your behaviour.'

Chloe rolled her eyes. 'What the hell, Mum. You told me to say away from my phone.'

'Well, why don't you invite her over? Emma's busy with work, but I'm sure Chanel would be happy to see Jessica.'

'And I'm sure Emma would be happy to meet Luke,' she countered. 'Or are you keeping him all to yourself?'

'What a silly thing to say, Chloe.'

'Is it? Then why don't you invite your tribe over?'

'That's exactly what I'm going to do,' I decided on the spot. It was time. Luke would love Emma. And Emma would drool over Luke.

I made a couple of phone calls. Jack was a no-go, much to my disappointment, but Emma was thrilled.

I pulled out all the stops and made my special ricotta, sugar and cinnamon-filled ravioli for lunch.

'What are you making? Can I help?' Luke asked as he loped into the kitchen.

'Ravioli. Oh and I'm inviting my best friend Emma and her daughter over for dinner Saturday night.'

'Ooh, sounds like fun. You are an amazing cook. You should open your own restaurant. Well, not anymore, because you won't need to once our movie hits the theatres.'

I flashed him a shy smile. 'I actually make *arancini* for some local restaurants.'

'Ara… what is that you said?' His voice was still pasty with sleep and I could smell "bed" all over him.

Despite myself, I giggled. '*Arancini.* Basically Sicilian rice balls stuffed with minced meat and all kinds of delicious things.' I was getting pretty creative and was working on ways to introduce Nutella into the scheme. I know, it sounds sick, but trust me, it's not. Something about the sweet and savoury works.

'So how is it that you are always on the go?' he asked as he reached for a couple of mugs above the sink.

'I don't know,' I said as I chopped up my onions for the minced meat. 'With kids, you have to be, don't you?'

'Tell me about it. Here's your coffee.'

'Thanks.'

He cocked his head and slid me an amused look as he poured a cup for himself.

'What?' I said as I scooped up the onions for the sauce, threw them into the sizzling olive oil, gave them a stir and rinsed my hands under the sink.

He passed me the tea towel and I smiled my thanks, glancing at him briefly. This felt so strange – almost like watching one of his movies (I'd caught up with his career in the few weeks before his arrival) where he and his lady had just come downstairs after a night in the sack.

I stopped as he was staring at me. 'What? What is it?'

'Dunno. For a minute you reminded me of… domestic bliss. My mother used to get up very early in the morning to cook.' He reached out a hand and squeezed my forearm, letting out a hearty laugh. 'Not that you remind me of her, God forbid!'

'No, God forbid,' I echoed.

'I miss her so much.'

'When… did you lose her?'

Again he laughed. 'Mary O'Hara is very much alive but would die laughing if she heard you…'

'Oh. Sorry.'

'Your face, Nina! It's… awh… incredibly expressive. I wish you could see it.' He lowered his head. 'I wish Jess could see it – see all of you. You are all so lovely. A true family. She loves you guys so much.'

I stopped and passed him a plate of cookies. 'We love her too – how could we not?' He stuffed one into his mouth and ran a hand through his thick hair, and suddenly, and completely out of the blue, I wanted to follow his hand with my own.

He shrugged. 'I'm a worrier, in truth. I have nightmares about Jessica being home alone, and the house catching fire. She wanders through the house, looking for an exit and in my dream I know she's not going to make it…'

I nodded, my heart suddenly pounding for no reason at all. What the heck was happening to me? Was I, in the end, and at my age, becoming a fan girl? I shook my head clear to follow our conversation. 'I have dreams like that about Ben, only he's down on the beach and the tide is rushing in and he can't get to higher ground quick enough.'

We stopped, a sudden silence invading the room. A silence where all our communal fears gathered and nestled within the deepest part of our hearts. He looked at me, and we both sensed something had shifted, somewhere in the universe.

23

La La Land

That afternoon Luke and I decided to go for a walk over to Mullion Cove. Ben was at Jack's, and the girls were finally at Chanel's. I was glad that Chloe had decided she wasn't too high and mighty to share her celebrity friend.

'This is such an inspiring landscape,' Luke said.

I nodded. 'Yes, some of my best work was born while dreaming of these cliffs. As a matter of fact, most of the classics that were set in Cornwall were because the author had spent some time here and couldn't bear to leave. I couldn't bear to leave it myself, even if—'

'Nina?'

'What?'

'Shush a minute. I'm inspired.'

'Oh. Did you just have a brainstorm? Good, because we need one like—'

And then he took me by the shoulders. 'Are you going to shut up a minute and let me kiss you or not?'

I stared at him. 'You want to kiss me…?'

'Ah, Nina, you don't know how much…'

I supposed asking him why that was would've ruined the moment, so I shut up and watched him watch me, his eyes twinkling, his lips nearing mine, and my heart began to beat a soft tattoo that I'd long forgotten.

'Brace yourself,' he murmured against my mouth, his voice so low I could barely hear him. But I felt his words inside me, like a vibration. 'I have a feeling this is going to be a good one.'

And then his lips touched mine in the tenderest of kisses. He was so sexy, yet delicate.

'How was that?' I asked and he rolled his eyes. 'I don't know yet. Give me another one.'

I closed my eyes and let him kiss me again. It felt exactly like the naughty moment with Kevin Nealson in third grade, when he asked to see my knickers. Only more delicious. I hadn't felt like this in so many years that it was almost new to me all over again. The awakening, the shivers, the excitement. Could I bear it when, very probably, a disappointment would ensue? Was I strong enough to let myself go again… and suffer the consequences if it didn't go well? How could it go well? I was a single mum from a Cornish village the size of a big family, and he was the Hollywood dream personified. Where was the common ground?

'Nina – you drive me crazy…' he murmured against my ear.

'So do you,' was all I could say.

'I think I'm falling in love with you, you know?'

I giggled. I didn't mean to, but it just happened.

'Is it so difficult to believe that love can blossom out of an ordinary encounter?'

'Love? Luke, we've only just met…'

'So?'

'But… you're a Hollywood star. I'm a writer from Cornwall with writer's block, to boot.'

'Nina, I know you weren't exactly crazy about me when we met. But I'm hoping that you may have grown fond of me lately?'

'You know that I am not totally indifferent to your charm.'

'That's a good start,' he whispered, his lips barely touching my jawline now, sending shivers up into my hair. Okay, maybe I had underestimated the situation. Maybe I would have to learn to rein in my emotions.

'What is it?' he asked.

'Nothing. I just wasn't, well, prepared for this.'

At that, he threw his head back and laughed. 'Prepared? Oh, Nina, you are a character and a half. You don't prepare for these things. You just let them happen.'

'I'm not… used to this stuff anymore,' I confessed. 'I don't know how to act.'

'Don't act. Just close your eyes and tell me what you are feeling.'

I swallowed and nodded. 'Excitement.'

'Me, too.'

'And… fear.'

'Of me?'

'No.'

'Of what, then?'

'Of myself. Of how I'll feel when this all ends.'

'It doesn't have to end, Nina. I'm very fond of you. This has never – and I mean never – happened to me before.'

'No?'

'I meet a thousand people a day. But none of them has ever had the effect that you have on me, Nina…'

I nodded, because I understood. 'I too, feel overwhelmed.'

I felt him smile. 'Me, too, sweetheart.'

As you can imagine, I spent the rest of the drive home in a complete daze. Had that really happened, or had I just dreamed up a scene for my next book? He said he loved me. As much as I wished it were true, I couldn't believe that love happened so quickly. In my mind, it took time, kindness, courage and years to blossom. I didn't believe in love at first sight. I was past that, at my age, and with what had happened to me.

If the father of my children had deceived me and hurt me in the worst of ways, leaving me destitute and in a ruin with our children, what could a stranger do to me? And a stranger from a completely different world? The list of possibilities was endless.

'You know, I have never in my whole life met someone that I've connected to like I have with you, and in such a short time,' he said when we got back to the house.

'But… but we argue all the time…'

He laughed. 'It's good arguing, very different from the "It's you turn to take out the trash" kind of arguing. It's *sexy*…'

I gulped and stood up, somewhat rattled and confused. A key in the front door turned and Chloe stopped in the entrance hall, instantly alert. In one jump I put the table between Luke and myself.

'What's wrong with you?' she said. 'You're traffic-light red.'

'Am I?' I asked as I flicked the kettle on for something to distract me. It wasn't every day of the week that a girl got kissed by a Hollywood superstar now, was it? 'It's just the cold.'

'Mum – it's the summer.'

'Let's have a cuppa and you guys can tell me what you've been up to.'

'You first,' Chloe challenged, her eyes swinging back and forth between me and Luke who busied himself with the cake tin. Bugger me, the kid knew by just looking at me. I must have had that rabbit caught in the headlights look again.

I shrugged. 'We checked out some locations. It's going very well.'

'This is going to be a great movie. Your mom wrote a fantastic book,' Luke said as Chloe reached for a piece of cake.

She shrugged. 'Never read them.'

Luke glanced at me, at a loss for words for once.

After dinner, and at least two hours of Ben flicking through documentary channels and Chloe complaining she wanted to watch MTV, I put an end to it. I was too jittery to put up with anything tonight.

'It's bedtime,' I said. Not because I was sleepy, but I didn't want Chloe to get bored fighting with Ben and turn on me with her accusatory innuendos. The kid had ESP. And I needed to go to my own room, away from his influence and charm. And mull over today's developments.

At that, Minnie and Callie, who were observing our exchange with alert eyes lest we dropped any food, shot to their feet and happily trotted to their night baskets under the staircase.

Chloe shrugged and climbed up the stairs, half-muttering a goodnight for Luke's sake.

'Goodnight, Mum,' Ben whispered, wrapping his little arms around my neck and kissing my cheek. He smelled so clean, so fresh. I wrapped my arms around his little body and squeezed him tight. 'I love you a million gazillion, baby…'

'And I love you a gazillion million, Mum.'

He raised a thumb up at Luke, a gesture he'd picked up from him.

'Night, buddy boy, sleep tight,' Luke answered as we watched him slowly climb the stairs.

Luke took my hands and pulled me close again with a broad grin. 'Bedtime – my sentiments exactly.'

'No. I meant, it's time for me to go to bed.'

'But it's early. At least share a bottle of wine with me.'

'Oh, no, no, no,' I countered. 'I'm really very tired. I'll see you in the morning, Luke.'

He stopped, disappointed, and I wondered just how many women had ever said no to him. Probably very few.

'I'm a gentleman, Nina. Nothing that you don't want will happen,' Luke said. 'But I'll sure as hell make sure you want it.'

God, I was so out of practice. Actually, I didn't think I'd ever even been good at this game at all. I was only nineteen when I got pregnant. The boyfriends I'd had until then were not actually even men, but just boys, really. Phil had been twenty and he was the oldest of them all. Luke was a man.

'See you tomorrow,' I said as I scooped up my mobile.

''Night,' he whispered, kissing the side of my face. 'Sleep tight…'

'Uh-huh,' I croaked as I turned my back and dashed up the stairs all the way up to the safety of my bedroom.

By the time I washed and got into my nightie, my heart was pounding like a girl's after her first date. What had just happened?

Luke wants to sleep with you, you silly cow, a voice inside me answered. *And… you are not just flattered.* True. I was also terrified.

I had to admit that. But how did it make me really feel? Good about myself? Was I only succumbing to Luke's Hollywood charm because he was a handsome famous actor, or to the human being behind the sexy face and body? And what a cat in hell's chance did I have – me, a normal single, frazzled, bedazzled mother of two with more problems than she could count – of having a real relationship with him, despite all his nice words? Would it even work between us? Would he move Jessica to Cornwall to be with me and the kids? Highly unlikely. I just couldn't see how it would work.

There you go, said that evil voice inside me again. *It wasn't a marriage proposal. Lighten up, have a little fun.*

Ah, said the angel on my right shoulder. *The last time you had "fun" like that was when you got pregnant with Chloe. As much as we love children, we don't want another unplanned pregnancy, do we?*

Leave her alone, said the little devil on my left shoulder. *A little sex never killed anyone.*

I don't know which little spirit won, because by that time I was so exhausted from all the emotion that I must have dozed off, only to wake with a start at the sound of Minnie and Callie barking. Burglars?

I tiptoed downstairs with a cricket bat and paused on the bottom step.

In the kitchen, Minnie and Callie were barking along with the fridge in another one of their howling matches, and I suddenly realised that I had a man in the house and hadn't even thought to wake him.

24

Stand By Me

Saturday night dinner for friends, and I was just about to light some tea lights when Emma and Chanel arrived through the back door.

'Hi, it's so nice to finally meet you,' Emma said, shaking Luke's hand. 'Nina's been keeping you under wraps, eh?'

Luke turned on the charm. 'And you. I've seen most of Cornwall incognito, and it's been pure bliss. You have a lovely corner of the world here.'

'We like it,' she said amiably as I came out with a tray of food.

'Chanel,' I said, 'I'm so happy to see you. You have to stay for a sleepover tonight. Chloe and Jess would love that, wouldn't you?'

'Absolutely!' Jess said, and Chloe nodded, hugging Chanel.

'Jess, I've brought some music for you. They're a pop band from Newquay.'

'Cool – thanks, Chanel! I love your name, by the way!'

Chanel's face brightened. 'My mum's, like, obsessed with fashion.'

Well, that one was sorted at least. I exhaled a sigh of relief as I put the dish down on the trivet, but not without a pang of regret. Jack should have been here as well.

The dinner with Emma went swimmingly well. She laughed at all Luke's jokes and asked all the right questions. Luke asked her for a few of her business cards and promised to brag about the beauties of Cornish wedding venues, saying that he had a few friends thinking about tying the knot, and would she be interested?

'Of course!' she said. 'I am already pretty much booked solid through for the next two years, but some celebrity names would skyrocket me to the top.'

'Oh, Em, that's fantastic!' I cried. 'I'm so proud of you!'

'Thanks, love. But if things got any busier I'd need to hire a secretary.'

'I'll help,' I offered.

Her hand shot to her heart. 'You would?'

'Of course. What's a few phone calls and a few pickups for a friend?'

She hugged me. 'Nina, you are the best! She's the best!' she said to Luke, who laughed.

'She certainly is.'

'Are you guys ready for dessert?' I asked, getting to my feet.

'I'll help,' Em volunteered, following me into the kitchen with the dirty dishes.

'What the hell is going on here?' Emma hissed as she put the dishes into the sink and ran the hot water.

I pulled out my tiramisu from the fridge. 'What do you mean?'

'I mean Luke O'Hara drooling over you…'

I giggled. 'He wasn't drooling, Em.'

'He can barely keep his eyes off you.'

I sighed happily. 'Okay, I'll admit it. There might be a little something. Just kisses. But please don't tell anyone. Not yet. It's way too soon.'

'Not even Jack?'

'No one.'

'It's not like he won't know. You know what Penworth Ford is like. You are the talk of the town.'

'Career-wise, maybe, but I don't want anyone getting any strange ideas.'

'That'll be difficult, seeing as he lives under your roof.'

I should have thought of that, if Nellie's reaction at the tea room had been anything to go by. Apparently a man and a woman couldn't be friends, according to them. How naïve of me.

'In any case, are you sure you know what you're doing? These Hollywood people are a bit flighty, aren't they? One minute they're married to one person and the next—'

'Like you and me, you mean? Look at me, you, Jack – we're all single. It must be a village curse. Alf, Deirdre, Bev, Carol, Stephen Nanfan. Even Old Nellie hankers for someone she lost years ago.'

'I'm just saying. You know how these show-business people are.'

I huffed. 'Why can't you be happy for me?' I whispered. 'At least now I know I'm still alive.'

Her eyes widened. 'Please tell me you and he haven't—'

'Of course not!' I hissed. 'What do you think I am, a hussy?'

'Of course not. I have never met anyone so staid as you, Nina. And that's why you, in particular, need to protect your heart from someone who will very probably hurt you.'

She had a point there. I was staid. But as far as getting hurt, something told me that I had already given in that department.

Because Jack's aloofness was annoying me, I went over there the next day to see how he was doing. I found him in the barn, going through a batch of apples, checking them one by one.

If he was pleased to see me, he didn't show it.

'Hi, Jack, how've you been?' I tried as I sat down opposite him on a bale of hay. It smelled nice in there, like someone's happy childhood.

'Busy,' he said, his eyes swinging to mine. 'Was Emma there last night, with you, no doubt flirting with your Hollywood bloke, too?'

'Em? You know her, the life of the party.'

'Don't I just,' he muttered.

'What's happening between you two? Have you fallen out or something? I never seem to get a hold of you at the same time.'

He shrugged. 'I've been busy.'

'What does that mean?' I asked. 'Are you seeing someone?'

'Maybe. And you? What's going on between you and your Hollywood star?'

'Luke? What do you mean?'

'Are you and he…?'

'Of course not.' I hoped he didn't notice the sudden flush rushing up my neck and into my cheeks. I was never a very good liar.

'You looked pretty tight to me.'

'You must be joking. There's not a day that goes by that we don't argue.'

'All the same, I saw the way he looked at you out at Predannack that day.'

I laughed. 'Absolutely not. In any case, I'm not one to fall for an actor. They're much too volatile. Not that I actually have time for a relationship, thank God.'

'Women,' he muttered.

'Jack, have Emma and I done something to offend you? Because I sense something's off.'

He shrugged. 'I told you, Nina. Things change.'

'I bet you Jack's got a girl and she hates us,' I said to Emma later. 'And we don't even know who she is.'

Emma gasped. 'He said that to you? That he has a new girlfriend?'

'Not exactly. But I tell you, if she's changed him like this in the space of a few weeks, I already don't like her.'

Emma coughed. 'I'm sure there's no one new, Nina. But if there were…?'

'Well then she'd better clean her act up. I don't want to lose him as a friend. Or you.'

'You won't lose me, Nina. At least I hope not.'

'Sweetie,' I said, 'nothing you could do would push me away from you, save hurting my children.'

'Or marrying Phil.' She laughed.

I shuddered. 'That would be your choice, but don't expect me to hang around him.'

'So... you would back me up, no matter whom I chose?' she asked. 'Even if it was the most unlikely candidate?'

'Of course!' I assured her. 'If you love him, then I'll love him.'

25

The Wedding Planner

The next morning found me sitting in my writing chair, waiting for the kids to surface before I started preparing breakfast. I'd been up since dawn, raring to get to work on our script. But Luke didn't come down to work for another hour, and by then I'd already outlined the next few scenes.

'Morning!' he said, making me jump with a kiss on the side of my neck. 'I thought we could all go for a drive today.'

'Ooh, no can do; we've got much too much work to do. I've got an idea of where to shoot a scene and—'

'Excellent. Let's go take a look at it.'

'But I already know the place, Luke. Trust me, it's gorgeous. Have breakfast and then we'll start, okay?'

'Nina, you've got me working like a slave here.'

I stopped. 'But I thought we were on a tight schedule?'

He poured himself a cup of coffee and shrugged. 'The production company is mine. I dictate the timeframe. Maybe I'll stay a little longer now. We can take our time. There's no rush.'

No rush? I had to get my cheque so I could get Ben's operation sorted. Of course I was in a bloody rush. But better to play it cool. At least for now.

A minute later Ben ambled in and sat down to his breakfast, absently mumbling a 'Good morning' when usually he was all kisses and hugs, happy to be up and alive. Luke, too, noticed this change and shot me a glance.

'Are you okay, darling?' I asked as I ruffled his hair.

'Yep.'

I bit my lip. Ben was sensitive, but not fragile. This listlessness was new and unsettling.

'Mum?'

'Yes, love?'

'If Dad came back and wanted joint custody, what would you do?'

Panic shot through my heart. If Phil was trying that on, it would only be to wind me up, because he already barely respected his visiting times as it were. I would have to deal with it immediately before he filled my children's heads with all his codswallop. I pulled up a chair and sat opposite Ben.

'Why do you ask, darling?'

Ben continued to shove his soldiers into his mouth and shrugged. 'I was just wondering. If he said he was sorry for leaving, and wanted to get to know Chloe and me better, would you be upset?'

I swallowed, glancing at Luke whose wide eyes betrayed his poker face.

'Is that… something your father's suggested?'

He avoided my gaze. He'd never done that before.

'Not really. I just wanted to know how you would feel.'

Was it possible that my kids were suffering whilst all

I was trying to do was protect them? Even a judge had decreed that twice a month with Phil was more than enough. My throat had gone very dry, but I took his hand gently and held it in both mine. 'Ben – what I feel is not as important as what you feel. Do you… want to see more of him?'

Please God, let him say no.

He looked up at me and I could tell he was troubled. 'No, Mum, not particularly. I think we work just fine without him.'

Thank you God. He wasn't the problem, then. 'And what about Chloe?' I asked. 'Does she still want to spend more time with him?'

I didn't know how the hell I was going to handle my whirlwind of a daughter if she made explicit, serious demands to see more of him. I couldn't hide behind a judge forever.

'Can I have some more toast, please, Mum?' he asked, his eyes lowered again, as that was all he was prepared to say.

'I knew it – I knew it,' I fretted as I watched him playing in the garden with Olly and Joe who'd swung by.

Luke's hands covered my shoulders. 'Easy, sweets. You're getting all worked up about nothing.'

'Nothing? Phil wants to muscle in, and I can't allow that. I can't let our delicate balance be disturbed. I'm barely hanging in there and I can't—'

'You're not barely hanging in there, Nina. I'm here with you. Every step of the way.'

I sank back against him, still not used to having a man under my roof. 'Thanks, Luke.'

'Anything for you, sweets,' he said, wrapping his arms around my waist and nuzzling my neck, sending a shiver through me despite my worries.

'Let's go upstairs,' he murmured naughtily into my ear.

I froze. He wanted to have sex with me? Now? I giggled off his offer like a consummate actress. Not that I didn't want to. Because I did, of course. Who wouldn't want to sleep with him? He was every woman's dream. But I had to pace myself, at least a little. 'Behave yourself. The kids are home. And we've only just woken up anyway.'

'Oh, I don't mean to sleep, hon,' he whispered, lightly nipping my earlobe.

'Hah, good one,' I shot back. 'The girls are still sleeping upstairs. Let's – take our time.'

He sighed and let his head drop onto my collarbone, exaggeratedly but playfully resigned. 'You're the boss, Boss.'

'And don't you forget it,' I played back, safe for the moment from making that huge leap of faith.

This man sure knew how to charm a woman, especially me. Because little by little, between POV predicaments and parenting, he'd certainly proved what a proper father he was – something sorely missing in our lives – and found his way into my heart. I don't know if it was quite love yet, but he certainly had my full attention as my body began to tingle like it hadn't in a long, long time.

That afternoon I got a call from Emma.

'Nina, please say yes.'

'Yes, whatever you need, Em. What is it?'

'One of Luke's friends has already contacted me. I showed her my work and she's hired me!'

'Em!' I gasped, warm waves of pride flowing through me. 'Congratulations!'

'Thanks, love. But now I need that help you offered. She has no idea what she wants, and for the first time in this job I'm at the end of my tether. Can I pick your brain?'

'Of course. What kind of wedding is it?'

'Very posh and very extravagant.'

'Budget?'

'Limitless.'

'Crikey, who is it, someone from the royal family?'

'Close. She's a pop star. But I can't say who because she's a freak about her privacy.'

'Okay. What's the dress like?'

'That's the thing. The wedding per se is rich and lavish, but she's a simple girl at heart, although still somewhat temperamental. I don't do simple, so I thought of you.'

'Gosh, thanks, I don't know whether to be offended or flattered. Well, how about a simple champagne-coloured dress, maybe in taffeta, with silk wildflowers or something?'

'That sounds nice. I'll have a look tomorrow. Would you come into Truro with me in the morning to look at some invites and flowers? I've got a gazillion things to do and if I don't get it right I'm afraid she'll go for someone else. With this commission I'll be fine for a whole year.'

'Sure, why not? It'll be fun. I haven't looked at wedding dresses since my own marshmallow disaster thirteen years ago.'

She laughed. 'Please, no stunts, Nina. If I can pull this off, I'm home free. She's got three single sisters!'

'Relax, I'll see you tomorrow.'

'Bye, luv!' she kiss-kissed me and we rang off. Emma was brilliant at her work. With her brains and sense of style, she'd establish herself in no time at all. Of course, the pop-star wedding would hasten her ascent. If anyone deserved to be up there, it was hardworking Emma.

So the next day I put Luke in charge of the kids and drove to Truro as promised. Emma was waiting at the entrance of Lemon Street Market and her face lit up when she saw me.

'Hey, you!' she cried and we hugged as if we hadn't seen each other in a million years. Which was actually quite accurate. I *missed* her.

'So what's the plan? Flowers or invites first?'

'Centrepieces,' she answered, steering me inside the market. We were always adamant in supporting the local economy and steered clear from the flagship stores. 'I've narrowed them down to a few, but I just can't decide and she's absolutely useless. We're looking at an autumn wedding.'

'This autumn? Can you manage it?'

'I'll have to, if I want the account.'

'Talk about pressure. Okay, then, no worries. We'd better hop to it.'

'See, that's why I need you, Nina – you never lose it. What do you think of these for the tables?'

I studied the options. The centrepieces that seemed most appropriate were old-fashioned glass jars containing pine cones and white fairy lights. Simple and appropriate for a Cornish autumn wedding.

'These ones are pretty,' I suggested, holding one up. 'Or these,' I opted, pointing to the tallish glass vase filled with dried wildflowers in the shades of gold and cream and about a dozen mini pumpkins and other gourds in each one.

'Jack could provide the gourds,' I suggested. 'He should almost be done harvesting by now.'

She huffed.

'Will someone tell me what it is with you two?'

She lifted the centrepiece with the pine cones and fairy lights, turning it this way and that. 'Let's just say that lately I'm beginning to be fed up with Judge Jack.'

'What do you mean?'

'You know what I mean. He can be really judgemental sometimes.'

'I've never heard him speak an ill word of anyone,' I said.

'Oh, not that he would,' she countered. 'But when he doesn't approve of something you do, you can just see it on his face, can't you? And when he ignores you, you know you're not on his Christmas card list anymore.'

And suddenly it all made sense. That was why he had distanced himself from me. He didn't approve of Luke being in the house with us. But it wasn't like I was cheating on anyone. All I wanted was to rebuild a life.

Granted, Luke wasn't the safest choice – larger than life, and definitely not your average Joe who had a nine-to-five job (at least he *had* one, as opposed to The Phil-anderer) plus there was potential for a new beginning. Even if he wasn't one of us, hailing as he did all the way from California and a life diametrically opposed to ours. Maybe, even like this, there was potential for hope. Hope for us and our little Cornish farmhouse and household to flourish.

Because I had a right to get a life of my own. I'd earned it. So just how justified was Jack in his attitude after all?

'Then why don't you talk to him? Clear the air?' I suggested, picking up a pretty bouquet of calla lilies, thinking that I should follow my own advice. 'This would look stunning against the champagne-coloured taffeta dress.'

Emma examined the bouquet. 'I was right – you are so the person to help in cases like this. If you ever get sick of slogging over a computer, would you go partners with me?'

I laughed.

'You'd be perfect, Nina.'

'I aim to please.'

'By the way, how's it going with Luke?'

I sighed.

'Was that a huff or a happy sigh?'

'A confused one.' I blushed. 'Let's say we're beginning to see eye to eye.'

She stopped. 'You've slept with him!'

An old woman checking out some candle centrepieces opposite the display table frowned at us.

'Of course not,' I whispered, pulling her to the next display table where some hideous frog centrepieces crouched, looking like they were ready to jump to the next table.

'But you want to! Has he asked? Oh, my God, Nina, tell!' she hissed.

'I want to,' I finally gushed. 'But I'm so frazzled.'

She put down the centrepiece and took my elbows, her face serious. 'Honey – whatever you do, don't ruin this! He is so the guy for you!'

I bit my lip. 'I really hope so, Nina.'

She wrapped her arms around me. 'If there's anyone that deserves the best, it's you, love.'

'After you, of course,' I said loyally.

We agreed to meet later in the week for the dress. When I got home, I found the girls in the living room watching some teenage movie while fiddling with their phones as Ben sat in his armchair reading his science book. 'Is this programme fit for Ben?' I asked.

He shrugged. 'Some drivel about a runaway princess. But I guess it's a formula that works on common minds.'

Luke, who was sitting at our work table, laughed across the hallway. 'Ben, I swear, you are a character.'

'She's the character,' Ben said, nodding towards the screen. 'I've never seen such a sap in all my life, waiting for her estranged mum to come home. It's not going to happen, and that can only be a good thing.'

'Ben, shush!' Chloe silenced him. 'We're trying to watch a movie here.'

Watching Ben out of the corner of my eye as I kicked off my shoes and hung my jacket in the hall. I decided to investigate that one later in private.

'What are you up to?' I asked Luke as I padded over to him, still keeping my eyes on Ben who went back to his book.

'Just writing down a series of approaches for Bill's point of view.'

Again with Bill. There was no moving this man. He was as stubborn as a mule. I huffed. I had eventually agreed to let Bill have a voice, but on condition that he didn't come on with any tommyrot. 'If you're determined to show his point of view, at least don't make him so bloody saintly.'

'You mean like your buddy?'

'Who?'

He nodded towards the window. 'Farmer Joe down the road.'

'You know his name is Jack.'

'Whatever. Just to make it clear, Nina. I'm not on a crusade to defend men. I just want them to get their say. Show their vulnerability as well. Just like Stella shows hers. And she has her faults.'

I bristled. 'Of course she does. Who doesn't?'

'And yet, you expect everybody to take her side.'

'Because she's the victim!' I said hotly.

He shook his head. 'Men can be victims of circumstances too, you know?' he said as he got to his feet and walked to the window overlooking the garden.

Uh-oh. Now I got it. 'How bad... was it, if I may ask?'

He snorted. 'It was purgatory. I was young and immature, working waiter shifts around the clock. Luckily my mom lived nearby, but she had my sick dad to deal with, and wasn't getting any money for him, so I had to take care of her financially, while she took Jess on my night shifts. So I ended up taking Jess with me whenever I found a charitable boss. She was practically brought up in all the dinners across Iowa.'

It was then that I realised that Luke was my exact male counterpart. His Lauren was my Phil, why we had done the lion's share of the slogging. Perhaps it was time for me to open my eyes to other people's difficulties in raising their kids, and not just mine.

'I'm sorry,' I said, standing next to him at the window. The kids had in the meantime migrated to the garden and Chloe was pushing both Ben and Jess on the swings, and they were all laughing as Ben incited her to push harder.

Jess closed her eyes, and the look of sheer happiness on her face was one to behold.

'I'm sorry you had to go through that. I know that you sacrificed your whole life for her.'

He shrugged, not taking his eyes off them. 'It's what parents do, isn't it?'

'Not all parents. But look at what you've achieved. She is such a lovely girl. You had Lauren to deal with, and I had my cross to bear. Many people in the world are dealing with the same issues as we speak, Luke. Both mums and dads.'

He turned to me and smiled a faint smile, somewhere between sad and hopeful. 'Well, Nina, at least you and I can now speak for both sides with our movie.'

Perhaps he was right. Even men suffered for love. Look at Jack. Clarissa had made a dog's dinner of his life. And he compensated by protecting himself from a new relationship. Different people fought back in different ways.

It was becoming clear to me now, bit by bit, that Luke didn't actually want to deride my heroine, but put her into a different context. One where she wasn't the only one suffering. Fair enough.

'Whatever. How about a truce? I'm totally exhausted tonight, Nina,' Luke said as he put his tablet down for the day. 'Let's go for dinner, just you and me. We can call a babysitter.'

'Dinner?'

He grinned that sexy, open-mouthed grin at me, the one I'd seen him give Marnie Jones in the final scene of *Burning Hearts* as, with a flick of his head, he tells her to get on his Harley Davidson and then they drive down that hill in San Francisco.

'Yeah, dinner. Give you a break from cooking.'

'And you'd, uhm, entrust Jess to a babysitter?'

'One that you picked, yes. You know I trust you completely, Nina…'

Damn, this man could make me blush with just one look. He was a time bomb, ready to destroy all the walls I'd put up against the opposite sex. I had to defuse him with a show of indifference. 'A break sounds good to me.'

He cocked his head to one side, peering closely at me.

'What?' I said. What had he seen now? It seemed I was always under his scrutiny.

'You've got the cutest little beauty mark on the bridge of your nose. How have I never seen that before?'

I felt myself go hot. 'It's hidden by the glasses.'

He got up and nuzzled my neck. 'Hmm, you smell amazing…'

'It's the fried onions,' I answered and he chuckled.

'No, I don't think so.'

He pulled me into his arms and I looked up at him through my glasses that were slowly fogging up as the temperature rose. 'Take these damn things off,' he said, gently reaching for them.

'But I can't see without them, Luke…'

'That's good…'

'What do you mean?'

He chuckled and leaned in, his breath on the side of my face. 'Because you might not want to see what I'm going to do to you…'

26

No Sex Please, We're British

Was two months too early to sleep with a bloke without betraying my self-image of responsible, single mother of two?

Let me rephrase that. Luke and I were attracted to each other; we were both single and both consenting adults, although I was a bunch of nerves. I hadn't been with anyone since Phil, nor had I ever felt the desire to. I had guessed I was just, well, dead, down there. But now, after all the good things that had happened to me, wasn't it time to start looking at life differently? Didn't I deserve to return among the living?

If it went well and our relationship developed, great. And if it didn't, we'd always have the movie deal. It was a win-win situation, although you might think that is a bit cynical of me. Perhaps it is. I have always put my family's wellbeing first, and of course I'd risk my own happiness for my children. What woman wouldn't?

So – we had the motive for the sex, and we had the suspects. All we needed now was the time and place. So I decided to go for it. Tonight. I would farm the kids off to Alice who was in Cornwall for her two days a month, and consequences be damned.

'Alice? I need a favour.'

'Anything, doll.'

'Can you come over and stay with the kids tonight? Luke and I are going out.'

'Oh, you naughty girl! Good for you!'

I blushed despite myself. Did that make me sordid, or calculating? Weren't these things supposed to happen naturally, without planning?

'Have you prepped?' she asked.

'Of course, there's loads of home-made stuff in the freezer. All you have to do is nuke it.'

She laughed. 'I didn't mean food, Nina.'

'What do you mean, then?'

'Oh God, what would you do without me? Are you prepped as in waxed, and all?'

Oh? Oh!

'I didn't think so,' she said, chuckling. 'Have you got a racy little number to wear in bed?'

I thought about my lime green fleece pyjamas. 'Uhm, no.'

'Jesus, Nina. Give me an hour to get everything we need and we'll sort you out.'

'Uhm…'

'Be there soon,' she said and rang off. Sort me out? I had a feeling it was going to be a very long afternoon.

★

'Yeowwh…' I hissed under my breath so the kids wouldn't hear us as Alice yanked off the wax strips. 'What are you trying to do, skin me?'

She laughed. 'I'll give you a lotion to lessen the redness and swelling. You should be okay by tonight. Oh, Nina, I'm so happy for you!'

I blushed. 'Maybe we're making such a big deal out of nothing. Maybe I should wait.'

'Are you nuts, Nina?' she barked. 'This is a one-time opportunity, and you mustn't let him escape!'

'Do you think he might want to?' I hadn't thought of that. And if I couldn't keep my own husband, what right did I have to try to hang on to someone I'd only just met?

'Of course, Nina. He's absolutely smitten with you. Who wouldn't be? You are gorgeous. A little rough around the edges, granted, but lovely all the same.'

'Gosh, don't smother me in kindness,' I play-scoffed.

'Come here, let me tweeze those eyebrows now.'

'I'd rather not,' I said. 'I've never tweezed before…'

'Relax, just a few stray hairs. You don't want him noticing them when he looks deep into your eyes, do you?'

'Ouch!' I yelped as she plucked away. 'No, but I don't want him noticing I'm missing a piece of my eye, either.'

'Silly, we're done. And now, for the pièce de résistance,' she said, whipping out an array of barely there baby doll nighties. 'Feast your eyes on the *lingerie*!'

'Where is it? All I see is two tiny pieces of confetti and a postage stamp connected with strings.'

She giggled. 'You cheeky cow. But I can guarantee it has worked wonders.'

'On who, The Invisible Woman?'

'Just try it on, already.'

'Uh, I don't really think I'd feel comfortable in that, Alice. But thanks anyway.'

She rolled her eyes. 'You're not supposed to feel comfortable, Nina. You're supposed to give him a coronary, or so to speak.'

'I don't know, Alice. I'm not actually sure that in this case less is more.'

She studied me. 'You know what,' she said, throwing them onto the bed. 'Maybe you're right. It isn't you. You don't need ornaments to dazzle men.'

I rolled my eyes. 'Please, I never dazzle men.' Maybe, when I was younger, but now?

'Of course you do.'

'Alice, I know you love me, but that's just not true. I haven't had a man look at me in years. Maybe every now and then on the high street, but that's just the traffic controllers to make sure I don't double park.'

'Listen to yourself. You're oblivious. Fine, have it your way. But I will tell you this. Luke is a keeper.'

'We'll see,' I said. I really hoped so, but I wasn't about to just assume anything anymore.

When Luke and I left Alice to babysit that evening, I closed the door behind me and realised I was shaking like a leaf.

Luke's arms immediately circled me from behind and I managed not to jump in panic.

'Jesus, Nina,' he said as we got into his rental. 'You are going to kill me tonight, I just know it.'

'Or the other way around,' I corrected him.

'I've booked at a gorgeous hotel in Marazion.'

Marazion? Good. No one knew me there.

'Nina? Are you okay? You seem kind of scared.'

'Who, me? I'm fine.' If you didn't count that I was about to pass out.

He leaned in and kissed me. It felt… deliciously naughty. And terribly exciting to get away from my rubber marigolds for once in my life.

27

Morning Glory

While the heat of the moment was one thing, the cold light of day was another.

Luke lay next to me, dead to the world, with his arm around my waist. I hadn't removed my make-up last night, and my hair was a rat's nest after all the acrobatics.

Luke was a considerate lover. Kind, respectful and fun. Not like the old Phil-anderer up in Truro. If the sex was anything to go by, we were definitely carburetting. And then I stifled a giggle of elation. After three years of celibacy, I was back in business!

But if he woke up and saw me like this... he'd run a mile. Not the right way to start a, ehm, relationship? Was that what this was: the beginning of a normal, mature relationship? Was I even ready for one, at this point of my life? I had to be, sooner or later, and judging by the way everything else was going, and that I was finally going places, maybe it was time to surrender to life as part of a couple after all.

So I slid out of bed as quietly as I could given how every muscle in my body was screaming at me *Why don't you do this more often*? and tiptoed to the en suite where I showered and lathered my hair, all the while trying to make sense of what had just happened. How had it felt? Like someone else, as if another woman had inhabited my body and taken it on a very, very pleasant trip.

And I was now myself again, ready to take on the world. Months back, I would never have contemplated sleeping with anyone, but now I liked the idea of waking up to someone that I had slowly grown to like very much indeed. But how we were going to have a repeat in the future – assuming Luke wanted one – without the entire world knowing was another story.

I had no idea how things worked in Hollywood, but in my world, sleeping together was pretty much a deal-sealer. Did he really want to be a part of my life? And if so, how would it even work, with him in California and me in Cornwall? I wish I could talk to Em about it, but I somehow felt she wouldn't understand. Nor would Jack, who had never really made an effort towards Luke aside from the day at Predannack Wollas. Knowing Jack, he obviously considered Luke a fake.

In fairness, any man compared to Jack would seem fake, because he was the epitome of the male protector. Anything dear to him was always safe: his dog Mac, his fellow villagers, Emma, Chanel, my children and me. I only hoped I wouldn't have to choose one day between his friendship and Luke, because Jack was a huge part of my life. He was my friend; part of my insides.

I would never forget the day Jack took us into his home

while our caravan slowly crackled away, leaving only a shell. The day Phil had left us was the day Jack had officially proclaimed himself our protector. I remembered silently crying myself to sleep as Ben and Chloe lay on either side of me in Jack's enormous bed, while he slept in one of the guest rooms. I remembered him cooking us a feast of a breakfast the next morning, and telling me he would rebuild my house and make it liveable as best he could, but in the meantime, his home was ours.

It had been a great comfort to have him there for us at a time like that, and I would cherish his presence in my life forever, especially now that I needed support.

Continuing to lather up, I jumped and nearly fell over in the shower as, undetected, Luke had slipped into the shower and slid his arms around my waist. It was such an unfamiliar feeling, so intimate. I couldn't remember the last time someone had touched me, as if I belonged to them.

'Easy…' he soothed into my ear as the water continued to pour down my hair. 'You okay?'

I nodded, but I was shaking. 'Aren't you full of surprises?'

'I have even more for you,' he whispered as his lips found mine again as the water poured down on us.

As Luke was checking us out of the hotel, wearing shades like the superstar he was, I stood near the exit, watching the morning traffic go by, absolutely out of place in my best evening dress and high-heeled shoes and feeling for all the world like Holly Golightly in *Breakfast at Tiffany's*, i.e. half hungover and empty-headed, but impeccably dressed.

'Are you sure you don't want to have breakfast?' Luke asked.

'Uhm, I'd rather get back to the kids, if that's okay.'

'Sure,' he said with a grin, kissing me on the lips in broad daylight. 'But you've made me ravenous now.'

I smiled. 'Let's go home. I'll cook you a huge breakfast. I hope Alice can stay a little longer.'

'She'll probably want the details if I know her,' he said.

I smiled up at him. 'I never kiss and tell.'

'Good girl. Our business is our business. Ready to go?'

'Ready,' I said and, his arm still around me, we walked through the hotel doors and out into the morning sun.

And that was when I saw him. Jack, hands in his pockets, talking to a circle of people in suits. He laughed at something and casually looked my way, doing a double take, and our eyes locked.

It didn't take rocket science to figure out what Luke and I were doing in front of a hotel in our evening wear at nine in the morning, especially with Luke's arm wrapped around me.

While I was wondering if Jack was going to acknowledge me, he nodded ever so slightly, looking so disappointed in me that I couldn't help but cringe.

'Nina?' came Luke's voice. 'You okay?'

'Never better,' I assured him as I straightened and crossed the road on his arm, all the while feeling Jack's disapproving eyes boring into my back.

28

The Secret Of My Success

'So, how's your dad?' I asked Alice back at the house as she sipped her tea and reached out for a Hobnob. I had slipped back into a pair of jeans, trying to look like I'd been there all night for when the kids woke up, still trying to get over the encounter with Jack. I should have still been overwhelmed by my night with Luke, but all I could think of was how I'd disappointed a friend.

It had saddened me to think that my friends didn't approve of my choices, especially when I always supported them in theirs. I knew nothing about his new flame, or even Emma's secret bloke, for that matter, but I didn't pry or judge. When they were ready to tell me who they had hooked up with, I would happily accept them within our circle in the hope that they would do the same with Luke. I just wanted everyone to be happy, and somehow I felt that it wasn't like that for Jack and Emma anymore.

'Never mind my dad, tell me about last night,' she hissed as Luke wandered around in the front garden, framed by the French windows. He was truly beautiful, with his sandy blond hair and all-American looks. 'You spent the night with him, and all you can talk about is my ninety-year-old dad?'

I shrugged, feeling myself blush. 'It's nice to have someone around the house.'

Alice gawped at me. 'Nice? Sweetie, you had the most desired man on the planet in bed with you, not to mention living under your roof, and all you can say is *nice*?'

I shrugged. 'It was more than that, of course. Luke is a good bloke. He's a lot of fun, and kind.'

'But?'

'There are no buts. It's just that we don't know where this is going, nor how long it will last. And I don't want our whole world to be shattered all over again.'

'Except for in between the sheets,' she cackled in delight. 'What does he say?'

'I'm taking each day as it comes.'

'Good girl. You do that. But keep him on a short leash, just in case.'

'A short leash?'

'Yeah – make sure he doesn't go too far or too long without you. You want to be a part of his life now. Do you and his kid get along?'

'Jessica? She's a dream.'

'Fantastic. You want to make sure she likes you enough to see her as her new mum.'

I shook my head. 'Alice, you're going too fast for me. I've only just got back on my feet. Technically, I'm not even divorced yet. Plus I don't know what's going to happen when the script is finished.'

'Then write a sequel while he's in your clutches. God knows you could use the money.'

'Actually, I'll be happy if we get to the end of this one without killing each other.'

'Still having problems?'

I shrugged. 'He's extremely headstrong. He's not easily swayed. This husband's point of view thing risks changing the story completely.'

'Don't you trust his talent?'

'Oh, he's a very good storyteller.'

At that, she laughed. 'I can just see it in the papers: "Luke O'Hara and novelist Nina Conte tie the knot in Cornwall".'

I snorted coffee through my nose. 'As if. But please keep this to yourself, Alice…'

'Mark my words. The only way for Luke to get rid of his bad-boy reputation is to marry a nice girl like you. It would make a perfect story.'

'Promise me, Alice. Your absolute discretion.'

She rolled her eyes. 'All right, but I'll be back on your case very soon. People want to know about Luke's love life. And it would sky-rocket your book sales, not to mention the movie. Imagine – staid novelist hooks up with the actor who made her book dream come true by turning it into a movie. It just doesn't get any better, Nina!'

There it was again, the word that described me best, according to everyone. Staid. Which implied that I was incapable of having wild fun. Which, of course, was true. I had already done the wild college thing. And now? Not so much. Now I needed to concentrate on being a good example to my children, and to teach them to believe in themselves at all times. Even if I, I must admit, didn't practise what I preached. The look in Jack's eyes was proof of that.

'What's he really like? The real Luke?'

I thought about it. 'He's kind. Intuitive. Fiercely fond of his daughter. But, you know… I get this feeling.'

'Yes?'

I shrugged. 'I get this feeling that he… wants out of Hollywood or something. That sooner rather than later he'll leave.'

'Leave? He'd be a fool. Hollywood loves him.'

'Well, he said he'd be interested in scripting the other books too if this movie does well.'

Her mouth fell open. 'And you tell me that only now?'

'There's nothing to tell. It was just a conversation.'

'Oh my Lord in Heaven, we're in the money, honey!' she cried.

'Easy, Alice. We need to see how *Written In The Stars* goes first, yes?'

Alice got to her feet. 'It will be a blockbuster, Nina, trust me. And now, I have to get back to London. Keep me posted, will you?'

'Ah, okay. Remember your promise.'

'Yes, all right.'

'And thanks for babysitting.'

'Thank you for your cannelloni. If you weren't going to be the next Nancy Meyers, I'd suggest you opening a restaurant. See you next month, doll!'

'Bye,' I said as I watched her from my front door, waving goodbye until her red Toyota disappeared down the hill. She had every faith in Luke. She was convinced my whole life and that of my children had taken a turn for the best. I certainly hoped so. Was I doing the right thing, or was I making a Bigger-than-Phil mistake?

As much as it killed me, Phil had visitation rights every other weekend and as usual, I mentally wrung my hands as I watched my kids prepare for the night over at his place. You might think I was nuts to leave my children in his hands, but the judge had decreed he was forgivable and therefore should be pardoned for his behaviour. Me, I'd connect him to a high-voltage socket while pushing him into a tank full of bloodthirsty sharks, but there you go.

'Have you both packed your toothbrushes? Your liquid soap? Your towels? Hand wipes?' I asked as I hovered between their two bedrooms.

'Mum, Dad's got soap,' Ben giggled as he packed a couple of his favourite tractors.

Judging by the state of him the last time I saw him, I doubted that.

With their bags ready to go, they waited for him at the bottom of the stairs, Chloe busy on her mobile and Ben reading through his portable dictionary.

'Mum, what's another word for tardiness?' he asked.

Phil Jenkins, I wanted to say but sealed my lips.

The doorbell went and Ben hopped to this feet, only to stop short upon opening the door.

'Hey, handsome, come and give Auntie Emma a kiss!' I heard Em say.

'Hey,' I called from the kitchen, utterly delighted. 'You want to stay for tea?'

She sauntered in, looking around as if she hadn't been in ages.

'Oh dear,' Emma whispered, eyeing the kids. 'Phil forgotten again?'

'Yes,' I whispered back.

She shook her head. 'He never changes, does he? Adam's the same, you know? They just can't be bothered, the pricks.'

I shrugged, fighting back the burning sensation in my eyeballs. It hurt so much to see my children wait in vain for someone who simply didn't care enough to remember. It wasn't the first time. When Chloe looked sideways at me, I smiled sympathetically.

'Would you like a biscuit while you wait?' I asked. Trust me to resort to the easy solution.

'No thanks,' she said, lowering her gaze to check her messages.

'Why don't I take them then? One of my clients postponed,' Emma offered. 'It'll give the girls a chance to hang out, seeing as we haven't been lately.'

'Please do, Em,' I said gratefully and hugged her. 'And thank you. As soon as things get back to normal we'll have a nice dinner, okay?'

She laughed. 'No worries.'

'How's the job going?'

'Oh, don't ask, I'm full up to here,' she answered, plucking an apple from the fruit bowl and biting into it.

'Hm, Jack's apples are the best, aren't they? I don't know what he does to them.'

I grinned. 'He probably sings to them.'

Emma cackled. 'I'm sure he does. That man is so dedicated to the things he loves. Have you seen him lately?'

'No, not lately,' I lied, feeling my ears burn. I so wanted to tell her about being caught out by him in front of that hotel, really, I did, but I felt that she wouldn't approve either. 'I expect he's busy with his new girlfriend and all that.'

'You don't mind, do you, that we're no longer Three's Company? Then again, why would you, seeing as you have that stud muffin Luke O'Hara?'

'I don't *have* Luke O'Hara.'

'Oh, I beg to differ,' she whispered, eyeing the kids loitering in the entrance hall.

I made a face. 'Who told you that? Jack?' There went my secret.

Emma frowned. 'Jack? I thought you said you hadn't seen him lately. Where did you see him? What was he doing?'

'I—I don't know,' I answered. 'It was just men, I think. But he saw me… and Luke.'

'What do you mean?'

'We were just coming out of that French hotel in Marazion,' I sighed. Le chat was out of le bag.

'I knew it!' she cried, slamming her hand against the table.

'Please keep your voice down.'

'Since when?'

I shrugged. 'It just happened. Please keep this to yourself. I already feel bad for Jack seeing me. He looked at me like I was a prostitute.'

'Jack? No, he would never.'

'Oh, he did,' I assured her. 'It was like I'd disappointed him or something.'

She shrugged. 'He probably misses you. Hell, *I* miss you.'

'Well then why don't we have dinner again this week? I'll cook something nice.'

'Sure, love to. Is Jack invited?'

'Oh. Uhm, I'm not sure he…?'

'Forget it,' she sighed. 'I'll see him in Truro.'

'You see him in Truro? You never mentioned.'

'Oh. I meant I'll see him around.'

'Em, what's going on here?' I asked.

She gave me a furtive look. 'What?'

I shrugged. 'I don't know. Have you guys solved whatever it was that was bothering you? You were practically at loggerheads at one point and now you're awfully chummy again.'

'What choice have we got? You totally abandoned us since Luke arrived, breaking the hearts of the whole of the female Cornish population who had hoped to have a chance with him.'

Hm.

'Auntie Em, can we please go?' Ben begged. 'It's lapalissian that Dad isn't coming.'

Emma frowned, her eyes swinging to me. 'What's he on about? What did you do, Ben, eat another dictionary for breakfast?'

'He means "obvious",' Chloe bit off, not looking up from her phone.

'Oh, I'm glad to see your vocabulary is improving too, Chloe,' I praised.

She smirked. 'It isn't. I just looked it up. Ben likes to show off when he feels neglected.'

At that, I knelt at his feet. 'Oh, my darling, you don't feel neglected, do you, love?'

He rolled his eyes. 'Mum, seriously? Chloe's only speaking for herself. She's angry that Dad has forgotten to pick us up again. I'd be much happier if I didn't have to go. I find him tiresome to say the least. And it's clear he doesn't care enough to remember.'

'Don't you worry about your father, sweetheart,' I said to Chloe. 'He's probably just still sleeping or something. 'But Auntie Em has offered to take you guys to Truro for the weekend.'

But instead of jumping up and down for joy as she would've in the past, Chloe was now eyeing me with suspicion. 'What are *you* going to be doing in the meantime?'

'Luke and I have got a script to finish,' I assured them as flashes of naked flesh raced across my mind.

'Yeah, right, the *script*,' she scoffed and marched out the door with her rucksack.

I watched her, slack-jawed, and Emma shrugged. 'Get used to it.'

'Good luck, Em. And thanks. Bye, guys,' I called out the door. 'Mummy loves you. Don't drive Auntie Emma crazy, behave yourselves.'

'Yeah, yada, yada, yada,' Chloe scoffed, getting into Em's car. After they drove off, I closed the door with a sigh of relief. I would have to sort her out when she got back. I didn't like her attitude at all. But for now, I finally had a moment's peace. Time to get to work.

I looked out the window. Luke was no longer in the garden. 'Luke?' I called.

His voice reached me from my bedroom. 'Up here, babe. You coming?'

I caught my breath in anticipation. I could really get used to this.

★

A couple of hours later, and still no sign of Phil, the doorbell rang as I was making parsley sauce with boiled ham for tea. Luke had never heard of it so I wanted to introduce him to England's culinary delights. With an Italian twist, of course.

Wiping my hands on a tea towel, I made for the door, nearly tripping over Callie who followed me everywhere. She knew who her breadwinner was. Or in this case, her boiled ham-winner.

When I opened the door, there was a girl of about, oh, maybe eighteen, if that, with pink and green hair in dreadlocks and a spike running through her nose, dressed in a polka-dot dress and biker boots. She would have been very pretty, if I'd been able to distinguish her features under all her make-up.

'Can I help you?' I asked.

She smiled. A rather nice smile, typical of the young and full of hope and naivety.

'Yah,' she barked, and I noticed she was chewing on a large glob of blue gum. 'Phil sent me to pick up the kids?'

I baulked. 'Phil?'

'Yah.'

'I'm sorry, you are…?'

'Tracy.'

'Tracy?'

'I'm his girlfriend. Phil can't make it because he's busy.'

Typical Phil. He begged me to have this day, and now he didn't even show. 'Busy?' Doing what, I wondered, getting drunk on the sofa?

She nodded, pulling on her long sleeves to reveal two enormous tattoos on each forearm as she blew a huge bubble and burst it. 'Yah. The big game's just about to start.'

'I see. So he sent you so he can watch a football game?'

'No, not football. Poker. We've got some friends around and Phil's preparing the drinks and snacks.'

'I'm sorry, uhm…?'

'Tracy.'

'Yes, Tracy. Please tell Phil that the kids waited and waited for him to show, and in the end they went to a friend's.' That should teach him. Or, knowing his track record, probably not. He had the memory of a pinhead.

'Okay. Just give me the address and I'll go pick 'em up, then.'

Not only did she speak like Phil, she even acted and thought like him. A female clone? His dream had finally come true, then.

'I'm sorry, Tracy, but my children are not available at the moment.'

Her face fell. 'What, you don't trust me then?'

'Trust you? I don't even know you.'

'But Phil sent me—'

'I'm sorry, Tracy, nothing against you personally, but I'm not in the habit of farming off my children to my ex-husband's friends. Especially after I've consigned them to perfectly capable parents whom I trust.'

Her shoulders drooped. She was just a young girl, infatuated with a guy, just like I had been. 'However nice they may be,' I added hastily, not wanting to hurt her feelings. 'Because I'm sure you're very nice.'

She perked up and smiled. 'Thank you. I'm sure you are, too, despite what Phil says.'

'Please tell my ex-husband that if he wants to spend time with his children, he can at least make the effort to remember the scheduled dates – and find the time to pick them up personally. And if he thinks I'm going to let them sit in his flat while there are other people I don't know, playing poker, drinking and smoking, he's got another think coming.'

She blew a giant blue bubble that covered most of her face and burst it with her teeth. 'He's not gonna be happy,' she warned me.

I smiled. 'Oh, believe me, he never is. I'm sorry you had a wasted journey. Nice meeting you.'

She shrugged. 'And you. Better luck next time, I guess.'

I watched her turn and get into a yellow Maserati. At least his gambling was going well. Until it wouldn't anymore, and he threw her out into the middle of the street, too. Because for a girl of her age, Tracy had already lumbered herself down with the biggest of losers. I knew because I had done all the legwork. Like many a young woman, she had stopped at the surface of Phil's charm and let the relationship go from there to its eventual endpoint, soon to arrive.

He may have been good-looking years ago, and, had we continued to be a couple, I'd have pushed him to eat healthily and take care of himself, but his girls didn't care about his health. They were enthralled by his now fading but still boyish looks, thinking themselves clever for having bagged an older bloke who drove a sports car.

That it wasn't even his was secondary. Far from them were the doubts and questions about the future, such as, is he going to love me forever? Is he going to be responsible and care for his family? Is he going to love me unconditionally, even when the kids have flown the nest and I'm old and grey?

Questions that I'd actually asked my younger self, believe it or not. But back then, Phil was different. We had had the same goals, the same will to conquer the world for the good of our family. But when my writing money started coming in, paying for the things we'd always previously had to do without, such as holidays and top-quality clothes and extras, Phil decided he could take his foot off and let me do all the pedalling.

And when the hill got steeper and I could no longer carry everyone's weight, he simply hopped off the back seat, taking the wheels with him, leaving me a single mum with two kids on a dwindling income.

The next morning, as Luke and I lay in bed, for once not having to jump up to feed the kids, my stomach gurgled.

Luke laughed. 'Starving you, am I?' he said as he kissed my mouth. 'You stay here and I'll go get us something to eat. Don't move.'

I wasn't planning on going anywhere. It had been an amazing night, and I wanted to see where this was going. If anything, he'd proven to me that a) I was not frigid as Phil used to say and b) that I still "had" it. Who knew?

And Luke, what a beautiful man. Kind and fun. A bit controlling, maybe, but that was probably just his being used to having his way, being a superstar and all that.

There was a muffled kerfuffle downstairs and I sat up, instantly alert.

'Oy! Who the bleedin' 'ell are you?'

Oh, God. This was all I needed – Pheral Phil unleashed in my home. What the hell was he doing here, and at this hour, to boot? The last thing I needed was for Luke to see what a prize I'd bagged in my youth. I threw on a pair of nearby jeans and a sweater, tying my hair back as I tiptoed downstairs.

There stood Luke in a pair of hip-hugging boxers, looking for all the world like his younger self in the Calvin Klein underwear ad, carrying a tray with two bowls of Honey Nut cereal.

Phil looked back and forth between us, slack-jawed. 'Nina! Are you serious?'

'What do you want, Phil?' I said, then turned to Luke. 'Phil, obviously.'

'Ex-husband, Phil?' Luke asked.

'Yes.'

'Not yet ex,' Phil ground out, then it hit him. 'You're the actor. Luke O'Hara, right?'

'Nice to meet you,' Luke said, suddenly as suave as they came. I looked for a sign of jealousy, but there was none. Luke was nowhere near intimidated by the presence of my almost ex-husband. Yet he had posited that Bill was based on Phil, only a consonant away from the monster that had ruined my life. And yet, there was no sign of animosity anywhere on his perfect face.

'I didn't realise you and my wife—' Phil began.

'Ex-wife,' I said again.

'—Were sleeping together.'

'Oh,' Luke said, sliding me a glance as I shook my head, but it was too late. It was obvious even to anvil-head here.

249

'Well, good luck to you, then. There's no one like my Nina,' Phil said, pseudo-wistfully, changing tactic, and I rolled my eyes at the line he used to pull out at the end of an argument to make sure I'd forgive him. Back then, it used to make me think twice about leaving him. Now, I could see right through him. And speaking of which, I suddenly realised why he was so accommodating. If I met a new man, Phil would be off the hook once and for all for child support, in his simple mind. Jesus, why was everyone always so calculating? Why wasn't I that fast on my feet? Emma would've figured that one out in a heartbeat.

Luke glanced at me, then lowered his eyes, but I could tell something had shifted. 'You're absolutely right,' he said, putting the tray down. 'There's no one like Nina.'

Phil hiked his jeans up higher. 'Well, I'd better be off, let you two… get to work.'

'Thanks, man,' Luke said.

When I closed the door behind him, I let out a sigh of relief. 'I'm so sorry, Luke…'

He ran a hand through his hair and fixed me with his stare. 'I didn't realise you still talked to each other. Nor that he was even still in your life.'

Ah. Finally, a bit of wholesome jealousy. Not that I wanted him to break Phil's nose or anything (hmmm, on second thought), but it would have been nice to see a bit of territorial in him.

'I told you, he isn't. But I won't let the children suffer by eliminating him completely from their lives. They believe he loves them, and I don't want to shatter that illusion.'

'I don't think he sees it that way, Nina. I think he still holds a candle for you.'

'Oh, he knew it was over the day he dumped me and the kids in that trailer.'

'I'm not so sure,' he said.

'Are you afraid he's going to do something to try and get me back?'

'Not in the least.'

Oh. Okay. Good.

'Are you *sleeping* with him?' Chloe asked out of the blue when they returned Sunday night. Not so out of the blue, on second thought, seeing as we had been alone in the house for forty-eight hours. I should have thought that one out better.

'Who?' I said, feigning distraction.

She rolled her eyes. 'Luke – who do you think, Mickey Mouse?'

'Chloe! What a question to ask your mother…'

'Well, are you, or aren't you?'

'Of course not.' What was that about little white lies turning into huge black mushrooms? 'Our relationship is strictly business.'

Chloe snorted. 'Dad said you'd better not be.'

'Well, sweetheart, your father no longer has any say over me. Nor does anyone else.'

I only wished I could shake the image of Jack's disappointed face out of my head.

Later that day I decided I needed to talk to Emma. So I got in my car, drove to Truro and knocked on her door. When she didn't answer, I pressed the doorbell. Sometimes she was out in the garden with her radio on. I knew she was in because her car was parked out front, and Em never walked anywhere. It had been a running joke between us since we met.

After a long moment, the door opened, but it wasn't Emma at the door. It was Jack, on his way out, and surprised to see me.

'Nina!' he said, and Emma popped her head out the door, her face flushed.

'Hi!' I chirped, my voice dying in my throat. 'Is something wrong? You guys look… angry. Have you been quarrelling or something?' They hadn't even heard the doorbell.

Jack's eyes swung to Emma's and then he forced a laugh. 'Of course not. I came to… sort Emma's Wi-Fi.'

I looked between the two of them. Neither seemed thrilled to see me.

'Guys,' I said. 'I know I haven't been around much lately, but I'm here for you both.'

Emma huffed. 'Thanks.'

'Would you like to come over for dinner tonight?'

'I'm sorry,' Emma said. 'I can't.'

'And I have to see someone,' Jack added.

'Hot date?' I said and his eyes swung to Emma's before he laughed. 'Me? Nah.'

'Oh, okay, then,' I said. 'Shall we, uhm, reschedule?'

Emma coughed. 'Yeah, sure. I have to get back to work now. I have a client from hell. Thanks again for your help, Jack,' Emma said as she ducked back inside to get her bag. It was like she didn't even want me to come in.

He waved her away. 'Don't mention it.'

29

Mystery Man

The next day I went to drop Ben off at his friend Joe's and also back to see Emma's new place in Truro where Chanel and Chloe would be having another sleepover.

This time I bought her a housewarming present, i.e. a gin tumbler and glasses for her fun fests.

She was behaving very oddly indeed lately. On a personal level, she seemed to be all over the place, but on the other hand, her job was going well. It was like she'd been injected with some energy drug lately as she bounced around the whole time and her eyes were bright with excitement. I wondered if it wasn't just her new client. And yes, she was definitely sleeping with someone. All the signs were there. But she had made it clear that she wasn't ready to talk about it. Who on earth could it be? Her bank manager? Her accountant? Those were the only men I saw her with on a regular basis, if you didn't count Jack.

'It's not a *house* house with a garden or anything, but it's conducive to our lifestyle,' she explained as she proudly showed me around. 'We go out the front door and straight into the thick of it. It's perfect for Chanel as it's only a bus ride away from Northwood, and it has huge bright rooms.'

'I'm so happy for you, Em. Even if I miss you, I know this is the right step for you to take. Your business will flourish in Truro and you might even meet a city bloke.'

At that, she paled. 'I'm sorry about yesterday, Nina.'

'Don't mention it. You'll talk when you're ready.'

'And this,' she said, moving towards the kitchen, a modern, glossy affair that spoke of fashionista Emma, 'is the largest waste of space as far as I'm concerned because, as you know, I don't cook much.'

It was almost clinical, but magazine beautiful – so far from my own drab and unfinished kitchen that always had something on the boil or in the oven.

'I'd die for a kitchen like this, Em! You should use it!'

'No, this is where my bread and butter is,' she said, gesturing to the living room that was decorated as an office. It had period features such as a fire and crown moulding, and a new glass desk, with a swivel chair and a super-modern but comfy padded bench instead of two guest chairs.

Everywhere there were pictures of her past weddings on show, giving the room a refined yet welcoming atmosphere. Her clients would indeed feel that she was worth their money, and much much more.

'Chanel and I use the third bedroom as a living space,' she explained.

'That's a great idea, Em. This place is gorgeous, congratulations!'

'And the bedrooms are upstairs.'

'Ooh, a duplex,' I chimed as we climbed the period staircase. 'How very chic!'

Chanel's room was practically a replica of Chloe's with the same uniform hanging from the wardrobe door, the same cosmetics scattered across the dresser, and the same pictures of each other and themselves wedged into the mirror. All in all, the standard teen-girl's den.

'Now that we've seen your bedroom, let's see Chanel's,' I quipped.

'Haha, I know I'm messy, but here is me,' Em said, pushing the door open.

I cast a casual glance, and stopped in my tracks. There, hanging from a hanger on the door, was a man's jumper. My eyes swung to hers.

'It's for one of my clients,' she explained hastily, but I knew her better than her own mother.

Her eyes darted from me to the door. 'No one, I told you.'

I shrugged. 'Okay, sorry, Em. I didn't mean to pry.'

On the drive home, I wondered about Em. Why was it such a secret? Had she been carrying on with someone at her previous company, and got sacked? Maybe that Nigel bloke? But Emma had always implied that he was gay. But there were literally no other men at her company, unless… her boss? No way. He was married, and Emma was not the kind of person to sneak behind people's backs. Her loyalty and honesty were what had won me over in the first place.

Suddenly, a pall of sadness descended upon me. In the space of a couple of months, we had drifted apart as each of us kept our lives secret, almost as if we were ashamed of our choices. It seemed we truly were no longer the Three's Company of Meadowbank Lane.

After three full years of supporting each other through thick and thin, births, deaths, and divorces, we had suddenly shot apart. Was it my fault, because I was so busy with the script? Or was it because Emma had moved to Truro, or because Jack met new people every day, leaving not even a tiny crack in the day for us to chat?

Or had Luke's monumental presence put a wedge between us all? I'd tried several times to organise another dinner so we could all sit around the table together, Jack included, but there was always something stopping it. How could a friendship like ours wither out and die like that? Were we like icebergs slowly drifting apart on a silent sea, going out without a fight on the gelid currents of life?

30

Gone With The Wind

Because I promised Chloe I wouldn't call incessantly like I always did when she was out and about the village, I *stalked* her instead. Chloe loved to post pictures of herself, and this time I saw with joy that she and Chanel were once again #BloodSisters as the post assured me they were alive but not kicking anymore, which was music to my ears.

About an hour before the kids were due home, Phil showed up on my doorstep, looking like something that the cat had dragged in.

'Hi, Nina!' he called, barely recognisable, when I opened the front door.

The red nose, not to mention the flabby abdomen, were a gift from too many beers and evenings on the settee when instead he could have taken the kids for a hike or a picnic, were all a result of the way he lived his life.

His boyhood beauty was rapidly fading, and knowing him as I did, I knew he was panicking about it, and if I had once found things about him endearing, such as his fondness for lounging around in bed on a Sunday morning, they were now the part of him that I resented most. And even the slowest girl on the planet would eventually come to her senses and ditch him before he put an unwanted baby inside her. I hoped, for Tracy's sake, that she would open her eyes and walk away before he ruined her life as well.

'What do you want?' I said, blocking the door with my body.

'To apologise for not coming to get the kids myself. That's why I came the other day, but I didn't want to say anything in front of your Hollywood friend.'

'You could have called them, Phil. They waited for you on the stairs. And what's this rubbish about you sending your girlfriend?'

'Jealous, huh?'

I rolled my eyes. 'Nauseated, actually. Did you really think I was going to hand my children over to a perfect stranger?'

'*Our* children, Nina. Our children.'

'Not that you'd know, Phil.'

'Look, I know I screwed up with you years ago. But I want to make it up to you.'

'Really? You mean you've found the money you took from me and a time machine to get back all my years wasted on you?'

He opened his mouth but then closed it again, defeated. And then he remembered his ammunition.

'I'm not happy about you and that Yankee rubbin' more than just shoulders,' he said, quite pleased with his new-found wit. 'Sleeping with him with the kids around and all.'

Which I didn't, of course. I took off my glasses and speared him with my best Cross-Mum look that put even him in his place. 'I beg your pardon?'

He looked at me, his once lovely forehead lined. 'When did I lose you, Nina?'

When had he lost me? Probably while I was holding down several jobs, preparing meals, scrubbing the floors (and his muddy sweatshirts fresh from a football game), managing the household and writing three novels all the while he sat on the sofa munching on junk food, completely ignoring me as I ran rings around him with my duster and mop while trying at the same time to help the kids with their homework.

'Because I see you have lost your way,' he said.

I had lost my way? 'Out.'

'What? I'm not even in yet.'

'Nor will you be. Now piss off.'

'Nina, all I'm sayin' is that… I'm jealous.'

'Don't be. For some reason I can't explain, the kids love you.'

'It's not them I'm worried about!'

I snorted. 'No surprise there.' And then I understood. He was jealous about the movie and the money I'd hopefully be making. It wasn't enough that I had never, nor would ever be dependent on him for survival.

'Nina – when are you gonna get it through your thick skull that I still love you! And it kills me to know you an' 'im are sleeping in our bed.'

'Oh, you don't have to worry about that,' I informed him. 'I threw that bed out three years ago.'

NANCY BARONE

He wrung his hands like a child about to get scolded. 'That should be me with you upstairs, Nina. Not him. I wanna come back, babe.'

'You what?'

'You heard.'

'So what happened to Tracy, then?'

He shrugged. 'She's just a girl, Nina. You're a woman. *My* woman.'

'Not anymore, Phil. You had your chance and blew it.'

'But I don't like you sleeping with that man. And you are legally still my wife.'

Dear oh dear. 'I owe you nothing, Phil, and what I do with my time or whom I sleep with is my business. Is that clear?'

He crossed his arms and slid me a sullen glance as if I'd taken his crisps from him.

'Now get out, I'm busy.'

'Nina, wait.'

'What now?'

He crumpled his face in his best I'm sorry expression, the one he used to make when he came home drunk or spent our weekly grocery money at the gambling tables.

'You will always be my love – no matter what you do, or where you go. You are the mother of my children. How can I ever forget you?'

I snorted, sad but also grateful that life had been so unkind to me as to make me wary of men. It was, after all, his fault that I could no longer believe that love conquered all. It was his fault that I was taking Luke one day at a time, rather than abandoning myself to the joys of a new relationship. And it was his fault if I simply couldn't commit to anything long-term without expecting to be dumped. If this sack of rubbish had considered his own children and myself a burden, how could someone like Luke want to stay?

Phil made to lift my chin to look into my eyes, but I stepped back. His was the gaze I didn't wish to hold. There were too many memories in there, and the past was somewhere I couldn't afford to go anymore. It had taken me too long to recuperate from the uphill journey, and now there was no way I was ever looking back upon all the hardship and pain.

'Seriously, Nina. You will always be the lovely girl I married thirteen years ago.'

'Seriously, Phil. You will always be the bloke who left me three years ago,' I said and closed the door on his face.

'What was that all about?' came Luke's voice from behind me.

I whirled around. 'Oh, nothing. Just Phil acting up again.'

'He still loves you. Jesus, Nina, what was the point of even writing this book if you can't put the past behind you?' he asked, coming to stand in front of me.

'Oh, I have, trust me.'

'You mean you're not still in love with him?'

What the hell was he talking about? 'Of course I'm not.'

'You wouldn't be the first. Women are so fickle.'

'Maybe your women are. I'm sure as hell not.'

He snorted. 'Your book was full of all sorts of stories about how your husband was a waste of space, and how you dreamed of ditching him. But not once did you ever mention still having feelings for him.'

'Because I don't. My book is fiction. A story.'

'There's always a piece of truth in fiction.'

'Like in all your spy movies and thrillers? Look,' I reasoned. 'Why would I lie about this?'

'Then what's stopping you from moving on? I feel like you're trying to not let go and ride the wave with me. Where are you?'

'I'm here, Luke.'

'Are you?'

'Yes. But I do have some reservations about us, now that you mention it.'

'I knew it. Like what?'

'Come on, Luke. Seriously? You're from bloody Hollywood and I'm from... Realville. How could it ever work?'

He huffed. 'When are you gonna understand that I want this? I want a normal life... with you.'

'Ah, you may want that *now*. But what happens when you wake up one day and look around yourself and see nothing but... un-Hollywood stuff?'

'Nina, will you cut it out with the Hollywood stuff? It's not who I am, it's what I do. And if you want to know the truth, I'm getting tired of it.'

I stopped. So my suspicions had been right. 'Tired? What do you mean?'

'I mean I want this to be my last movie. At least for now. I need a break, I want to raise my daughter and be free to love. I want you to be able to love me without having a lens shoved in your face every time we step out for dinner or go for a walk.'

Whoa, whoa, whoa – his last movie? Hadn't he said he wanted to do all three books if the first one went well? Not to be greedy, but this was a total U-turn I was not expecting.

He took my arms. 'Why the face? You think my feelings for you won't last? What are you so worried about? That I'll be dying to run back to Tinseltown?'

I shrugged. 'I don't know, Luke. I just don't want all of us to get used to having you around and then… you know.'

'Listen to me, Nina. I have a daughter too. You think that if I had one tiny doubt I'd tell her about us and let her become attached to you only to never see you again? I haven't brought a girl home in years. What does that tell you?'

'I… I don't know.'

'I think we know what the real issue is here, Nina. It's not bloody stardom, is it? It's Phil.'

I felt my jaw drop. 'Again with *Phil?*'

He crossed his arms in front of his chest. 'Yes, Phil, and the fact that you never got over him.'

'Oh, come on, Luke, I thought you understood…'

'I know what it's like – you think you're over someone. You start dating someone else who seems to be perfect for you. You're actually doing fine. But then, all it takes is one tiny memory and whoosh, it all comes back to you. With a vengeance.'

I stared at him. 'Is that what you think is happening?'

He nodded and looked at me with something between pain and anger. 'Yeah. Yeah, I think it is, actually…'

'You're wrong. *So* wrong.'

'Am I?'

'Luke, please don't be like this…'

'I'm not being like anything, Nina. Can't you see? The guy's pulling out all the stops to win you back.'

I took his hands. 'Luke, listen to me. Even if you weren't

in my life, I still wouldn't get back with Phil. Not even if he was the last man on earth. And furthermore—' I stopped in mid-sentence as I recognised the dialogue I had written more than three years ago and it dawned on me that we were having that very same conversation. He had steered me straight into Stella's words and I'd walked right into it.

'You sneaky bastard. I can't believe you'd do this to me!'

'Ah, I was waiting for you to recognise your own words…' he half-accused.

'Luke, my life is serious, and so is my work. But one has nothing to do with the other.'

He shrugged. 'I just wanted to see how far I could take you, that's all. It will make for great dialogue.'

'Luke – seriously? You are actually playing with my feelings? Yes, of course I made a huge mistake in marrying Phil. But you can't turn my life into a Hollywood drama.'

'Why not? You turned it into a romcom.'

'Well, at least I was optimistic for a happy ending.'

'Did you get one?' he wanted to know.

I huffed. 'I'm going to sleep. Goodnight.' I'd had enough wittiness out of him for one day.

And yet, as I lay in bed under my eaves, I couldn't help but wonder how much of that conversation came from Luke the man, and how much came from Luke the entertainer. Was there at least a tiny bit of jealousy in there?

The next day I pulled on my jacket and sneakers and trudged up the hill to Jack's, a bit of trepidation rising up inside me. How do you break the ice after weeks of not seeing each other after being practically joined at the hip for years?

His SUV was not in the garage, but I had a look around anyway, just in case. When he wasn't in the barn, I swung back to the farmhouse and peered through the windows. Nothing. I remembered the days when the three of us always knew where the other two were. He had always been there, whether to give Lottie – or me – a boost, or for me to spoil him and Emma with a nice meal.

But since Luke's arrival, I only saw them rarely, and I began to understand how Ben and Chloe must have felt torn, going back and forth between their parents. The idea of being estranged from Jack was scary. I never wanted to be without his friendship.

It suddenly struck me that I had been horrid to him by not inviting him because of Luke. Jack, who had saved my life more than a thousand times in a gazillion ways, was slowly drifting away. I had to stop it before it was irreversible and we were only nodding at each other frostily in the village, if that at all.

I pulled out my mobile from my back pocket and dialled his number, waiting, anticipating what I'd say.

Hi, Jack, how's it hanging?

All right?

Want to come around mine for dinner? I've missed you. We all miss you.

But when he didn't pick up and my call went to voicemail, I couldn't leave a message. My throat hurt too much to speak. Maybe he'd only think I needed something. It would have served me right if he'd picked up and given me a piece of his mind. He'd have been right. I did need something. I needed to hear a friendly voice. *His* voice.

So I called again, and this time he finally answered.

'Jack!' I cried, almost weeping with relief.

'Nina, what's wrong?' His voice was alarmed, and still charged with all the affection between us.

'Oh,' I croaked, drying my eyes. What the hell was wrong with me? Couldn't I cope with change? 'I'm so glad you're there. I came looking for you a few days ago, and then yesterday and today, but you were nowhere to be found.'

'Me? Oh, I went to, uhm, Truro...'

'Oh? Did you call on Emma?'

'No, I had no time,' he said with a cough. He always coughed when he was uncomfortable, and even over the phone I could tell something was off.

'Jack? Are you all right?'

Why was he lying about something so normal? Unless... of course. My birthday was coming up soon and they were probably organising something for me, the two sneaks.

'I'm fine, thank you, Nina. How are the Ben and Chloe?'

I baulked at his formal tone. And then I understood I should have of course invited him over for dinner to give him the good news of my budding romance, and probably get him and Luke to make an effort and forget their pissing contest. But Luke and I weren't yet ready to tell the whole world. Luke had warned me that the minute the press found out, they'd be on our house like bees on honey, and I didn't want that for my children.

'I'm fine, we're fine. Chloe and Chanel are still a bit iffy over Jessica's presence here. Chanel feels threatened. But she should know that they will always be best friends, no matter what.'

Callie, who had been studying me with her intelligent eyes, abandoned her nook behind the AGA and settled herself on my feet, whining. She, too, knew the state I was in.

Silence at the other end, and then: 'Sometimes things change, Nina.'

'Only apparently,' I said in earnest. 'And only temporarily. Then things go back to normal, once the storm has passed.'

'Has the storm passed yet?' he wanted to know.

'It doesn't have to go away completely, does it? We can still continue in the rain, through thick and thin. Isn't that what good friends do, Jack? Thick and thin? Jack, are you there?'

'Yep,' he said, sounding distracted.

'When will you be home? Can I come over then? I've made you your favourite, peach cobbler.'

'So your actor is still there, then.' It was a logical deduction, not a question.

'Luke? Of course. We're still writing the script.'

'Then you finish writing your script, Nina.'

Ouch. 'Okay, I understand. But can't I just bring you the cobbler? If you're busy I'll just leave it and—'

'I'm not home,' he said with finality.

'Oh.'

I would have, a thousand years ago, let myself in and surprised him with a dinner as I used to, back in the day. But he was right: so many things had changed in the space of a summer.

'Okay, Jack,' I croaked. 'Goodbye.'

At that, he groaned, albeit under his breath. When had he ever, ever groaned at me? Not even when I called on him several times a day for trivial things. He had always been happy to see me, but now I realised I had offended him by cutting him out from my happiness. As if I had been too high and mighty to spend some time with old friends. It served me right. I had absolutely no excuse for neglecting my friendships, especially the people who had always cared for me.

What could I say? It was as if I'd been momentarily swallowed up by a parallel world where only good things happened to me, and where I managed to obtain everything I'd always aspired to in order to better my kids' lives. And was it now too late?

'Jack?'

'Goodbye, Nina.'

'Goodbye, Jack…'

Swiping at tears of humiliation and sadness, I stuffed my phone back into my pocket and shuffled home, the weight of my stupidity on my shoulders.

Goodbye, my dearest, kindest friend in the entire universe.

31

Miss You Already

A t least at home things were improving with our script.
'This is gonna be great. I can already see Stella's slim
figure set against the Cornish cliffs, waiting for Dylan to
return.'

If he ever returned. Would she ever see him again, I
wondered?

'Nina? What's with you lately? You've been moping
around as if you'd been given a death sentence.'

I picked myself up and forced a smile. 'I'm sorry, Luke.
I'm just – just tired. You were talking about Stella?'

'Yeah. I was saying that it would be beautiful to see her
tall, slim figure set against the sunset waiting for her lover
to return.'

'Not too slim, though,' I countered. 'Real women aren't
a size zero. We have flesh and organs, remember. Otherwise
you might as well cast a paper doll.'

'Yeah, but we also want to appeal to the younger
audiences.'

'If it's a good story, you won't need to. Everyone can relate to a well-written story, as long as it establishes a connection with the reader. But usually all good stories do.'

'But what about the younger fans? They're my safer bet.'

'And that's where you're wrong. As girls mature to womanhood, their tastes mature as well, so if you have mostly young fans, they'll grow out of you, whereas if your target audience is, as you say, middle-aged, they'll stay with you forever. Emma's mum still goes to David Essex's concerts. Mature women are more faithful, and don't easily forget their first crush.'

'Is that what you expected to happen with you and Phil?'

Ah. Here we were again, nosy sod. 'No comment. But I will tell you this. I never write for a target audience. If a story is good, it will resonate with people from every walk of life, age and religious faith. So I really wouldn't worry about how old your fans are, Luke. You should be grateful for every single one of them, as I am.'

'Uh, speaking of fans, Nina…'

'Yes?'

'You understand that we still have to keep this a secret a little while longer,' he said. 'From the paps, I mean. If they find out I'm dating an English woman I'll never hear the end of it.'

I bristled. 'Yet I can take you in under the very roof my children sleep under, toss their lives upside down like a salad, and you're okay with that.'

'I'm sorry, Nina, but I have to follow the rules in my contract. I have to do everything I can to protect my career.'

His career? What about us?

'Mum?' came Chloe's voice from the threshold.

'Dad?' came Jess's like an echo.

We turned to look at the pair of them and instantly knew something was wrong.

It wasn't just the way Chloe was folding one foot over the other like she did when she knew she was in deep trouble, nor how they were clinging to each other. It was their pale faces and their enormous eyes that made my heart lurch.

We shot to our feet. 'Ben? Is he okay?'

'He's fine, Mum, he's at Jack's remember?' Chloe said.

Yes, of course I remembered. Jack and Ben were still as close as ever, but you never stopped worrying in any case as a parent.

'Are you guys okay?' Luke said as we covered the few feet between us and them, meeting in the hall.

'Yes, yes.' Jess nodded, biting her lip as Chloe glanced at her, then turned to me. 'But we have something to tell you both and you're not going to like it.'

A knock on the door saved them – for the moment – but I noticed the way they kept glancing at each other, cringing. If it wasn't health-related, they'd have to wait until I got rid of the unexpected caller.

I opened the door to a beautiful woman about my age.

'Hello,' she said.

I had no idea who she was, but it was instantly obvious to me that she was troubled.

'Hello,' I answered, desperate to get back to the girls. 'Can I help you?'

'Is this Cornflower Cottage?'

'It is. Can I help you?'

'I'd like to speak to Luke O'Hara, please.'

Ah. Emma had been right about his fans. It was only a

matter of time until he was tracked down, even in our quiet little neck of the woods. Unless…

'Are you a reporter?' I asked politely. That was the last thing Luke wanted, someone to know he was living with an English woman, as if we were the Antichrist.

She chuckled. 'Me? No. I'm—'

'Who is it, Nina?' Luke said as he padded into view behind me, then: 'L-*Lauren?*'

I looked back and forth between them, frozen like two statues, facing each other.

Lauren? As in ex-*wife* Lauren? How was that even possible? After thirteen years?

'Mom?' came Jess's voice from behind us.

Luke turned to Chloe, all colour drained from his face. 'Jess – upstairs. Now.'

'But, Dad—' Jess said.

'Now, Jess.'

'No, Dad. Please. I-I called her.'

Luke turned to stare at her. 'You *what?*'

'Please don't be upset, Dad. I just wanted to meet her…'

'It's my fault, Luke!' Chloe said. 'We were on Facebook a while ago, and I suggested looking for her mum so I could at least describe her to Jess – and next thing you know we were writing her a message.' Chloe left Jess's side and came to stand straight in front of our visitor. 'We asked you to *wait* until we could speak to Luke!'

'I need to speak to you, Luke,' Lauren said quietly.

'Chloe,' I said, taking her hand in mine and Jess's in the other. 'Let's go upstairs and give them a chance to talk.' Chloe, slack-jawed for once, nodded and did as she was told. 'Come on, Jess,' she whispered and together the three of us ascended the stairs, the weight of the world in our every step. Goodness knew what Luke was feeling right now.

'Are you angry, too, Mum?' Chloe wanted to know as the three of us sat down on her bed.

I took a deep, deep breath. 'I understand why you did it, girls. Truly I do. But you can't just do something so monumental behind our backs.'

They nodded, crying twin tears.

'It's just that Jess has been saying how lucky Ben and I were to have a mother. Jess never told her dad, but she was dying to meet her mum. And it turned out she was holidaying in Paris. Wouldn't you have asked to see her?'

Would I? Absolutely. *But.* 'You understand that you've both put him in a very difficult position. He's been protecting you for years.'

Jess dried her eyes. 'But, Nina – she seemed really nice. And sorry for what she did. She was only nineteen.'

So was I, when I had Chloe, but I didn't run at the first difficulty.

'And then? Go on,' I said.

'Well, we didn't even know if it was the same Lauren O'Hara – we thought she might have changed her surname, but she never did.'

'And we never really expected her to answer anyway.'

'But then she did.'

'And then she kept messaging. She wanted to come and meet me and talk to Dad.'

I ran a hand through my hair. My head was killing me.

'Will you talk to Dad, Nina?' Jess pleaded. 'Will you make sure he doesn't stay angry with us – or my mother? Please?'

I sighed. This was not good. They had opened a can of worms that would not go away all that easily. I wondered what was happening downstairs. From what I knew about Luke, he was never going to let Lauren anywhere near Jess.

I nodded. 'I'll see what I can do. I suggest you two stay out of the way for the rest of the day.'

Chloe nodded, tears filling her eyes as Jess wrapped her arms around my neck and kissed my cheek. 'Thank you, Nina,' she whispered into my ear.

I held her, trying to still the tremors in her little body. But I knew that there was nothing that Luke wouldn't forgive his daughter. 'It'll be okay, Jess. Just give your dad some time, okay?'

Still clinging to me, she nodded fiercely.

I eyed Chloe, who was perched on the edge of the bed, and held out my other arm for her. She gingerly neared me, her eyes studying my face, her own a mask of shame.

'You don't hate me, Mum?' she asked.

'Chloe, sweetheart – I made you. How could I ever hate you?' I said as I kissed the side of her face.

'Then it's true that my own mum still loves me even if I disappointed her by being blind?' Jess asked.

I squeezed Jess. 'Honey – your mother didn't leave because she was disappointed. She left because she was too young and confused. She just need to do some growing up, is all.'

Chloe wiped her eyes. 'Well, it took her long enough.'

'Better late than never, girls. Isn't that what I always say, Chloe?'

'Actually, Mum, you always say, "If anything's worth doing, it has to be done properly."'

'Hm – happy you listen from time to time.'

Chloe rolled her eyes, much happier now that she had proof that she was loved unconditionally.

'So now what happens?' Jess asked.

'You wait until your dad's ready to make a decision. I suggest a couple of long movies,' I said, giving them a light pat and getting to my feet to make my own self scarce. Luke would want to speak to Lauren alone, if I knew him at all. 'I'll call you when it's time.'

When the front door closed much later, followed by the sharp pinging of the pebbles of gravel hitting the front door, I poked my head into the living room where Luke was standing facing the fireplace.

'Hey…' I whispered, and he whirled around.

'Do you want to be alone?' I said, stuffing my hands into my jean pockets.

He sighed. 'Of course not – come here, you…'

He wrapped me up in his embrace, but I could tell that his muscles were still very tense.

'Do you want to talk…?' I said.

'In a minute,' he said. 'Just let me hold you for a while.'

'Okay.' I drew him closer and kissed his shoulder. 'People make mistakes—' I began, but he shook his head.

'Mistakes that can't be forgiven, Nina. I will never forgive her for what she did to my baby – not a day didn't go by that Jessica didn't wonder why her mother didn't love her enough to stay.'

'So don't you think that maybe now she might honestly have wanted to meet her? To make amends?'

'I just don't get it,' he said, following his own train of thought. 'Jessica has never said she wanted to meet her mother. Never.'

'Maybe she never said anything because she didn't want to upset you. You know she lives for you, Luke.'

'I know,' he said. 'But it doesn't make it any easier.'

'So what are you going to do?' I asked.

'If Lauren had shown up without Jess knowing, I'd have told her to get lost. But Jess wants to get to know her and I—' He growled raking a hand through his hair, his eyes meeting mine. 'I can't bring myself to accept it, Nina.'

'But you have to. Because when Jess grows up and is free to contact her for herself, she'll be all the more angry with you for all the time she could have spent with her.'

He raised his head angrily. 'It wasn't my choice to separate my daughter from her mother, Nina.'

'But it is now. How do you think Jess will feel when you, her entire world, deny her the one thing she really wants?'

'And what's that? A flake of a mother?'

I shook my head. 'No, Luke. The knowledge of a mother. However imperfect, it's always better than not knowing anything at all.'

He ran his hands over his face and grabbed his jacket from the coat stand.

'Where – uhm…?'

'Out for a walk,' he answered. 'I need to think.'

'What's this I hear about Luke's wife? Is it true she's in Cornwall?' Emma asked me over the phone the next day. It was good to hear her voice, at least. I didn't dare mention my sort of falling-out with Jack. It hurt too much.

'True it is,' I answered.

'I don't get these people bouncing back – even Phil. What makes him think he even stands a chance after all he did to you? And Clarissa, too. What was she thinking when she left Jack?'

'I don't know. But I do know that he's being a bit cagey lately.'

'Does he look like he's in love to you?' she asked.

'Some friendship we have here,' I said, 'if we can't even ask one another about our love lives.'

She shrugged, 'Maybe some things are better left unsaid.'

I knew she was talking about herself again. 'Em? What's causing you so much stress? Do you think we wouldn't approve of your new man? I'm here for you.'

She groaned. 'I can only hope to be as discreet as you.'

'Nonsense. But please don't tell me it's someone I already know, because I'll kill you.'

'Huh? What do you mean?'

'I mean, that you'd had him under your nose all these years and it's taken you all this time to realise he was The One?'

'What about you? How are things with Luke? Are you two getting serious?'

Terrific question. 'I have no idea, Em.'

'Well, how do you feel about him?'

I thought about it. 'The truth? Besides the fact that I'm grateful to him for singling my work out, and the opposite fact that it took quite a while to adjust to each other as writers, as a man, he is actually the breath of fresh air I needed.'

'Really? That's fantastic, Nina! But it's true that you haven't really dated much at all – what makes you think, besides being Luke O'Hara, that you and he will be happy together?'

'Whoa, Em. I don't know how long this is going to last. That's why I'm not letting the kids in on it.'

'You mean they don't know?'

'All they know is that we're working together. Although I suspect Chloe is onto us.'

'If things were to get serious, how do you think they'd react? Do they like him enough?'

I smiled although she couldn't see me. 'Oh, Em – they adore him. And Jess.'

'And you, Nina? Do you adore him, too?'

I thought about it. His easy-going attitude, the way he waggled his eyebrows to get his way or when he said something flirty. The sheer love he harboured for his daughter. 'Yes, Em – I adore him, too. Although I doubt it's the same for him. Not completely, at least.'

She was quiet, thinking. 'And what about his ex-wife? Is there any chance she's come to rain on your parade?'

I hadn't thought of that. How stupid of me. Of course she'd want him back.

'You'd better stake your claim, Nina. You don't want her stepping in and ruining everything.'

'Em, let's take it easy. I don't even know where this is going, if it's going anywhere at all. So I just want to sit back and enjoy it for once.'

'I hope you're right, Nina, and that this woman is no threat to you. Stars can be so fickle.'

When I was silent, she cleared her throat. 'Forget what I said. We really should learn to enjoy and take like one day at a time without worrying ourselves sick about what may happen tomorrow. Carpe Diem and all that.'

Carpe Diem. 'You're absolutely right, Em.'

'Good girl. You enjoy. How's the sex by the way?'

I gushed. 'Pretty amazing, actually.'

'Yay!' she cheered, and I could hear her clapping her hands.

'And you, Em? Are you ready to tell me about you yet?'

'Uhm, not quite yet. But I will. I promise. Even if you'll think less of me.'

'Oh, Em, you know I could never do that,' I assured her. But if I was waiting for her to open up and tell me all as she used to in the old days, juicy details that made me blush included, I was going to have a long wait. And again that same sadness pervaded me. I was losing Emma as well. The three singles of Meadowbank Lane simply were no longer.

When I got home from grocery shopping later that day, I realised I'd forgotten the bread for my crostini.

'Do you want me to go get it?' Luke volunteered, but I could tell his heart wasn't in it. He still hadn't made a decision about Jess.

'Better not. Alf would probably take a swing at you.' At the look on his face, I burst out laughing. 'I'm kidding. I'll be right back.'

'Okay, then, don't be long. Take my keys.'

'No, that's okay, I'm going to take Lottie out. It's been a while.'

'Lottie?'

Jack knew Lottie very well. 'My car. It's just… an old joke. I'll see you later.'

And with that, I swung out the door and straight to my car that started on the first try. Jack had taught her well, I thought with a tiny pang of longing and regret.

At the shop, I parked and went in.

'All right, pet?' Deirdre said as she was sorting some postcards on one of the racks by the till.

'Just forgot something,' I called as I headed for the bread shelves.

And, of course *you* can guess what happened next, but how was I supposed to know? I only went back to buy bread. There he was, undecided as usual between the whole wheat and the granary, Jack Marrak in the flesh. His hair was longer, and his handsome lean face was covered in dark stubble, but besides that, he looked pretty much the same in his The Smiths T-shirt.

I gasped, unable to help myself, and he turned around and did a double take.

'Nina…' he breathed, our eyes locking the same way they had in Marazion.

I gushed with happiness and it was all I could do to keep from throwing myself at him. 'Jack…' I whispered. 'How've… you been?'

He studied me, and I hoped he didn't find me too different from his old bosom buddy.

'I'm all right,' he whispered back, his eyes never leaving mine. He was so close I could smell his familiar soap, and memories of all our good times flooded back to me, overwhelming me in an instant

'You… you look pale,' he said.

My hands went to my face. 'Do I? I'm all right, just tired, really.'

He continued to study me, and I wanted to say something – anything – but was afraid to ruin the moment.

'How are the kids?' he asked, his large hands still wrapped around the bag of sliced bread.

And what about me, I wanted to ask, but didn't dare.

'Oh, same old, same old.'

'And Minnie and Callie?'

I rolled my eyes. 'Always the attention-seekers.'

He chuckled, and his long lashes fanned his cheeks.

'They miss you, too, Jack.' *And I miss you. Desperately,* I wanted to add, but it stuck in my throat. *I miss the laughs and the jokes and feeling safe with you nearby, knowing you were a holler away, day or night. And now, you're not my friend anymore, at least not how we used to be, and you very probably are becoming serious with your mysterious girl and I…*

He caressed his chin as he always did when he was embarrassed. 'I, uhm, have to run, Nina. Take care of yourself.'

'You too, Jack,' I answered. And then, because fortune favours the brave, I bit the bullet. Just like that. If you don't ask…

'Would you… come over for dinner, or a coff—?' I began, but he had already moved back up the aisle, out of my reach, and halted only briefly, a look of sadness in his eyes as he turned away to pay at the till.

I rounded the shelf, out of sight, and tried to compose myself. This was ridiculous. So we'd had a misunderstanding. We'd be friends again one day. Also because in Penworth Ford, there was no one else to talk to.

Outside, I opened the door and sat in my car, waiting for Jack to drive off, as I didn't want to appear to be following him.

When his SUV took off I turned on the ignition. But of course, the car didn't bloody start. I looked up, watching with a sinking heart as Jack's tail lights disappeared in the distance. In the old days, he'd have waited for me to catch up, or let me go first, as the gentleman that he was. I debated whether to call him on my mobile for help as he was only a minute ahead of me. He knew Lottie better than any mechanic. But then I realised I'd have to explain to Luke why I had called Jack and not him, so, slumped in my seat, I watched him disappear and, unable to control myself, bawled my eyes out.

'I was about to come and get you,' Luke said when I got in an hour later after finally getting the car started and driving around the village ten times, too red-eyed to be seen by Luke. 'What happened, did you bake the bread yourself?'

I turned from the door. 'Oh. I… had to call the garage.'

'I don't know why you don't scrap that piece of junk and get yourself a new one,' he said.

A new car? I didn't even have the will to snort inwardly. I could barely afford to get this one even looked at. Luke was completely oblivious to my situation, despite the fact that I'd told him the script was what would save me financially. And here he was, dragging his heels. Just like Phil was dragging the divorce. I was sick and tired of depending on a man to get my own life into gear. First Phil, and then Luke. Only Jack had never left me hanging. He had always been there when I needed him. Except for now, when I needed him most.

'Nina?'

'Yes?'

'Where's the bread?'

I stared at him, and for the second time in an hour, I burst into tears.

He drew me into his arms. 'Nina, baby, it's okay. I know what's worrying you. You think I'm going to get pulled in by Lauren's charms now that she's moving back to LA. Well, let me make this clear right here and now. You won't lose me, sweets. I love you.'

At that, I began to howl. I had a man like Luke who loved me. And I loved him back. So what the hell was wrong with me?

32

Revenge

'Nina?' Luke called up the stairs the next day. 'I have got some business to tend to in Exeter. I'll be back late tonight, will you be okay with Jessica?'

I poked my head over the banister. 'Oh? Okay. I didn't know…'

'Neither did I, but he's a producer I've always wanted to work with.'

'Okay. Any special instructions regarding Jess?'

He looked up as he put on his jacket, tossing his keys from one hand to the other. 'Just don't let you know who anywhere near her in case she comes back. I trust you completely. I'm sorry but I have to do this. I'll let you know how it goes, okay?'

'Okay, good luck, then!' I called, but he was already out the door. No doubt about it, when Hollywood called, Hollywood got an answer. And a quick one at that.

Luckily I had planned a nice afternoon with the kids blind-building with Ben's Lego set. We would all choose something to build like a house, or a tower, and then, blindfolded, we would have to assemble it. I already knew that Jessica was going to win this one, and giving her a head start filled me with joy. Besides, it was a rainy day and I didn't fancy traipsing along the coastal path in my Mac and wellies.

As we were finishing up, the crunch of gravel made me turn to the front window. It couldn't possibly be Luke so soon, also because he usually parked where I could see his car. Could it possibly be… Jack?

I got up, my heart in my throat, as I opened the door.

'Are you alone? I need to talk to you.'

I sagged in disappointment. The last person I needed to see. *Lauren*. I thought she'd left England.

'Luke's out,' I managed.

'All the better. Have you got a moment?'

I pulled the door shut behind me, not wanting the kids to hear.

She smiled. 'I would do the same – don't feel bad.'

'Look, Lauren – I know why you're here, but I don't have any influence on Luke. And even if I did, I wouldn't use it. He has to do what he thinks is right for his daughter.'

She nodded, looking down at her feet. 'She's my daughter, too, Nina,' she said, her eyes getting moist.

Please don't. Oh, please don't.

I would have invited her in, but more than complying with Luke's request, I didn't want to give Jess any false hopes if she saw her mother inside the house. 'Look, uhm, Lauren. I'm sorry. Really I am.'

'I was too young. I was only nineteen. You must have had your first around the same age, am I right?'

I nodded. 'Yes. And it was difficult for me, too.' *Only I never abandoned them.*

'I made a huge mistake,' she said. 'Unforgivable. And now I'm paying for it twice.'

She looked up. 'I can't have children. Call it karma, or "what goes around comes around". The fact that I will never ever have another child made me rethink my absence from Jess's life. For so many years, I battled depression, and thought she was better off without me. Now I know I made a mistake. I should've accepted Luke's love, and his help. But it all just got bigger and bigger until it overwhelmed me and one day I couldn't even breathe and... I simply left.'

'Lauren – I understand what you went through, truly I do. But you don't have to justify yourself to me. Just talk to Luke.'

She studied me. 'Yes. You're right.'

'I'll tell him you called. Good luck, Lauren.'

'Thank you. Goodbye.'

I waited for her to get into her car and then quietly closed the door.

'And that's it?' Alice said over the phone a while later. 'You're not going to talk to him?'

'Believe me, Alice, I tried, but he just clammed up. I have no power over Luke's decisions.'

'Oh, honey, if you only knew. When he first called me, he told me he wanted to meet this wonder of a woman who was so brilliant and who loved her children so much.'

I waved away her words. 'What woman doesn't love her children?'

'Don't you see, Nina, his wife doesn't. That's why he loved your book so much. Because it's about a woman who puts her children first, rather than herself. And you did it with such wit and warmth. That's why he loves you. And that's why we love him. Although your Jack fellow isn't a fan.'

That was the understatement of the year. 'How did you know?'

'I have my sources.'

'You're not talking to the Ice Cream trio, are you?' They were a first-hand source of what was happening in my life, apparently. Shakespeare was right when he said that life was a stage. At least mine was. You couldn't beat small-village life for private information. Or imagination.

'You mean those charming old biddies? Yes, of course. They have been keeping an eye on you since you signed up with me years ago.'

'What?'

'Good God, Nina, how else am I going to keep watch on you from London? I'm only down once a month because of my dad. You don't expect me to schlep all the way down to Cornwall every time there's a crisis. I may be your agent and dear friend, Nina, but I'm a busy woman. I have other authors too, you know?'

'Ah, but none with a Hollywood deal, correct?'

I could feel her grinning on the other side of the nation. 'None, my dear duck of the golden eggs. Now hang up and get writing that blockbuster.'

'Alice?'

'Yeah?'

'Thanks so much for believing in me when no other

publisher did, all those years ago when I came to you with three chapters and a synopsis.'

'And a badly written one at that,' she said with a giggle. 'I love you, kid.'

'I love you too, Alice.'

'Now go. My other line is ringing. This better not be my Australian author Mary Morris with another tax question again, after I've only explained it to her five times.'

Chuckling to myself, I wandered into the conservatory, where I found Jessica lying back in an armchair, soaking up the last rays of sunshine for the day.

'Are you cold, Jess?'

She opened her eyes and turned her head in my direction. 'No, I'm fine, thanks, Nina. I was just thinking…'

I sat on the arm of the chair opposite her. 'Good thoughts, I hope?'

She shrugged. 'I was thinking about my mother.'

Ah. 'Sweetie, what she did doesn't reflect on you. She didn't even know you when she left, really.'

'I know. But sometimes… sometimes I wonder what things would be like if she hadn't left.'

'It's normal for you to wonder. But maybe you should tell your dad when he comes back?'

She nodded. 'I will, eventually. I'm just not sure it's what I want yet.'

'Well, when you are, make sure you don't keep it from him. He deserves to know how you are really feeling inside.'

She smiled. 'I will, I promise. And you? How's the script going?'

I smiled. 'Some days better than others, but yes, it's going very well.'

'He's driving you crazy, I bet. He's such a perfectionist.'

'Ye-es…'

'It'll be a great movie, Nina,' she said. 'I'm sure of it. I've listened to all your books. I love your style.'

'Awh, Jess, thank you.'

She shrugged. 'Chloe and Ben are lucky to have you as a mother. I guess I was lucky with my father. You can't have everything, I suppose…'

'Well, you're right about that, Jess. Spaghetti for dinner?'

She sat up. 'Ooh, yes, please!'

'Want to keep me company while I cook?'

She stood up and reached for my arm. 'Absolutely. I love being in your house, Nina. It's so warm and lovely.'

'Just like you, Jess. You've done wonders for my children. I can barely recognise Chloe. Well – some days.'

She giggled and rested her head on my shoulder as we went into the kitchen. She was indeed a joy to be with. I only wish she hadn't suffered so much in her life. If I had a magic wand, there were plenty of people I'd help. I'd give Jessica her sight, Carol her hearing, Ben the use of his legs, Alf his memories back and Jack a shot at happiness. I'd make Old Nellie young again so she could relive her love story with her first love. I'd give everyone all those things they hankered for and that money couldn't buy.

As I was getting dinner ready, Chloe hollered down the corridor, running into the kitchen. 'Mum! Mum! Callie's sick!'

'Oh dear, you didn't feed her any of your junk food, did you?'

'No, Mum, she's really sick! Her eyes are rolling around and she's foaming at the mouth!'

I dropped my oven mitts and ran through to the conservatory where Ben and Jessica were kneeling over her as she convulsed and yelped at the same time. I ran back and grabbed the throw from the sofa and wrapped her up in it, but she showed no signs of quieting down or even recognising us.

Even Minnie, who had been slurping at her water, stopped and stared at her, turning her head in confusion, sniffing her, and then hunkering down next to her, as if to offer her support.

'Ben, grab the keys, we're driving her to the vet's. Chloe, Jessica,' I said as I reached for my bag, 'I'm calling Jack from the car so he can come and stay with you.'

'Why can't we all come?' Chloe called out the front door as I settled Callie in Ben's lap and rounded back to my door.

'Because Emma is due later to drop Chanel off, remember?'

'Mum, it's okay, we don't need Jack to babysit us anymore! We'll be fine!'

I got behind the wheel and called back through the window. 'No, I'm sending you Jack.' He wouldn't allow the girls to be left on their own, even if he was angry with me. Always assuming he was in the vicinity.

'Call us!' Jessica said as I took off, flooring it. This poor little pup had already had a crap life. When we found her she had been beaten, neglected and God knows what else she had been through in her young life. I wasn't about to let her go down without a fight.

I looked down as Ben caressed her head, his tears plopping

down onto her. We had all fallen in love with her the very day she had loped into the front garden one evening a few months back, starved, dehydrated and emotionally derelict and had immediately found a place in our home. After an initial sniff here and there, our dog Minnie had decided that she was harmless, and not big enough to take up too much space in our hearts.

'Keep talking to her in a calm voice, love,' I said in soothing tones. 'She needs to know she'll be okay.'

'You hear that, Callie Coo? We're taking you to a nice doctor who's going to make you feel as good as new…'

But the poor pup just continued to roll her eyes.

'Mum?' Ben whispered.

'Yes, darling?'

'I'm scared.'

'Oh, sweetheart, don't be. It's probably just a bug. I've had loads of dogs go through this when I was a kid. She just needs a good vet.' And a miracle, I thought to myself, as I had omitted to add that I had lost that load of pups this same way.

Poor Callie. From the moment that she had entered our front garden, that little drenched tail between her skinny legs, and collapsed at my feet with those huge, sad eyes begging for help, I knew none of us would ever be the same again. Ben and Chloe had helped me nurse her back to life, and in the space of a few months Callie, who had been a nameless stray, had become a trusting, loving and happy member of our family with her very own clean water bowl, food bowl, basket and loads of chewy toys, and who sometimes royally pissed off Minnie, our baby number one.

I reached for my mobile and hesitated. I really had no one else who could come running.

Alf was busy at the Post Of ice and the Ice Cream Club ladies would take too long to get there. Annie had a tea room to run and Emma was in bloody Truro.

I only had one choice. Despite all that had passed between us, I knew he wouldn't say no. So I called him, my heart in my mouth, hoping he wouldn't avoid me.

'Jack?' I said, relieved he was still answering my calls at least.

'Nina – what is it?' he answered, slightly alarmed, because he, too, knew it would take something serious for me to contact him after the last time.

'I'm so sorry to bother you, Jack, but I can't ask anyone else. Callie is convulsing and I have had to rush her to the vet's and I have Chloe and Jessica home on their own.'

Pause. *Please don't hang up on me,* I silently begged, but knowing that he wouldn't.

'Where's Ben?' he asked.

'He's with me.'

'I'll be there in five minutes,' he said and I sagged against the steering wheel in relief.

'Oh, thank you, thank you. I'll be back as soon as I can.'

'All right, then.' No good luck or anything. But I supposed I was asking for too much now. He was coming, and that was good enough for me.

'Four minutes,' he informed me. 'I'm already in the car. Go. It'll be okay.'

'Oh, bless you, Jack,' I said and rang off, flooring it even more now.

When we got to the vet's, they gave her a sedative and we sat and waited for about an hour.

'Best to leave her overnight,' the vet suggested. 'I'll call you in the morning.'

'Is she going to be okay?' Ben whispered, stifling his tears and patting Callie's head as my own lower lip trembled.

'She's been poisoned, but we've pumped it out of her system, so now we're rehydrating her. Best to go home and get yourselves some rest.'

'I don't want her to die,' Ben hiccupped, grabbing my hand. 'Mummy, please don't let her die…'

I got down to my knees and squeezed my son's hands in mine. 'Darling, Dr Richards will do everything she can,' I promised. 'She'll be fine, you'll see.'

Lisa Richards shot me a sidelong glance and I widened my eyes. 'She's getting the best possible treatment, Ben. I promise you that.'

Together, Ben and I leaned over Callie, tiny and fragile in a sterile basket, and covered her with kisses and caresses while the drugs kept her under. I hadn't been this scared since Minnie had had her hysterectomy.

After long moments, we got to our feet and left Callie in Lisa's care, not without a silent prayer for my baby number four.

'Tell you what,' I said to Ben in the car on the way back. 'When we get home we'll make popcorn and watch a movie all snuggled up together on the sofa. What do you say?'

'Yuh…' he said, wiping his eyes.

'Yeah?' I asked. 'What would you like to watch?'

'*Marley and Me*,' he said without hesitating.

As we approached the house, I expected to see Jack's 4x4 parked out front, but by God, there were also a fire truck and an ambulance.

'Oh, my God! Ben, stay here!' I ordered as I flew through the front garden, frantically looking for the kids and found them next to a paramedic who was giving Jack the thumbs up. They all looked unharmed.

'I'm here, I'm here!' I cried as I reached out to hug them. 'Are you all right? What happened?' I asked, checking them as if for broken bones.

'This bloke arrived to save the day,' the paramedic informed me, beaming at Jack.

'It was the electrics,' a firefighter explained, removing his gloves. 'It's dodgy to say the least.'

'Nothing to do with the fridge?' I asked.

'No, not in the least,' he answered me.

Jack and the two men shook hands, complimenting one another for the nice work as Ben came over, his eyes wide.

'Thank you, I'm so sorry, thank you all,' I croaked as tears welled up in my eyes. I left them for four minutes and this happened? What the hell was wrong with me? I risked the lives of two young girls by abandoning them.

'Everything's okay, mate,' Jack said, folding Ben into his arms when he reached out to him for a hug. 'Just a tiny spark.' And then he turned to me. 'How's Callie?'

'Not out of the woods yet,' I whispered as Ben limped on ahead to join Jessica and Chloe on the sofas.

I threw a blanket over the three kids, making sure they weren't in shock, but they were very brave and downplayed it.

'Mum – it's fine, really,' Chloe assured me. 'It was only a tiny fire and Jack arrived three minutes after you left.'

'Nina, please don't be upset,' Jessica said. 'We were never in any danger.'

'Never in any danger? The kitchen was on fire!'

'But only for a minute, really, Mum. It's not as bad as it looks,' Chloe insisted.

The kids could have been hurt, seriously hurt, and it was all my fault. I should have hired someone more reputable to check the wiring, instead of Bert and Harry from the phone book. When was I going to do something right? Whatever I did, whatever decision I made, it always seemed to be the worst.

And just because I couldn't feel any worse, Lauren's BMW rounded the corner in a screech and braked just across the road. Within seconds, the howling started.

'Jessica! Oh, Jessica!' she called, bursting in, beating her way past us all to Jess who went from chilled and relaxed to alarmed in a nanosecond.

'Oh, my God, are you okay? I was in the village and someone said, "Fire at Cornflower Cottage," and I drove over immediately!'

Luckily for us, it hadn't been a real fire, as Jack had repeated to me. We had already given in that department three years ago.

'I'm okay,' Jess answered, taking Chloe's hand.

Lauren looked up at me.

I wrung my hands in helpless frustration, willing her to go away, and for Luke to return so I could explain what had happened without Lauren possibly poisoning his judgement.

'How could you not take care of my daughter?' she cried.

'How could you be any more qualified than me? Do you see why I can't imagine not being with her? Life is so precious, and it could slip through our hands any minute. And I don't want to waste another day. Do you understand?'

I huffed. Of course I understood.

'Miss, calm down,' came Jack's voice. 'Jessica is perfectly fine as you can see.'

'Who the hell are you to talk to my mother like that, Lauren?' Chloe cried. 'You're the one who dumped Jess, not her! If anything, she's been like a mother to her. And you! You, her own mother, can't even be bothered to send a bloody birthday card once a year!'

I stepped forward and took my daughter into my arms. 'Sweetheart, hush now. It's okay.'

'No, Mum, it's not okay! This woman is just trying to make you feel bad with her good manners and sob story! She's been doing it for weeks to Jess, too! *Oh, my poor baby, I had to leave you, even if I didn't want to!* It's all a crock of shit, Lauren! A real mother, a mother who loves you *stays*, no matter *what* the cost!' And then she burst into tears. 'And that goes for fathers as well!'

'Chloe, don't get upset because of me,' Jess pleaded, catching her hand again.

'What do any of you know about it?' Lauren bawled at Chloe who stood back in surprise, not expecting Lauren to break down in front of them.

'Please stop,' Jess whispered.

'Miss, I think you should leave now,' Jack said, moving towards her, and I knew that if she continued, he would personally escort her off the property.

It felt so strange for him to be here, once again taking

action, or at least shouldering the load with me like he used to. I had missed that. And tonight was not his fault at all. If anything, he had deflected what could have been a tragedy. I shuddered at the thought, and he put his arm around me, which strangely, made it better.

'Leave?' Lauren honked. 'I'm not going anywhere without my daughter!'

'Now there's a first,' came a voice from behind us. Luke.

I spun around, which caused Jack's arm to fall off my shoulder.

'Oh, Luke…' I whispered, but he strode straight over to Jess and took her in his arms. 'Are you okay, sweetie?'

And then he noticed the blackened corner in the kitchen. 'What happened here?' he demanded, and as I opened my mouth to answer, Lauren threw herself into a tirade against us all. When she was done, Luke looked up at me in shock. He said nothing, but the expression on his face was clear: *You left my daughter with your neighbour?*

It was my fault, and my fault only. And I shouldn't have trusted an electrician who had only glanced at the wiring.

After a few moments, as I stood by the kitchen sink, still wringing my hands like a useless git in contrition, Lauren took Luke aside and informed him that she was back, and had no intention of going away again.

She followed him through the front door and they paused on the threshold, as – I could tell by the slant of his body – he was becoming angrier and angrier. I had blown it big time. I had put his child's life in jeopardy. Had there ever existed a woman as stupid as myself? Lauren was right. I had no right to be in charge of Jess.

'Jack,' I croaked. 'You'd better go.' I didn't want him to hear any more of this.

He turned to me. 'You must be joking. I'm not leaving you with those two.'

'It's okay, really. She's just upset. I'd be the same. So go.'

He wasn't convinced. 'Are you sure?'

I nodded. 'I can handle it. I'll just explain everything to him.'

Jack took my elbows and looked straight into my eyes. 'I'm a phone call away, Nina. If you need me, I'll come running. Okay?'

''Kay,' I sniffed. 'Thank you. I don't know what I would have done if you hadn't been there…'

'I'll always be there, Nina. Always.'

I hugged him. He felt solid and warm and strong. He felt like… home within a home.

'Okay, then. I'll call you tomorrow morning.'

I swiped at my eyes and attempted a smile. 'Tomorrow morning…'

With one last look and a lingering caress of my arm, he stalked out the front door, but not without stopping to say something to Luke, who shook his head.

When Lauren finally left, not without one last venomous look my way, Luke came back in, his face ashen.

'What? What is it?' I asked, pulling out a chair for him.

He plonked himself down, his eyes unfocused. 'She's moving back to LA and wants back into our lives and if I put up a fight, she's going to contact her lawyer.'

33

The Crying Game

After a sleepless night, the dawn seemed even grimmer as I crept downstairs to make some coffee. And to take Luke's temperature. He had been odd with me last night, and I had waited for him, if not to come to my room as Ben was sleeping with me, but to at least send me a text where he said that he wasn't angry with me, and that it was just all one big mess-up. But I guessed it was a little too much to ask of him.

While the kettle boiled, I called Dr Richards to ask about Callie, hoping that it hadn't all been for naught, and that at least one good thing would come of that horrible night.

'She's in and out of it because of the drugs, but her vital signs are stabilising. Hopefully you can come pick her up tomorrow, by which time we expect her to be out of the woods.'

'Oh, Lisa, thank you, thank you!' I nearly sobbed all over again. 'Can we come by today?'

'Best to let her sleep, plus she's riddled with tubes – it would only upset the kids to see her like that.'

'Okay, I understand. See you tomorrow then. And thank you so much, Lisa.'

A moment later Luke surfaced, his expression stony, and I smiled weakly as I passed him a steaming cup of please-forgive-me coffee, which he took with a soft grunt. Now Luke had to fight Lauren to keep the child he had raised since she was a baby, and it was all my fault.

'I just checked in on them. They're fast asleep,' I whispered, not because I was afraid of waking anyone, but because I could barely speak over my sense of mortification that had accompanied me all night, weighing down on my heart like a demolition ball.

'She's young and resilient, Luke. She'll get over it.'

Luke put his mug down on the counter and turned to me, his face set. 'I've made a decision. I'm taking Jessica back home for a bit. I'll need my wits about me, and I'll need to be on home turf to fight Lauren. I'll call you when this has all blown over, okay?'

He was leaving, just like that? Not asking my opinion about any of it, just… leaving. He blamed me. Only he was too polite to come out and say it.

I nodded. 'Of course.' What else could I say?

'Okay.'

I swallowed. 'Luke, for what it's worth, I am truly, truly sorry.'

He patted my hand. Quickly, cursorily. 'I know. But it's not your fault, really. I'm going to book my flights now,' he said and padded across the open space and up the stairs again. The bit of dialogue that changed my life had lasted less than a minute.

Luke and Jessica's flight was the next evening. We were all a wreck, of course, but not as much as Jessica and Chloe.

'I don't want to go, Dad,' Jessica pleaded as Luke brought their luggage to the front door and turned to us to say goodbye.

He sighed. 'I know, sweetheart. But it can't be helped for now.'

'Please tell her that it's nobody's fault,' Jess said.

'Will you ever come back?' Ben wanted to know.

'Of course,' he said.

'When?' Ben insisted.

'When Jessica's mother and I become friends again, Ben.'

Jess snorted. 'That's not happening any time soon, Dad. We both know that.'

'Yeah, well…' he muttered more to himself. And then he turned to me.

'Good bye, Nina. Thank you for everything.'

That was it? No, *I'll keep you posted – don't worry, we'll beat her together*. Nothing?

I swallowed and nodded. 'Good luck, Luke…'

'Yeah. Thanks.'

'I'm going to miss you, you little munchkin,' Jess sobbed into the top of Ben's head.

'Me, too. I like you much better than my own sister.'

At that, Chloe, who was wiping her eyes, swatted him

softly across the back. 'Don't worry, Ben, she'll be back before you know it. Won't you, Jess?'

Jessica sniffed, facing upwards. 'Dad?'

Luke looked at me, and I knew it would be a long time before I saw him again. 'Let's hope so, Jessica. Bye, guys.'

Jess spread her arms and Ben and Chloe hugged her, the two girls sniffling, while Ben held tight onto her skirt. Then they hugged Luke, who kissed their cheeks. 'I'm going to miss you too,' he said. 'But I'll be back before you know it.'

Ben looked up at him. 'Promise?'

'Cross my heart and hope to die, buddy boy.'

At the door, Luke stopped and turned so only I could hear him.

'I'm sorry it had to come to this.' His voice lowered just enough so only I could hear him. 'Take care, Nina... kids.' And without a backward glance, he disappeared.

Completely numb, I wanted to crawl into the safety of my bed under the eaves and cry for a week. But my children needed me, so we all piled into the car and I drove them down to the animal clinic to retrieve Callie.

The minute we burst through the doors, she spotted us and, although she was too weak to shoot to her feet, her tail swished back and forth, her eyes following us as we all knelt by her side, Ben scooping up the entire basket containing her as delicately as possible.

I turned to Lisa who winked. She was out of the woods! 'You are a star,' I croaked as I passed her secretary my bank card. 'I'm going to make a huge donation.'

'You already have,' she beamed.

'I beg your pardon?'

'Jack swung by this morning. I offered to give him Callie,

but he said he'd rather you and the kids come down and got her.'

Was he or was he not the best? A minute later, my mobile went. It was a message from Jack:

How are you guys? And Callie?

And it suddenly occurred to me that Luke hadn't even asked, nor known about Callie's brush with death. He hadn't even noticed her absence.

If the days were less than tolerable, the nights spent in the company of guilt were endless, as I cursed myself over and over again.

That evening, Jack stopped by, solemn like I'd never seen him before. 'Luke's got quite the battle ahead of him. I feel guilty in some way. I didn't really care for him, but he was a great father,' he whispered.

I sniffed, trying to keep my composure. 'It's not your fault, Jack. Not in the least. You were only trying to help out as you always do. I'm the one who messed up. I'm a terrible mother and a terrible human being.'

'Hey, don't say that. You're a fantastic mother. It was just one of those things, you know? If I had arrived three minutes earlier—'

'Do not make this your fault, Jack. You've been nothing but kind and loving to us and I…' I swallowed the boulder in my throat. 'I screwed everything up. I'm so sorry, Jack. I'm a terrible friend.'

'Come here,' he whispered, wrapping me in his arms,

and it was like going home after a long journey abroad. I'd *missed* him.

Later, as if she had sensed something was wrong, Alice phoned and I gave her the low-down on all that happened. But she already knew as it was all over the papers. Apparently Lauren had told the press I was keeping her family from reuniting.

'How are you doing, sweetie? Is everyone okay?'

'Physically, we're okay, but we're all upset, of course.'

'Yes, I can understand that,' she answered. 'I'm just glad no one was hurt.'

I nodded as if she could actually see me over the phone.

'So when's he coming back to finish the script?' she asked.

'I don't know. I'll be working on it in the meantime. God knows how long.'

'I'm so sorry. Luke's a great dad.'

'Jack was saying the exact same thing.'

'Maybe we should let things settle for a bit. Hollywood is a cruel place, but also fickle. When this blows over they'll forget,' she soothed.

'You were wrong about something, Alice.'

'And what's that?'

'You once said there was no mud in LA. But actually, I have come to see that there's lots and lots of it.'

The people of Penworth Ford, who had been used to seeing a Hollywood star ambling around the village and surroundings, were now slightly confused, especially after word of Lauren's return to her family had spread to the Post Of ice – and the papers.

Alf was sitting behind his counter, barely visible behind his broadsheet as usual and completely absorbed.

I smiled at the lovely old man who had been like a father to me.

'Good morning, Alf.'

'Mornin', Emma.'

I paused and swallowed. It hurt to see him not completely sharp of mind, even if it was for just brief moments.

'I heard yer fella left – 'spect you'll get over him soon, bein' plenty o' suitable men around,' Alf said in the hope of cheering me up.

'You offering?' I quipped, but inside I was falling apart. All my dreams of a better future, of selling my script and having our own Happily Ever After had been put on stand-by for who knew how long.

'Ah, I'd gladly accept, but my heart's already spoken for by a special lady.'

'Oh? Who?'

'Discretion, pet. Discretion. I've got to preserve my lady friend's reputation.'

Well, that made me almost keel over in a fit of giggles despite everything.

'You, on the other hand, should not be searchin' anywhere else,' he asserted.

'How do you mean, Alf?'

'You have everything you need right here.'

Everyone else I met in the village just kindly smiled at me, patting my shoulder as they passed, sending me their silent messages of solace, which made it even worse. Because I didn't need them to say anything. They knew my life well, and had been there when it had fallen apart the first time. They had seen me pick myself up and dust myself off. They were the people who had been so kind to me, and for them to witness another downfall of mine was not only humiliating, it was also devastating, and only flashes of humour managed to save me from total depression.

When a week had passed and no news had come from Luke, I sent him a text:

Hi Luke, how are things?

And waited. It was still daytime in California, so unless he was driving or with his lawyers, he'd see it.

After a few hours, he finally answered:

Real battle.

I could only imagine. Lauren was on a mission, judging by the look on her face the evening of the fire. I truly felt for Luke. I texted back:

Good luck, keep me posted xxx.

But there was no "Will do" or "Thanks" in a return. Not even a single x.

Over the weeks, everything had changed and nothing had changed. The kids had gone back for another term at Northwood, and the leaves had turned to orange while the sea had whipped itself into a greyish-brown brew, and I had turned the heating up and started making soups instead of salads.

I expected a phone call any minute with either some

news, or even a simple "How are you?" But again, none came, just like every time I asked him a question, I rarely got an answer back. I didn't dare ask about the script, of course. That was secondary to him. But to me, it was vital.

After week four, exasperated, I typed:

How is the battle going?

To which he answered almost immediately:

A bloodbath.

So he was alive after all. I waited for him to elaborate. And waited. And waited. And then in the end, I got on with my evening. Sod that for a game of soldiers.

'Come on, Nina, pull yourself up,' Alice said during one of her visits. 'It's just a temporary glitch. He'll be back. There's a contract.'

'Gee, thanks for your faith.'

'Well, it's true. Listen, I know there was something between you and Luke, but these people are fickle. One day you're their world, then the next, not so much.' Could she have said anything worse?

'You think this is just about the script? Do you really think me that vain? This wasn't just about the money anymore. I actually thought we'd found happiness. That I'd found…' I swallowed, unable to say it out loud. I thought we'd found something good.

I thought that from here on, with somebody to live and

laugh with, we could rebuild two broken families. Jessica was a wonderful girl that had touched our hearts, and Luke was genuinely fond of Ben and Chloe. So many good things had happened these past few months. Picnics, walks along the coastal path, frolicking with our lovely dogs, days out and about… and promises of a better, fuller life.

And now? Now my heart was breaking, and everything, all the responsibilities and burdens that I'd shouldered all these years up until now seemed unbearable. The forest dream now made sense to me.

Forget *Written In The Stars*, *Abandonment* should be the title of the movie, the story of my life. Not to throw a pity-fest here, but who, in my same situation, wouldn't feel at least a tiny bit sorry for themselves?

I wanted to kick myself in the head. I'd shown all my cards upfront and Luke had probably decided the movie was too much of a hassle and I wasn't worth the trouble. It served me right. What was I thinking, hoping to get my family out of this predicament? Things like that only happened to J.K. Rowling, not Nina Conte. And now, because of my damn pride, I'd jeopardised my children's future. Could I be more stupid?

Although I couldn't hear them, I could feel my fellow villagers' thoughts that, despite being kind, stabbed me in the back like little daggers dipped in pity. Of course they couldn't understand how I'd come across such luck. Not even I could make sense of it.

'Why are they looking at us so sadly, Mum?' Ben asked.

I shrugged. 'Maybe they think we're sad, sweetheart.'

'Are you?' he asked.

'Absolutely not. Are you, darling?'

NEW HOPE FOR THE LITTLE CORNISH FARMHOUSE

'Absolutely not, Mum.'

'Good. Then let's go home now.'

Okay, so for the moment, the deal might be postponed, but I still needed to pay my bills. Utility companies didn't care what fantastic, ultimately lucrative (one hoped) project I was working on; they just wanted their money. Money I didn't have.

And that was when I caught sight of the brochure for the *Poldark* tours Emma had left on my desk.

Except for some snippets she had shown me on her phone, I hadn't seen the show, but when I was pregnant I had read all twelve books. And, given that I'd been trawling Cornwall flogging my *arancini* for years now, I knew every inch of this county.

I could do that job with my eyes closed (even by the cliffs). It would be a great addition to our income, especially as I wasn't getting any great humongous light bulb moments for a book and, on top of everything else, the price of beef, my main ingredient, had gone up. All I needed was another bout of mad cow disease and I was screwed forever. So yes, it was wise to have a back-up plan. Hedge my bets, just in case. So I called their head office in Charlestown and offered my services. They were thrilled to have an Italian-speaking guide for the flocks of Italian fans, but would I send a résumé? Of course. *Certamente.*

Although Emma's appearances were becoming as rare as Halley's Comet, at least Jack had migrated back into our lives.

'Any news about Luke's custody battle?' he asked me, code for *Are you still together?*

I shook my head. 'I don't know. I don't even know if

he's coming back. I understand he's got problems and all, but it wouldn't hurt to text me actual sentences now and then, would it? All I get is… Oh, forget it. And you? Is there anyone on the horizon for you, Jack? We always talk about me and the kids. What about that girl?'

He shrugged. 'There's nothing to know.'

'So there's no one…?'

'There's only been one person ever since. But she hardly knows I exist.'

'Well, then tell her.'

'What? No.'

'Tell her your feelings.'

'I would, but I don't think she feels the same.'

'Then she's an idiot, Jack. Tell her. What have you got to lose?'

'Her friendship? Her respect?'

I shook my head. 'If she cares for you at all, even as a friend, you will never lose her.' Of that, I was certain. Whoever this woman was, she would give him a chance. What woman wouldn't? Jack was everything a woman could ever want.

He sighed. 'I wish I had your confidence.'

'You should be more assertive, Jack. Hell, you're a successful businessman and you can't handle your love life?'

'Ouch,' he said. 'Okay. I'll try. Have you seen Em lately?'

34

Nine To Five

The next Monday was my first day as a *Poldark* tour guide. Each day I'd be carrying out a different tour with different starting points dislocated across the county. It was roughly a four-hour tour across the whole of Cornwall at the best of times, but I had no choice. I donned my stupid red cap and blue dress, courtesy of Holsworthy Poldark Tours that had done me the favour of hiring me, and drove to Charlestown where the bus driver was waiting for me to collect the fans from their hotels.

As it were, my first batch straight off the bat happened to be indeed Italian, so after our Hellos and Where are you froms and Why you speak Italian so wells, we got into the nitty-gritty. It was a young group, mainly couples who were up for a trek and dressed for the Vietnamese jungle.

Our first stop was Truro Harbour from where we went on to Falmouth, then off to Porthcurno and, getting familiar with the lingo of the trade, to the magical Minack Theatre, from which you could enjoy the best views featured in *Poldark* Series 1. (Or so the brochure said.)

Then we went down to Porthcurno beach featured in *Poldark* Series 2. The views from there were among the most iconic in Cornwall. After a quick lunch we headed on Porthgwarra, the tiny cove used in *Poldark* Series 1 for the pilchard boats scene, and also from where Demelza spies on Ross bathing in the sea.

Later, as I stood out on Gwennap Head waiting for them to take their selfies and making sure they weren't going to selfie themselves off a cliff, I did some of my own dramatic gazing out into the sea, just like Demelza (minus the optimism) waiting for her beloved Ross to return, the irony of it occurred to me. Because as sure as hell, I wasn't Demelza, and Luke, as much as he may be someone's Ross, certainly wasn't mine anymore. Because he wasn't coming back.

As I stood there, I remembered Ben explaining to Luke about the daymarks, and a sense of nostalgia enveloped me. 'And this is where Ross Poldark said he would be happy to leave California and live here with her and the kids,' I heard myself say out loud.

'Ross Poldark in California?' I heard someone say, scratching their heads. 'Wasn't it Virginia?'

If only I hadn't screwed up. Luke would be here, the script would be finished by now and maybe production would have even started. And Ben's operation would be on the horizon. Boosted by the movie, I'd probably have started my next book and watched the royalties ca-chinging from the comfort of the dining room table by the window. But instead I was clad in a cheap, blue polyester dress and a red cap and still making *arancini* on the side to make ends meet. So much for California Dreamin'. So much for any dreamin'.

'Ehm, *Signorina*?' one of my couples addressed me.

I sighed and turned around. '*Sì*?'

'Are you okay?'

'Fan-Pold-*astic*,' I chimed.

'*Signorina*?'

'Yes?'

'Please come away from the edge, you're scaring us.'

After a gruelling day scarpering over hill and dale in the cool Cornish winds, I decided to take Lottie to the mechanic's in Truro on the way home. I had to make sure that at least *she* would be able to endure the commute into work and back.

I would have loved to have swung round to Emma's while waiting for the verdict, but I was too tired and didn't want to drag her down with my misery.

'It's bad,' the mechanic warned as he wiped his hands on an old filthy cloth.

I groaned. 'How bad?'

He shrugged and said something about the carburettor and that it was an old car and when was the last time I'd changed the oil? Apart from the last time Jack saw it? How the hell was I supposed to know? I took it to the petrol station, asked them to give it a once-over and they poured stuff into it. I didn't get into the details as long as the engine started.

Besides, we'd got the clunker thirteen years ago before Chloe was born and even then it was a second-hand deal. And now it was either spend a whole cartload of money on it or wave it goodbye. I did a rapid calculation. With the way things were going financially, we'd have to sell the house before the end of the school year just in time to find a hovel on a bus route. There was no way the kids were leaving Northwood Academy as long as I pulled a breath.

And so I left old Lifeless Lottie at the garage and walked to the bus stop and waited for the next bus. And waited. And waited. Thirty minutes later, I decided that if my feet hurt that much from standing, maybe walking might help. I was wrong. Walking only made it worse, and soon I was limping, agonising at every single step of the way. A car full of yobbos slowed down to take a look at me, their dashboard covered in take-away food, and the bloke in the passenger seat was licking his fingers allusively.

'Yorrite, luv? Want a ride?'

'No thanks, I'm meeting someone,' I lied and they guffawed and sped off with a screech. I supposed I was lucky they didn't throw their leftovers at me.

In the end I called Emma, wondering if she might come and pick me up because I couldn't take another step.

'Of course, where are you?'

'Uhm, not quite sure. Definitely on the outskirts of Truro.'

Silence. 'What the hell are you doing down there?'

'Long story,' I said. 'Oh, wait, there's a pub, Smuggler's Rest. I'll wait for you in there, okay?'

'Won't be a mo,' she promised.

'Thanks, Em.'

Shoes in hand, I walked into the place, fitting in immediately with the misfits in there. Smuggler's Rest was right. It looked as if every down-and-out in the whole of Cornwall had found its way out here. And then I realised

I was in the middle of a movie set. Not shooting at the moment, but all the cameras and props were there.

The male lead, handsome but nowhere near Luke's stature, was practising a scene with his co-star in which he was begging her over a ploughman's to marry him. I wanted to cry. *Go for it,* I almost said. *Somewhere, there's someone for everyone. You just have to find him.*

'Nina?' came a familiar voice, but not Emma's.

I looked up. Jack…?

He slid into the booth opposite me. 'Are you all right? Emma sounded concerned. She said you didn't know where you were?'

'Hmmm…' I nodded absently.

'What the hell are you doing here?'

'I went to the mechanic's.'

'Stuart's? You know he's a thief. Why didn't you call me?'

'Because I'm always calling you, Jack. I can't do anything on my own, and that's not good. Ever since Luke disappeared it's like I don't know how to do anything anymore…'

His mouth tightened. 'Nonsense. You don't need him, Nina. Look at what a good job you've done raising your children on your own.'

'Yeah,' I half-snorted, half-bawled. 'Look what a proper job indeed. My house is falling apart, my finances are practically null, my son is disabled, my daughter is running riot shoplifting, and there's absolutely nothing I can do to fix it all! What a mess I am, Jack! Stay away from me before I screw you up, too!'

Jack put his hand on mine. 'First of all, that was just an isolated incident of Chloe's.'

'No, you don't understand, she did it to attract my

attention. I'm so focused on survival that I've forgotten how to savour the good moments in life.' I buried my head into my arms on the table. 'One day when I'm old I'll be looking out the window of an old folks' home wondering why my kids don't ever come and visit!'

He laughed. 'Nina, stop. Your kids love you. And for the record, Ben is not disabled.'

'He will be, because I can't afford all his treatments. They're so expensive that not even ten advances would cover it! I can barely afford the flights to the US, let alone the surgery!'

'You don't need any flights to the US. I've found someone in France.'

I lifted my head, barely able to focus through my tears. 'What…?'

'I've been reading wonders about him from all over the world. He's in Normandy. But I wanted to talk to you first. Will you allow me to make an appointment so he can have a look at Ben? I'll drive you to France.'

I almost rose from my seat, ready to go to Normandy in my bare feet. 'He can help Ben?'

'He made no promises, but I've explained Ben's situation, and he said his condition is more common than you'd think, and that he's helped loads of people.'

I clutched at my heart. 'Really? He said there's hope?'

Jack squeezed my hand. 'There's always hope, Nina.'

I accepted the tissue that magically appeared in his hands with a timid smile. If Ben could walk freely, without that bloody contraption around his leg, I would be the happiest woman on earth. I'd forgo anything just to give my kids the right tools to carve out a decent life for themselves. Ben wanted to be an explorer, climb mountains and jump out of planes. Not that I was happy with that last scenario, but, oh, I'd give my right arm if only he had the same opportunities as everyone else!

'Will you let me take you home, now, Nina?'

I nodded, wiping my eyes and reaching for my bag as we left the pub to get into Jack's SUV. 'Of course, thank you.'

'But first, I want to swing round to Stuart's and make sure he knows who he's dealing with,' he said, driving up the steep hill again. No wonder my feet were killing me.

He parked across the street from the garage. 'You stay here, I'll talk to him,' he said, and I sat back, grateful for once that I wouldn't have to speak to that awful man again.

He was back in two minutes. 'It'll be ready tomorrow, free of charge.'

'Free? How...?'

'Well, let's just say that it was a small problem, Nina.'

'Oh my God, thank you, Jack. I don't what I'd do without you.'

'Of course you do.'

We drove home in a companionable silence, and I was reminded of when he had come to retrieve us at Heathrow and driven us all the way home. It was always Jack who stepped up to the plate when this damsel was in distress. The woman who had bagged him was very fortunate indeed.

At the house, I turned before I got out of the car. 'Thank you, Jack. For everything. Can you stay for dinner?'

He grinned. 'Love to. Do you need help making your *arancini* tonight?' he asked. 'I've got some extra time on my hands.'

'Uhm, no thanks. I already made them because I won't be home all day tomorrow. I've got a new job.'

'Oh?'

'Yeah – Italian-speaking tour guide for *Poldark*.'

'That would explain the cheesy outfit. I was wondering.'

I slapped his forearm lightly. It felt good to be back in this place again. 'Silly.'

'There it is, the Nina smile…!'

'I don't remember the last time I smiled.'

He sighed, shaking his head. 'Nina… you don't need to work this hard. I can't bear to see you like this.'

'It's nothing, I'm used to it, Jack. Plus it's only during school hours. I'll be home by four, and Deirdre's already agreed to fetch and keep the kids until I get home.'

'But, sweetheart, you shouldn't be killing yourself making *arancini* or doing tours across the county. You should be sat at your desk writing your next blockbuster. That's what will make your fortune.'

I shrugged.

'Why don't you let me help you?' he offered. 'Just enough to keep you going while you write your book.'

'No! No, thank you, Jack. I haven't got a book in me at the moment.' And I realised I had been saying this for years now. Even Alice would have had a right to give up on me, but she never did. One good thing that I had was my people. My tribe. I was so lucky to be surrounded by the salt of the earth. People I was now, however, disappointing – my kids first of all.

'I'd be surprised if you did, the way you tear across the county for everyone else except for yourself. Nina, just take some time off. Forget the *arancini*, forget *Poldark* and just… *be* a while.'

There was nothing that I wanted more – the chance to just "be" a while. But I couldn't take his offer, not while I was still paying Alice's advance off. The ten grand had gone to the school fees and new uniforms and school supplies for the kids and Ben's consultation in the States, but I didn't have enough for the follow-up and pre-op visits, let alone the operation itself. It would be good to check this French doctor out.

And then something hit me. Why, if I'd called Emma, had Jack come in her stead? Had they been together?

35

Phoenix

If there was any bright side at all to Luke leaving, it was Chloe's transformation from resentment to sympathy for me. Instead of being her usual rebellious and selfish self, she found the time to talk to me without asking me for money, or for permission to go somewhere absolutely unfit for a girl her age.

'Do you miss him?' she asked softly, rubbing my back like I always did to her when she was down.

I was always one to protect my children from my own problems. But if they had brought Chloe back to being my sweet little girl who would hug me just for being me, then I would always be honest with them.

'Yes,' I said. 'But I am also sorry for disappointing you and Ben. I so wanted to make your lives better, and I promise you, I will, Chloe. I'll get back in the saddle and write my heart out. Full time. I won't stop until I've finished a book. An entire series, in fact.'

'Mum,' she said. 'You haven't disappointed Ben and me.

We are so proud of you, of everything you've done since Dad left us.'

I looked into her eyes. Was she serious?

'Oh, Mum,' she sobbed, rubbing her forehead against mine. 'I'm so sorry for being a monster to you! All these years and I blamed you for him leaving.'

I fought back the tears. My baby was growing up. Enough snivelling. It was time to be strong. 'Oh, no, my darling. You were angry. We all were. But I'll do everything I can to make sure that scumbag doesn't get to your money, either. I'll put it in your names for your college funds.'

At that, she giggled through her tears. 'Mum! You've never talked like that before!'

'Yes, well, sorry. I can't always be perfect.'

'No one ever asked you for that.'

Well, that was a good thing.

'Can I read your books?' she asked, blowing me away. She had never ever expressed any interest in my work, always dismissing it as "rubbish".

I swallowed. 'Of course. You're a young woman now. You understand women and their feelings.' Of which there had been an abundance.

'Is there a lot of… sex? Because I don't want to read about you and Dad—'

Was there a lot of sex in my marriage? 'Absolutely not. It's more about relationships and problems.'

'Like money problems?'

I smiled and nodded. I was a specialist in those. I mean, in having money problems. Not solving them. At least not yet.

'Those, too, yes. And again, it's fiction. It even says so

at the beginning of the book: all characters are purely fictional.' (That one had got a good laugh out of Alice.)

Chloe eyed me, still unsure. 'So it's not about you?'

'It's about women like me, Chloe. Maybe even half of the mothers at Northwood, the ones who bad-mouth me. You know how many of them are divorced or unhappy in their marriages and put on an act, just so they can swim in the family money?'

Her blue eyes widened. 'Really? Maybe that's why they're so gossipy?'

I winked at her and she hugged me. 'I'm sorry for being such a brat, Mum...'

'I love you, sweetie,' I reassured her as I breathed in her fresh scent of youth and bubble gum and lip gloss. 'Always remember that. No matter how difficult it is for your dad and I to get along, I will always love you and Ben to pieces.'

'Does Dad love us too?'

In his own, twisted, intermittent way, maybe. 'Of course he does!' I chimed.

'So then why did he leave us? Emma told me that he stole all the money that you had earned from your books and put away for our education, and the renovations of the house. And that he even took the rent money you had saved for us to live in a flat so we wouldn't have to live in a trailer. She told me he left you with nothing, and that the trailer even burned down. Oh, Mum! You must have suffered so much!'

'Emma told you that?'

Chloe nodded, swiping at a tear. 'I called her a couple of weeks ago. I had no idea that Dad had done all those bad things to you. He always said he left you because you were boring and you never let him have any fun.'

Oh, he had his fun. 'It doesn't matter anymore, Chloe.'

'Now I understand why you never wanted him back!'

'Sweetheart, men are not as complicated as we girls tend to think.'

Chloe extracted herself from me and nodded, sniffling. 'Okay. I'll read the books. Maybe it'll help me understand why Simon acts like an arseho— I mean a jerk,' she corrected herself.

'Well, if my book doesn't help, maybe I can?' I offered.

Chloe looked up at me, the doubts still lingering on her face. 'Guys aren't like they used to be, Mum,' she explained. 'They're shallow, mean and inconsiderate…'

'Not all of them, sweetheart. One day you'll meet one who will change your mind about the male gender completely.'

Of course I didn't believe it either, but if you couldn't have hope for something, what else did we have to live for? Besides, thirteen was way too young to be jaded and disillusioned.

A week later, Jack swung by with a huge grin. After we'd chatted for a while, he said, 'Nina, I have a solution for you.'

'Please, no charity,' I begged. 'No loans, no help.'

'Agreed. I won't help you. But you have to help me.'

'With what?'

'I am considering a business idea, but I can't do it alone. I'll put in the capital, and you help with the legwork. What do you say?'

'I'm listening.'

'You know the cider side of the business is doing well.'

'Yes?'

'And I'm breaking into the apple crisp market, too, now.'

'That's wonderful, Jack! Your parents would be so proud of you.'

He grinned shyly. 'I'd like to think so. But my real apple passion is about pies.'

'Pies?'

'Yeah. Big pies, bite-sized – everything. I'm thinking about getting into the market. I've already made a business plan and everything and the numbers are promising. But there's one not so minor thing.'

'Being?'

He grinned. 'I can't bake to save myself. Would you teach me?'

'You want to bake the pies yourself?'

'Initially, yes. My kitchen is massive but I only use it for my apple experiments. If things go well…'

'Of course I'll teach you, Jack. It's the simplest thing in the world.'

'Thank you. I know it's a silly request, but I'd like to be able to make my own product, like you do with your *arancini*.'

'Shit!' I swore as I jumped to my feet. I had been enjoying his company so much I had completely and utterly forgotten to prep! I ran to the freezer to peer inside. Luckily I had the ingredients in stock: rice, minced meat, peas, eggs, breadcrumbs and tomato sauce. All I lacked was the willpower.

Jack rolled up his sleeves and washed his hands under the kitchen tap. 'Come on, Nina. I'll help you.'

'But you don't know how to shape them.'

'You're welcome.'

I laughed. 'You want to help me by squishing raw meat and egg yolk between your fingers?'

'Yeah.'

'Okay, then. You start out with a sheet of rice on the palm of your hand, curving it gently inwards so as to make the bottom side of a pear.'

'I thought they were called *arancini* because they looked like oranges?' he asked as he gently patted the rice in his huge hands according to my instructions.

'Those are the ones with the mozzarella and cheese filling. These ones are peas, eggs and ragù sauce.'

'Is this the right shape?' Jack asked after we had worked in silence for a few minutes. 'It looks a bit wonky…'

'Your hand pressure is slightly too strong.' I covered his hands – or tried to; they were like shovels – with mine in order to close the *arancino*. 'You have to make sure that you don't squeeze too much when you shape your rice ball. Apply more pressure at the end, but don't squeeze the tip too much. You want it to look like a rounded pyramid, see? Plus, you don't want to flatten the poor thing.'

He grinned. 'No, we wouldn't want that. How am I doing now?'

'Perfect,' I said.

He looked up and smiled again. 'Christ, I thought it would be easier.'

'Jack?'

'Hm?'

'Thank you. So so much.'

'For what?'

'For being you. You are our knight in shining armour.'

He smiled. A smile that went deeper than teeth and dimples. 'My pleasure.'

The next day I got a call from the United States – precisely from Dr Ellenberg's surgery in Los Angeles. I had an appointment for next month. Did I wish to confirm?

To say I had forgotten about it would be untrue. But that had been a long long time ago when I had a perspective on having the means to afford it.

'Or do you want to cancel?'

If the doctor in Normandy didn't work out, did I want to completely cancel my son's dreams of being able to run across the back fields? Never. Even if I didn't know how the hell I was going to pay for it? The flights, the consultancy, the hotel. But I knew that, one way or another, I'd manage to sort it out. I had to.

And then I started worrying all over again. What if it didn't work, and I'd brought my boy all the way across the ocean only to disappoint him?

In a parallel universe, it would have been so nice to have Luke meet me at the airport, drive me there in his black convertible, the wind in my hair again, a big ol' smile on Ben's face as we drove back from the appointment to his home where Jessica and Chloe would be waiting for us, snuggled up in front of The Disney Channel.

But that was then and this was now. I still had Normandy. Better to play with two decks of cards and keep both possibilities.

'No, please don't,' I begged her. Either way, I'd sort him out. Even if I had to sell the shirt off my back.

'Of course. Have a great day!' she said and rang off.

'Yeah,' I said to the ether. 'You have a great day, too.'

Later, I swung by the Post Of ice for some crumpets. Stephen Nanfan was there, talking to Alf at the counter.

'And of course everyone knows Jack's sweet on Emma.'

I leaned back against the crumpet shelf. Jack… and Emma? There it was, that tiny, minuscule seed of suspicion that had always been there, in the back of my mind, although I had never even wanted to think it, let alone say it. And now I had to hear it from Alf?

I felt left out, if not betrayed. What they did behind closed doors was their affair. But they could at least have been honest about the relationship. The Three's Company joke had always been just that – a joke. So why were they playing silly buggers? They had both changed drastically in the last couple of months, since Luke had arrived, actually. I guess that my being busy with him had forced Jack and Emma into an intimacy they hadn't seen coming and bam. It all fitted perfectly – the embarrassed silences, their secret rendezvous in Truro. Now all the invisible pieces had fallen into place.

The next day Alice came over for coffee and a catch-up on my work. She was as annoyed as I was that Luke had gone AWOL. It seemed to me lately that men just couldn't be trusted. Every time I went near one, it was a disaster. Better single, in the end.

'And not one word about the script?' Alice asked me when I told her about my worries about Ben and about Luke's messages (or lack of) over the past months.

'Not a word about anything. I know he's busy and frustrated, but *Jesus…*'

'Of course, you should sue him if he doesn't come back by the end of the month,' Alice suggested.

'Sue him? Why on earth would I do that?'

'Because he's in breach of contract. You have to protect yourself, Nina.'

I lowered my head. 'I just thought… I wanted to be able to finally trust someone.'

'Oh, honey, don't we all? But this is unacceptable, running off from a job – and you – like that without a word except for cursory texts.'

'Alice, you know what happened. His wife threatened to take his daughter away. He could really lose her. He needs time and space.' Or so I kept telling myself.

She sighed. 'We all have problems, Nina. And I sympathise, even if his decision is affecting me as well, long-term. But he has responsibilities he can't just shake off. Every day that goes by without that script loses us money.'

I knew she was right. She was the money side of everything. But sometimes, I wished she understood that it wasn't always about the money. What about love, dreams, pride, honour, hope and happiness? Was there really no room left for such things in our modern-day, hectic, vain lives?

But as much as I hated to admit it, Alice was right in a way. Luke had behaved like Phil, leaving me hanging in a hot mess. Granted, Luke had no responsibility towards my children but he did to our project. I didn't want to rock the boat with demands I wasn't quite sure I had a right to make. On the sentimental level, at least. But work-wise, Alice was right. I had to protect my family's future.

'Especially after he stopped us from making the deal with Ben. We'd practically be in production by now if it wasn't for Luke.'

I shrugged, unsure of what to say. She did have a point, but this entire showbiz thing was definitely not for me.

'Nina, face it, he's gone, and what has he given you in return?'

I was silent. 'It's not like the project is dead. He told me to keep writing in his absence.'

Silence.

'What, you don't think I can do it?' I asked.

'Of course I do. But you're not Hollywood. We need Luke's name – and money – to back us up.'

I knew she was right. Three *Sunday Times* bestsellers did not a scriptwriter make.

'I'm calling Ben Stein.'

'What? No.'

'Why not? He wanted that movie badly. I'm sure he'll gladly take it off Luke's hands.'

'But that's unethical!' I cried.

'Unethical? Honey, you need to wake up and smell the coffee here. Luke is – make no mistake – in breach of contract. If you sue him, not only do you get a settlement, but you could still get a new deal with Ben Stein.'

'I don't like it, Alice…'

'Nonsense. It's a win-win situation. What's not to like?'

'What about the clauses? Wasn't there something in the contract about delays?'

'Yes, but not regarding delays this long, Nina. It's been months now.'

Sue Luke? I could never do that to him. Even if he could afford it and I was in desperate need. My mind simply didn't work that way.

She huffed. 'Did he promise you anything?'

'Like what?'

'A ring?'

'A ring? Of course not, we've only just met.'

'Well, then make sure he returns and gives you one. Either that or the contract. You can't be left empty-handed.'

I groaned. 'Alice, I can't think like you. Can we just drop this for now?'

'For now,' she conceded. 'But it will rear its ugly head again before you know it.'

While I was wrapping up my next batch of *arancini*, all two hundred of them, my mobile phone went. Chloe was at Chanel's and Ben was with Jack, working on their secret project, so I didn't have to worry about them.

But then I saw it was Jack's number. 'Mum!' Ben cried.

I clutched the phone, already horrid thoughts of disasters flooding my mind. Was there another fire? 'Ben, what is it?'

'Can you come over, Mum? It's ready!'

I sagged in relief. For once it wasn't a broken nose or a fractured collarbone. 'What is?'

'Our project, Mum! You have to come and see it. We're in the warehouse!'

'I'll be right over,' I promised, smiling to myself. He sounded so happy. I grabbed my keys, the cake I'd made for Jack to thank him for his kindness towards Ben, a shawl, a jacket for Ben and then finally pushed my feet into my wellies before letting myself out the door.

Up ahead, the setting sun had smeared the sky with lashes of pink and purple. Ah, sometimes it really was the free things that gave us pleasure in life. I wished Jessica could see this. I wished Luke could see it as well.

As it turned out, the surprise was nothing small. It was humongous, covered with an olive green tarpaulin. Ben jumped around, almost tripping as Jack steadied him. 'You ready, mate?'

Ben nodded eagerly. 'Ready!'

I looked back and forth between the two of them, wondering if they had gone completely mad.

'Now, you know that Ben has been working on this for months now,' Jack said.

'Yes, yes, unveil it already!' I cried, as excited as Ben, if not more. For months now, my baby had spent all his afternoons working on something for me.

Jack walked up to the edge of the tarpaulin. 'Here goes!' he cried, and yanked it down.

I stepped back, ready to faint.

36

Triangle

'**M**um! Mum! You okay?'

'Nina, are you all right?'

I opened and closed my mouth. 'How… where… did you *get* this?' I cried as I looked upon a large vehicle, something between a van and a trailer. It was bright red, green and white, like the Italian flag, with a sign that read *Nina's Arancini.*

'Like it, Mum? It's your brand-new food truck! No more cooking for restaurants for you!'

I hugged Ben to me, feeling the flood of tears gushing down my cheeks and into my mouth. 'Oh, it's absolutely gorgeous!' I bawled, and Ben jumped up and down on his longer leg, clapping his hands in glee, his face bright red with joy.

'Well, not brand-new, really,' Jack confessed. 'It's what was left of your trailer, remember?'

I gasped. 'Oh, my God, Jack! And you've kept it all these years?'

He blushed. 'Sorry it took so long, but Ben and I had, uhm… artistic differences.'

'Ohhh,' I cried as I grabbed them both, smothering them with kisses. 'Thank you, thank you, thank you so much, guys! I'd have never been able to do this by myself! I wouldn't have even thought of it!'

They led the way into the food truck and showed me the cooker, the deep fryer and the work surface, along with the fridge and all the clever shelving.

'And now you can sell your *arancini* and keep the profit for yourself instead of giving more than half of it to those greedy restaurant owners who pass your little miracles off as their own!' Jack said.

I stepped back and beamed at them as I patted their hair down and restored their clothing to their initial position.

'You two have made me the proudest, happiest woman alive.'

Jack stuffed his hands into his pockets. 'Thank Ben – he did all the hard grafting.'

I hunkered down and took Ben's hands in mine, and he sobered, understanding the importance of what I was about to say.

'Never,' I said, swallowing back my tears, 'has a mother ever been so proud of her son, as I am of you, my darling Ben. But even without this marvellous, selfless gift, you would still be the best son a woman could ever pray for. You and Chloe are the reason I live.'

He looked at me for a long moment, and then threw his arms around my neck with all his might. I kissed his baby cheeks over and over again, aware in the background that Jack was swiping at his cheek nonchalantly.

And after we all had our sob session, I stood up and wiped my eyes, laughing like a lunatic. 'I'm calling Truro town hall for a licence tomorrow, and I'm quitting the restaurants! And you two are going to be my first guests!'

'Already done,' Jack informed me. 'You can get out there for tomorrow if you want.'

'You didn't!'

'I did. Hey, where are you going?' he said as I headed for the door.

'To type a letter of resignation to the Poldark Tours company!' I called over my shoulder. 'Come on, we're going to celebrate!'

I invited Jack over for the afternoon, just so we could take our time talking, but he insisted on helping me make dinner.

It was still so strange, having him back in the house again, but it also felt right, as if the very house was exhaling in relief, and telling him, both with its silences and sounds, that it had been waiting for him to come back. And he listened to it in return, his eyes meeting mine.

'It's so good to have you back, Jack,' I whispered. 'It just wasn't the same without you. It was quite rubbish. Absolute shit, in fact.'

Even Minnie and Callie monopolised him by lying each on one of his feet as he sat working away at the table. He should have never disappeared from our lives in the first place, and I wanted him to know that.

His eyes crinkled as he smiled, and I thanked our lucky stars.

As promised, the next day I went over to Jack's to teach

him to bake an apple pie, as it was the least I could do for him.

When I got there, he was already at the kitchen island, surrounded by every known cooking ingredient and implement his mum had ever owned. His kitchen was amazing, with all the proper copper pots hanging above, and a triple oven and a fridge the size of my entire kitchen.

'Hey, right on time,' he said as I put my keys down on the counter. 'The oven is pre-heating and the kettle is boiling.'

'What's the kettle for?'

'Coffee,' he answered. 'You don't expect me to bake without any caffeine in me, do you?'

'Okay, I'll make it,' I offered, busying myself. When I looked up, he was sticking his head through one of his mum's old aprons – precisely one with a Toile de Jouy pattern.

To see a man like Jack, who was six feet, had a permanent five o'clock shadow and shoulders the size of a Bentley, wearing such a dainty little number was just too much and I bent over in a fit of giggles, nearly spilling our coffees as tears slid down my face.

'Wha-at…?' he said, laughing along as he took a sip. 'I find it rather suits me, don't you think?'

I wiped my eyes, paused to look at him once more, and started giggling all over again.

'Laugh it up,' he chuckled, shaking his head. 'It's easy for you to talk. There's nothing you can't cook, while I don't know how this kitchen is still standing.'

'I told you, it's easy. Here,' I said, bumping him aside with my hip. 'Watch the real experts at work. The first thing is your filling. Have you got your apples ready?'

'Has the Pope got a Bible? Fresh from the orchard,' he assured me, sweeping a large hand over his bounty of colloget pippins covering the opposite end of the island.

'Might have been useful to start peeling them, you lazy toad,' I said, reaching for a knife. 'Or at least peel them and put them in water so they don't oxidise.'

He grinned. 'I like it when you talk dirty, Nina.'

'Come on, you, start peeling,' I said, and soon we fell into companionable silence as we worked through the mountain of apples.

'Christ, how many do we need for one pie?'

'We should make more than one. Try different sizes and stuff,' I said. 'Now you add just a touch of sugar, a bit of cinnamon – at least that's the way I do it. And you can freeze the filling for next time, too. That's the beauty of it. Where's your flour?'

He put his knife down and looked at me in panic. 'Shit.'

I laughed. 'I'll go home and get mine. I always have some on hand.'

'No, let me check the pantry,' he said, wiping his huge hands on the tiny apron and I wanted to laugh all over again as he filled the entire pantry with his person, looking like a giant in a dollhouse as he rummaged around the top shelf, knocking over boxes and jars in the meantime. 'Got it!'

'Check the expiration date.'

His eyebrows shot up. 'Flour expires?'

'Usually when the weevils arrive, yeah.'

He stuck his head in the bag. 'No weevils in here.'

'You sure? Then we're good to go. Sieve?'

He joined me back at the island, where I showed him

how to dice the butter and, using only his fingertips, mix in the flour. 'You need to be very delicate so the butter doesn't heat up.'

'Like this?' he asked dubiously, his huge fingers gently plucking the flour and butter.

'Perfect. Now pull it all together into one big lump and gently knead it. Like this,' I said, taking over as he sat on the stool and observed me.

'You watching carefully?' I prompted.

'Huh? I was actually looking at your hands. They're so tiny.'

'Says the Jolly Green Giant. Yours could whack a man back to yesterday. Then you take your rolling pin and even out your pastry. Depending on the diameter of your pie, you thin it out accordingly so you don't get paper-thin wagon wheels or tiny pies that are so thick you can't even eat them. Here, have a go.'

'Like this?' he asked as he delicately spread the pastry out.

'Hey, you're actually good at this. Sure you've never done it before?'

'No, but I used to watch my mum.'

Next, we filled our pies and I taught him to crimp the edges with a twist of my fingers. It was funny how many things were second nature to me but presented a problem to him. Anyway, his hands were too big. 'I'll get you a crimper to make it easier for you.'

When we had made enough shapes and sizes to fill both ovens, we bunged them in and set the timer, bearing in mind that the tiny pies only need a few minutes, so we placed them at the front of the oven.

'Satisfied?' I asked, as we knelt to the floor to peer through the glass door, his head level with mine.

'Absolutely chuffed, Nina. Thank you.' He turned to me, his eyes twinkling and crinkling at the corners. I had never noticed that they were actually a dark hazel, and not brown. And there was an inner ring of golden flecks just around the pupil. The things you could see up close. How had I managed to spend all these years in his company and never notice that?

And why, all of a sudden, did any of that matter? Why, after three years, were his good looks and charm having such an effect on me now, of all times? How had I never noticed that he was so manly, sexy but at the same time impish and adorable? It had to be the dimples bracketing his lips. When he smiled they danced like... April showers in a ray of sunlight.

'I couldn't have done it without you,' he continued as he moved in to kiss my cheek, but at the same time I turned my head, and his lips accidentally smacked mine in a kiss. I froze for a moment, suddenly unsettled.

'Oops, sorry!' I then tittered, but he was looking solemnly, deeply into my eyes as if searching for something, his eyes darting to my lips, and before I knew what he was about, he took my head in his hands, and with an urgency I never knew he was capable of, caught my mouth in a long, deep, utterly delicious and knicker-melting kiss. Dizziness and confusion overwhelmed me as my heart hammered its way up into my head, which was swimming in naughty, naughty sensations.

All I wanted was his mouth on mine forever, and his arms around me. What was happening to us?

I hung on to him as the room spun like mad.

'Nina,' he whispered against my lips between our kisses. 'Stay with me. I love you…'

I love you, too, Jack! I wanted to cry. I also wanted him to take me upstairs. But I fought against my instincts and wrestled myself back to sanity. *Stay with him? He loved me?* How could he even say such nonsense, and how could I even contemplate the idea when he was secretly involved with Emma? I couldn't do that to her. It would break her heart all over again! What was the matter with me? And Jack? I knew he'd been a bit of a playboy in the past, but how could he think he could play with me and Emma like that? Where was the respect for her – and me? This was not the Jack I knew.

I sat up and pushed him away softly, and he instantly let go as if I'd slapped him. 'Please don't do that again, Jack, if you value our friendship.'

He sat back, lowering his eyes. 'I'm sorry,' he whispered solemnly, like a little boy being reprimanded by his headmaster.

I would never want to ruin a friendship because of a kiss, so I cleared my throat and whispered back, 'Then let's just forget it ever happened, okay?'

He ran a hand through his dark curls that had grown back, nodding as he stood up – 'Okay…' he finally croaked, holding out his other hand to help me to my feet, which was fortunate as I was still shaking. The contact with his body sent my hormones – if not my dignity – in sudden overdrive, and I had to step back.

This was ridiculous. This was Jack in front of me, my best male friend, who had saved my life and whom I'd shared meals with more times than I could ever count. He was like a brother to me, having seen me in every guise, from my pyjamas to my work clothes, to my tear-smudged make-up on a bad day, and even in hair rollers once, and I had never thought about it twice. So now, how could this happen so suddenly, that I wanted him to continue? How could I ever justify it to myself, let alone Emma?

I needed to put some distance between us, because it had been all too sudden, as if I'd just noticed his physical and inner beauty entwined for the first time ever. Because of the man that he was on the inside. I would be attracted to him even if he wasn't so beautiful. And now that I had made this new discovery, how to ignore it, for the sake of our friendship with Emma? She had finally found a dependable man who would be there for her every day of the week. I couldn't interfere with that. Nor did I want to be his bit on the side. And he had even said he loved me. Could a man love two women? And, more to the point, could a woman love two men? Whichever way I looked at it, there was heart-break ahead.

'I think I'd better go, now,' I whispered.

He nodded.

I cleared my throat again. 'Keep, uhm, an eye on the smaller pies and bring them out as soon as they turn golden.'

If I hadn't stopped him… if I hadn't stopped myself… just what would have happened between us? Had we both suddenly gone mad? What about Luke? Although I had lost any hope in that dog's dinner of a relationship, had I actually given up on him?

37

Dazed And Confused

As I tried to go about my busy day the next morning, I was still in a zombie-like state after a night of tossing and turning, reliving that deliciously decadent kiss over and over again.

This was supposed to be the beginning of the rest of my independent life, and yet, I couldn't stop thinking about his hot mouth on mine, and the way we instantly responded to each other. I had only seen that kind of stuff in the movies and certainly had never ever thought I would experience such an intense, real moment like that myself. How messed up was he, as well? I bet he was regretting that moment of madness now, too. But he didn't have to worry – his secret was safe with me. Besides, who would ever believe me? *I* didn't even believe it.

For a brief moment, we had been in a bubble of our own, where responsibility towards others and morality didn't exist. It had just been Jack and myself, where he represented the centre and the borders of my consciousness, where nothing mattered but the scent of his skin and the banked strength vibrating in his body, the sparkle in his eyes and the warmth of his proximity.

Like most women, I had never been indifferent to Jack's good looks and charm, but never had I thought it even remotely possible that he could be interested in me. Deep down, beyond the running Three's Company joke, I always knew it would have eventually been Emma, and that it was only a question of time until they sorted themselves out. And nowhere did I see myself in that equation. Even now that his lips were still burning on mine, it made no sense. He and Emma were an item. The kiss, however naughty and arousing, had been just that – an instinct, felt by a lonely woman kneeling on a flagstone kitchen floor inches away from a sexy man. End of.

So I shook the thought out of my head and concentrated on reality as I parked my food truck on the Belvedere overlooking the sea.

I sighed deeply, wistfully, regretfully, trying to get the luxurious sensation of him out of my head, and like an automaton, flicked my generator on and pulled out my deep fryer. I had five hundred *arancini* ready to fry upon request, plus another fifty sweet ones containing Nutella, my recent invention. Financially, thanks to Jack, I was home free. Plus, I'd already committed to writing my fourth novel in the evenings.

To think that this same vehicle had let me down, burning all our worldly possessions and leaving us practically homeless – and now, more than three years later, it represented our rebirth. A new chance in life. If, as it now was apparent, the movie wasn't going to be made, at least I had a proper business to keep my children's bellies and minds full of good things. Anything for my kids. I could do this.

All thanks to Jack. He was a good man. Perhaps a bit confused himself, but a good man. If Emma and he had not been an item, and if Luke hadn't left me heart-broken… maybe we could have had something good. Even though entrusting myself yet again to another man's sensitivity, to be emotionally involved and to involve my children, and allow them to once again invest their own fragile hearts and affections in someone who wasn't their father, only to be disappointed and hurt all over again, was not something I could stand. I was still trying to get over Luke. Which would take me a very long time. You don't just touch the sky and forget about it immediately.

But Jack's kiss, I had to admit, had stirred within me feelings that I had thought long buried. But his words: *Stay with me. I love you*? They could have turned everyone's world upside down. I had done the right thing, on one hand. But on the other, I wished I hadn't fled. I wished I had let him explain what was happening to him, but I didn't want to be party to anything against Emma. She was like a sister to me, and Jack – he must have been in a very fragile place, too. That was the only explanation I could understand. Because Jack couldn't really be in love with me. Not with the way he'd been carrying on with Emma. They were exact opposites, yes, but made for each other. Maybe it was better that way.

'Can I get a Nutella *arancino*, please?' said a voice above me and I looked up, my heart ba-booming like a fire-cracker factory. It couldn't be. *Impossible.* But there he was, leaning on my little counter with his enormous baby blues, Luke O'Hara, his usual larger-than-life self.

'Oh my God!' I cried. 'What the hell are you doing here?' So much for the glamorous leading lady acting out her memorable lines, because, for the life of me, I couldn't remember what I had planned to say if he were ever to return. Not that I had expected him to, given his state of incommunicado-ness.

He threw his head back and laughed. 'Awh, Nina! I really, *really* missed you.'

I shrugged, my pride keeping me from melting at his feet like he expected me to, no doubt. What should you say when your male lead ditches you for who knows how long, without so much as a phone call for months on end, but only lawyer bulletins? And when you've been pretty naughty yourself? Glad you agree.

'Piss off, I'm busy,' I said as I checked my fryer again.

He raised his hands. 'Look, honey, I know you're angry—'

I whirled around in the cramped space that was at least my own. Angry? Did wanting to throw all my *arancini* at him mean I was angry? Then yes, I was absolutely furious.

'Why did you never answer my texts?' I demanded. 'Three months, you kept me waiting with nothing more than your legal bulletins!'

'I'm not very text-friendly.'

'Not very text-friendly? I had to ask Chloe for updates from Jess, for Christ's sake!'

'I'm sorry. I was in a bad place.'

'So was I. I had no idea what was going on, whether it was good news, or bad.'

'It's all good news, Nina,' he assured me. 'The battle is ongoing, but my lawyers assure me that there is no way in hell that Lauren is getting Jessica.'

I stopped, stunned. 'What? How can they be so sure?'

He grinned. 'Because no judge in the world would award full custody to a parent who abandoned their kid.'

I gasped.

'Don't make that face, Nina,' he said. 'I'm fighting for my daughter, here. You'd do the same if it were for Ben and Chloe.'

'Of course, absolutely,' I said. I'd do anything to protect my kids. Just like my heroine in my books. And speaking of books... 'Are you here to finish the script?' I asked tentatively.

He grinned. 'Everything is back on. You, me and the script.'

Oh, thank God! I couldn't begin to tell you how relieved I was inside. Immediately our lives turned sunny again, and I actually saw Dr Ellenberg's face in my mind's eye. But what about us? Did he really mean what he had said? Was there even an us at all, after his absence, and after Jack's kiss?

Jack was a mistake, said The Voice of Reason inside me. *A momentary lapse of reason.*

So you're just going to forgive Luke and fall into his arms like nothing happened? argued the other side of me. *Ladies,* I begged. *Please. There will be no falling into any man's arms.* Inside me there was a riot, but on the outside, I managed to stay cool.

'Nice truck you've got yourself,' he observed.

I shrugged, not feeling the need to hurry and explain everything to him. If he'd missed out on things happening in my life, it was his fault.

'But you won't need this little gimmick once your royalties start flooding in.'

I was silent, still trying to shush the two women arguing inside my brain.

'Okay, I can see I have a lot of ice to break. I deserve it. Now how about an *arancino*? They look delicious.'

'I am so confused,' I confessed to Alice when she swung by the house the following afternoon. I had told her about Luke's return and everything about Jack, holding back nothing. I needed a friend and I certainly couldn't confide in Emma. To have someone love you was a gift. But to have two men interested was pure danger to one's soul. What if I had made the wrong choice, and had got involved in a triangle with my two best friends? How had I even got myself into this situation?

'Did he ever use the word "love"?' Alice asked.

'Yes. He told me he loved me. But how can he if he's seeing Emma?'

Alice studied me. 'I was talking about Luke, not Jack.'

'Oh. Yes, of course.'

But when Jack had told me the same, albeit in a fleeting moment of passion, and even if it had caused a moment of guilt towards Emma, and panic, it had warmed me down to my very soul.

And I knew that he also loved the kids. And just then, it dawned on me that Jack always referred to them as "the kids", whilst Luke always said "your kids".

'So what are you gonna do?' she asked.

'Nothing. Live my life. Write the script. Get Ben's op sorted. These are the things that count most to me.'

But in truth, I was mind-blown. Never in my life had I

thought I'd be in this quandary. To have no man under my roof for years, during the darkest, most difficult period of my life, and then suddenly, out of the blue, to have two paths ahead of me, albeit the one with Jack fraught with guilt? Emma would never get over it, especially as she had been hiding it from me for so long. How could she ever forgive me for technically beating her at her own game? It was something I just couldn't do to her.

And Jack? How confused was he, if he was sleeping with her, and kissing me? He was never one to act lightly, nor was he one to throw around the word love, so I knew it had to have been the heat of the moment. What he had with Emma had been going on for quite a while now.

And Luke? He was great on so many levels. He loved my work and had opened the door to success for me.

But then again, Jack had everything that Luke lacked. He was thoughtful, kind and sexy as hell without Luke's glamour, pretentiousness or dominating attitude. Jack was dependable, quieter than Luke and very soulful, although he could be a real pain when he wanted to as well. Once offended, he did not easily forgive. And yet, he was not for me. Because you couldn't fall in love with two men.

Luke was the one for me, no doubt. He had opened up a whole new world to me, given me the confidence to reach for the stars, given me the chance to earn enough to not fear for my children's future, for their education and Ben's leg.

But to become a stranger again to Jack? I had barely survived his absence the first time. He was a take it or leave it kind of bloke. If I got back with Luke again, there was no way Jack and I could ever be real friends again. But I needed him, *wanted* him in our lives. And the kids adored him as well. So enough. I had given that accidental kiss way too much thought.

Yes, that was what it was, a silly moment of weakness, never to be repeated. Jack would get on with Emma and hopefully they would finally announce they were an item, and I could then put all this behind me.

After Alice left, Chloe came into the kitchen and flopped into a chair, her head in her hands.

'Sweetheart, what's wrong?'

'I'm confused, Mum. Chanel still wants me to choose between her and Jessica as my best friend, but I love them both. Who do I choose?'

Terrific question. But at least she had a way out.

'Why do you have to choose? Can't you have them both?'

'Jess is really cool and has taught me to be a better person, I think.'

I smiled and caressed her head, 'You have changed, Chloe.'

'Because I've seen how hard Jess has it, even of she's being very strong about her parents. Plus she knows the kids of half the celebrities that count. Do you know that she knows Will Smith's daughter? And then there's Chanel, who's like a sister to me. We've been together through thick and thin. When you and Dad split up, she was there to pick me up all the way. When I broke my arm, she was the one who brought me all my homework and didn't go to the school trips or dances just to stay with me. How can I forget that?'

She had a point. Do you choose the new, passionate and exciting person who is bound to take you places and heights you'd never seen, or do you choose the stable, loving and caring one who would rather hurt themselves than you?

Chloe's Chanel was my Jack, steadfast and true, whilst her Jessica was my Luke, new and exciting. But in friendship, you were permitted to have more than one person. In love, not quite so.

'I say talk to her, and tell her that you can't choose because you love them both. If she loves you as much as I think she does, she'll accept it.'

'At least you've got it right,' Chloe said.

'What do you mean, sweetie?'

'Well, at first, I thought there was hope for you and Dad,' she admitted. 'But then I met Tracy, who is not exactly Einstein, but she loves him and she makes him laugh. You and Dad never used to laugh together, he said.'

We used to, before the kids were born, but I wasn't going to put the blame on them. It wasn't their fault if I had grown out of Phil.

'Sweetie, your father and I… we were too young when we got married. And after we had you and Ben, we continued to grow, each in our own way. And in opposite directions. Do you understand?'

Chloe nodded. 'I do now. Like I've grown out of Simon. Now I can see what a toss— uhm, jerk he is. Mum, all these years I've blamed you for the end of the marriage because Dad kept saying all sorts of bad things about you, like you didn't care about us. But I see every day that you do, much more than he ever has. You are the one who talks to us about our future, who cheers us up when we're down, and who tells us to not chew with our mouths open and to brush our teeth. Not Dad. You should see the pigsty his flat is, Mum. He doesn't care about himself, let alone us. I now see that you were meant to be happy with someone else.'

'And who might that be?' I asked cautiously.

She rolled her eyes. 'Come on, Mum, even the flagstones know the answer to that question.'

Dinner had been delicious that evening. Chanel was downstairs with Chloe and Ben and Jess, all watching TV. It had been a gloriously sunny day and they were now exhausted and as the sun had gone down I'd fed them dinner on trays and wrapped a soft throw over their legs, and scattered it with mini Cadburys. I loved to spoil them when I could. And the look on Chanel's face as I patted her shoulder was priceless.

As I was doing the washing up and pondering on having a chat with Emma – provided I could do the entire Avoiding The Pink Elephant In The Room thing – she rang me instead.

'Hi, it's me.'

'Hey, Me,' I chimed as I scrubbed the sticky bits off my oven dish.

'Listen, Nina, I have a huge favour to ask you.'

'Shoot,' I said.

'I'm going to be busy… tonight.'

I'd been right about Jack after all. It had been only a moment's madness. Everything was once again how it should be. 'That's great, Emma.'

'Would you mind terribly keeping Chanel with you? I'll come and pick her up in the morning. Tell her I had to go away for business or something.'

'Sure, no problem. Good luck with—' I bit my lip.

'Thanks. But I might not need it this time.' She laughed.

Of course not. She had every right to search for happiness in a new man.

I hung up and went back to my dishes, but I dropped one on the flagstone floor and it shattered to bits. I knelt down to pick up the pieces, silently bawling my eyes out.

38

Once Upon A Time In America

'I have news, Nina!' Luke said the next day, swinging me off my feet as soon as he came in, happy and flushed with excitement. 'Lauren's given up her claim to for custody! I get to keep my daughter!'

I clutched my chest, feeling it open with joy. 'Oh, Luke, that's amazing! I'm so happy for you! Oh, my God!' And suddenly my eyes welled with tears. He so so deserved to keep Jessica! He lived for her, and rightfully so. Lauren could never be to her what Luke was – father, mother, friend, mentor. Luke was Jessica's world.

I hugged him. 'Things are finally going your way, Luke, the way it should be. Now you don't have to worry about anything anymore. I'm so pleased, Luke!'

He held me close. 'Thank you! And now we can think about us!'

I pulled away to look up at him.

He took my hands. 'You have been very patient, but now it's your turn. I want you and the kids to come live with us in California. We'll get a new house, one that you actually like!'

I stared at him. 'You want us to move… to California? With you and Jess?'

'Yes, I do! We can finish the script there, sort Ben's leg out and enrol them into their new schools.'

'But… but… what about everything here? All our friends, the children's friends, and Northwood Academy?' I'd nearly killed myself to keep them there, and they loved it. How could I just let them leave it after all that?

'But I've found a fantastic new school for them, you'll see.'

He'd found a fantastic new school for my kids? There he went again, making my decisions for me. 'But… I can't do that to the kids. They'd miss Cornwall terribly. They're English through and through, and adapting to a new life would destabilise them, especially at this age…'

'Well, then why don't we take it in stages? Why don't you move for only, say a year? We'll see how it goes, and if they don't like it, you can come back.'

That was a very generous offer, despite my views on it. But where did it leave us, as a couple? He was asking me to go and live with him. I had made that mistake the first time with Phil. For my children, I needed to make the right decision this time.

'But if we don't like it and come back after a year, what does that mean for you and me, Luke?'

He frowned. 'I think by then that we'd know what was what. You wouldn't be my prisoner, Nina.'

Meaning that he wasn't asking me to marry him, thank God. But I had to ask myself if I truly was relieved. Had I expected more from him – a true commitment – or was it wiser to just go with the flow, move lock, stock and barrel to California, and be free to come back if it all went pear-shaped? I had already made that mistake of tying myself to a man and look how that had gone.

'What about Cornflower Cottage? And Minnie and Callie? Is there a quarantine? I couldn't put them through that.'

His smile faded as he took my hands. 'Nina, do you want to come with me or not? I'm offering you a life of luxury, free of financial worries and the best of everything. Are you seriously considering staying here? Think about the opportunities for your kids!'

'Yes, I know and I truly appreciate the offer. But there are some things I would need to do first. I want to sort out Ben's leg, and Chloe and Chanel are still having a difficult time in their friendship, and Emma still won't admit—'

I stopped myself as his eyebrows raised. 'You're right, you're right. The kids would benefit tremendously. But it's a huge decision, Luke, too big to make on two feet. Can I mull it over for a bit at least?'

He shook his head, but he was chuckling. 'That's what I love about you, Nina. Everyone else always comes before you. I've never known anyone as selfless as you.' He kissed me. 'Okay. Take some time to think about it – but not forever! I want to leave at the end of the month. Now get everyone ready – I've booked a restaurant for lunch. I want the kids to know and be part of this decision.'

But there was one thing I had to do first.

As Luke was showering upstairs, I called Jack's mobile. I needed to tell him in person, before anyone else found out. I owed him that much to say the least. And I needed to make sure he was still on my side.

'Come on, come on, pick up...' I begged, but voicemail kicked in. I took a deep breath and said, 'Hey, Jack, I need to talk to you, Can you call me back? Bye...'

That would at least give me some time to think of how to word it. And beg him to back me up, because I needed my friends.

When the doorbell rang, I was relieved to see it was him, and just in time. With Luke upstairs, minutes away from leaving for the restaurant where we would discuss it with the kids, I still had a tiny and distinct margin to save both Jack's and my own dignity while trying to do as little damage as possible to our friendship.

'Hey,' he said softly, eyeing me, sizing me up, wondering what could be so urgent when I had already told him to stay away in that sense.

I took a deep breath. It was time to make things clear for all of us, so we could hope to go back to the way we were. If that was even possible after that kiss.

'Luke's back...' I stammered, unable to look him in the eye. It was, oddly, as if I'd betrayed him in the worst way possible, when I knew that couldn't be further from the truth, because Jack had Emma.

He just stood there, dumbfounded. I wrung my hands, helpless. 'Jack, I told you, you need to – to forget about what happened between us.'

And that was when, like in the cheesiest of movies, Luke came whistling down the stairs. In his bathrobe, to boot, towelling his floppy hair dry.

'Hi, Jack!' he said cheerfully as I wanted to bury myself under the floorboards and die. 'Good to see you again. How are your apples doing?'

Both Jack and I stared at him.

'Good, thanks,' Jack answered politely, although I could see his jaw muscle twitching.

'Nina, did you tell him?' Luke asked as he threw the towel onto the back of the chair.

I bit my lip and shook my head, my eyes swinging to Jack's.

'We were gonna tell the kids tonight at dinner first, but what the hell, you're like family anyway, right? Can you believe our girl's agreed to move to California with me?'

Jack's eyes widened and his jaw tightened. 'Is this true, Nina?' he whispered.

'I haven't quite decided yet,' I stammered.

Luke put his arm around my neck and pulled me to him. 'You know Nina – always thinking about everyone else first,' he said. 'Naturally I'll sell my house and we'll choose a new one together.'

I could hear, rather than see, Jack's intake of breath. But his face remained completely impassive. He cleared his throat. 'Well, then it seems that congratulations are in order.'

'Thanks, man.'

And then Jack's eyes swung to me as he murmured, 'I hope you'll be happy, Nina…' And with that, he turned on his heel and marched out the door.

'Well, that oughta make things clear for him, once and for all,' Luke said.

'What?' I whispered.

'Oh, come on, Nina, the guy's gaga over you. All these years and you haven't noticed? You really are naïve.'

I cleared my throat. 'Naïve? Yes, it would seem so. There

was no need to say anything to Jack yet. I haven't even made my decision. We were supposed to discuss this over lunch with the kids. Plus there are so many things I want to do first, like finish my renovations with my movie royalties.'

'Sure, you can renovate your farmhouse and then sell it once you've decided to stay in California.'

'Whoa, what? Sell Cornflower Cottage? Why would I do that?'

He shrugged. 'Why would you need it? If you ever want to come back, there are tons of beautiful hotels.'

'But we agreed we'd try it first, for a year, did we not? I told you I don't know if I could raise the kids there.'

He shrugged. 'I did.'

'But I can't! Chloe and Ben were born and bred here. I can't just drag them across the world.'

'But I can do that to Jessica?'

I bristled. 'No. Of course not. But is it my fault if I prefer Cornwall to California? Holywell Bay to Hollywood?'

He chuckled. 'You'll change your mind.'

I moved away. 'I don't think so, Luke.'

'Nina, think of all that they'd be gaining in LA. A mansion, great schools, the best restaurants.'

'And absolutely no heritage. We both know Hollywood is dubbed Tinseltown. And FYI, we have amazing schools here. Northwood is number one in the Southwest and we have museums, heritage sites, excellent restaurants. And culture, loads of it.'

'So? Hollywood's an industry, a business like any other. Which, incidentally, has changed your life.'

Maybe so, but I hadn't as of yet seen a single penny from his production company.

'Yes, but I don't want it to change my life that much.'

He sighed. 'Nina – if you come with me, your life is going to change for the better. Accept it and let's move on, okay?'

For the better? With this weight on my heart, how did I even know that?

At the Post Of ice for a packet of crumpets, I parked and yanked on the brakes lever so hard I almost pulled it out.

'Evening,' I sighed to Alf as I approached the counter.

'Evenin' Emma!' he greeted me. I eyed him. He seemed all right, though.

Deirdre saw me from her ice cream parlour across the street and hurried over. 'Hullo, pet,' she said breathless. 'Alf here seems to think that Jack is doing the right thing. What do you think?'

'About what?' I asked as I pulled some mint candies off the rack. Let him be with Emma, if he wanted. I was sick and tired of all this subterfuge.

'About going. We all think he's barmy. Don't you?'

I turned around. 'Going? Going where?'

'To London. You didn't know?'

I shook my head. 'No. When's he coming back?'

Deirdre removed her glasses. 'Well, pet. I suppose never. He's accepted an offer on Crooked Hill.'

I almost dropped my mints. 'What? He can't! His place is here! It was his great, great-grandfather's!'

'We think so, too, pet. But he's not having any of it. He's moving to London. Got a fancy engineering job there already.'

London? That was a whole world away!

'The lad is definitely moving on with his life,' Alf said.

'But… but… he always said he was happy here!' I countered. 'That this was his place!' And moreover, what about Emma? He was leaving her, too? Or was she going and didn't want to tell me? Chanel would have said. How complicated relationships were. Why couldn't we all just be honest with each other?

'I don't know what to tell you, Nina,' Deirdre said, shaking her head.

'Why didn't you tell me Jack was moving to London?' I asked Emma on speakerphone as I drove back home in a panic.

'Because he asked me not to, Nina.'

'What? Why? Am I so out of our circle that I'm supposed to find out he's gone only if I go over there and ring the doorbell?'

'Not that you would,' she said. 'Seeing as you're so wrapped up in your script and your actor boyfriend.'

'What's that supposed to mean?'

'That you no longer have time for anyone anymore. He has totally enwrapped you in his charm, and all you can think about is that bloody script.'

'That bloody script, as you call it, is my one chance at getting out of the mess my life is in! I can't afford Ben's surgery unless we make this movie. So you'll all have to forgive me if my priority is my son!'

'What about us?' she said.

'Us? You pretty much have all moved on from our friendship. You have secrets you don't trust me with and Jack hasn't even bothered to tell me he's moving away.'

'Because you don't deserve our confidence!' she cried. 'You are not the same person we used to know.'

'What's that supposed to mean? I only want you to be happy, Emma.'

She snorted as she inhaled.

'Oh, Em! You haven't started smoking again…?'

'You know what, Nina? Get off my back!'

'Em, what's happening to you?'

'I am sick and tired of everything, and I'm sick and tired of you!' she shouted and I listened to her angry breathing. Was this really the end of a long friendship?

Once home, I wiped my eyes and stuffed my hands into my pockets as I marched up the road to Crooked Hill Farm.

Jack's SUV wasn't there, nor was there any sign he'd slept at home, as all the shutters were closed. He always opened them first thing in the morning. Was he ill? I hated to think he was inside, sprawled on the floor or in bed, unable to help himself, so I called him on my mobile. And on the third ring, he hung up. Okay. He wasn't in the mood for any conversation. But if he had made a mistake, it was only right that I should clear the air with my friends – leaving out, of course, Jack and my little moment of weakness.

So the next morning, I baked some Peace Muffins and drove to Truro to see Emma, hoping she'd calmed down a bit. If she was working with a client, I'd wait in a café or something. On the way, I thought about Jack, and his kiss. How could he do that to his best friends, kiss me while he was seeing her?

I parked in front of Emma's flat and was about to call her when the front door opened, and out came Jack, still throwing his shirt on. His hair was sticking out in every direction and there was a look of bed in his eyes. I sank back against the wall, my heart beating a trillion beats a second.

I made to move away, but he turned his head in my direction and did a double take and our eyes met and locked, but only for a moment, because Jack nodded briskly and went the other way, his shoulders stiff with indignity.

I could have gone up the steps and rung the bell to Emma's flat, but suddenly, I wasn't feeling so talkative anymore.

When I got home, Luke was tapping away at his laptop and I poured us a cup of coffee, when really what I needed was a double chamomile.

'Hey, hon,' Luke said, not looking up. 'My lawyer just called. He wants you to sign a cohabitation agreement.'

'Oh yeah, what's that?' I asked distractedly as I kicked my shoes off and into the hall closet, followed by my bag.

'It's something similar to a pre-nup, only for unmarried couples.'

I padded into the dining room and fell onto a chair, forcing myself to calm down. I'd had enough of being talked down to and pushed and pulled in every direction. This was all I needed. I took a deep breath, and shifted my mind to this new issue. There was always something.

'Ah. And… what do you think?' I asked.

'I think it's a good idea.' He shrugged. 'After all, anything could happen. We are all *Under the Sky*, Nina. Good quote, huh?'

Under the Sky being one of his earlier movies, I'd learned from Google. Which had absolutely nothing to do with our conversation. Was he actually contemplating the end of us before we even started?

'Luke, be serious.'

He sat back from his laptop and folded his arms. 'I am being serious. Listen, it's no biggie, really. Everyone in the business has them.'

'That's because in the business, almost everyone's relationships fall *apart*,' I countered. 'Or is that what you're envisaging?'

'Of course not,' he assured me.

'How can you be so sure? Look at us both, with failed marriages behind us.'

'Hey, why are you all so doom and gloom now? It'll be fine. Just relax and go with the flow.'

'I can't just go with the flow, Luke. This is not a simple matter between you and me.'

'I thought it was, actually.'

'You know exactly what I mean. There are three children to consider. Have you actually asked Jess if she's happy with this arrangement? Did you consider that maybe she's wondering what life would be like if she could actually spend time with her mum?'

'Yes, but that has nothing to do with us, Nina.'

'Doesn't it? I think that Jess would be thrilled if you and Lauren patched things up again, at least as friends, so she could see her. She is her mother, after all.'

Luke snorted. 'Like Phil is the father of your kids, you mean?'

I bristled. 'That's different. Phil has had years and years to change, but he's refused to.'

'Yeah, well at least Phil tried for a few years. Lauren left us the second we realised that Jess was blind. And, as opposed to Phil, she never returned, never looked back. So you'll excuse me for thinking they're not the same.' And with that, he got up, sauntered into the living room and turned on the TV. Loud. Our first non-script-related quarrel?

I followed him in there. 'Luke, can we please not argue? I quarrelled with Emma last night and don't have the strength for another fall-out.'

He jabbed the remote towards the TV set to mute it. 'Why, what happened?' he asked.

'I'd rather not talk about it.' I really didn't want to relive the ghastly conversation, nor what was happening in my trio.

At that moment, the doorbell rang. It was a courier with a large envelope.

'Is that for me?' Luke asked, getting up and peering behind me as I signed for it.

I turned it over, and almost froze. Oh God. *Smythe and Associates.*

'What is it?' Luke wanted to know, following me as I carried the envelope horizontally into the dining room like it was the sacred ark.

I sat down, still unable to let it go. 'M-my divorce lawyers,' I stammered as I carefully opened the envelope and pulled out the contents. They were, oh my God, my divorce papers – signed by Mr Philip Jenkins himself. Finally!

I dropped the papers onto the table and threw back my head. 'I'm free…' I breathed. 'I'm finally free…'

'You mean your divorce went through? Oh my God, Nina, that's fantastic, sweetheart! It's a sign, you see?'

And before I knew it, tears of joy (in case you had any doubts) were sliding down my face.

39

My Best Friend's Wedding

That night, I had a dream. I didn't know what it meant, but it was quietly horrific.

I had gone walking and found myself in a clearing with a small path leading down into the woods.

This path was overgrown with juniper and all sorts of clinging vines and suffocating plants that had soon pulled me to my knees.

I had no reason to go in there whatsoever. I wasn't searching for anything, but I found myself, within seconds, lying supine on the bed of the forest, plants closing in on me, and in my mouth and nostrils. I had no willpower, no strength to get to my feet and fight my way out of the woods. I knew I was going to die, and the worst part was that the plants were going to continue to grow and cover me so that no one would ever find me. They'd look and look and even dogs wouldn't be able to catch my scent as I lay dead, putrefying on my own.

But then, a sudden instinct, a burst of energy from within,

gave me the strength to fight back and get up. And I knew that the moment I was on my feet again, I could fight the vegetation and be back on my way, scarred and afraid, but alive. Which was all that counted.

'Cheer up, Nina,' Luke said over breakfast the next morning. 'You're a free woman now – Emma didn't mean all those nasty things she said, I'm sure.'

'Oh, you don't know Emma,' I countered. 'When Emma's mad, she's mad.'

'Do you want to tell me what it was about? Me?'

'You? No.' But in a way, I guess it was. 'She and Jack were my two best friends besides Alice, and now she's mad at me and Jack…' I swallowed. 'Jack is moving away.'

'Really? What's happening to Crooked Hill, then?'

I shrugged. 'Dunno… but I'll never see either of them again.'

He chuckled. 'I think you're exaggerating. If they really love you, you'll see them again. Now come on. I've got a surprise for you.'

'Sorry, but I'm not in the mood for surprises.'

He looked at me. 'Oh, come on, sweets. We've got an invitation to a really posh party. I've already asked Deirdre to babysit, and if the Versace dress I got you doesn't cheer you up, nothing will.'

Cheer me up? I had lost my two best friends, and I was supposed to smile?

'Luke, I'm really not up for a party. You go.'

'Uh-uh. If you don't go, I don't go.'

I sighed. 'How do you even know my size?'

He turned to look at me as if to say *Get real*. 'Now get going. The party's at three.'

'So early?'

'It's a black and white charity ball,' he said. 'I want you to look fabulous. Hair, make-up. Everything.'

Fabulous? Oh, goody. Just the way I was feeling.

'Chop chop, the clock is ticking,' he said, clapping his hands. I didn't like him when he got bossy like this.

I groaned and got to my feet. 'I'm going, I'm going.'

Upstairs, I stared at the black dream of organza. It must have cost a fortune. When had he had it delivered? I slipped out of my clothes and tried it on. It fit like a glove. Luke really did have a good eye, in every way.

I threw myself in and out of the shower and in twenty minutes I was finishing my make-up while sticking my tongue out at myself in the mirror. I was not my favourite person at the moment.

Luke called up the stairs. 'You ready, Nina? It's time to go.'

I stared again at my reflection in the mirror. I looked like the miserable cat from *Breakfast at Tiffany's* when Holly Golightly abandons him in the rain. The last thing I needed was to attend a party and pretend I was happy.

Already anticipating the moment I'd come back through the door and slip back into my jeans I gathered my skirts, checked my boobs were inside the scanty bodice, and waved my reflection goodbye.

'I need to call another babysitter to be here when Deirdre drops the kids off,' I said once we were in the car. 'I can't expect her to stay too long. She'll be wanting to get home and cook Alf's dinner.'

'Good idea,' Luke agreed as the car rounded the bend, Saint Piran's church coming into view at the top of the hill that dominate the village and countryside. Today it was festooned for a wedding celebration.

'Why are we here?' I asked. 'Didn't you say we were going to an important party?'

'I did,' he said, pulling me out of the car. 'But first, a little detour.'

There were white calla lilies in pots on each tread leading to the open front door of the church, everywhere and bows on benches and practically everyone I knew was there, including Alf and the Ice Cream Ladies, including Deirdre. What about my children? Wasn't she supposed to be with them?

'Who's getting married?' I asked, but Luke just smiled.

'Someone very important. You'll see.'

And then, I saw her. Emma, coming towards me in a dream of pearl grey silk. She was radiant, absolutely stunning and laughing with the guests. She was getting married! Here, today, in this fantastic setting, and hadn't bothered to invite me. Granted, I hadn't been around lately, but to completely bypass me like this? Did our friendship really mean nothing to her anymore? If so, it was really the end of an era. And where was Jack? Why wasn't the groom there? Shouldn't he precede the bride?

I stepped towards her, feeling myself going. She may not have wanted to talk to me, but I still loved her. 'Hi…'

She turned to me, still smiling. 'Hey…' she whispered, hugging me, her eyes moist.

'I'm sorry we quarrelled, Em. I'm so, so sorry. You are my BFF on this whole earth and I never want to quarrel with you again.'

'Ditto,' she said, dabbing at her eyes.

'See, I told you they'd be friends again!' Deirdre cried to everyone, clutching her handkerchief.

'Where's the uh, lucky man?' I asked. I couldn't see him anywhere.

'Here he is,' came Luke's voice at my side, and to my shock, he bent down on one knee in his Brioni suit and proffered me a Tiffany ring box. I knew that it was Tiffany because I'd seen it on TV and in the movies a thousand times.

'What... *Luke?*'

'Marry me, Nina! Marry me now!'

40

Breakfast At Tiffany's

I swallowed, looking around for any indications of a *Candid Camera* crew. There were none.

He was serious, and so, apparently, was the entire village who had dressed up for a wedding. *Our* wedding.

'What? You want to marry me? Now...?' I croaked. 'Here?'

He took my hands. 'Yes, Nina. Here. Now.'

I was aware of everyone watching me, and caught sight of, oh my goodness, Chloe with Jessica and Chanel, all decked out in pastel colours. They were all so beautiful! Were they... my bridesmaids? And Ben, bearing a ring cushion? It was all too much!

'But I only got my divorce papers yesterday...' I mumbled.

Luke nodded. 'Yes, well, I gave Phil a little incentive, and we were all on stand-by for the minute the papers arrived. The whole village was waiting for this moment, Nina!'

The whole village had been keeping this secret from

me, including my best friends? And Alf, and my Ice Cream Ladies? And even my own children? Had they all gone mad?

'But... but, I can't marry you just like that, Luke,' I whispered.

'Why not, Nina? I love you and you love me, right?'

'But... but... I don't even have a wedding dress...' I stammered. You'd think I'd come up with something better than that, right?

'No problem,' he said. 'Emma's got one for you, haven't you, Emma?'

I turned to her. 'What? Emma...?'

'Say hi to your personal wedding planner,' Luke said. 'She thought of everything – the invitations, and the wedding reception. And—' he raised his eyebrows repeatedly '—even the honeymoon. Surprised?'

'Gobsmacked is more like it.' I stared at her, expecting some help, but there was none. 'Seriously? What were you thinking, Emma?'

The whole mood suddenly changed from festive to hushed. By now everyone's eyes were trained on us, as if watching some Hollywood romcom that I, incidentally had had no part in writing.

'I was thinking that was what you wanted,' Emma said. 'A fairy-tale wedding.' She took my hand solemnly while swallowing and darting her eyes to Luke. 'But now I'm begging you not to go ahead with it. Don't marry Luke.'

Luke's mouth fell open. 'Emma, what the fuck...?'

'Language, my son,' Father Briarley chided as he approached us.

Emma's face was contrite and pleading. 'Sorry, mate,'

she said. 'Turns out I made a mistake.' And then suddenly, without a word, she dragged me inside the church.

'What the hell is going on here?' I hissed, my voice echoing. 'And how was it possible for you to organise a wedding in the three weeks Luke's been back? And why not warn me? And now you're asking me to not marry him after all this?'

She huffed. 'Luke hired me a few months ago, on condition that I wouldn't tell you.'

I couldn't believe my ears. 'Months? He was so sure I'd say yes that he actually hired you to organise my wedding *before he even proposed*?'

'He was sure you would say yes. We all were. But now I'm begging you, Nina. Don't! I don't care about my bloody commission! Jack is more important!'

Good God, had she found out about our kiss? Was that why she had been distant all this time?

Tears welled into my eyes. 'I'm sorry,' I sobbed. 'It was all my fault. I know the three of us had agreed to be friends forever, but it just happened. Give him a chance.'

Her jaw dropped. 'What happened?'

'I know, blame me. We kissed, and it was horrible. Not the kiss, I mean, which was actually the best I've ever had – lucky you – but the fact that we kissed is horrible, because we betrayed you! But it just happened, Em! And it will never ever happen again. I promise you. Please forgive him…'

'Oh, my bloody *God!*' she cried. 'You think that Jack and I… Are you crazy? What's the *matter* with you?'

I stared at her. 'You and Jack are not… he's not your secret bloke?'

Father Briarley appeared again at the end of the aisle in my line of vision, followed by the crowd that had migrated inside to listen in.

'Ladies?' he whispered. 'So sorry to interrupt, but I have another wedding in Marazion in an hour…'

'No, Jack's not my secret *bloke*!' Emma yelled, ignoring him. 'I was shagging Paul Carruthers, you daft cow!'

Our audience snickered.

'Paul Carr— one of the Northwood Dads?'

'Yes!' she said, slapping her thigh in frustration.

'But Jack – I saw him come out of your house one morning.'

'That's because he was in pieces after Luke returned! And FYI, he slept on the settee!'

'In pieces? I don't—'

'Ladies, please – it's getting late,' Father Briarley reminded us.

'Just a minute more, Father, please?' I begged before turning back to Em. 'But Alf said you and he were an item…'

All of the faces that had been glued to us, now swung to Alf accusatorily.

'He said that Jack was in love with you.'

'What?' Emma crowed. 'Rubbish!'

'That's exactly what he said, "Jack's sweet on Emma"!'

Alf looked around him in a panic, raising his hands. 'Emma, Nina… what do I know? These girl names are all the same!'

Beverly, Deirdre's sister, put her hands on her wide hips in a teapot stance. 'Oh, Alf, how could you?'

'So what, I got confused!' he shouted. 'Can't a man at my age make a mistake?'

'But why didn't you tell me you were dating Paul?' I cried.

'Shagging – not dating!'

Someone behind me gasped, while someone else hissed 'I told you so!'

'What? What do you mean? Are you not an item, then?'

'Not really. I didn't want to tell you because I knew you wouldn't approve because basically, I'm the reason he and his wife split up. And Jack was furious with me. But he has been very supportive while I was ending it.'

'Bloody hell, Em,' I said. 'You could have told me! I would have helped you, too! And all this time I thought you and Jack… First I thought that you and he had problems, and then I thought that you and he were seeing each other in secret, and that he didn't care anymore and… What are you going to do now?'

Emma's eyes popped open wide. 'You're standing in a church with a man waiting at the altar, and you're asking me what *I'm* going to do?'

And then it dawned on me. 'So all those times you asked for my opinion on your pop star's wedding, it was actually mine…?'

'Exactly!' she cried. 'It was killing me to keep it a secret!'

'Ladies, please…' Father Briarley insisted. '*Tempus Fugit.*'

'*In a minute*!' everyone roared at him, sending him scurrying down the aisle again, hopefully for good this time.

'Nina, you can't marry Luke. Jack's in love with you!'

My hand shot to my heart. 'Me?'

'Yes, you, you muppet!'

Jack was in love with me? Real love?

'But that night when you got drunk and started to kiss him, you said he had a very huge—'

'Crush! He had a very huge *crush*! On you! And I'm sick and tired of hearing him bang on about it, so get your arse down to Crooked Hill, already!'

'Nina!' came a familiar voice, and we turned to see Alice scrabbling up the aisle in a cloud of yellow. 'Sorry I'm late! Don't listen to her! You have to marry Luke. He is so the guy for you!'

'Shut up, Alice!' Emma shouted. 'Jack is the one for her! It's always been him!'

'Absolutely not!' Alice proclaimed. 'Luke O'Hara—'

'Shut up, Alice!' the crowd echoed.

I couldn't believe my ears. How the heck did I get caught in the middle of all this?

Suddenly, exclamations and expletives erupted in the church, topped by Father Briarley's voice. 'Folks, please watch your language, this is holy ground! Take your swear words down to the Bobbin' Buoy, for heaven's sake!'

I turned to Luke who was hovering just outside the church doors, eyeing me every now and then anxiously. I left Emma and Alice and reached him. 'Luke? Can we talk? In private?' I whispered as the entire village of Penworth Ford watched the exchange, some oblivious to my predicament (at least I hoped my love life wasn't completely public) some waiting for the bomb to explode.

Reading what was next, he reluctantly followed me outside to the church steps.

'Are you dumping me for Jack? Are you giving up California and Hollywood, for an *apple farmer*?'

'A *Cornish* apple farmer,' Alf corrected him from just inside the door.

We turned around to see that everyone had followed us

again, and were now all lined up in rows like the church choir, the little ones in front, and Alf and the Ice Cream Ladies, Annie and Old Nellie bringing up the rear, all hands clasped to their breasts in anticipation as if their very life depended on my answer.

You'd think my fellow villagers would have some more respect for our privacy, but then again, I was reborn here and they were fiercely protective of me. Plus, they always loved a bit of drama.

'Folks, would you *mind*?' I pleaded.

Beverly studied me, almost as if to read my mind. 'Come on, then,' she said, shooing everyone out the door again amidst "awhs" and "just a minutes".

When the door closed behind them with a loud echo, I turned to Luke, overwhelmed by the sudden silence, and the enormity of what was happening to us.

'Please, Luke, forgive me, but I can't accept your marriage proposal.'

'Oh, thank God,' I heard Old Nellie from behind the door. 'I was hoping she'd finally pull her head out of her arse and see the light!'

'Nana!' Annie half-hissed, half-wailed, but everyone burst into a hearty laughter. Feeling my ears burning, I ignored them. 'You're fantastic, Luke, and Jess – you're both practically perfect and I truly, truly love you both! And I *want* you in our lives. But not in the way I thought. I'm so so sorry for not being the woman you really need in your life, Luke, but it's better this way!'

'You call that acceptable?' he croaked.

My heart went out to him. I would have never in my life wanted to hurt Luke. 'I'm terrible, I know, but you just sprung this on me, and I haven't even had the time to think about it when only yesterday we were still talking about moving to California...'

'So then think about it, Nina. I'm offering you another chance.'

Another chance to grab at Hollywood. Who wouldn't go for it?

But I shook my head. 'I'm so sorry, Luke. I can't ruin your life. Or anyone else's...'

'Mum! Mum!' Chloe thundered, emerging from the church and pounding down the stone steps in a blue dress I'd never seen before. 'You have *got* to come and see this!'

We exchanged glances and dashed out through the side door of the church where everyone had assembled, craning their necks, all looking at the other side of the valley, across the fields to where Crooked Hill lay. The farm he was abandoning to its own destiny.

And then I stopped, dead cold, as something rushed from my calves up my legs, settling into my stomach. Something between ice and fire. In any case, it mollified me and froze me to the spot and all I could do was stare out at Jack's fields, unable to speak as my heart leapt into my mouth.

Alice followed my gaze and jumped. 'Holy fuck!'

'Nina, *please*!' Father Briarley shrieked, grabbing the few hairs left on his head in desperation.

'Yay!' Emma cried, jumping up and down and almost tripping in her heels. 'I knew he'd find the balls to do it!'

I could feel the tears sliding down my face as I fought to catch my breath.

'Is he fuckin' kiddin' me?' Luke wailed.

'Holy shit!' Ben said for the first time ever.

'Ben, watch your language! We're in church,' Chloe said, much to my surprise.

'What is it, Chloe?' Jess asked. 'What's happening?'

There, in the square field, was Jack, on his tractor, ploughing, carving actual letters. *I (heart) you Nina.* And so I lost it. I couldn't stop the silent tears, no matter how hard I shoved my fists into my eyes. I had to take a deep breath because the pain in my heart was so wrenching that I could barely stand. Jack really did love me after all. Jack, who had always been there for me, selfless and dependable, loved *me*.

Luke turned to me and his face softened. 'Bloody hell, Nina,' he whispered as he caressed my wet cheeks. 'I knew I had a rival in him, and that you both had chemistry, but this? There's just no contest. So just go to him already.'

'What?' I wiped my eyes with my indexes and they came away black and runny. I didn't know I was supposed to wear waterproof mascara today.

He sighed. 'I love you, Nina, but now I understand why I could never fully reach you. You love him too.'

Yes. I did. I *loved* Jack. With every part of me. I could no longer deny it.

'I don't want you to be unhappy, Nina.'

I wiped my eyes again and looked up at him. 'C-can you ever forgive me, Luke?'

His face was sombre as he cupped my chin and kissed my lips for one last time. 'Go. Go to him, that lucky sod.'

'Ohhhh…!' I threw my arms around him and kissed the side of his face. 'You're learning British expressions *now*? Oh, Luke!'

'But if you ever change your mind…'

'Oh, Luke, you're the best! I do love you.'

'Ah, Nina?'

I pulled away, sniffling. Had I got snot on his shirt or something?

'Before you go, you might want to use some make-up remover or something. You got a little... stuff around...'

'What?' I said, as I pulled out my compact mirror.

'Oh, my God!' I looked like the bloody Joker. And there was lipstick all over Luke's shirt. I dabbed at it with my sleeve and then turned around towards the fields. Jack was now ploughing another heart around his message.

Luke shook his head. 'The bugger's thorough, though, you gotta admit it.'

'I love you, Luke,' I cried, hugging him again.

He sighed. 'I love you too, babe. But I understand it just wasn't meant to be. Now go.'

'Oh, my word!' Deirdre said in the background. 'He's adding an arrow through his heart! Awh, the poor lad!'

Chloe turned to Jess. 'I guess that's the end of that, Jess. We won't legally be related. But you and I will always be blood sisters.'

Jess squeezed her arm and grinned. 'Definitely. You okay, Dad?' she asked on second thought.

Luke took his daughter by the shoulders. 'Nina and I are both okay with it.'

'Well, then what the bleedin' 'ell are ya waitin' for?' Alf shouted into my ear. 'Go!'

I looked around me and all I could see were the beaming faces of my support system cheering me on, telling me I was making the right decision. And in my heart, I knew they were right.

'Car! I need a car,' I panted, and a sudden burst of cheers

echoed throughout the church as Father Briarley shook his head and crossed himself.

'Go, go, go!' Emma cried, pushing her keys into my hand, while Alice hung on to me like in a tug of war.

'Nina, no! Are you nuts?' she shrieked.

'Yes, Alice!' I shrieked back. 'I'm nuts! But now at least I know what I want!'

And who I wanted. It had taken me three years to realise it. Maybe I had been testing him, familiarising myself with the idea of him being in my life, I don't know. All I knew was that when I had heard Jack was leaving, my heart had hurt so much I thought it would shatter into a million pieces. And now I knew why.

I scooped up my haute couture and made a mad dash for Emma's van that was still full of wedding paraphernalia, wedding presents and oh my God, what was supposed to have been my wedding dress.

As I drove up to the top of Crooked Hill, my heart in my mouth, I saw Jack stop the engine, jump off his tractor and make his way towards the edge of the field. All this time I'd had the perfect man right under my nose and failed to see the wood for the trees, as he always said.

'Jack!' I cried. Really cried, tears gushing down my cheeks all over again. I could barely see where I was going.

He looked up, and froze, and oh, the look on his face!

'Nina…? What are you doing here? It's your sodding wedding day.'

'A sodding wedding you tried to ruin!' I cried.

'Did I manage?'

'I'm here, aren't I?'

'Are you here to give me a bollocking?'

'Absolutely. Why didn't you ever tell me before?'

'I did – but you told me to never do that again.'

'You should have explained things to me!'

'You never gave me the chance!' he shouted.

'Well, here's your chance!' I shouted back.

'Nuh-uh,' he said. 'The ball's in your court, now. It's your move.'

'What is this, a game of chess?' I quipped through my tears.

'An extremely long one, Nina. I'd like to kiss you and marry you before I turn eighty. Do you think that might be possible?'

'Then go ahead and propose,' I challenged.

He took my hand and guided me through a gap in the hedgerows.

'Is this your idea of a proposal?' I asked. 'A romp in the hay?'

'No,' he said as we emerged to the other side. 'But this is.'

I turned from him and started. And there it was, in the lower field, ploughed into the earth, another message:

Will you marry me?

I gasped. 'How did you know I'd say no to Luke and come up here and see this?'

His eyes twinkled as he grinned and ducked to look into my face. 'I didn't. But I thought I'd pull out all the stops just in case. Did I do good?'

I turned to look at the message again and ran to his tractor.

'What are you doing?' he called after me.

'I'm giving you an answer,' I shouted over my shoulder as I scrambled up onto his tractor in my Versace. 'Jack! How the hell do you start this thing?'

'A verbal answer would suffice,' he said, as he ambled over, stretching his arms up towards me. 'What do you say, Nina? Will you let me love you for the rest of our lives?'

In response, I stepped down from the tractor and he caught me, just as he always did, Jack. *My* Jack. 'Yes, Jack! I'll marry you!'

'Not so fast, Nina. First, let me hear you say it.'

I rolled my eyes and laughed. 'Okay. I love you.'

'That's it? Try a little harder.'

'Okay.' I took his hands, my heart beating like never before. 'I love you, Jack Marrak. I love you like I've never loved any other man in my life and it's taken me much too long to realise it. But I don't want to waste another second. You make my knees shake, but you also make me stronger, if that even makes sense, and I'd be thrilled – and honoured – to marry you.'

At that, he pulled me into his arms and delivered me another one of those knicker-melting kisses that made me dizzy with excitement.

'What did Luke say when you left the church?' he asked as an afterthought.

'He's okay with it.'

'Oh, how nice for us all,' he said, half sarcastic, half relieved.

I punched him lightly. 'You like him.'

'I do,' he admitted. 'But I don't like him enough to give you up, thank you very much.'

'Jack, why the hell did you not say anything after Luke left for California?'

He shrugged. 'I figured I had time. But then, after I kissed you, I realised I had scared you away.'

'Because I thought you were sneaking around with Emma. And I thought that our kiss was just, you know…?'

He cocked his head. 'Emma?'

'I know, I know,' I said, hiding my eyes. 'She told me about Paul. I misread the situation.'

'I'll say. So you thought that kiss was just the heat of the moment?'

'And then, you never said anything again,' I said.

'Because Luke arrived and swept you off your feet…'

'Not exactly. I was in absolute hell after you kissed me.'

'Gee, thanks.'

'Silly. I was just so confused about us. You were my best male friend. All this time, you've been watching over me.'

'What does that tell you? I wanted to win you, fair and square, even if Luke was around. I wanted you to choose me because you wanted me, not win by default.'

'Default? Oh, *Jack*…'

'I'm no Hollywood star, nor a gentleman, Nina,' he said. 'I don't know how to make small talk and I don't know what the right fork is and what wine goes with… beef bourguignon.'

I smiled. 'Neither do I, Jack.'

He took my hand and guided it to his heart. I could hear it beneath his shirt, pounding in overdrive, as with his other hand he caressed my lips.

'I love you,' he said with solemnity. 'I didn't even really understand love before you, but I do know that I can't imagine life without you. I love the children. I want to marry you and be there for all of you. I can't promise you Hollywood lights, but I can offer you all of me, my attention, my loyalty, everything that I am. I will love you forever.'

'Forever sounds good enough,' I sighed happily, resting my hand on his chest, still stupefied by the truth that had been staring me in the face all this time. My destiny had not been written in the stars after all, but carved into a small corner of a Cornish field.

Epilogue

Los Angeles, one year later

In the movies, time and season jumps are the norm, which, while practical for the screen, is a real shame, because fictitious characters don't get to enjoy every moment of happiness, every smile, every laugh and every loving caress like real people do.

Fictitious characters only *appear* to love their newlywed husbands, or rejoice at their son's first real run across the green fields on a hot summer's day, or bask in the warmth of their daughter's embrace. And yet, movies are what I do now, while other times I just write my novels from my desk by the dining room window.

As the crowds gathered outside the theatre for the premiere of *Written In The Stars*, Jack squeezed my hand. 'How are you feeling, love?' he whispered into my ear as he smiled for the cameras on the red carpet. He loved being taken for Mr Conte, and even more, he loved spoiling us all rotten.

'A bit nauseous,' I admitted, caressing my huge tummy.

His eyes followed my hand and his eyes widened. 'The baby? Is it coming now?'

I laughed. 'No, silly. It's just stage fright. I have no idea whether the audience is going to like the film or not.'

'They'll like it, stop fretting and enjoy Hollywood for once,' came Luke's voice at our side, his daughter Jessica on his arm, radiant in a blue dress.

Luke raised a glass to me. 'You look beautiful tonight, Nina, you and your bump.' He clapped Jack on the back. 'Nice work, man.'

'Thanks, mate,' Jack answered.

Jessica smiled and turned to Chloe. 'I told you it would all work out. Dads are the best.'

Chloe eyed Jack, and lifted herself on tiptoes to kiss his cheek. 'They sure are, Jess…'

'Mum!' called Ben. 'We have front-row seats and our *names* are on them!' And as I watched, he jumped over them with great agility, just like Roberto Benigni had done when he won the Oscar for best foreign film.

Our French surgeon had performed a miracle on my baby. In the space of three months, he was up and really running like mad, signing up to all the sports Northwood offered, excelling in each and every one. I had always known that he could do anything he wanted, my boy. And it had been worth the tears, the anguish and the wait.

'Look over there, is that… Oh my *God*!' Chloe cried. 'Is that Kate Winslet? Sitting next to… Jude Law?'

Luke shrugged. 'They do star in the main roles, don't they?'

Jack grinned down on me with enormous pride. 'You did it, my love.'

'*We* did it, Jack. I wouldn't be here without you.'

'And me,' Luke butted in, raising his glass.

'To love and friendship!' Jack toasted, his arm firm around me.

'To love and friendship,' we all echoed.

To think that only a little over a year ago, I had been a practically destitute, single mum killing herself to survive. And now I was a happily married woman, full-time writer, and a mum of almost three. If you didn't count Minnie and Callie.

Nina Conte Marrak lives in her newly renovated farmhouse on the outskirts of a beautiful Cornish seaside village with her husband, three children and dogs Minnie and Callie. Her first novel, Written In The Stars, *has been made into a motion picture, while her subsequent books,* The Chocolate Wardrobe Girls *and* Storm In A D-cup *have already been optioned for the screen by Hollywood actor and producer, Luke O'Hara. Nina is currently working on her fourth novel.*

And because I promised you earlier, here it is, my mum's recipe for Sicilian *Arancini*:

Ingredients

1 kg of rice
1 hard-boiled egg, diced
Ground beef, fried in finely chopped onions and just a touch of tomato sauce. (You can use what's left for a Bolognaise.)
Peas, 250 grams
Breadcrumb, toasted in a pan with a touch of olive oil
Olive Oil for deep-frying

Procedure

1. Boil a kilogram of rice (leave it al dente) and place it to drain on a wide surface until it is dry and at room temperature.
2. Flatten two ice cream scoops of rice onto the palm of your hand. If they're too sticky, put a drop of olive oil in your palms. Gently curve your hand up to create the first half of your rice shell.
3. Having mixed together the egg, beef and peas in quantities and proportions according to taste, place them in the centre, and wrap another scoopful of rice to close the *arancino*, rolling it gently so that it has a pyramid shape.
4. Once ready, roll in the breadcrumbs so they are coated, and then deep-fry or bake until orange.

Buon Appetito!

Acknowledgements

Many thanks go to, first and foremost, my lovely editor Rhea Kurien, who 'got me' from the very start, is always available, and is an absolute dream to work with. You are the best, Rhea!

Thanks also go to Hannah Smith, Vicky Joss and Nikky Ward at Aria Fiction for pulling this one off while in times of lockdown.

Also many heart-felt thanks go to Jade Craddock who guided me through all sorts of industry mysteries!

Thanks to my family on both sides of the pond, and particularly my Mum and sister Lidia, along with Natalie, Dean and Becky.

Massive thanks to my dear friend Michéle for taking me to Cornwall. We know what amazing memories we have of that time.

And always, thanks so much to my dear old friend Alex Husic who spent hours on end with me in the 90s under that old mulberry tree eating, drinking and fantasising about this very moment. And who even designed my website.

Last but not least, many thanks to you, Dear Reader, who

took a chance on this book. Whether it was the gorgeous cover or the fantastic setting, I thank you for taking me on, and I hope to see you again on a new journey!

Nancy Barone

About the Author

NANCY BARONE is literally all over the place, in body and heart. She's an Italian-Canadian author of romantic comedy who lives in a farmhouse close to the Mediterranean sea but returns to the UK every time she can.

In her spare time she manages to work as an English teacher in a tiny Sicilian fishing village, and join her British husband on long walks with their dogs on the beach, all the while savouring Mayan chocolate and ricotta ice cream.

She also has the gall to classify her visit to Cornwall as 'research' for her novels.

Nancy loves to receive your messages – drop her a line anywhere here:

Website - www.nancybarone.com
Twitter account - NancyNBW
Facebook - Author Nancy Barone

Hello from Aria

We hope you enjoyed this book! If you did let us know, we'd love to hear from you.

We are Aria, a dynamic digital-first fiction imprint from award-winning independent publishers Head of Zeus. At heart, we're committed to publishing fantastic commercial fiction – from romance and sagas to crime, thrillers and historical fiction. Visit us online and discover a community of like-minded fiction fans!

We're also on the look out for tomorrow's superstar authors. So, if you're a budding writer looking for a publisher, we'd love to hear from you. You can submit your book online at ariafiction.com/ we-want-read-your-book

You can find us at:
Email: aria@headofzeus.com
Website: www.ariafiction.com
Submissions: www.ariafiction.com/
we-want-read-your-book

@ariafiction
@Aria_Fiction
@ariafiction